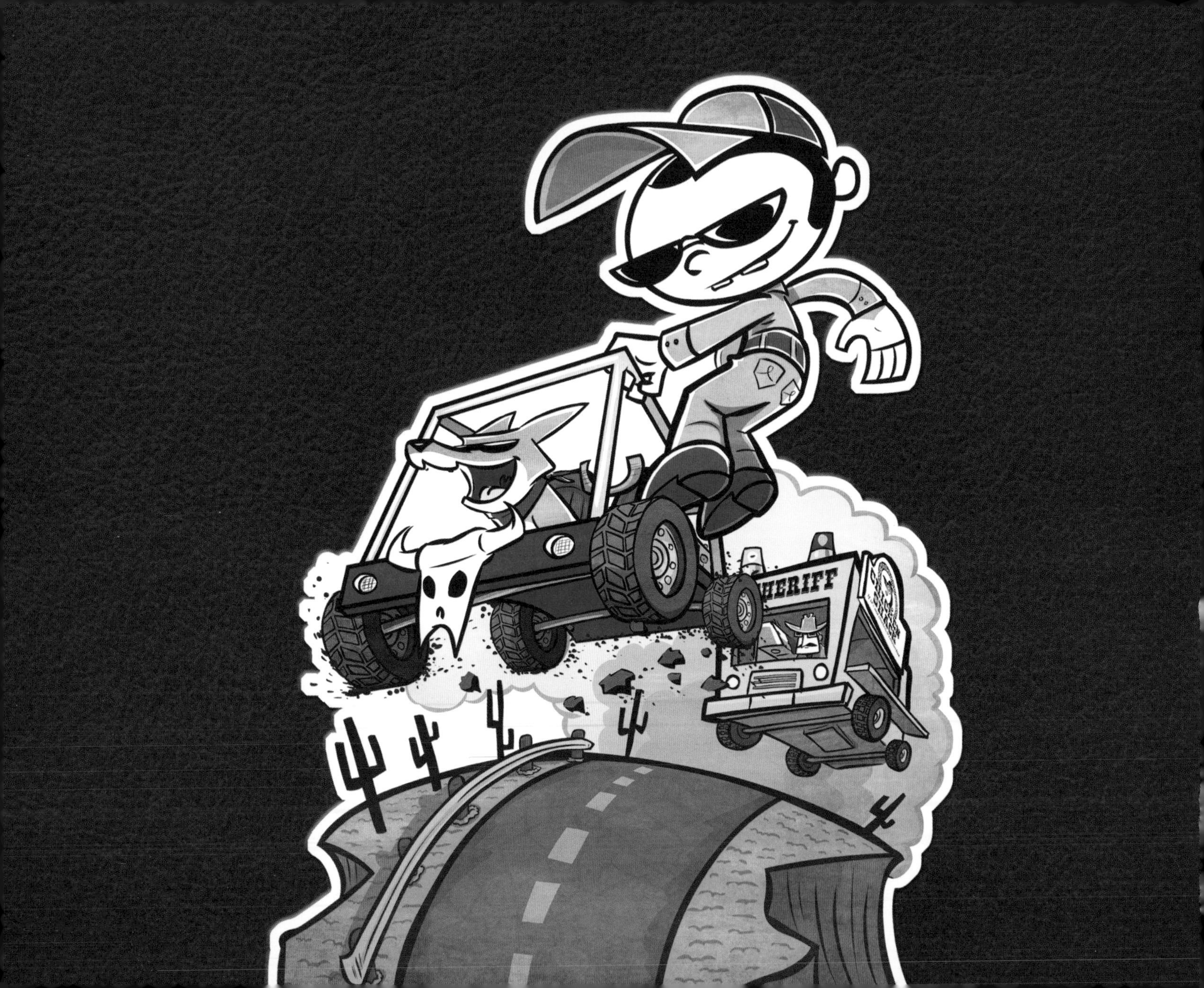
HERIFF

YEHUDI MERCADO

PANTALONES, TX™

DON'T CHICKEN OUT

ARCHAIA ENTERTAINMENT LLC
WWW.ARCHAIA.COM

SUPERMERCADO COMICS
WWW.SUPERMERCADOCOMICS.COM

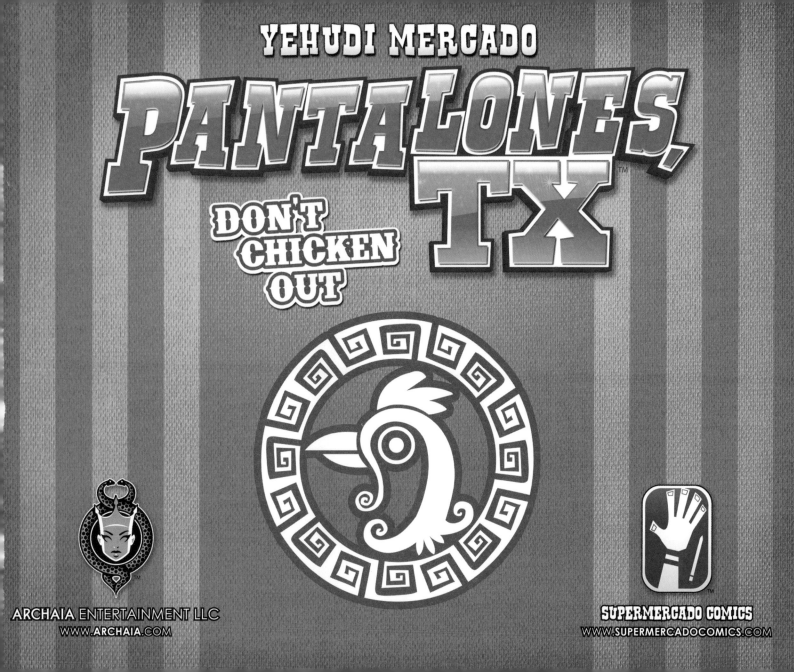

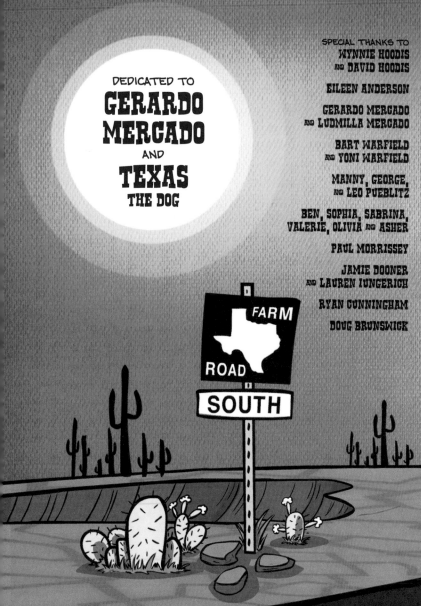

DEDICATED TO

GERARDO MERCADO AND TEXAS THE DOG

SPECIAL THANKS TO

WYNNIE HOODIS AND DAVID HOODIS

EILEEN ANDERSON

GERARDO MERCADO AND LUDMILLA MERCADO

BART WARFIELD AND YONI WARFIELD

MANNY, GEORGE, AND LEO PUEBLITZ

BEN, SOPHIA, SABRINA, VALERIE, OLIVIA AND ASHER

PAUL MORRISSEY

JAMIE DOONER AND LAUREN IUNGERICH

RYAN CUNNINGHAM

DOUG BRUNSWICK

Rebecca Taylor, *Editor*
Scott Newman, *Production Manager*

Archaia Entertainment LLC
PJ Bickett, *Chairman*
Jack Cummins, *President & COO*
Mark Smylie, *CCO*
Mike Kennedy, *Publisher*
Stephen Christy, *Editor-in-Chief*
Mel Caylo, *Marketing Manager*

Published by **Archaia**

Archaia Entertainment LLC
1680 Vine Street, Suite 1010
Los Angeles, California, 90028
www.archaia.com

ARCHAIA™
NEW **STORIES**. NEW **WORLDS**.

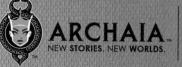

PANTALONES, TX: DON'T CHICKEN OUT Original Graphic Novel Hardcover. February 2013. FIRST PRINTING.

10 9 8 7 6 5 4 3 2 1

ISBN: 1-936393-90-5
ISBN 13: 978-1-936393-90-9

Printed in **China**.

WWW.PANTALONESTEXAS.COM

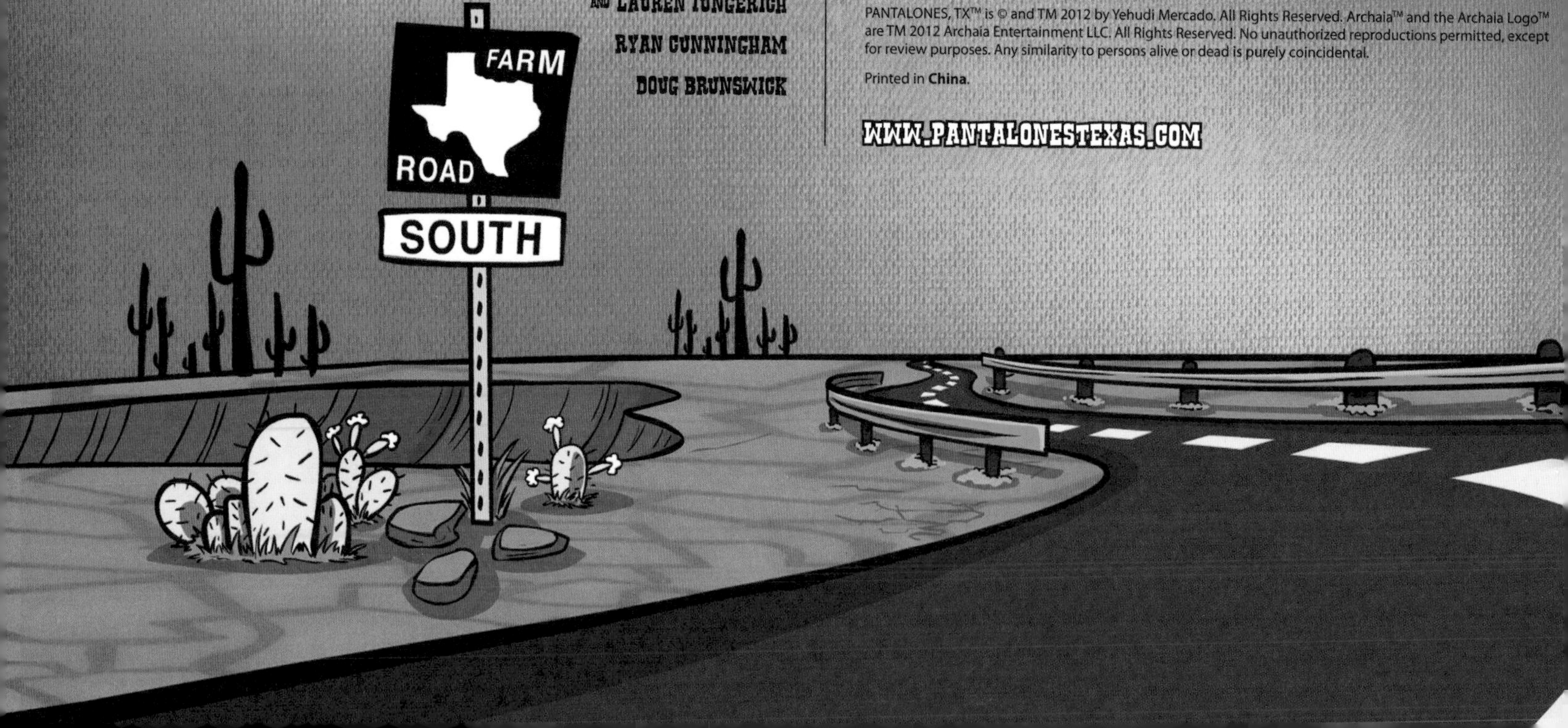

FARM
ROAD
SOUTH

PANTALONES, TX™

DON'T CHICKEN OUT

WRITTEN & ILLUSTRATED BY

YEHUDI MERCADO

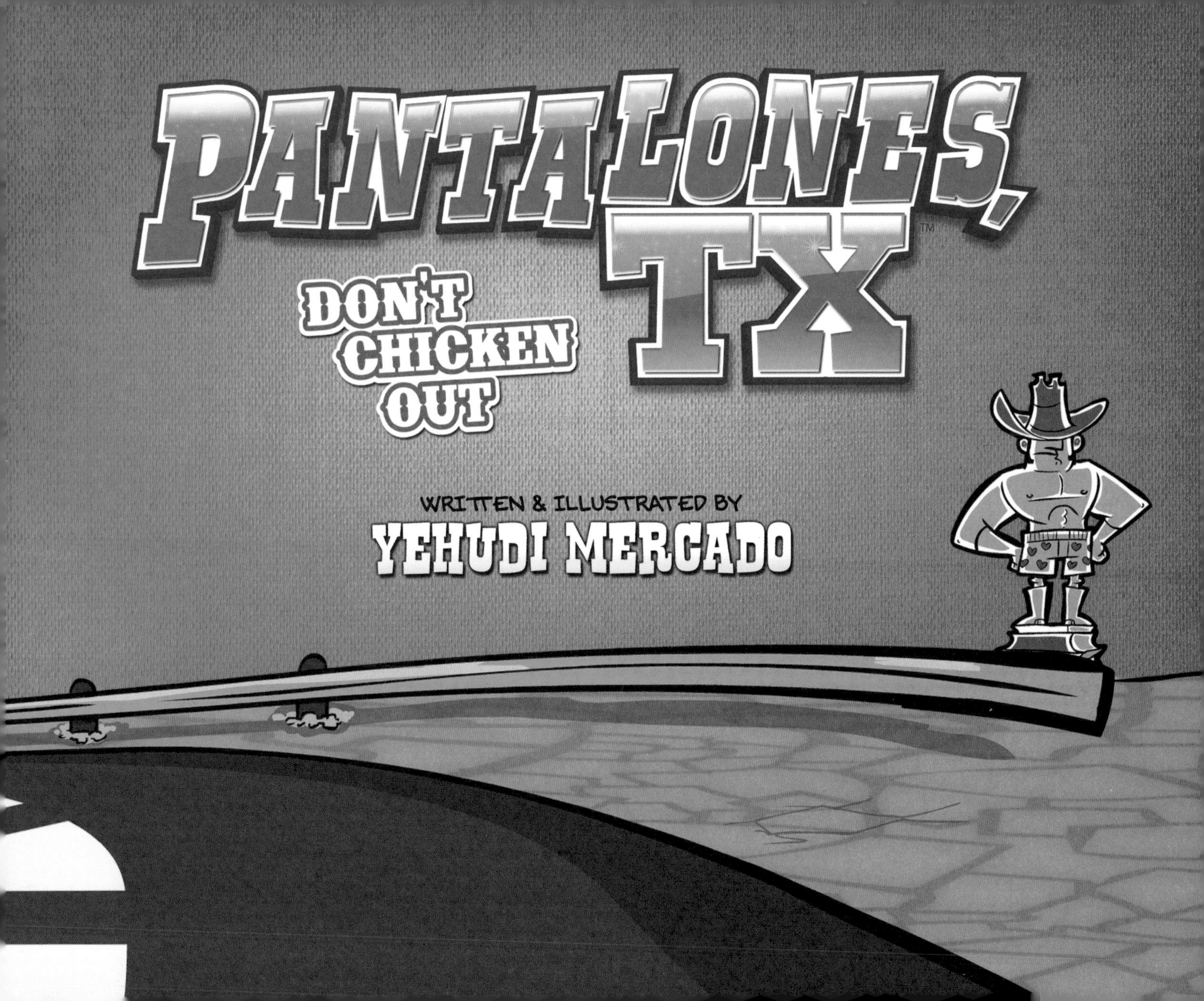

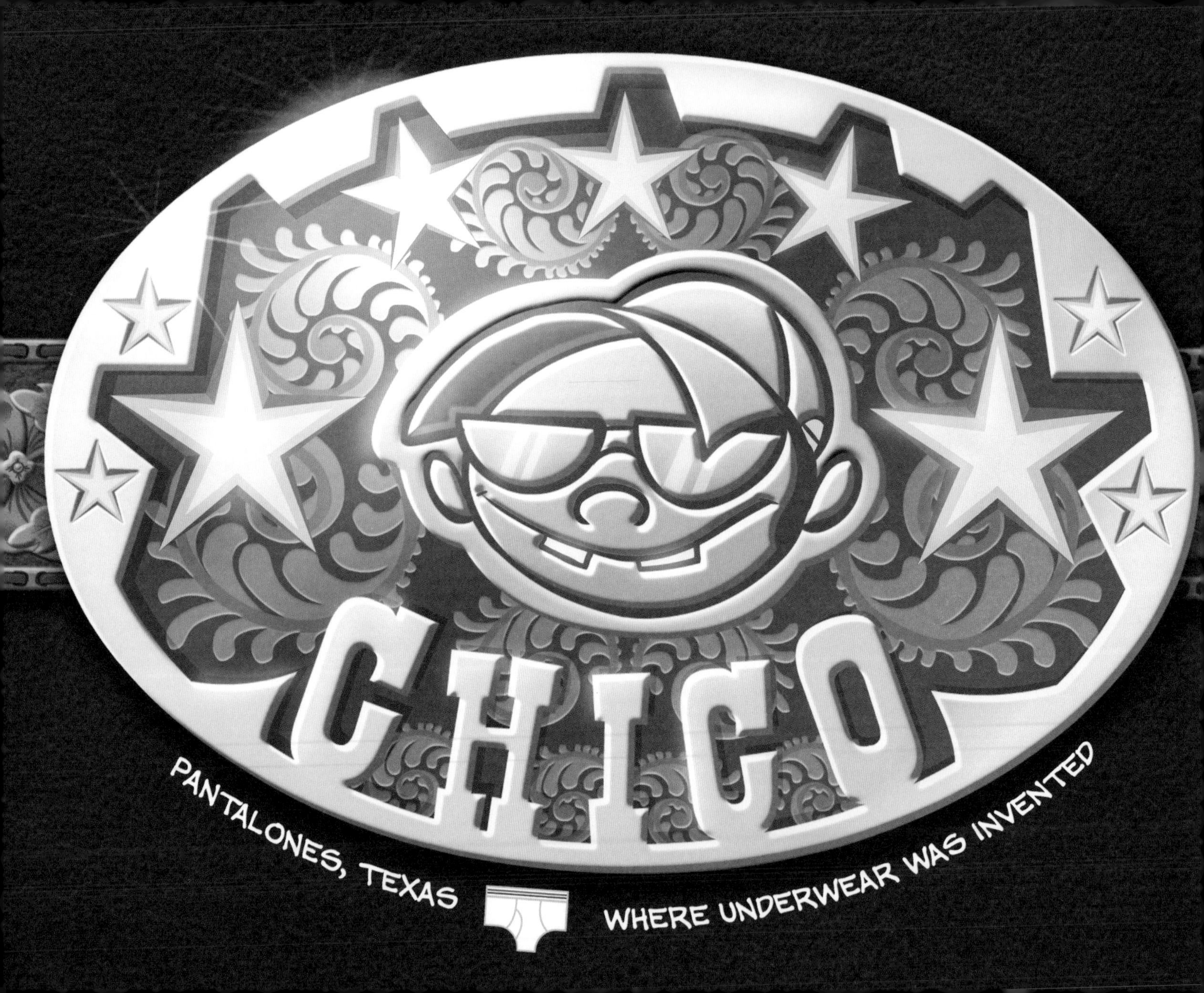
CHICO
PANTALONES, TEXAS
WHERE UNDERWEAR WAS INVENTED

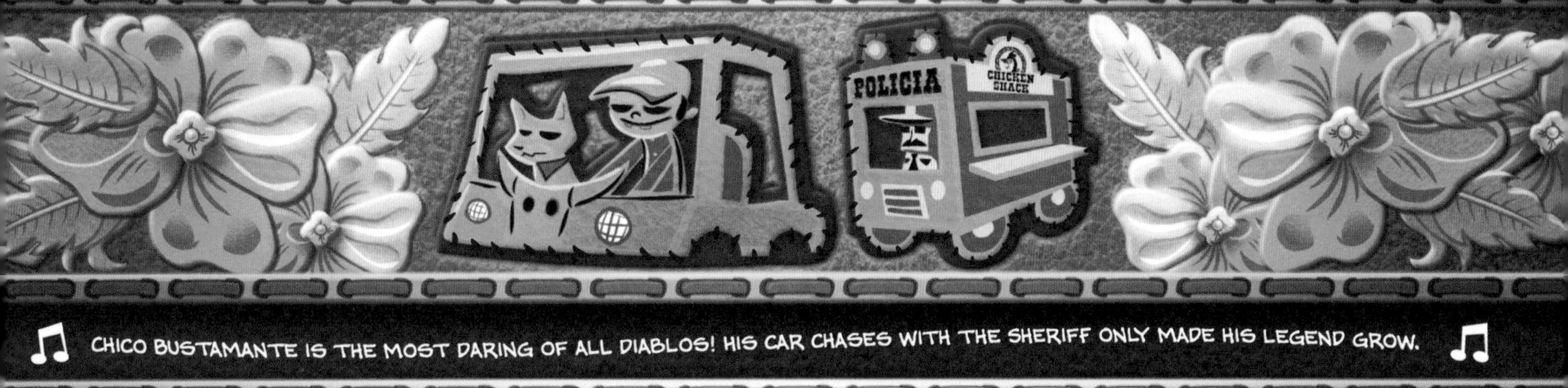
POLICIA
CHICKEN SHACK

♫ CHICO BUSTAMANTE IS THE MOST DARING OF ALL DIABLOS! HIS CAR CHASES WITH THE SHERIFF ONLY MADE HIS LEGEND GROW. ♫

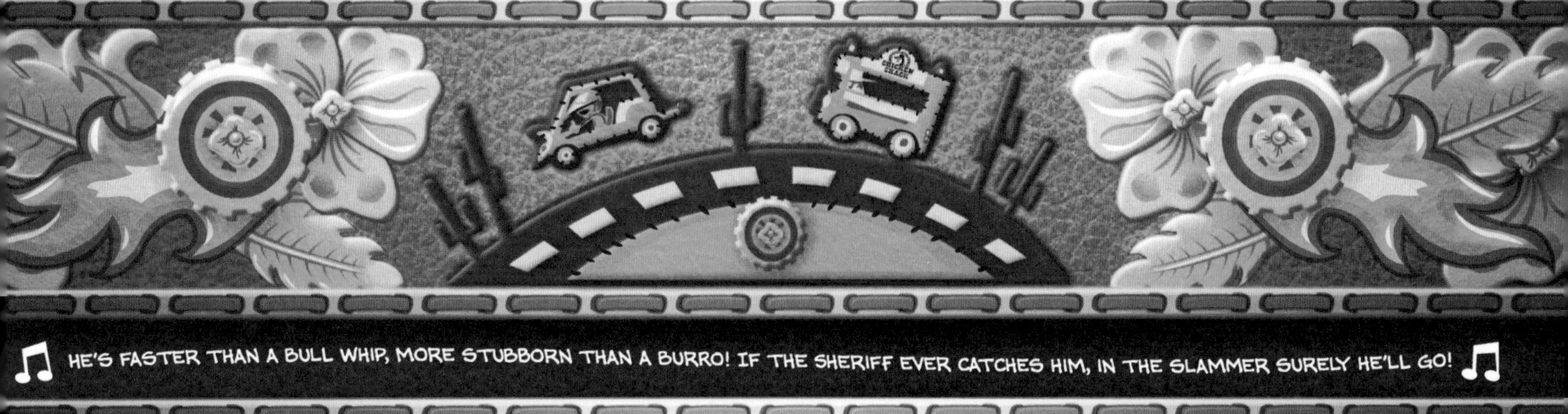

♫ HE'S FASTER THAN A BULL WHIP, MORE STUBBORN THAN A BURRO! IF THE SHERIFF EVER CATCHES HIM, IN THE SLAMMER SURELY HE'LL GO! ♫

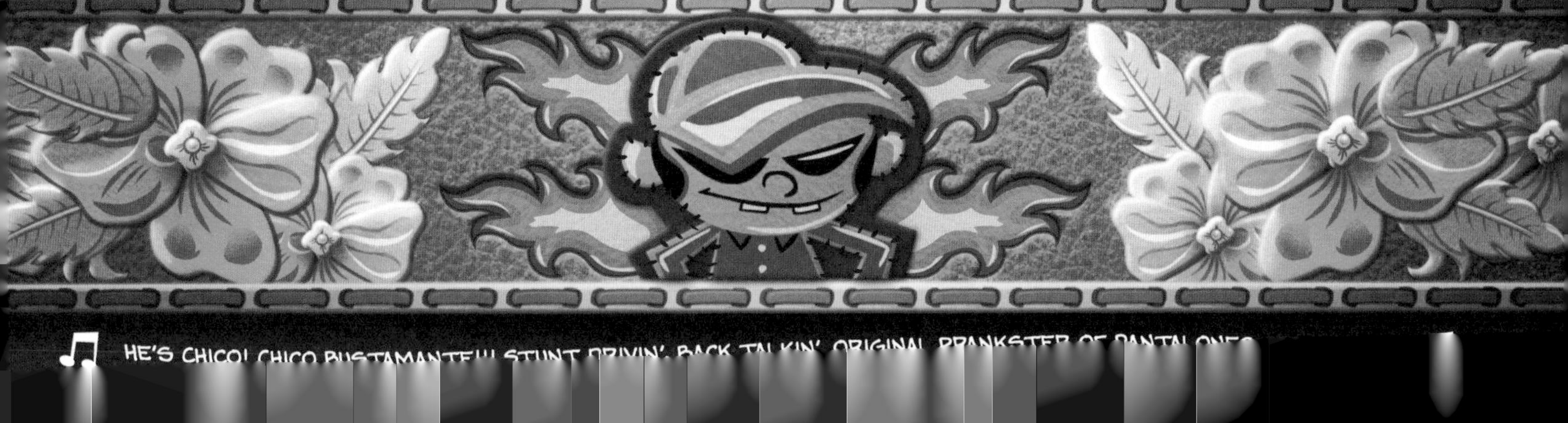

♫ HE'S CHICO! CHICO BUSTAMANTE!!! STUNT DRIVIN', BACK TALKIN', ORIGINAL PRANKSTER OF PANTALONES

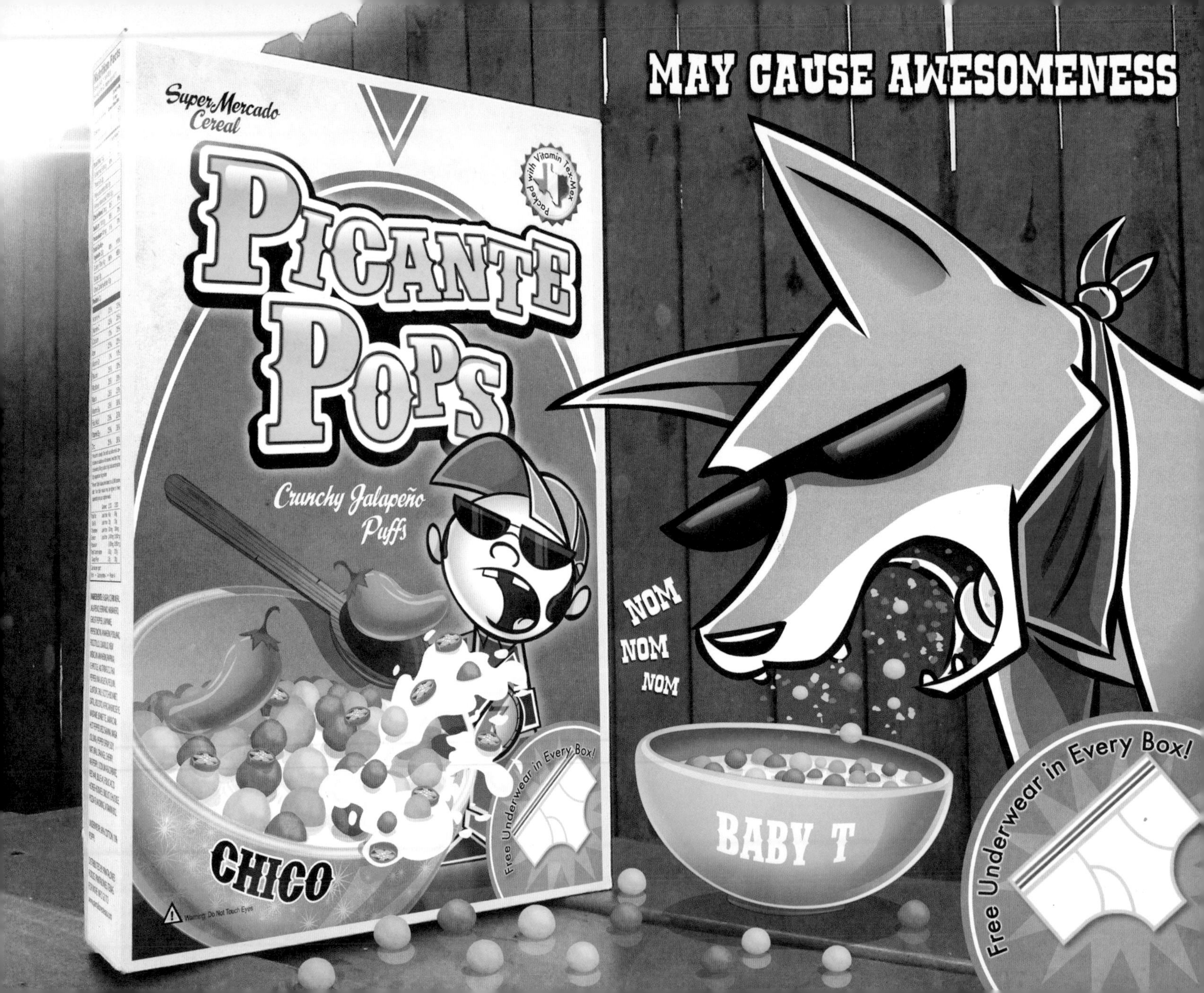
MAY CAUSE AWESOMENESS
Super Mercado Cereal
Packed with Vitamin Tex-Mex
PICANTE POPS
Crunchy Jalapeño Puffs
CHICO
Warning: Do Not Touch Eyes
Free Underwear in Every Box!
NOM
NOM
NOM
BABY T
Free Underwear in Every Box!

CHAPTER UNO

SCHOOL BELL RUN

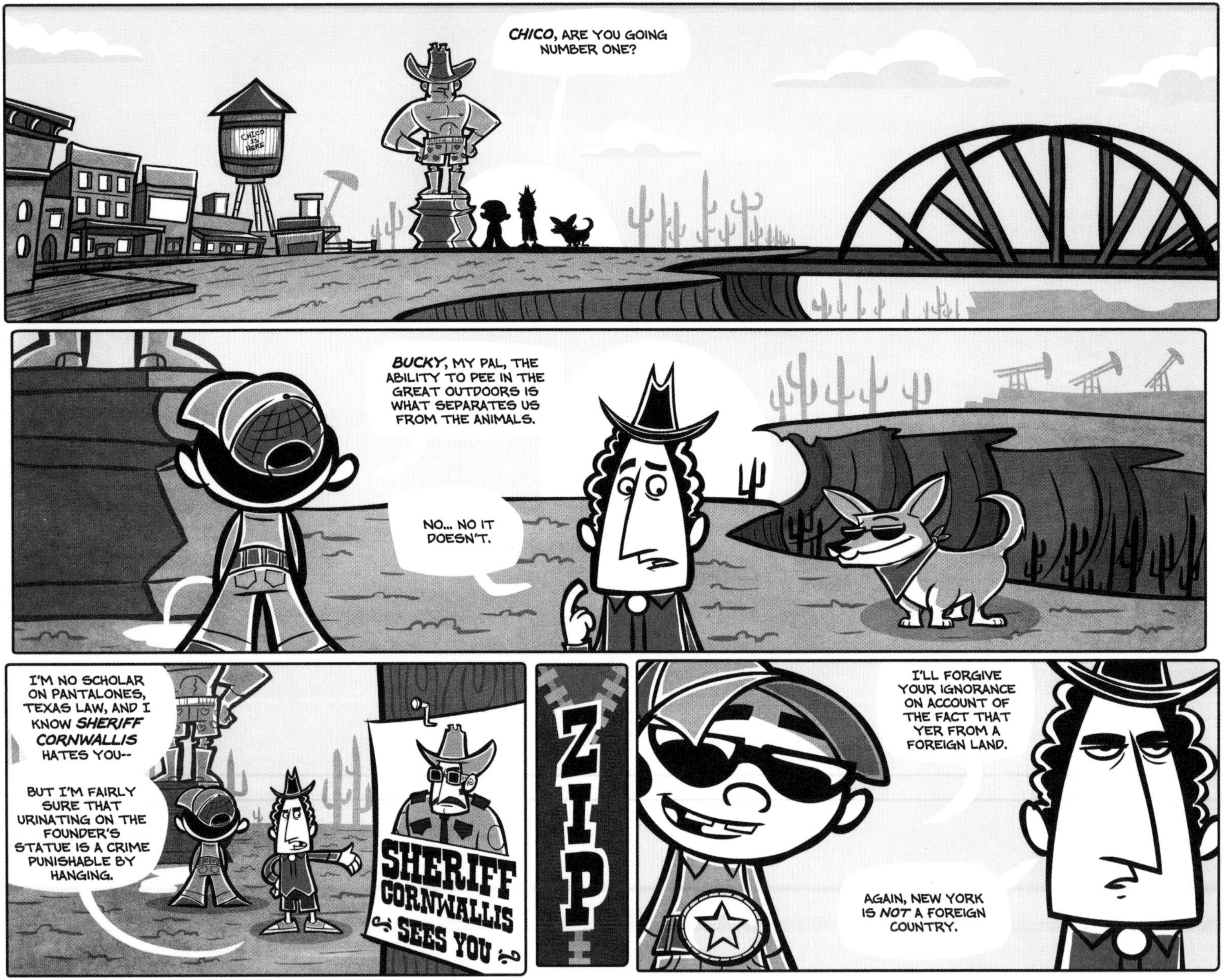
CHICO IS HERE
CHICO, ARE YOU GOING NUMBER ONE?
BUCKY, MY PAL, THE ABILITY TO PEE IN THE GREAT OUTDOORS IS WHAT SEPARATES US FROM THE ANIMALS.
NO... NO IT DOESN'T.
I'M NO SCHOLAR ON PANTALONES, TEXAS LAW, AND I KNOW *SHERIFF CORNWALLIS* HATES YOU--
BUT I'M FAIRLY SURE THAT URINATING ON THE FOUNDER'S STATUE IS A CRIME PUNISHABLE BY HANGING.
SHERIFF CORNWALLIS SEES YOU
ZIP
I'LL FORGIVE YOUR IGNORANCE ON ACCOUNT OF THE FACT THAT YER FROM A FOREIGN LAND.
AGAIN, NEW YORK IS *NOT* A FOREIGN COUNTRY.

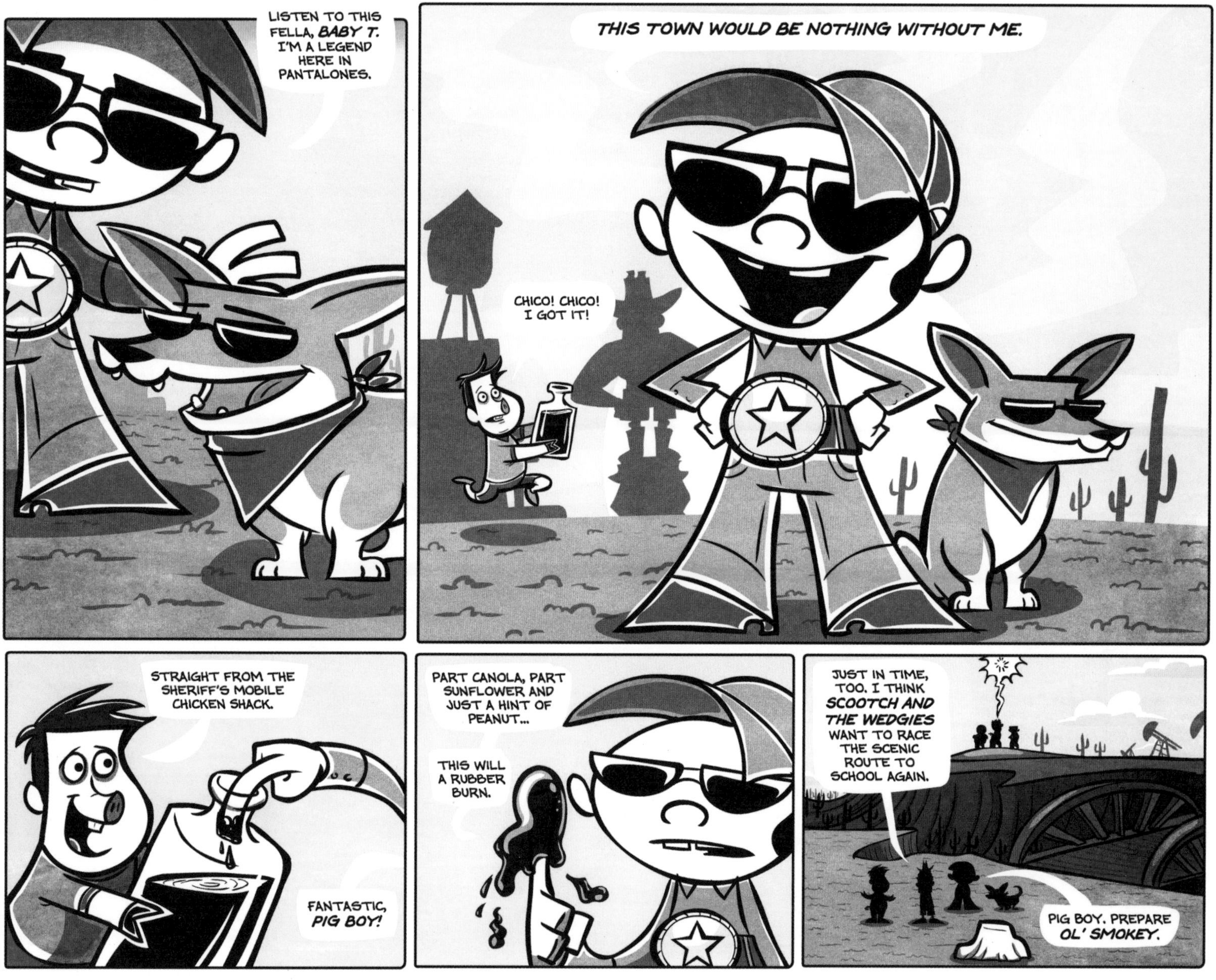
LISTEN TO THIS FELLA, *BABY T.* I'M A LEGEND HERE IN PANTALONES.
THIS TOWN WOULD BE NOTHING WITHOUT ME.
CHICO! CHICO! I GOT IT!
STRAIGHT FROM THE SHERIFF'S MOBILE CHICKEN SHACK.
FANTASTIC, *PIG BOY!*
PART CANOLA, PART SUNFLOWER AND JUST A HINT OF PEANUT...
THIS WILL A RUBBER BURN.
JUST IN TIME, TOO. I THINK *SCOOTCH AND THE WEDGIES* WANT TO RACE THE SCENIC ROUTE TO SCHOOL AGAIN.
PIG BOY. PREPARE *OL' SMOKEY.*

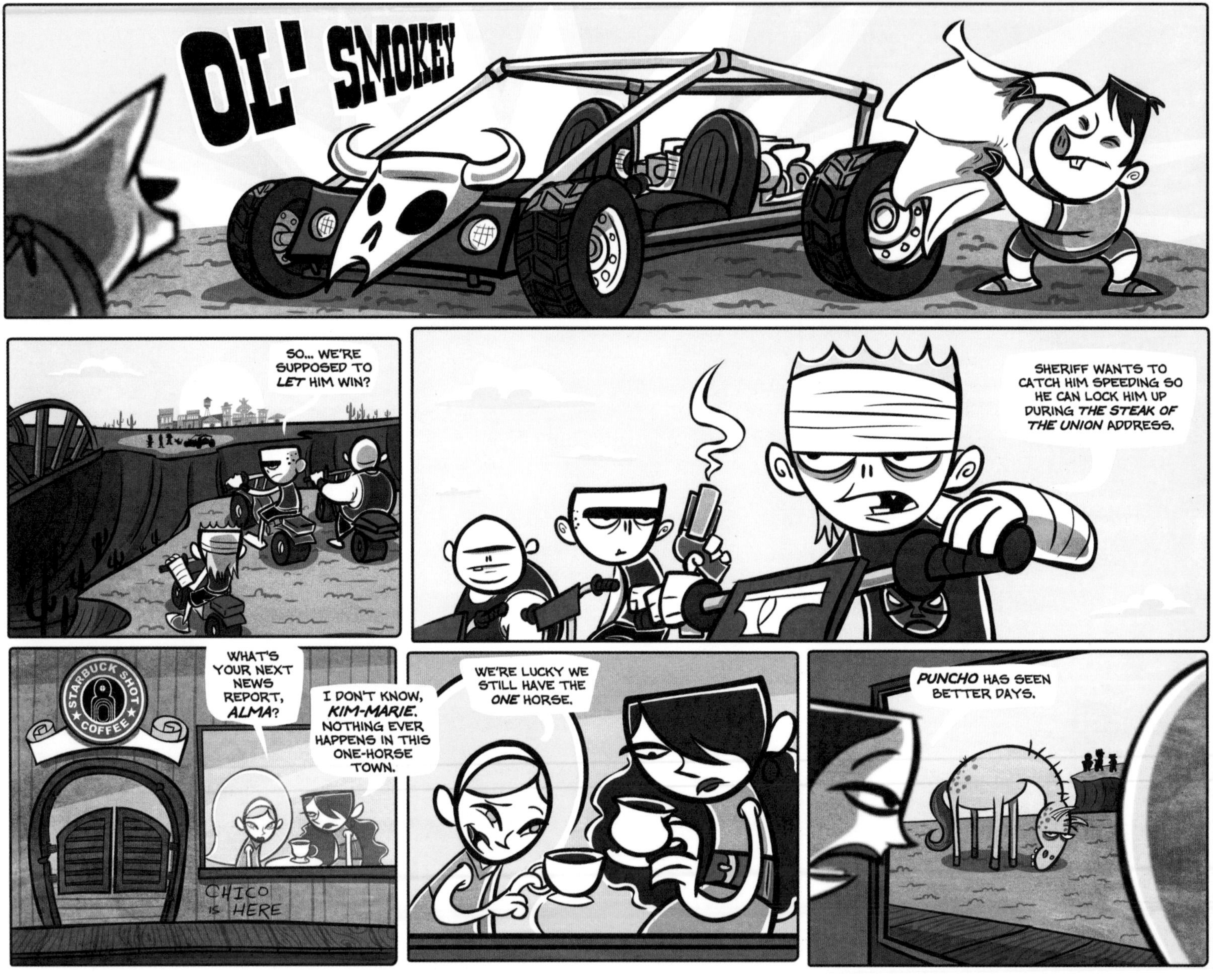
OL' SMOKEY
SO... WE'RE SUPPOSED TO LET HIM WIN?
SHERIFF WANTS TO CATCH HIM SPEEDING SO HE CAN LOCK HIM UP DURING THE STEAK OF THE UNION ADDRESS.
STARBUCK SHOT COFFEE
WHAT'S YOUR NEXT NEWS REPORT, ALMA?
I DON'T KNOW, KIM-MARIE. NOTHING EVER HAPPENS IN THIS ONE-HORSE TOWN.
CHICO IS HERE
WE'RE LUCKY WE STILL HAVE THE ONE HORSE.
PUNCHO HAS SEEN BETTER DAYS.

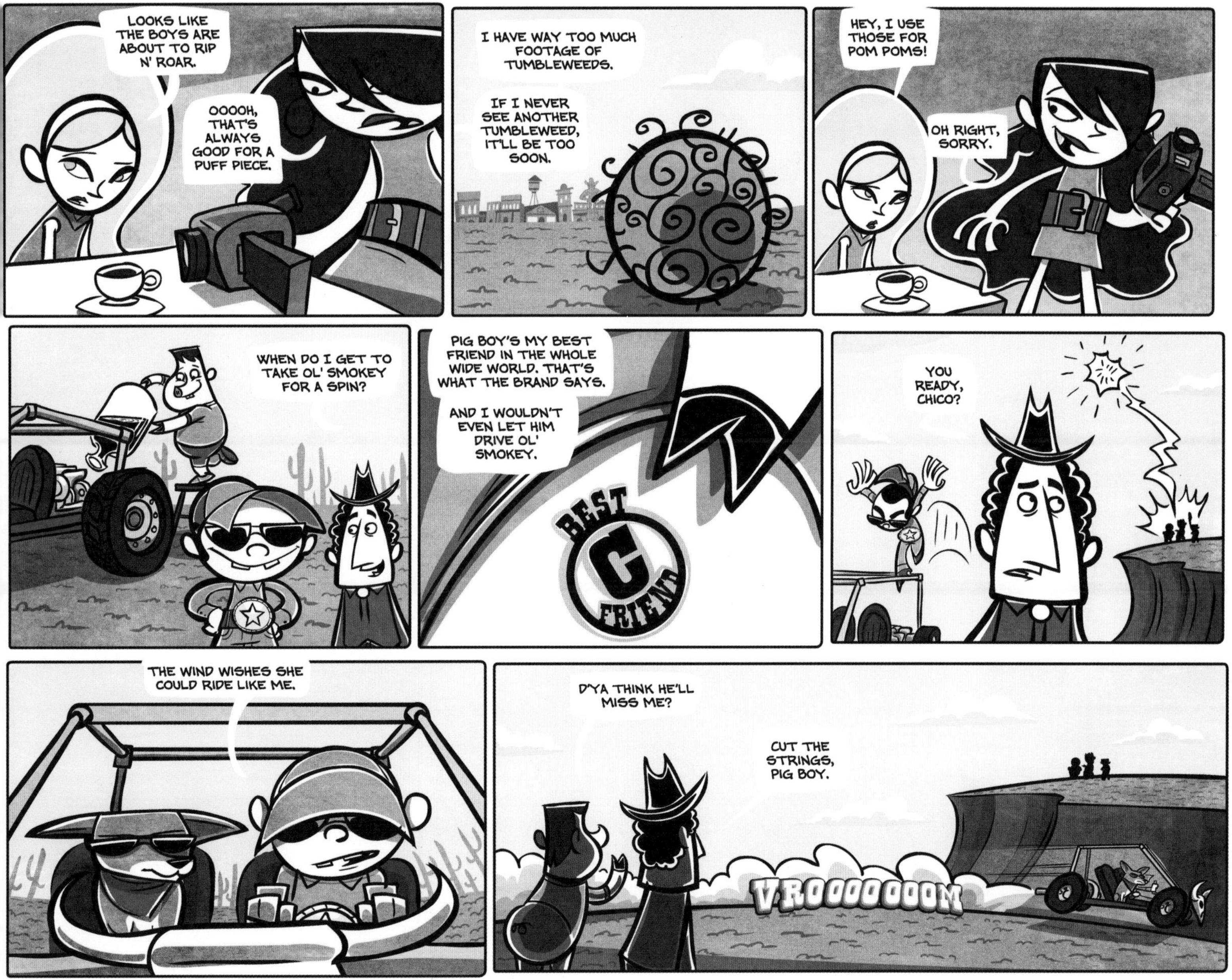
LOOKS LIKE THE BOYS ARE ABOUT TO RIP N' ROAR.
OOOOH, THAT'S ALWAYS GOOD FOR A PUFF PIECE.
I HAVE WAY TOO MUCH FOOTAGE OF TUMBLEWEEDS.
IF I NEVER SEE ANOTHER TUMBLEWEED, IT'LL BE TOO SOON.
HEY, I USE THOSE FOR POM POMS!
OH RIGHT, SORRY.
WHEN DO I GET TO TAKE OL' SMOKEY FOR A SPIN?
PIG BOY'S MY BEST FRIEND IN THE WHOLE WIDE WORLD. THAT'S WHAT THE BRAND SAYS.
AND I WOULDN'T EVEN LET HIM DRIVE OL' SMOKEY.
BEST C FRIEND
YOU READY, CHICO?
THE WIND WISHES SHE COULD RIDE LIKE ME.
D'YA THINK HE'LL MISS ME?
CUT THE STRINGS, PIG BOY.
VROOOOOOOM

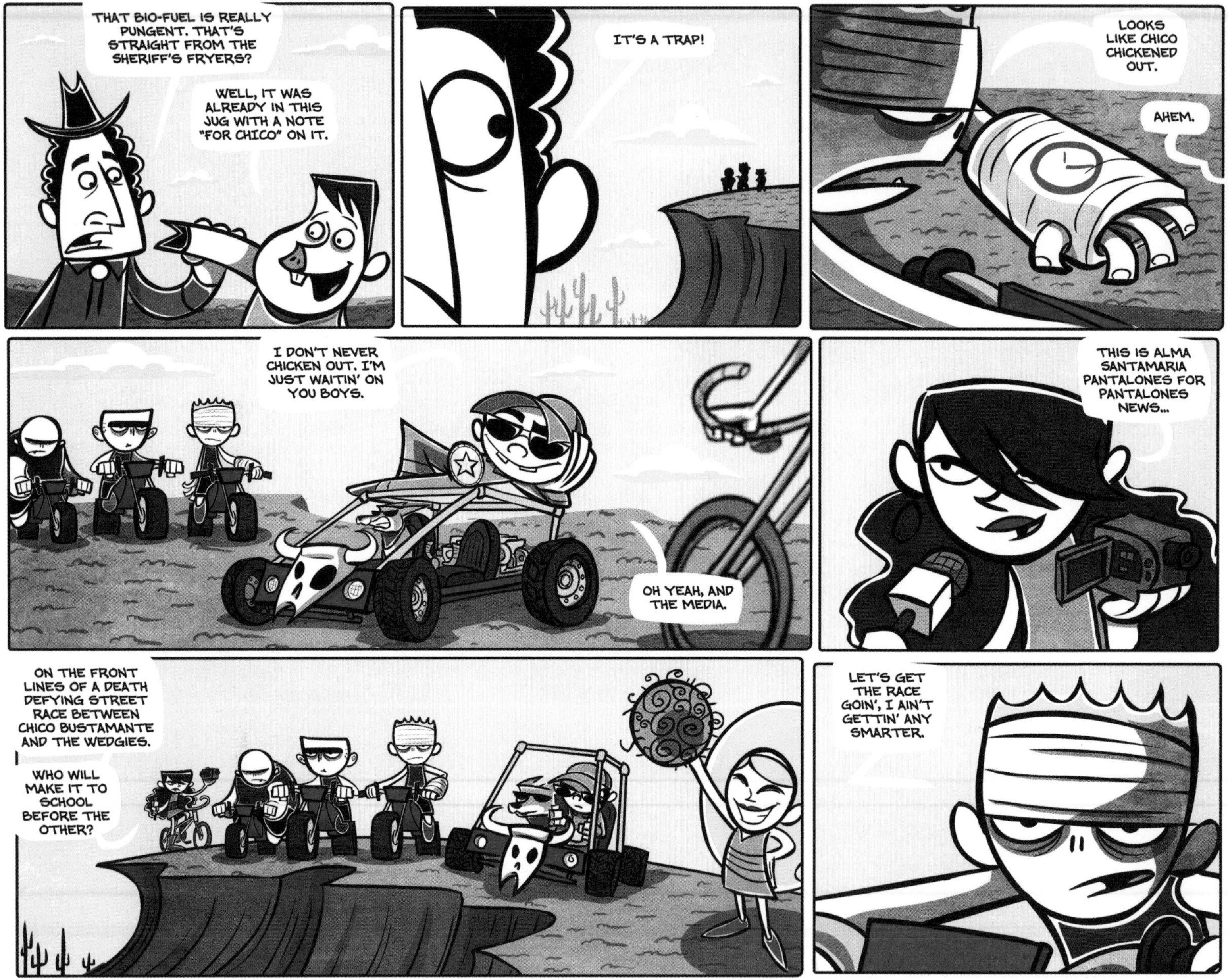
THAT BIO-FUEL IS REALLY PUNGENT. THAT'S STRAIGHT FROM THE SHERIFF'S FRYERS?
WELL, IT WAS ALREADY IN THIS JUG WITH A NOTE "FOR CHICO" ON IT.
IT'S A TRAP!
LOOKS LIKE CHICO CHICKENED OUT.
AHEM.
I DON'T NEVER CHICKEN OUT. I'M JUST WAITIN' ON YOU BOYS.
OH YEAH, AND THE MEDIA.
THIS IS ALMA SANTAMARIA PANTALONES FOR PANTALONES NEWS...
ON THE FRONT LINES OF A DEATH DEFYING STREET RACE BETWEEN CHICO BUSTAMANTE AND THE WEDGIES.
WHO WILL MAKE IT TO SCHOOL BEFORE THE OTHER?
LET'S GET THE RACE GOIN', I AIN'T GETTIN' ANY SMARTER.

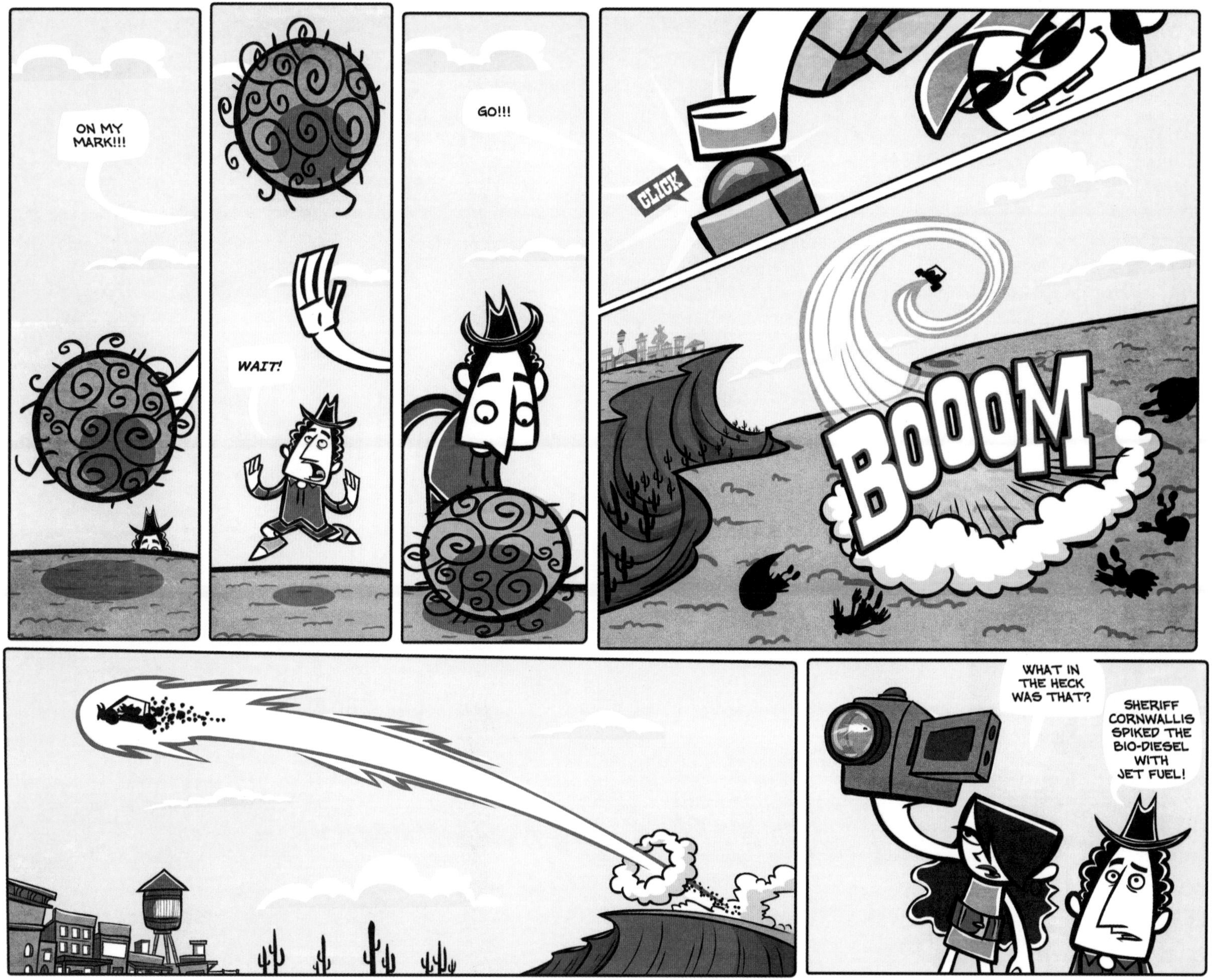
ON MY MARK!!!
WAIT!
GO!!!
CLICK
BOOOM
WHAT IN THE HECK WAS THAT?
SHERIFF CORNWALLIS SPIKED THE BIO-DIESEL WITH JET FUEL!

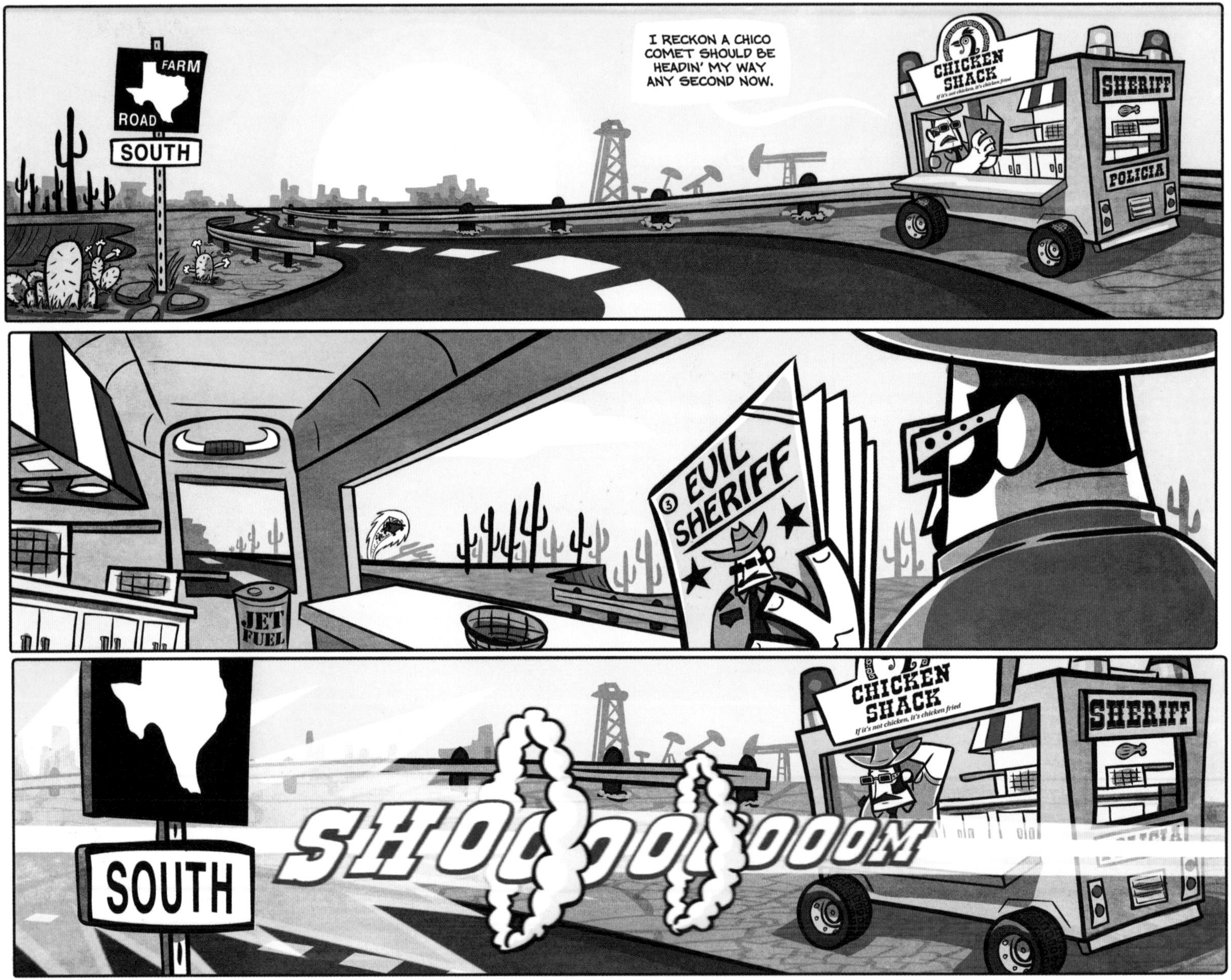
FARM
ROAD
SOUTH
I RECKON A CHICO COMET SHOULD BE HEADIN' MY WAY ANY SECOND NOW.
CHICKEN SHACK
If it's not chicken, it's chicken fried
SHERIFF
POLICIA
JET FUEL
3 EVIL SHERIFF
SOUTH
CHICKEN SHACK
If it's not chicken, it's chicken fried
SHERIFF
SHOO OO OOOOM

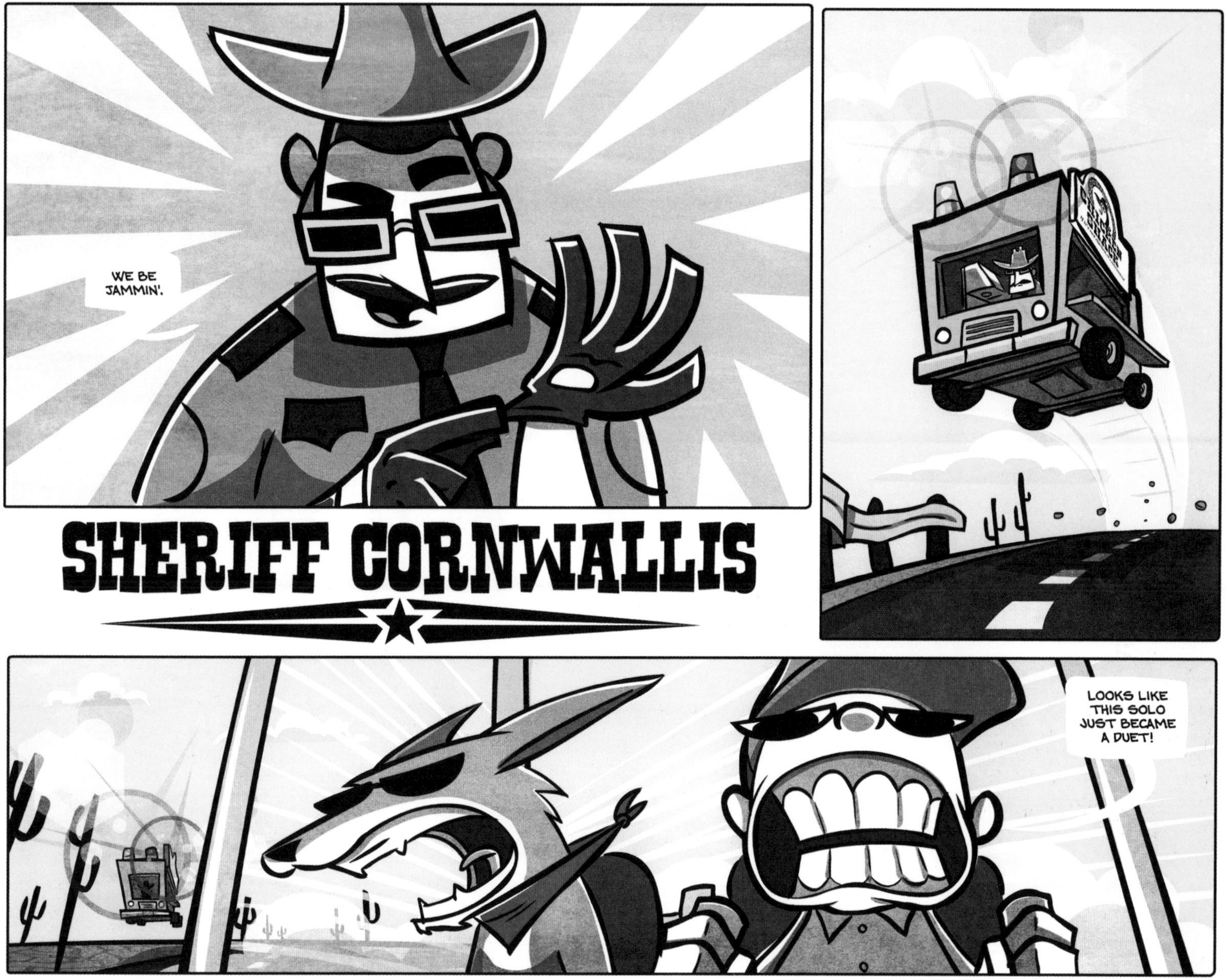
WE BE JAMMIN'.
SHERIFF CORNWALLIS
LOOKS LIKE THIS SOLO JUST BECAME A DUET!

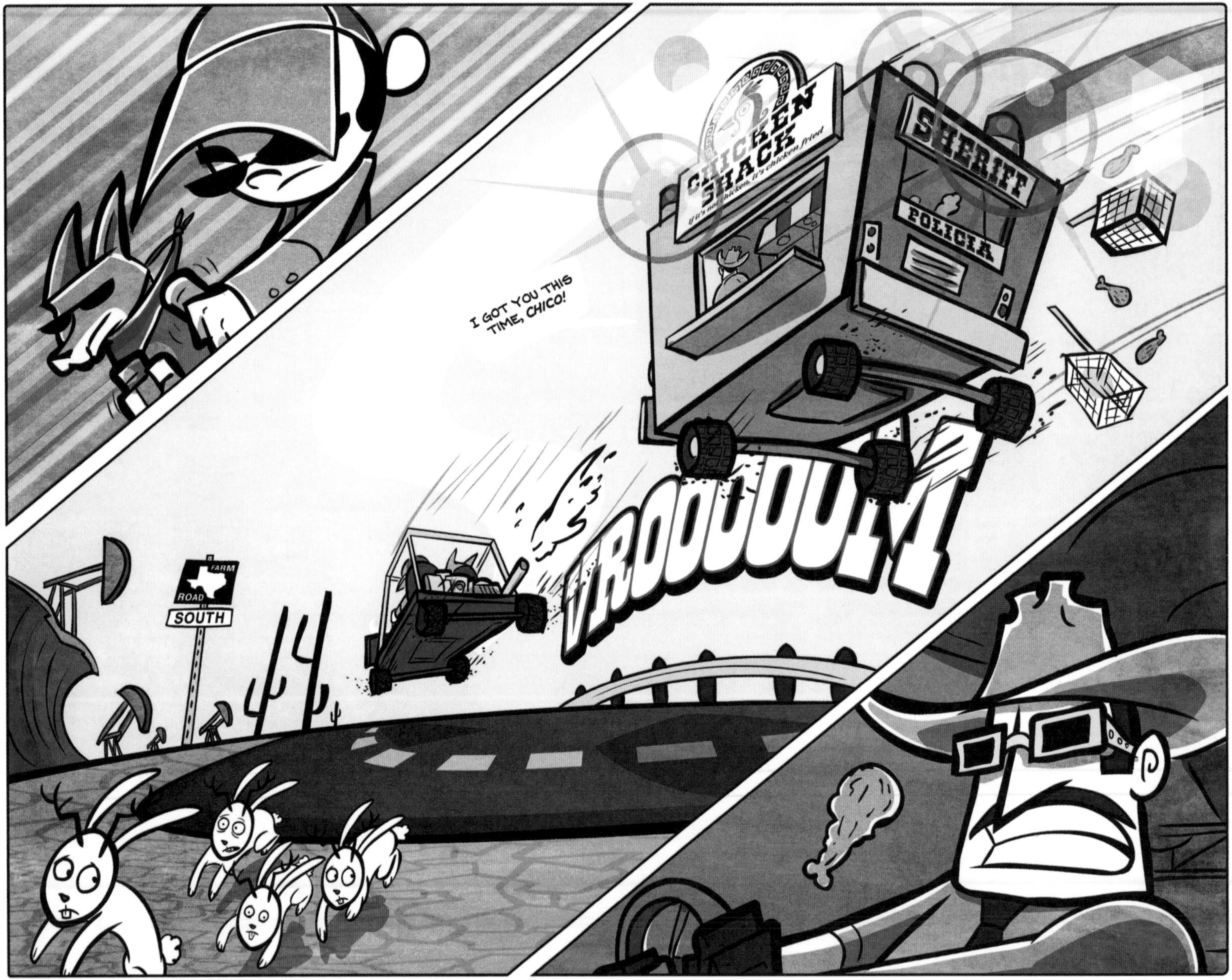

CHICKEN SHACK
SHERIFF
POLICIA
I GOT YOU THIS TIME, CHICO!
VROOOOOOM
FARM ROAD
SOUTH

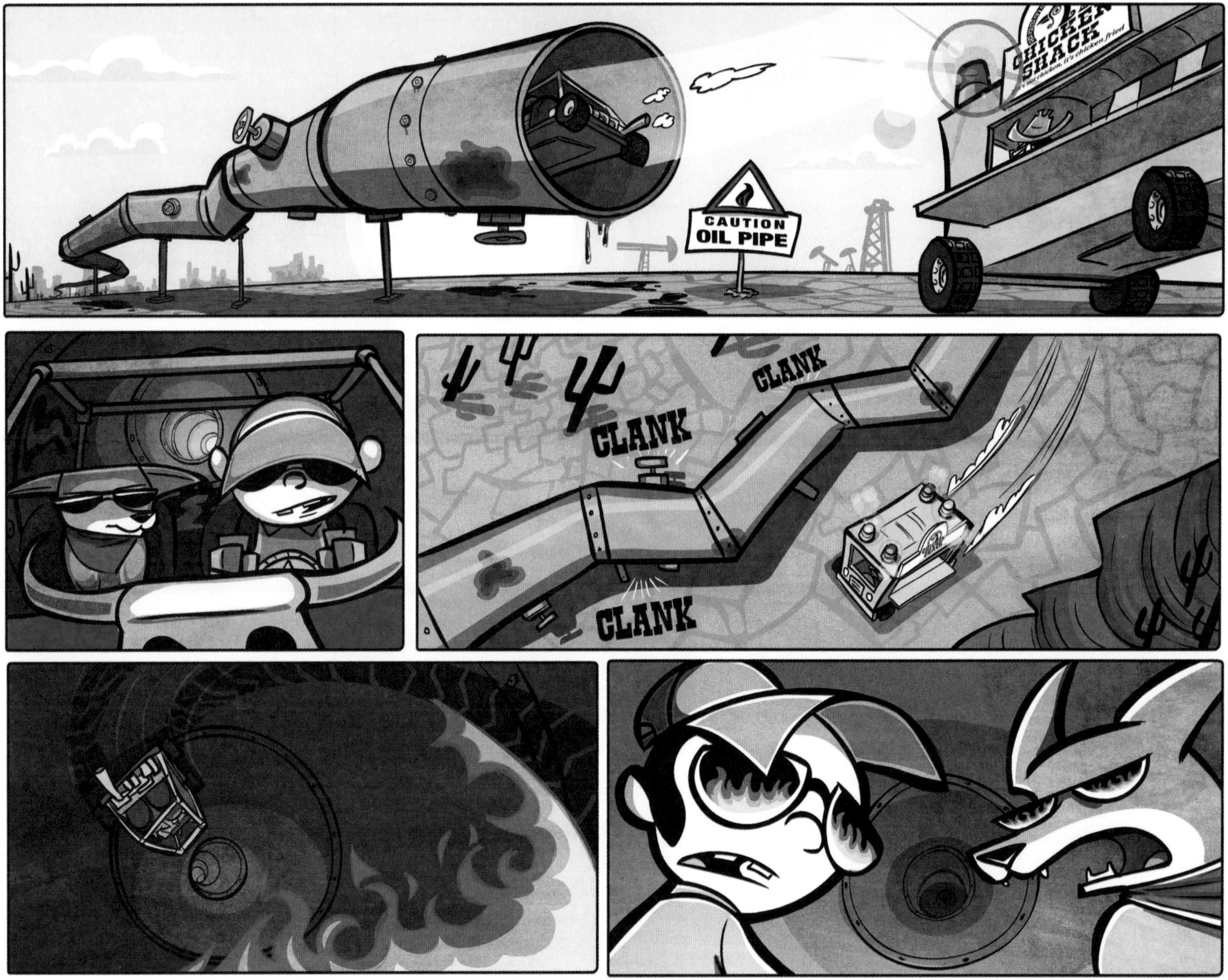
CHICKEN
SHACK
CAUTION
OIL PIPE
CLANK
CLANK
CLANK

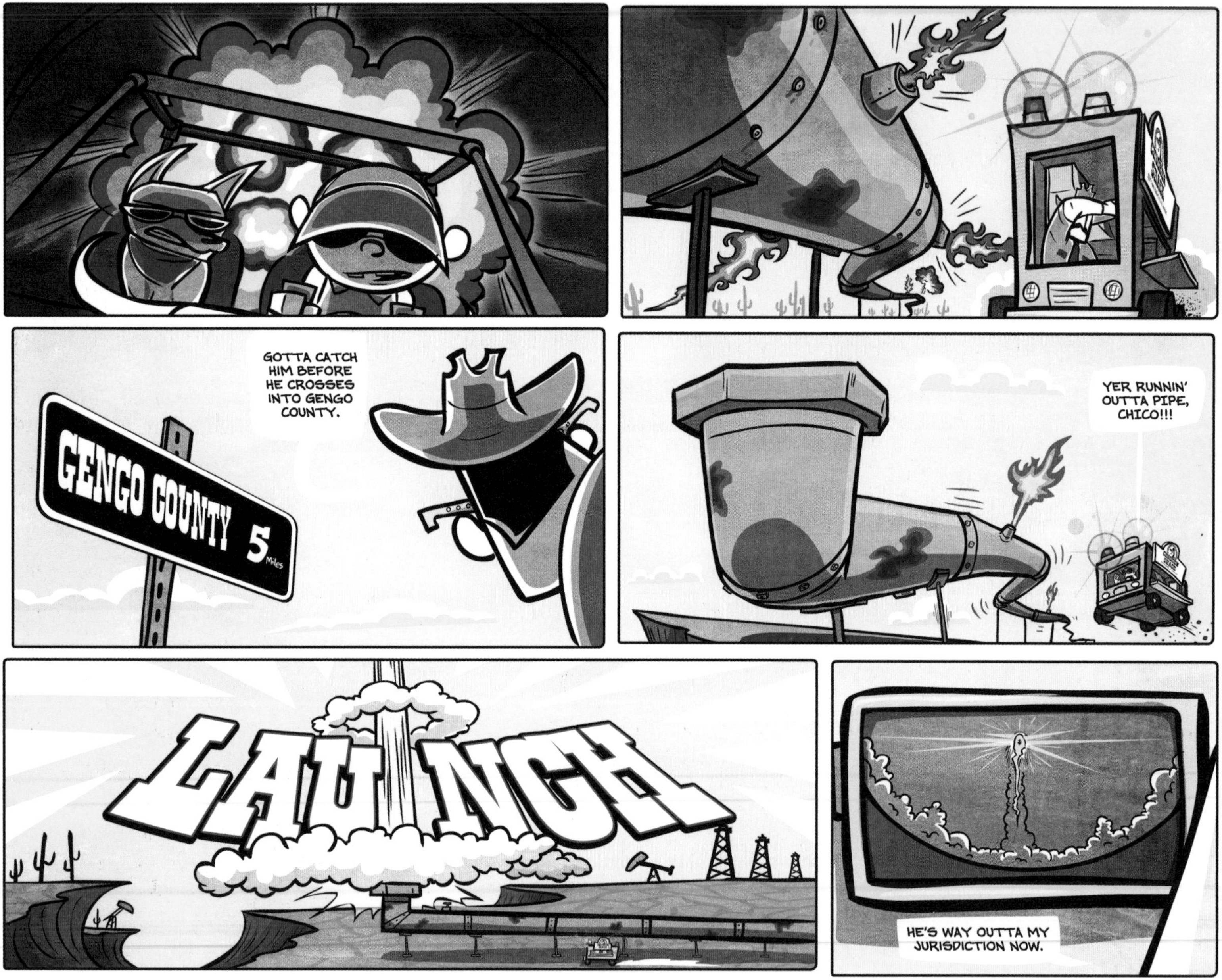
GOTTA CATCH HIM BEFORE HE CROSSES INTO GENGO COUNTY.
GENGO COUNTY 5 Miles
YER RUNNIN' OUTTA PIPE, CHICO!!!
LAUNCH
HE'S WAY OUTTA MY JURISDICTION NOW.

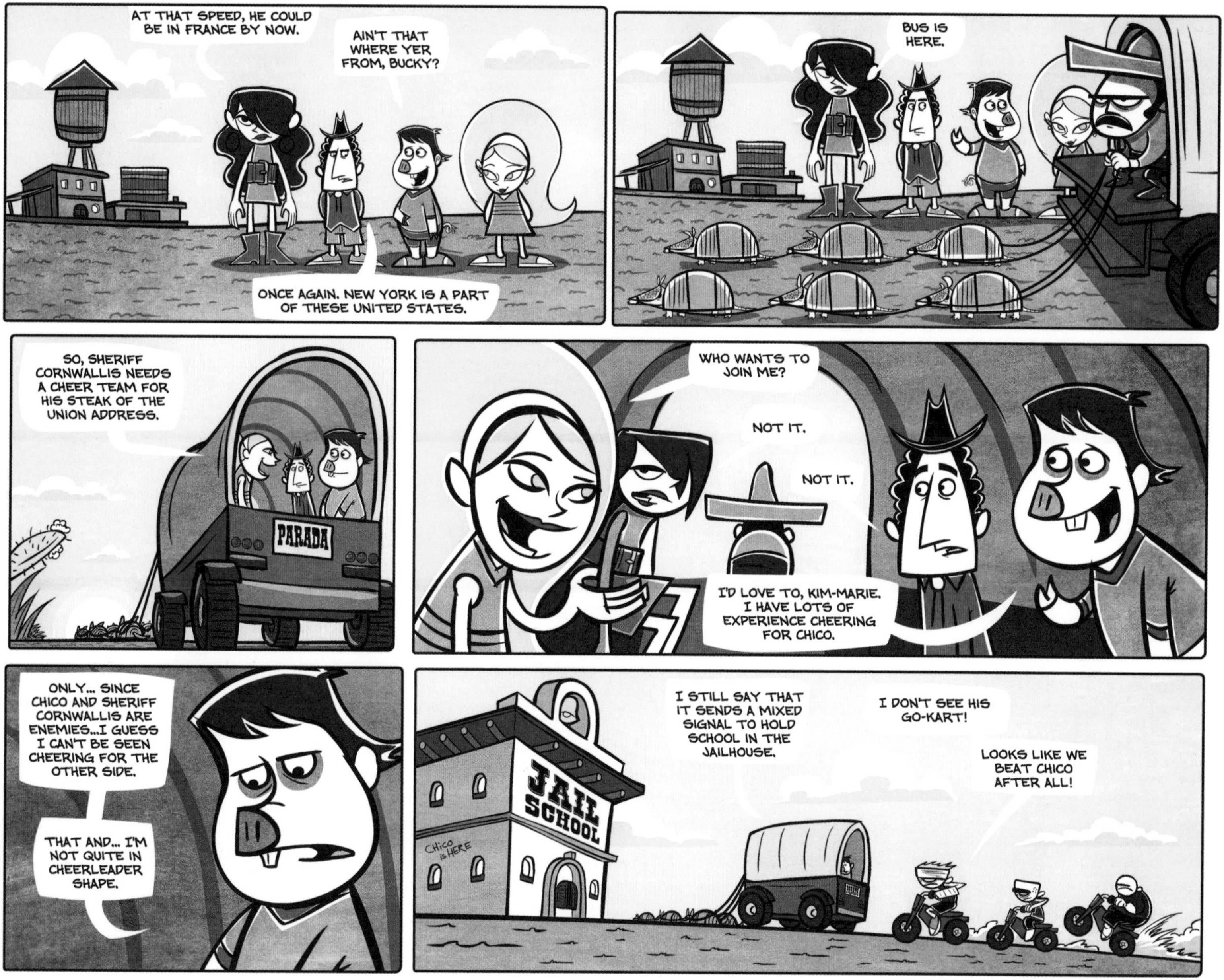

AT THAT SPEED, HE COULD BE IN FRANCE BY NOW.
AIN'T THAT WHERE YER FROM, BUCKY?
ONCE AGAIN. NEW YORK IS A PART OF THESE UNITED STATES.
BUS IS HERE.
SO, SHERIFF CORNWALLIS NEEDS A CHEER TEAM FOR HIS STEAK OF THE UNION ADDRESS.
PARADA
WHO WANTS TO JOIN ME?
NOT IT.
NOT IT.
I'D LOVE TO, KIM-MARIE. I HAVE LOTS OF EXPERIENCE CHEERING FOR CHICO.
ONLY... SINCE CHICO AND SHERIFF CORNWALLIS ARE ENEMIES...I GUESS I CAN'T BE SEEN CHEERING FOR THE OTHER SIDE.
THAT AND... I'M NOT QUITE IN CHEERLEADER SHAPE.
JAIL SCHOOL
CHICO IS HERE
I STILL SAY THAT IT SENDS A MIXED SIGNAL TO HOLD SCHOOL IN THE JAILHOUSE.
I DON'T SEE HIS GO-KART!
LOOKS LIKE WE BEAT CHICO AFTER ALL!

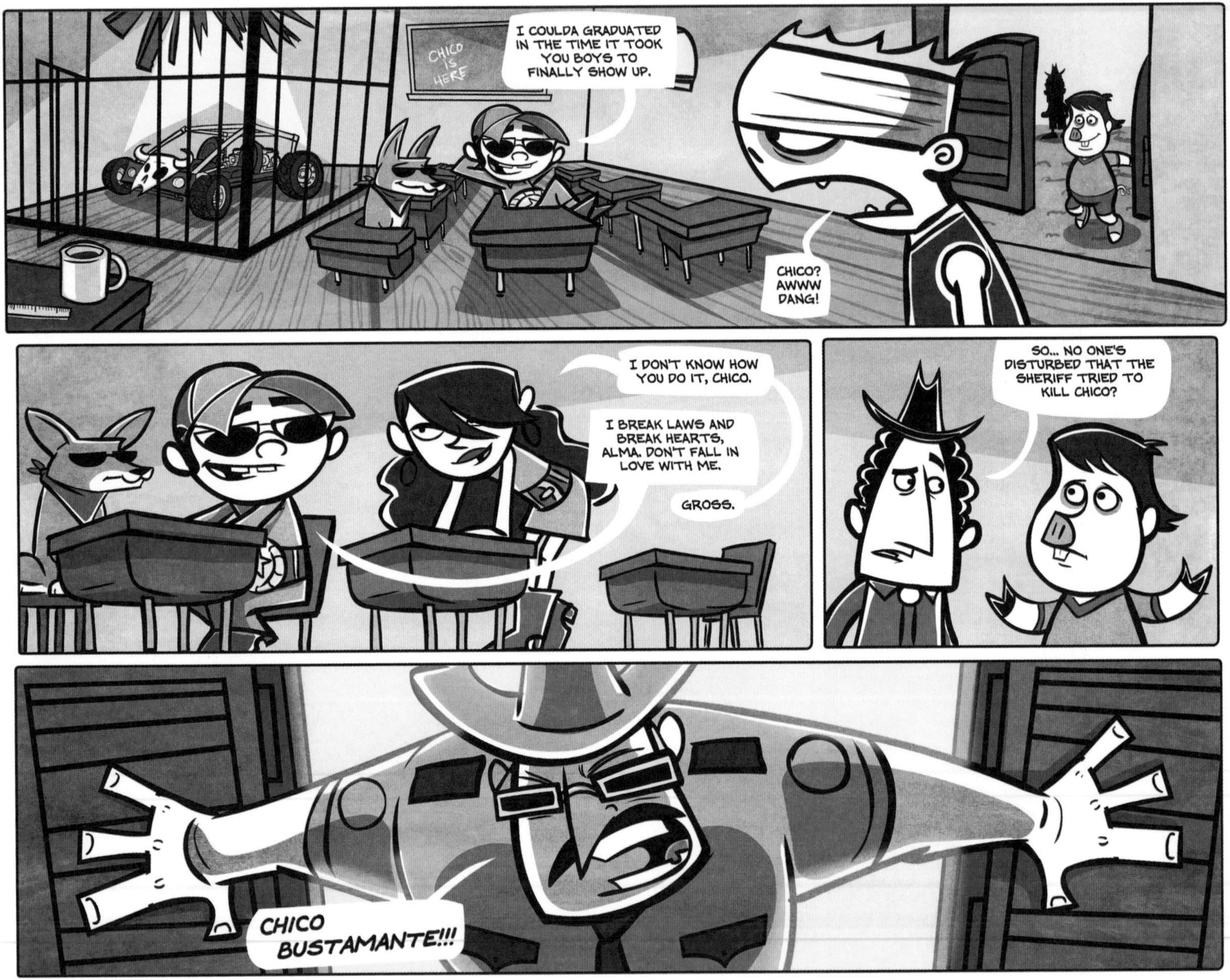
CHICO IS HERE
I COULDA GRADUATED IN THE TIME IT TOOK YOU BOYS TO FINALLY SHOW UP.
CHICO? AWWW DANG!
I DON'T KNOW HOW YOU DO IT, CHICO.
I BREAK LAWS AND BREAK HEARTS, ALMA. DON'T FALL IN LOVE WITH ME.
GROSS.
SO... NO ONE'S DISTURBED THAT THE SHERIFF TRIED TO KILL CHICO?
CHICO BUSTAMANTE!!!

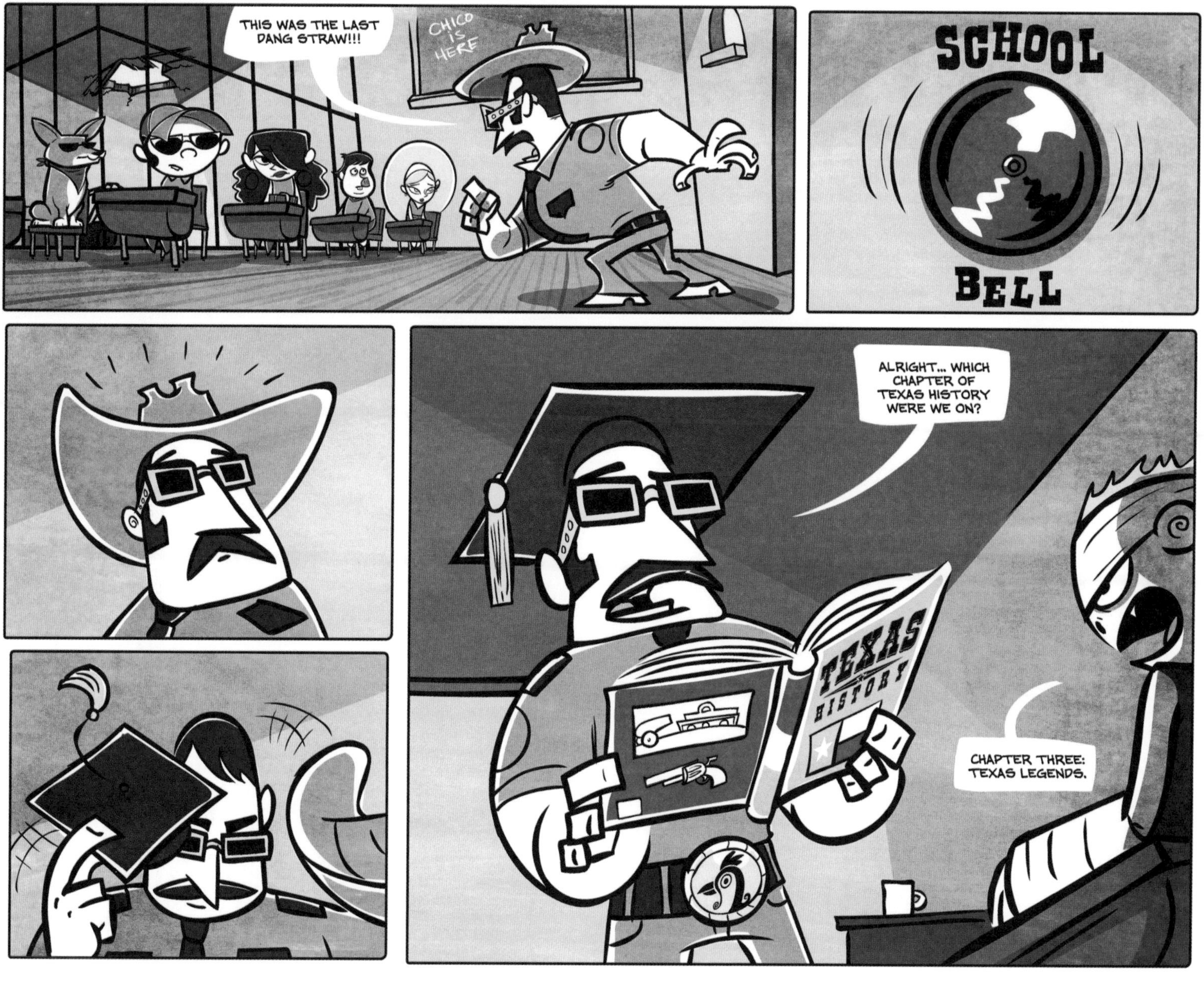
THIS WAS THE LAST DANG STRAW!!!
CHICO IS HERE
SCHOOL
BELL
ALRIGHT... WHICH CHAPTER OF TEXAS HISTORY WERE WE ON?
TEXAS HISTORY
CHAPTER THREE: TEXAS LEGENDS.

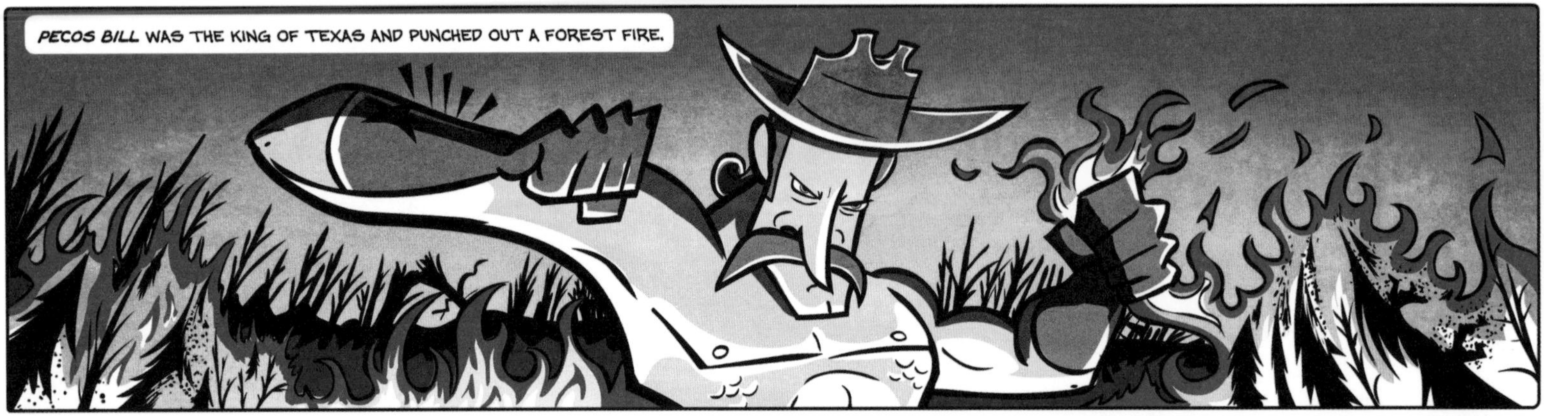
PECOS BILL WAS THE KING OF TEXAS AND PUNCHED OUT A FOREST FIRE.

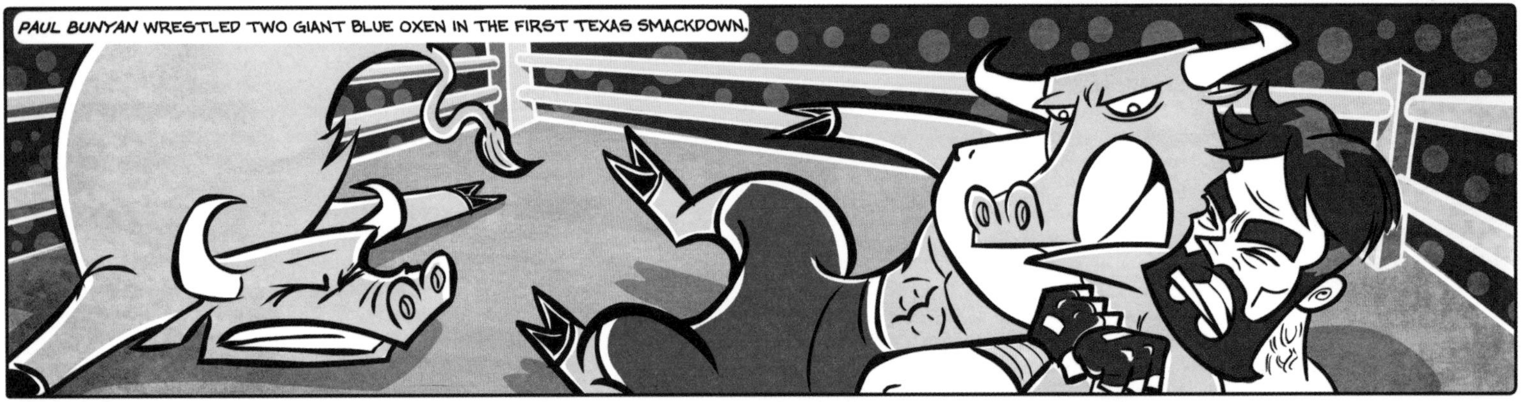
PAUL BUNYAN WRESTLED TWO GIANT BLUE OXEN IN THE FIRST TEXAS SMACKDOWN.

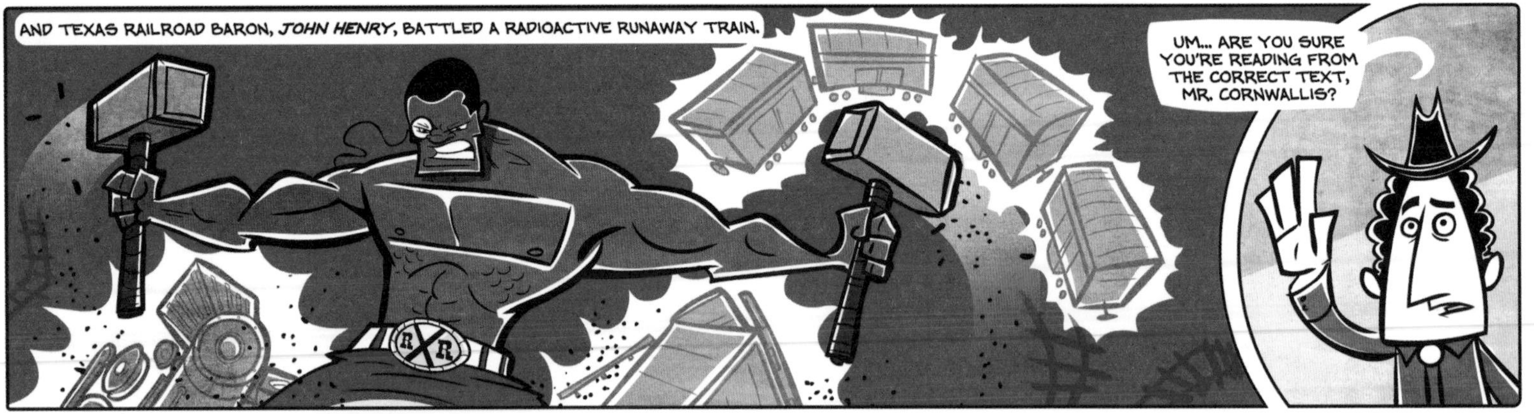
AND TEXAS RAILROAD BARON, *JOHN HENRY*, BATTLED A RADIOACTIVE RUNAWAY TRAIN.
UM... ARE YOU SURE YOU'RE READING FROM THE CORRECT TEXT, MR. CORNWALLIS?

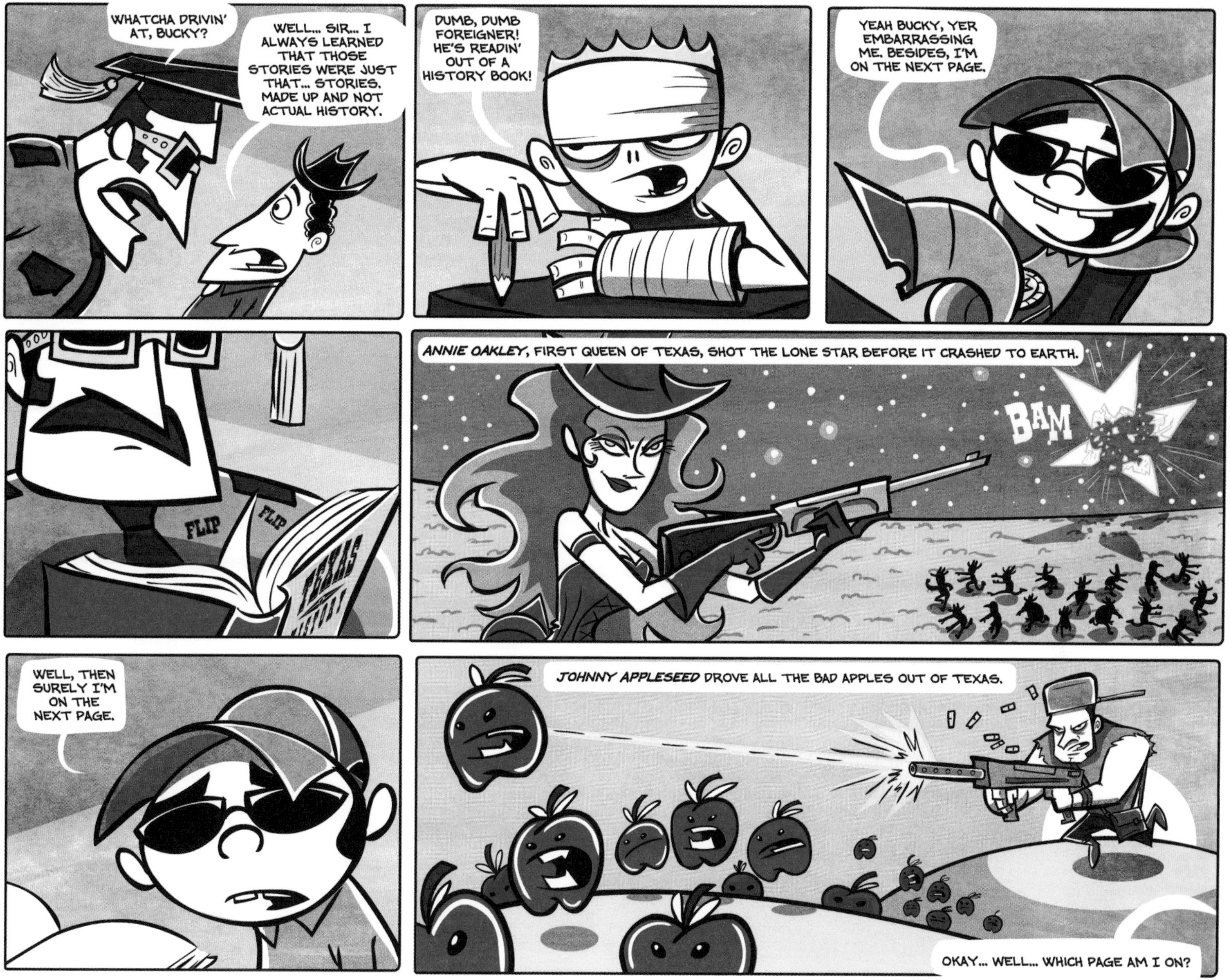
WHATCHA DRIVIN' AT, BUCKY?
WELL... SIR... I ALWAYS LEARNED THAT THOSE STORIES WERE JUST THAT... STORIES. MADE UP AND NOT ACTUAL HISTORY.
DUMB, DUMB FOREIGNER! HE'S READIN' OUT OF A HISTORY BOOK!
YEAH BUCKY, YER EMBARRASSING ME. BESIDES, I'M ON THE NEXT PAGE.
FLIP
FLIP
TEXAS
ANNIE OAKLEY, FIRST QUEEN OF TEXAS, SHOT THE LONE STAR BEFORE IT CRASHED TO EARTH.
BAM
WELL, THEN SURELY I'M ON THE NEXT PAGE.
JOHNNY APPLESEED DROVE ALL THE BAD APPLES OUT OF TEXAS.
OKAY... WELL... WHICH PAGE AM I ON?

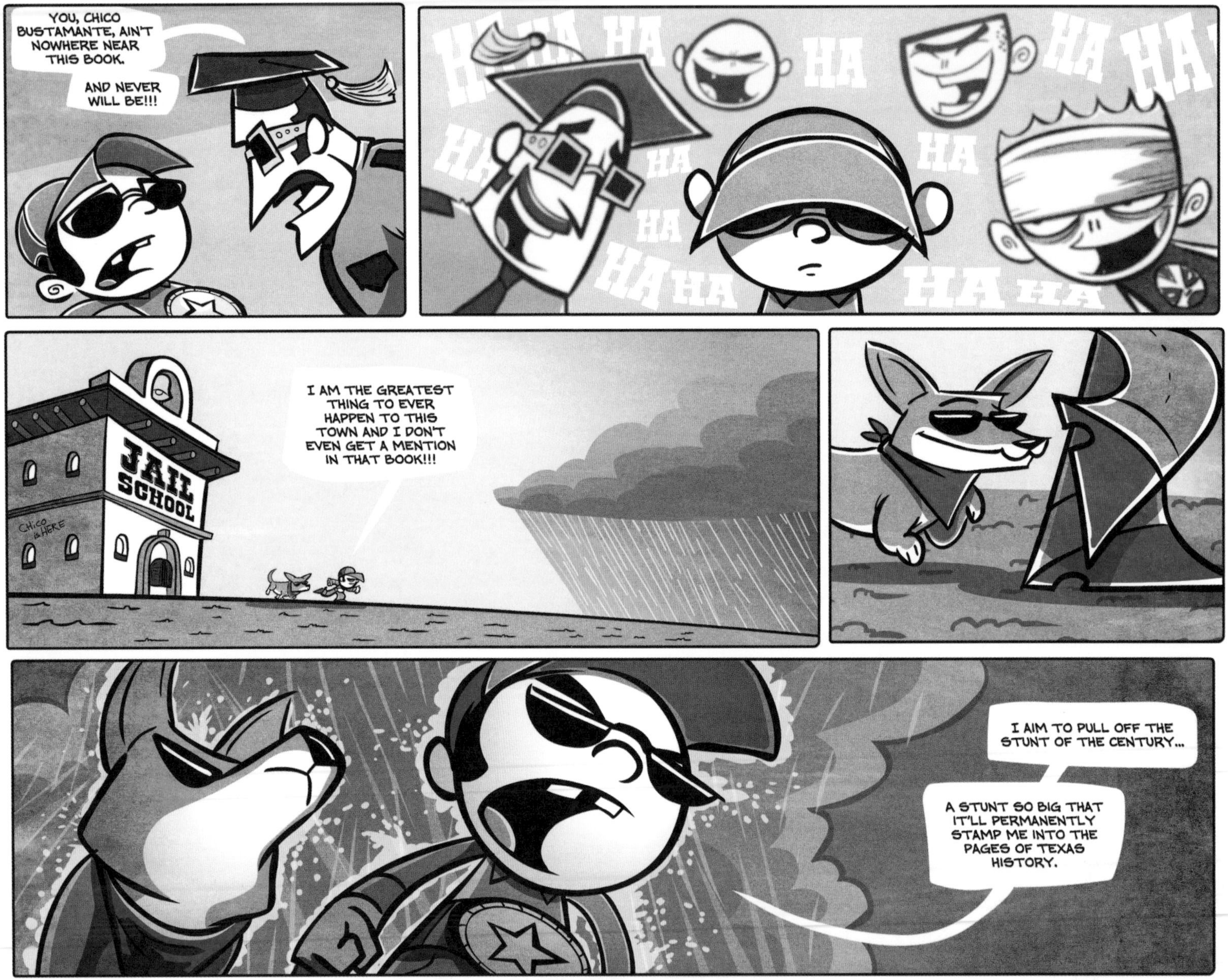

YOU, CHICO BUSTAMANTE, AIN'T NOWHERE NEAR THIS BOOK.
AND NEVER WILL BE!!!
HA HA HA HA HA HA HA HA HA HA HA HA HA HA HA HA
JAIL SCHOOL
CHICO IS HERE
I AM THE GREATEST THING TO EVER HAPPEN TO THIS TOWN AND I DON'T EVEN GET A MENTION IN THAT BOOK!!!
I AIM TO PULL OFF THE STUNT OF THE CENTURY...
A STUNT SO BIG THAT IT'LL PERMANENTLY STAMP ME INTO THE PAGES OF TEXAS HISTORY.

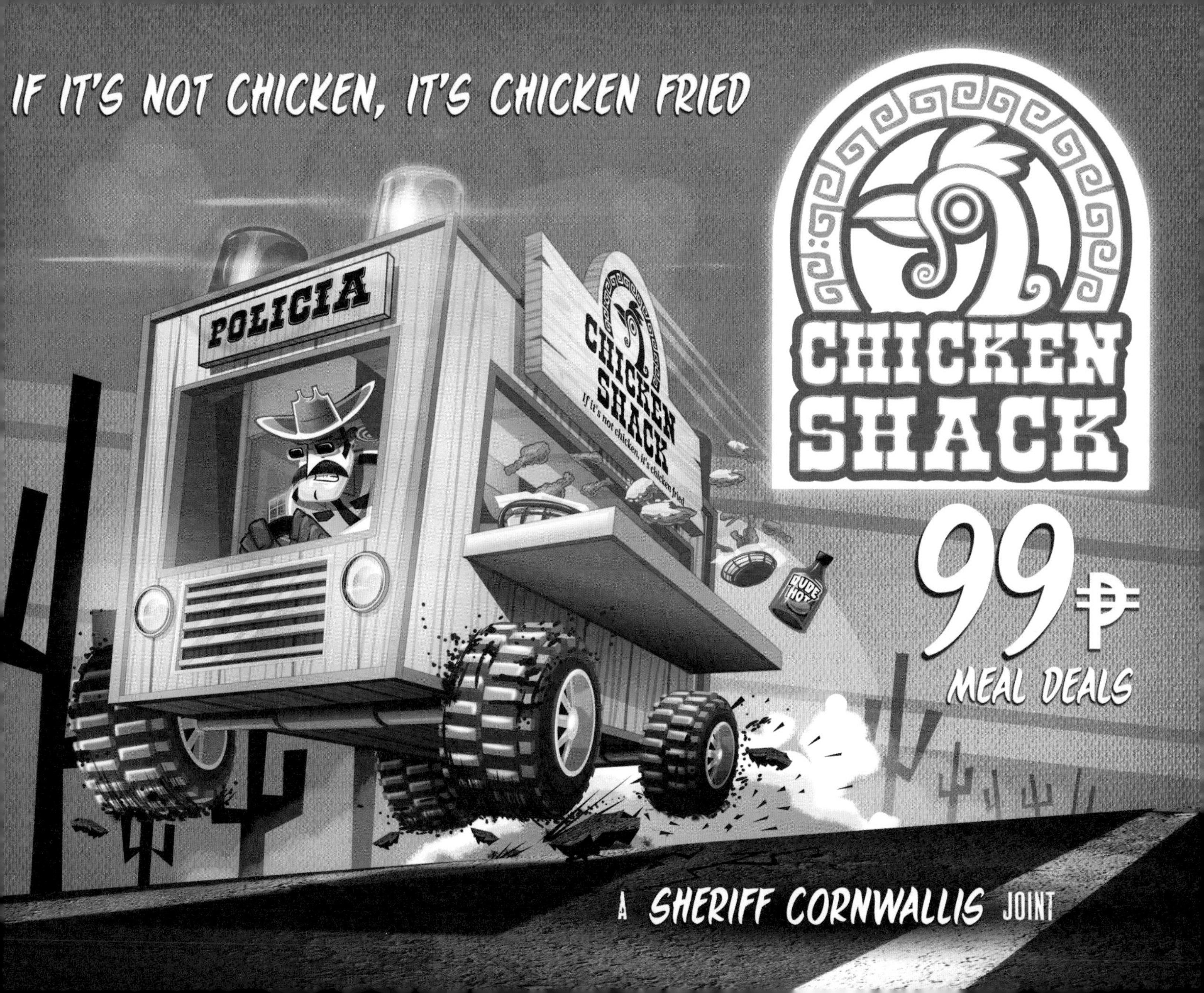

IF IT'S NOT CHICKEN, IT'S CHICKEN FRIED
POLICIA
CHICKEN SHACK
If it's not chicken, it's chicken fried
DUDE HOT
CHICKEN SHACK
99₱
MEAL DEALS
A SHERIFF CORNWALLIS JOINT

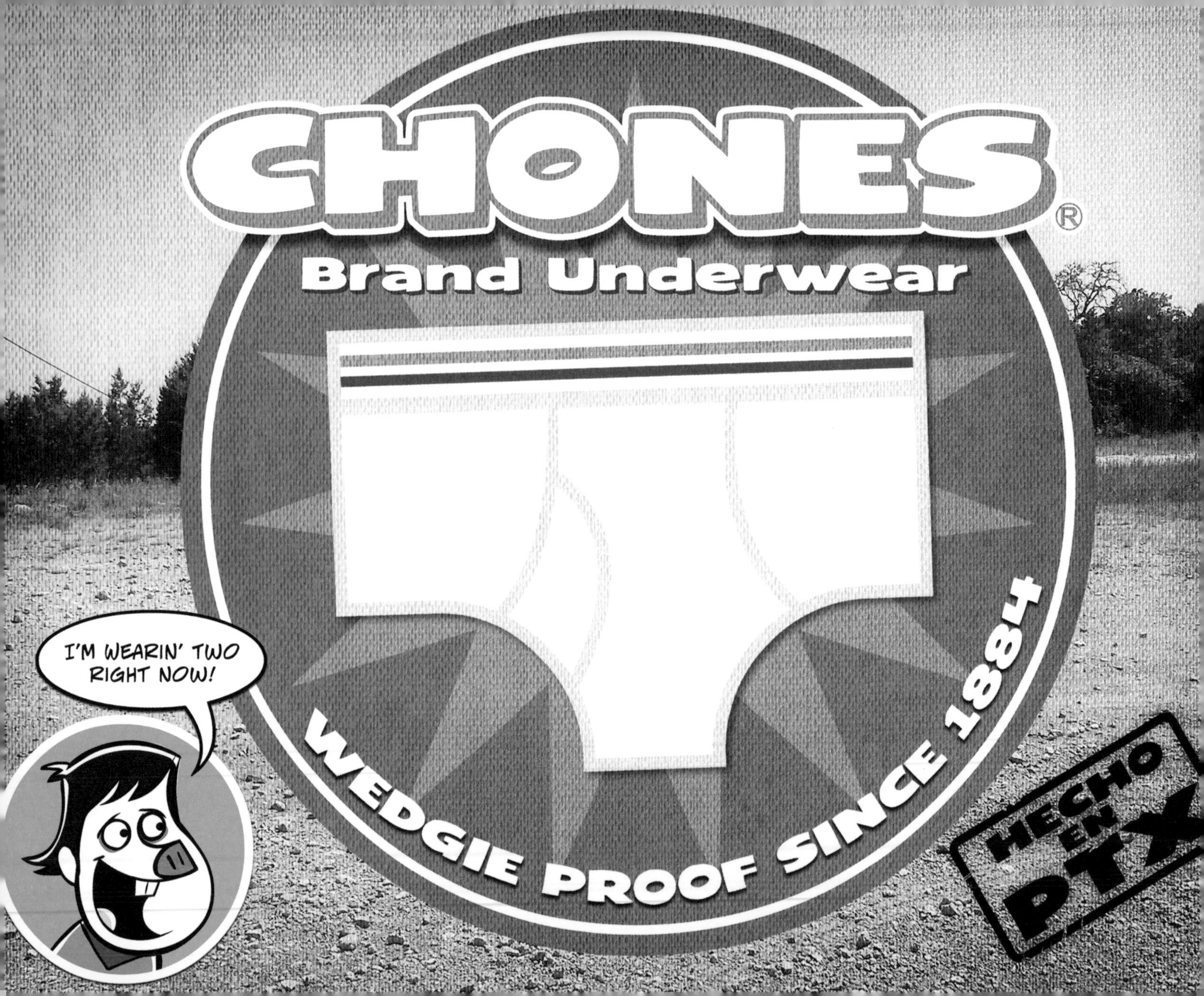
CHONES®
Brand Underwear
WEDGIE PROOF SINCE 1884
I'M WEARIN' TWO RIGHT NOW!
HECHO EN PTX

CHAPTER DOS

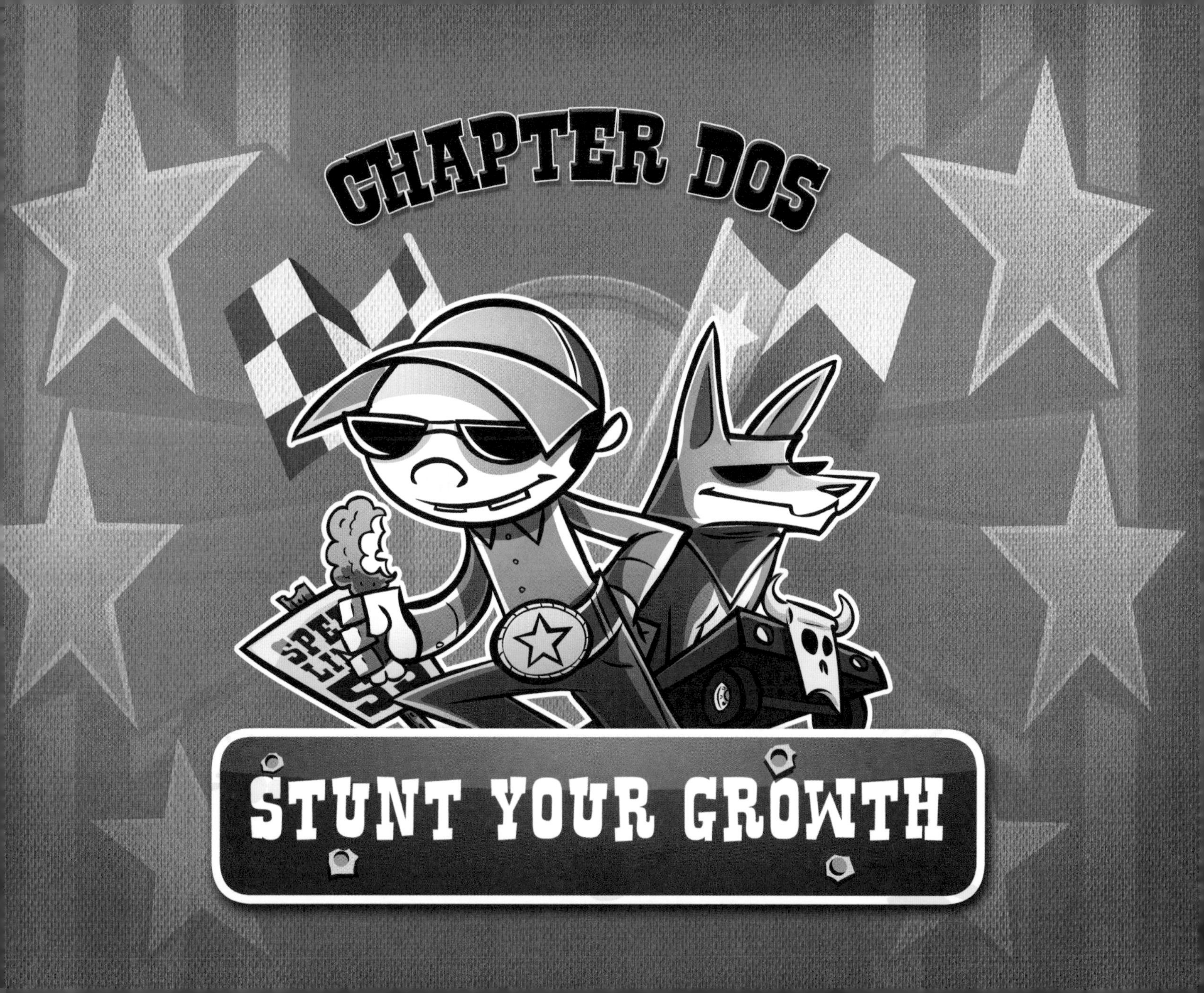

STUNT YOUR GROWTH

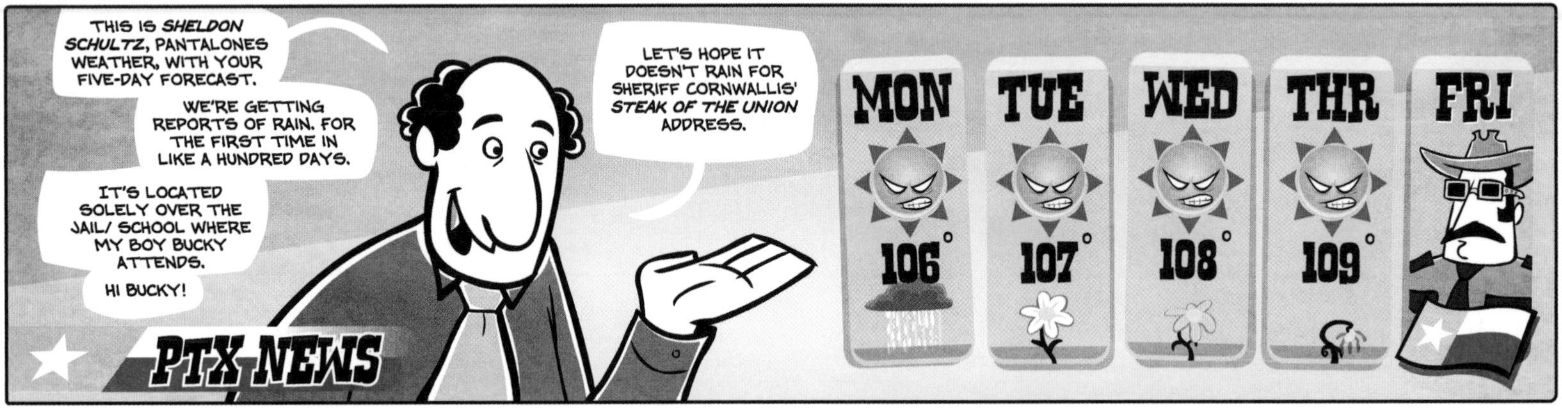
THIS IS SHELDON SCHULTZ, PANTALONES WEATHER, WITH YOUR FIVE-DAY FORECAST.
WE'RE GETTING REPORTS OF RAIN. FOR THE FIRST TIME IN LIKE A HUNDRED DAYS.
IT'S LOCATED SOLELY OVER THE JAIL/ SCHOOL WHERE MY BOY BUCKY ATTENDS.
HI BUCKY!
LET'S HOPE IT DOESN'T RAIN FOR SHERIFF CORNWALLIS' STEAK OF THE UNION ADDRESS.
PTX NEWS
MON 106°
TUE 107°
WED 108°
THR 109°
FRI

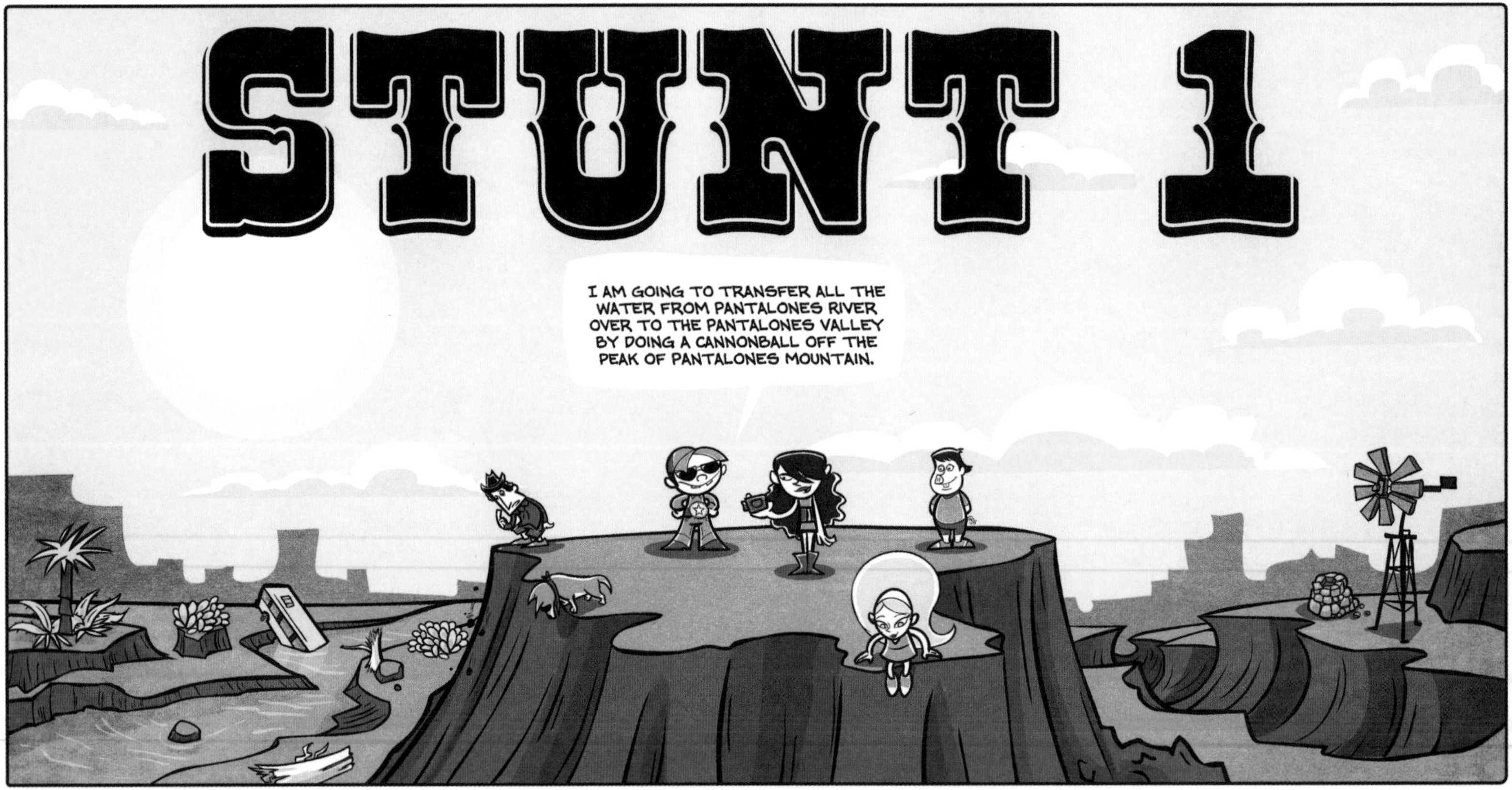
STUNT 1
I AM GOING TO TRANSFER ALL THE WATER FROM PANTALONES RIVER OVER TO THE PANTALONES VALLEY BY DOING A CANNONBALL OFF THE PEAK OF PANTALONES MOUNTAIN.

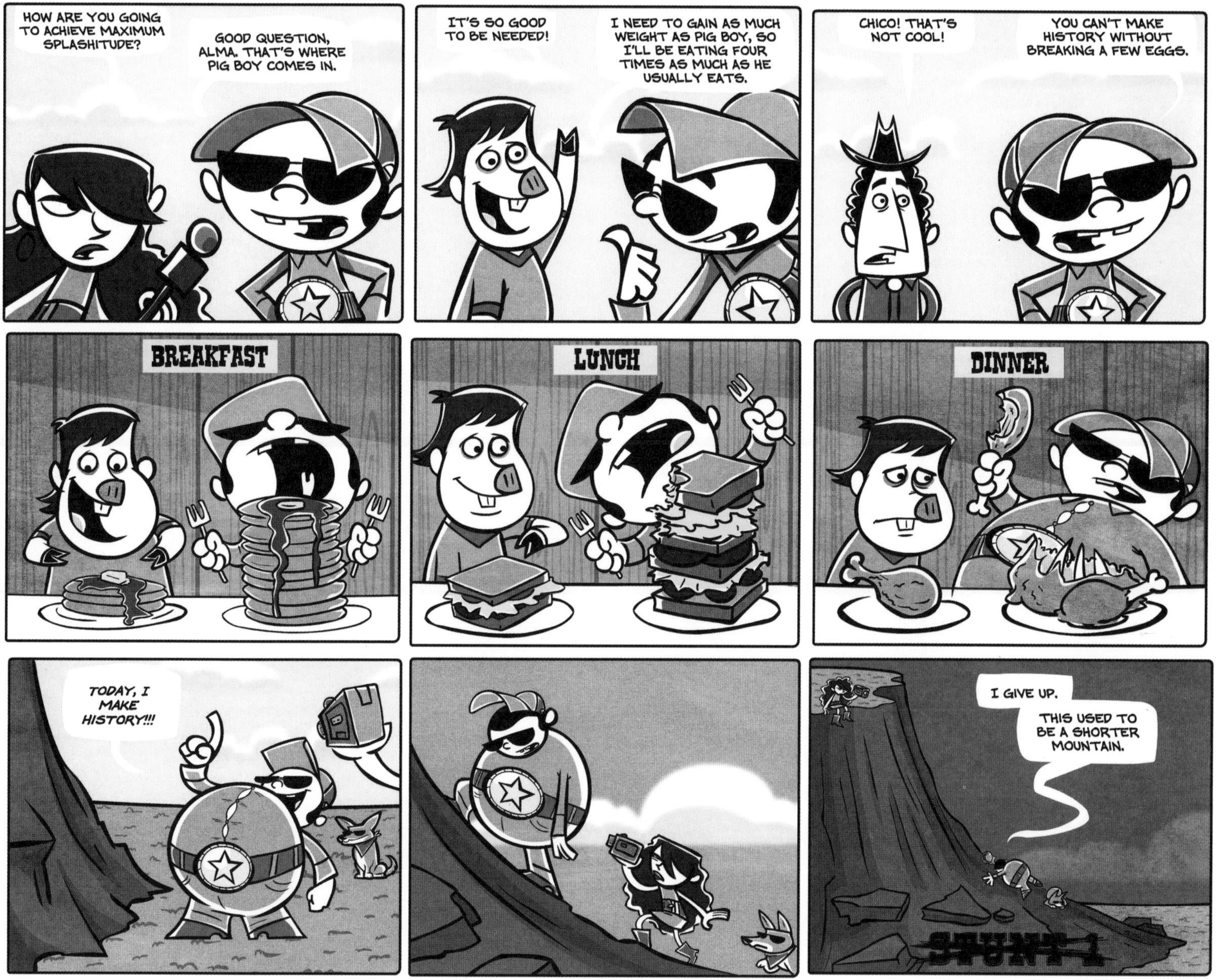
HOW ARE YOU GOING TO ACHIEVE MAXIMUM SPLASHITUDE?
GOOD QUESTION, ALMA. THAT'S WHERE PIG BOY COMES IN.
IT'S SO GOOD TO BE NEEDED!
I NEED TO GAIN AS MUCH WEIGHT AS PIG BOY, SO I'LL BE EATING FOUR TIMES AS MUCH AS HE USUALLY EATS.
CHICO! THAT'S NOT COOL!
YOU CAN'T MAKE HISTORY WITHOUT BREAKING A FEW EGGS.
BREAKFAST
LUNCH
DINNER
TODAY, I MAKE HISTORY!!!
I GIVE UP.
THIS USED TO BE A SHORTER MOUNTAIN.

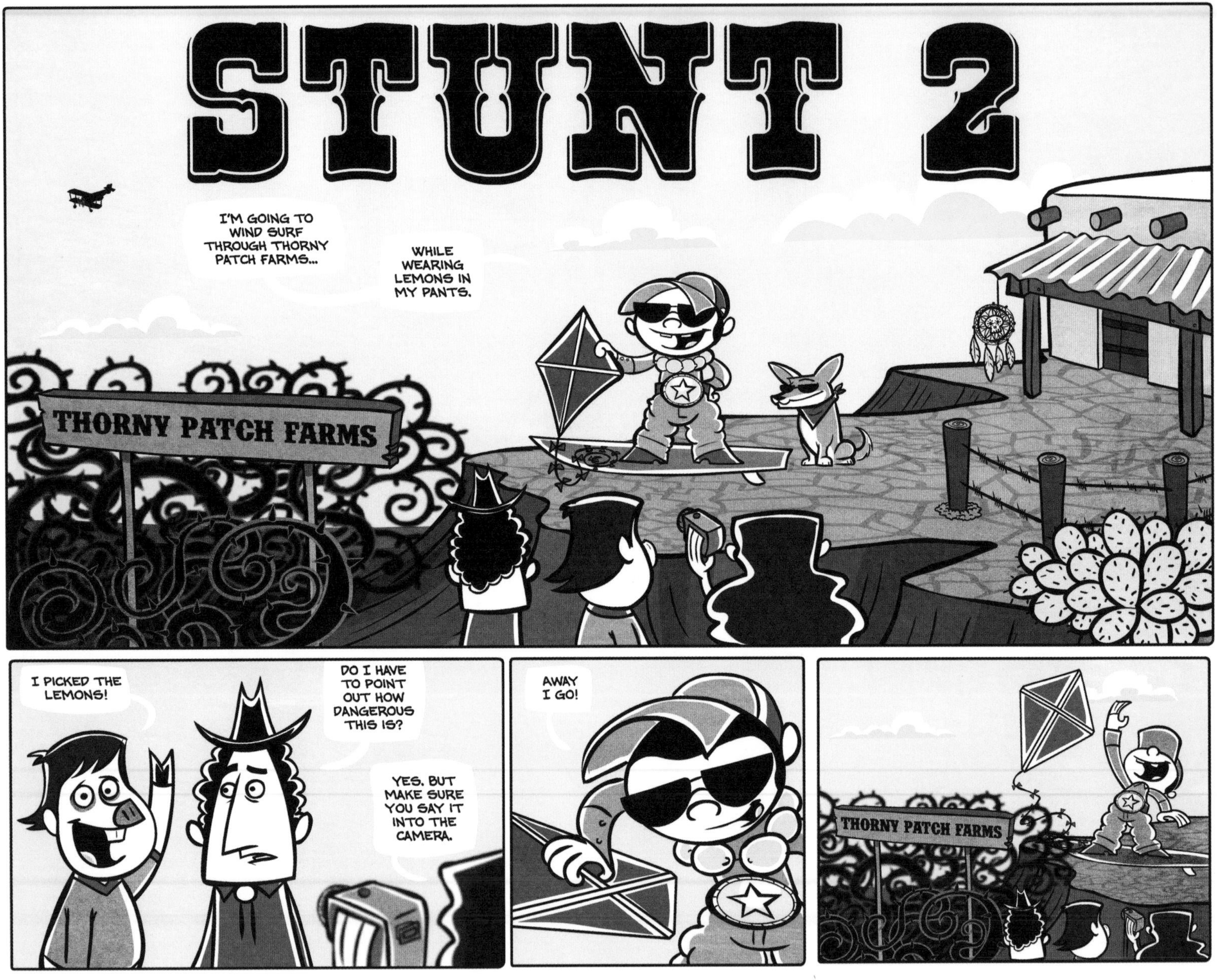
STUNT 2
I'M GOING TO WIND SURF THROUGH THORNY PATCH FARMS...
WHILE WEARING LEMONS IN MY PANTS.
THORNY PATCH FARMS
I PICKED THE LEMONS!
DO I HAVE TO POINT OUT HOW DANGEROUS THIS IS?
YES. BUT MAKE SURE YOU SAY IT INTO THE CAMERA.
AWAY I GO!
THORNY PATCH FARMS

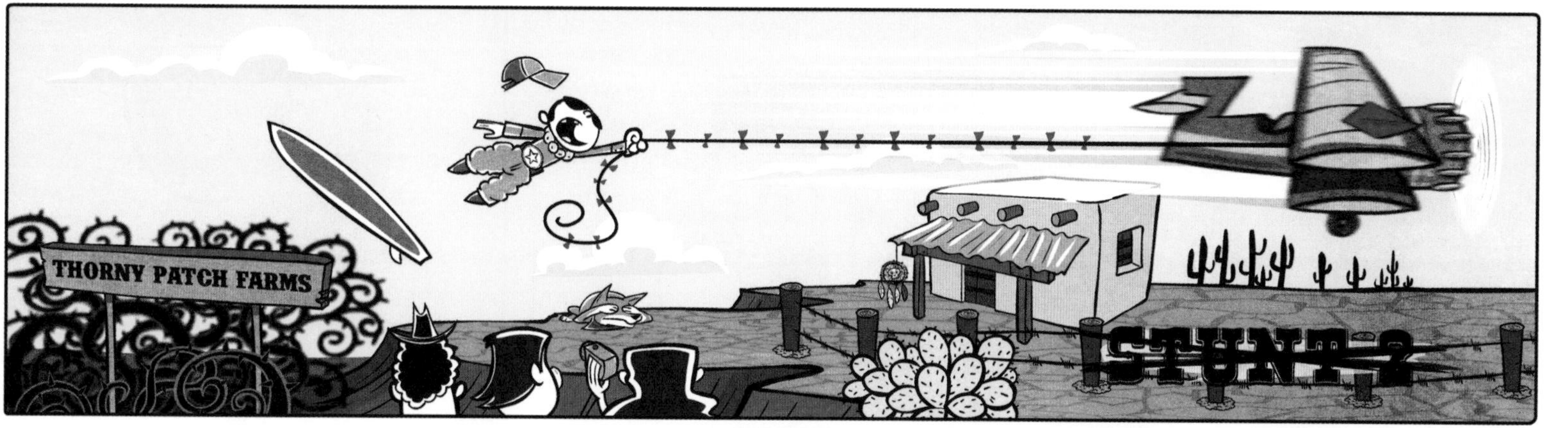
THORNY PATCH FARMS
STUNT 2

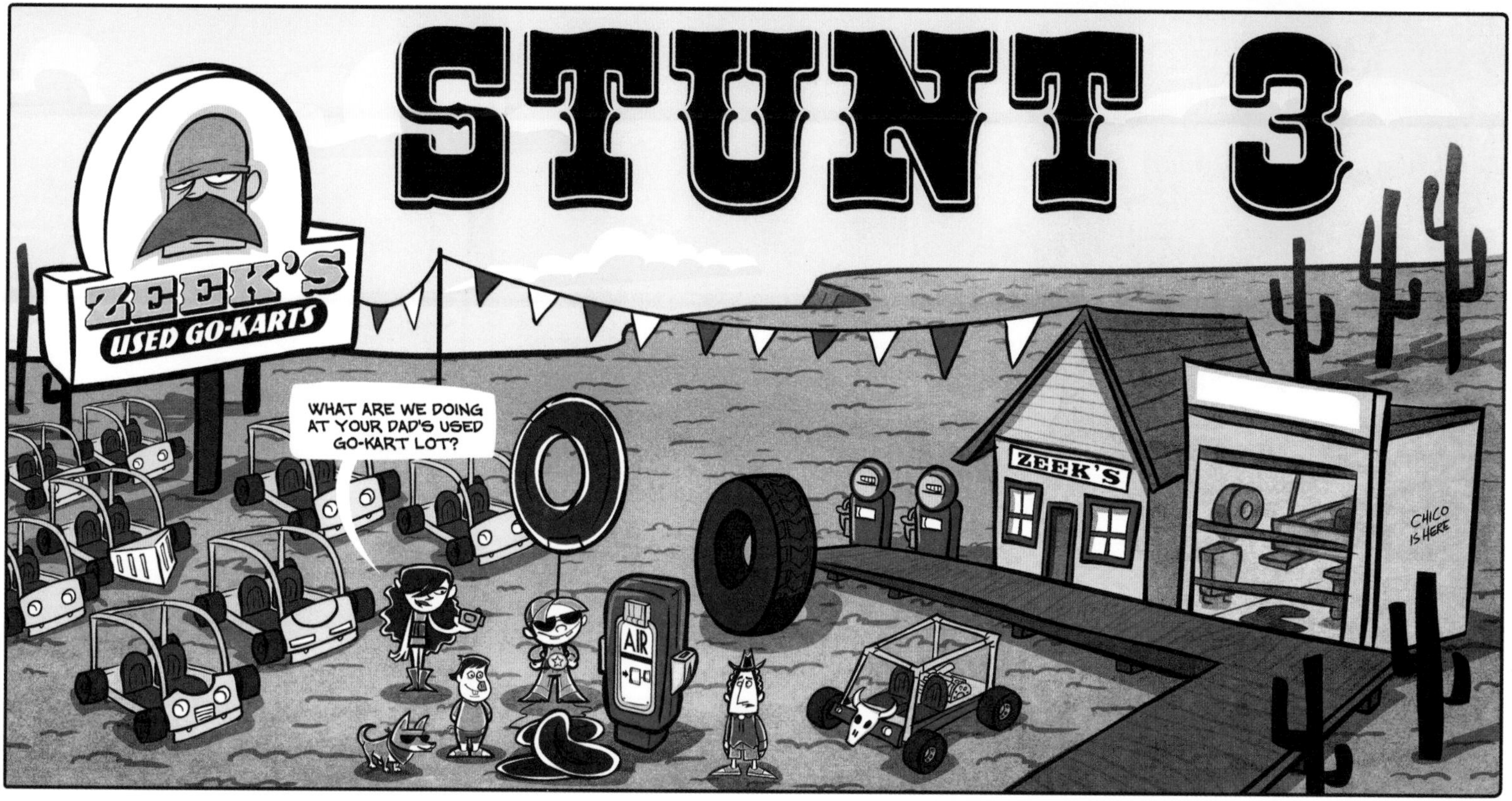
STUNT 3
ZEEK'S
USED GO-KARTS
WHAT ARE WE DOING AT YOUR DAD'S USED GO-KART LOT?
ZEEK'S
AIR
CHICO IS HERE

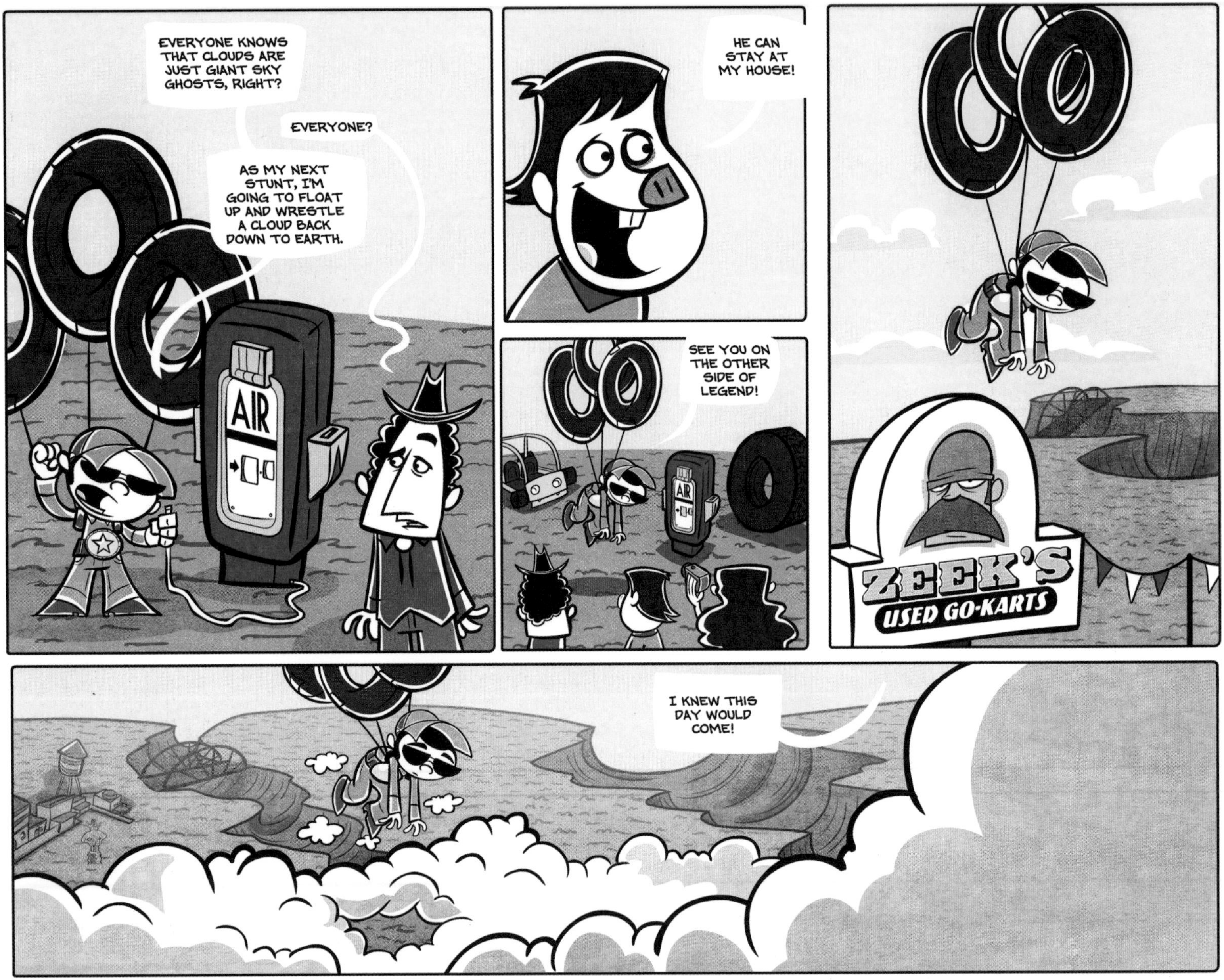
EVERYONE KNOWS THAT CLOUDS ARE JUST GIANT SKY GHOSTS, RIGHT?
EVERYONE?
AS MY NEXT STUNT, I'M GOING TO FLOAT UP AND WRESTLE A CLOUD BACK DOWN TO EARTH.
AIR
HE CAN STAY AT MY HOUSE!
SEE YOU ON THE OTHER SIDE OF LEGEND!
ZEEK'S
USED GO-KARTS
I KNEW THIS DAY WOULD COME!

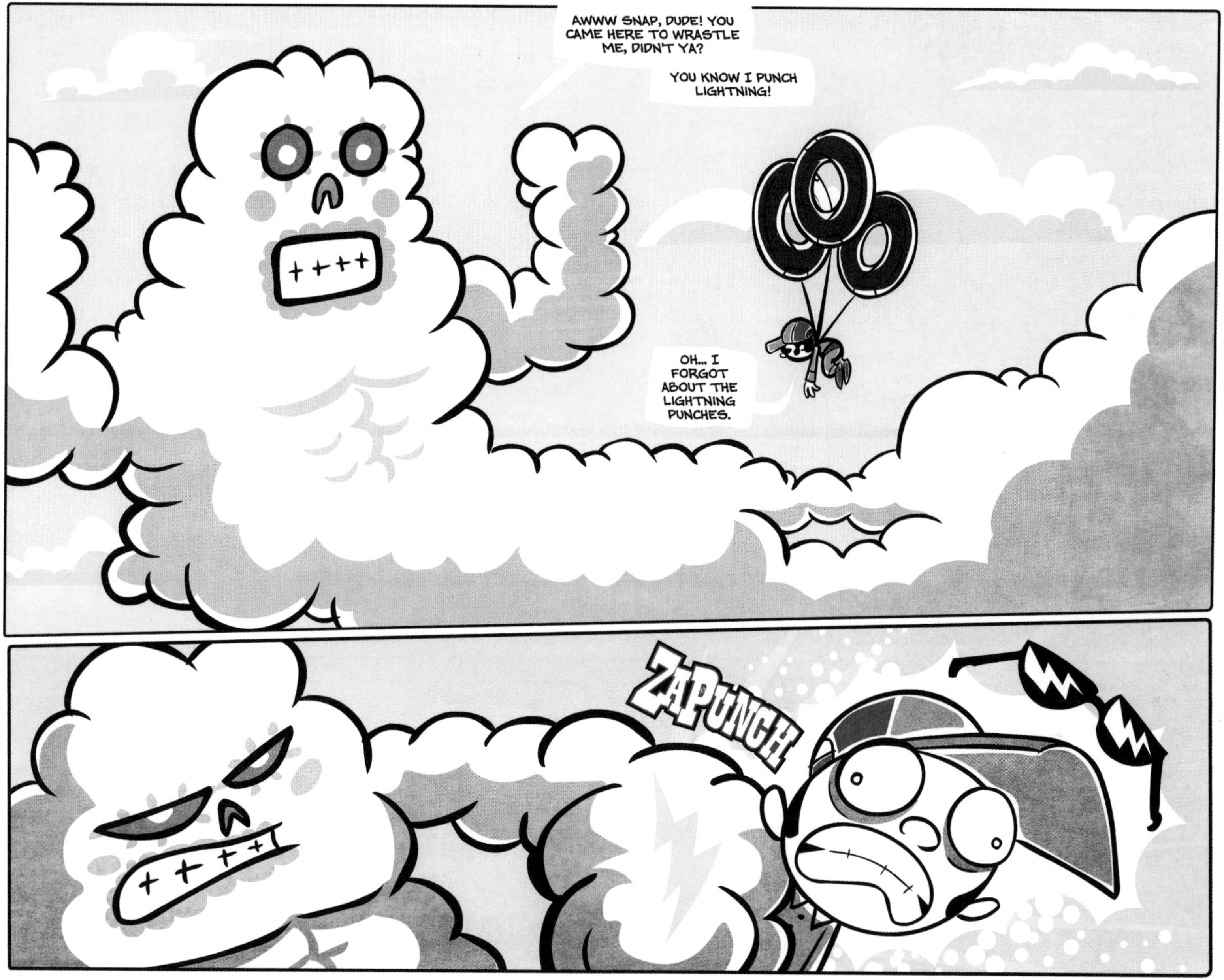
AWWW SNAP, DUDE! YOU CAME HERE TO WRASTLE ME, DIDN'T YA?
YOU KNOW I PUNCH LIGHTNING!
OH... I FORGOT ABOUT THE LIGHTNING PUNCHES.
ZAPUNCH

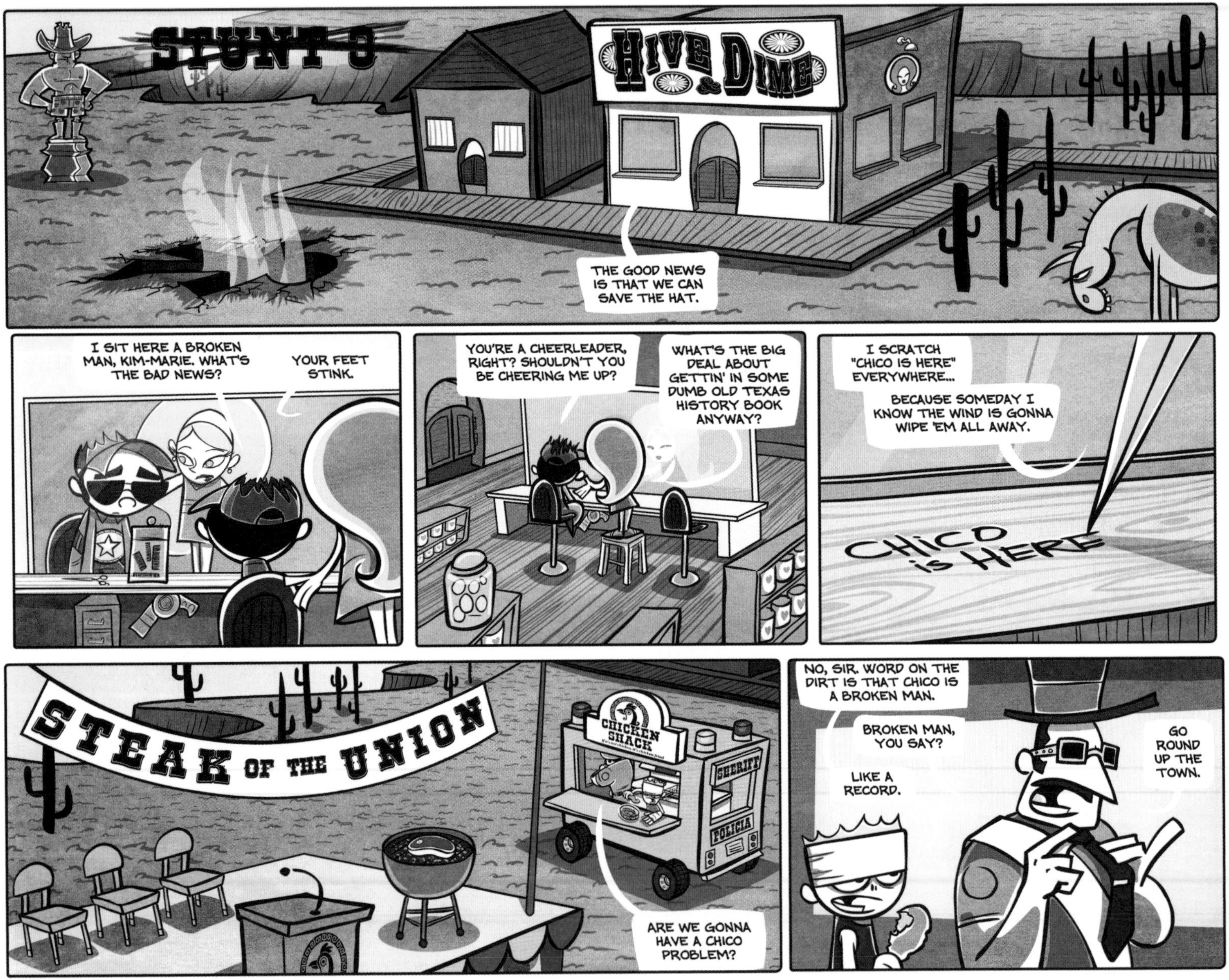
STUNT 3
HIVE & DIME
THE GOOD NEWS IS THAT WE CAN SAVE THE HAT.
I SIT HERE A BROKEN MAN, KIM-MARIE. WHAT'S THE BAD NEWS?
YOUR FEET STINK.
YOU'RE A CHEERLEADER, RIGHT? SHOULDN'T YOU BE CHEERING ME UP?
WHAT'S THE BIG DEAL ABOUT GETTIN' IN SOME DUMB OLD TEXAS HISTORY BOOK ANYWAY?
I SCRATCH "CHICO IS HERE" EVERYWHERE...
BECAUSE SOMEDAY I KNOW THE WIND IS GONNA WIPE 'EM ALL AWAY.
CHICO IS HERE
STEAK OF THE UNION
CHICKEN SHACK
SHERIFF
POLICIA
ARE WE GONNA HAVE A CHICO PROBLEM?
NO, SIR. WORD ON THE DIRT IS THAT CHICO IS A BROKEN MAN.
BROKEN MAN, YOU SAY?
LIKE A RECORD.
GO ROUND UP THE TOWN.

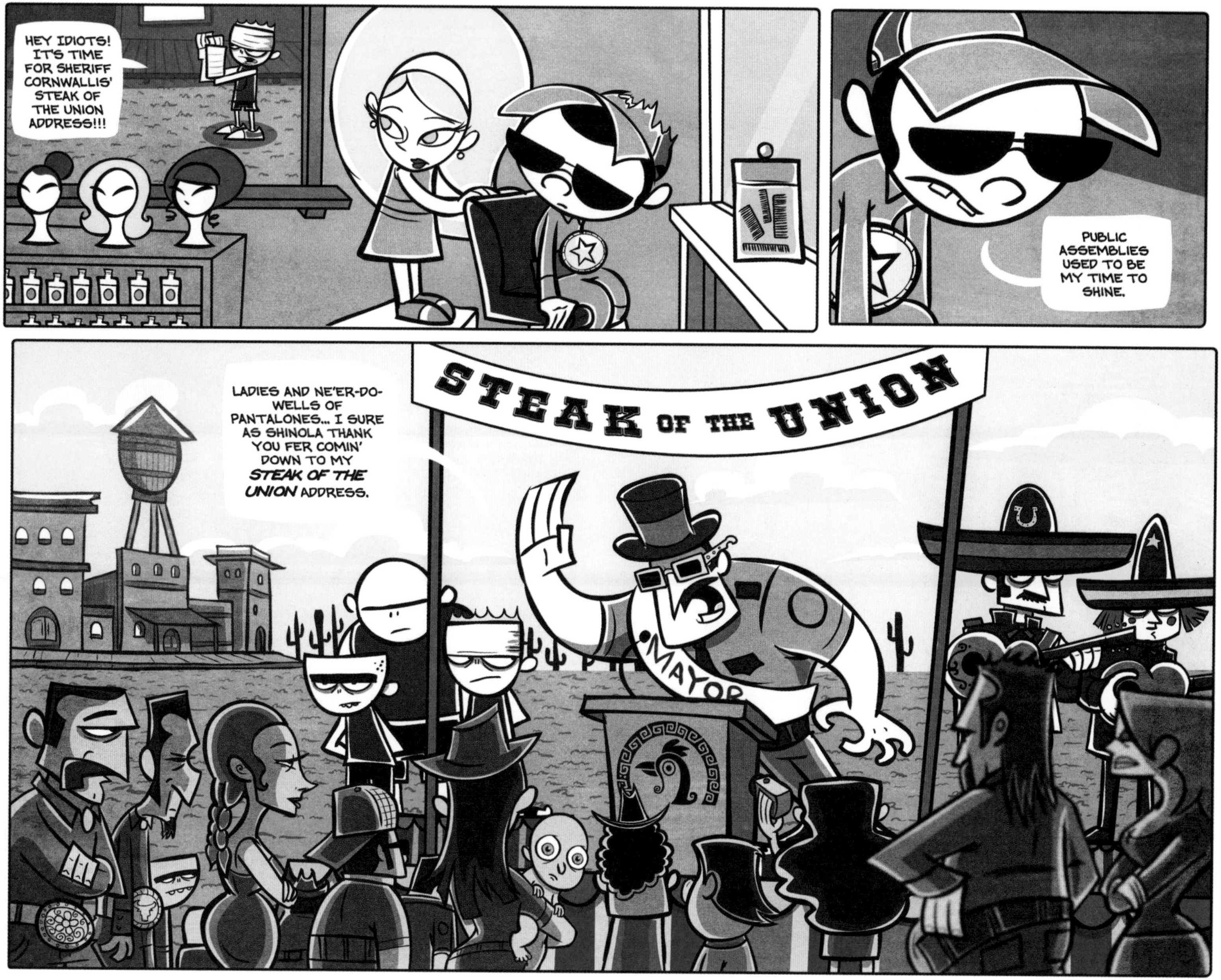
HEY IDIOTS! IT'S TIME FOR SHERIFF CORNWALLIS' STEAK OF THE UNION ADDRESS!!!
PUBLIC ASSEMBLIES USED TO BE MY TIME TO SHINE.
LADIES AND NE'ER-DO-WELLS OF PANTALONES... I SURE AS SHINOLA THANK YOU FER COMIN' DOWN TO MY *STEAK OF THE UNION* ADDRESS.
STEAK OF THE UNION
MAYOR

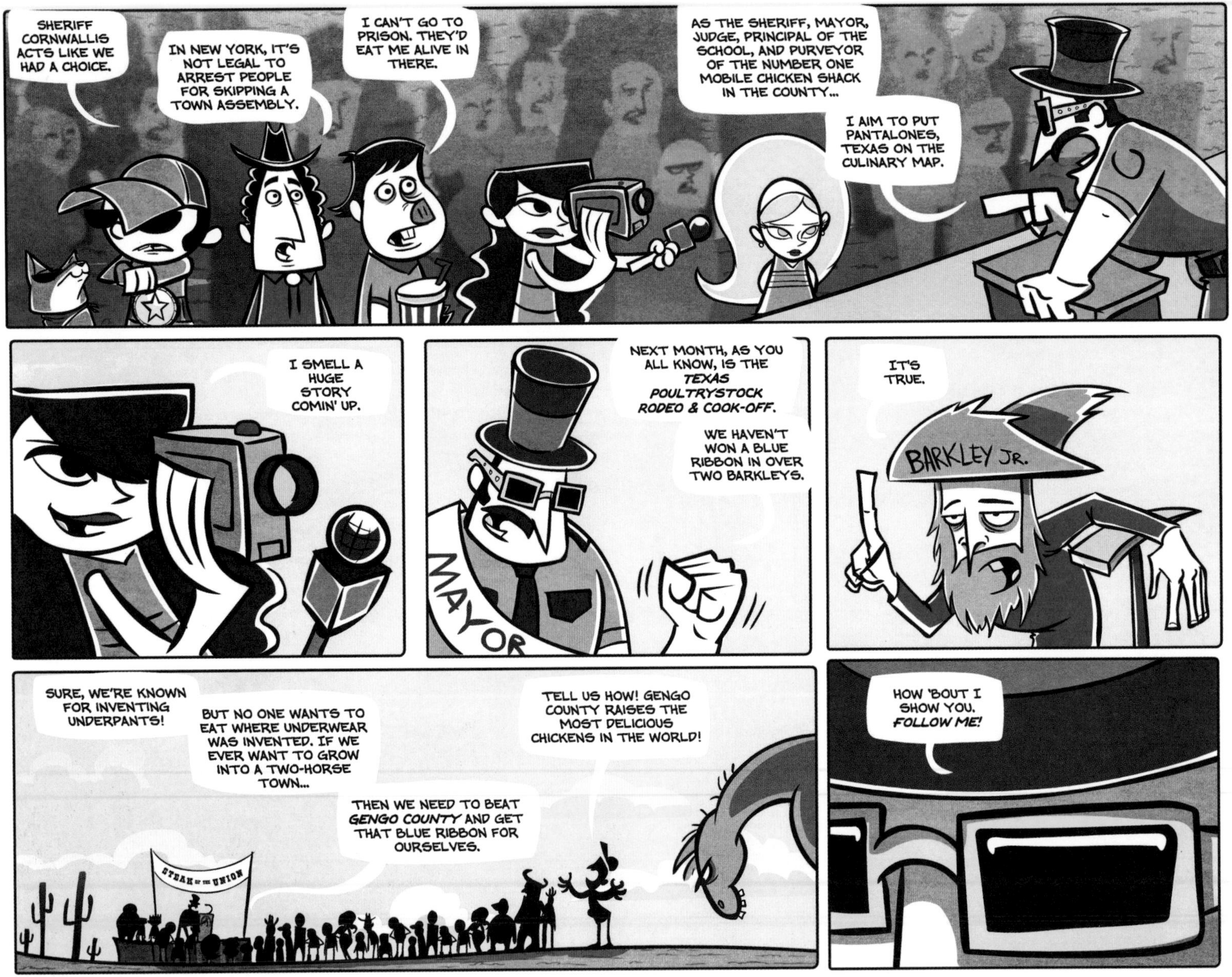
SHERIFF CORNWALLIS ACTS LIKE WE HAD A CHOICE.
IN NEW YORK, IT'S NOT LEGAL TO ARREST PEOPLE FOR SKIPPING A TOWN ASSEMBLY.
I CAN'T GO TO PRISON. THEY'D EAT ME ALIVE IN THERE.
AS THE SHERIFF, MAYOR, JUDGE, PRINCIPAL OF THE SCHOOL, AND PURVEYOR OF THE NUMBER ONE MOBILE CHICKEN SHACK IN THE COUNTY...
I AIM TO PUT PANTALONES, TEXAS ON THE CULINARY MAP.
I SMELL A HUGE STORY COMIN' UP.
NEXT MONTH, AS YOU ALL KNOW, IS THE *TEXAS POULTRYSTOCK RODEO & COOK-OFF*.
WE HAVEN'T WON A BLUE RIBBON IN OVER TWO BARKLEYS.
MAYOR
IT'S TRUE.
BARKLEY JR.
SURE, WE'RE KNOWN FOR INVENTING UNDERPANTS!
BUT NO ONE WANTS TO EAT WHERE UNDERWEAR WAS INVENTED. IF WE EVER WANT TO GROW INTO A TWO-HORSE TOWN...
THEN WE NEED TO BEAT *GENGO COUNTY* AND GET THAT BLUE RIBBON FOR OURSELVES.
TELL US HOW! GENGO COUNTY RAISES THE MOST DELICIOUS CHICKENS IN THE WORLD!
STEAK OF THE UNION
HOW 'BOUT I SHOW YOU. *FOLLOW ME!*

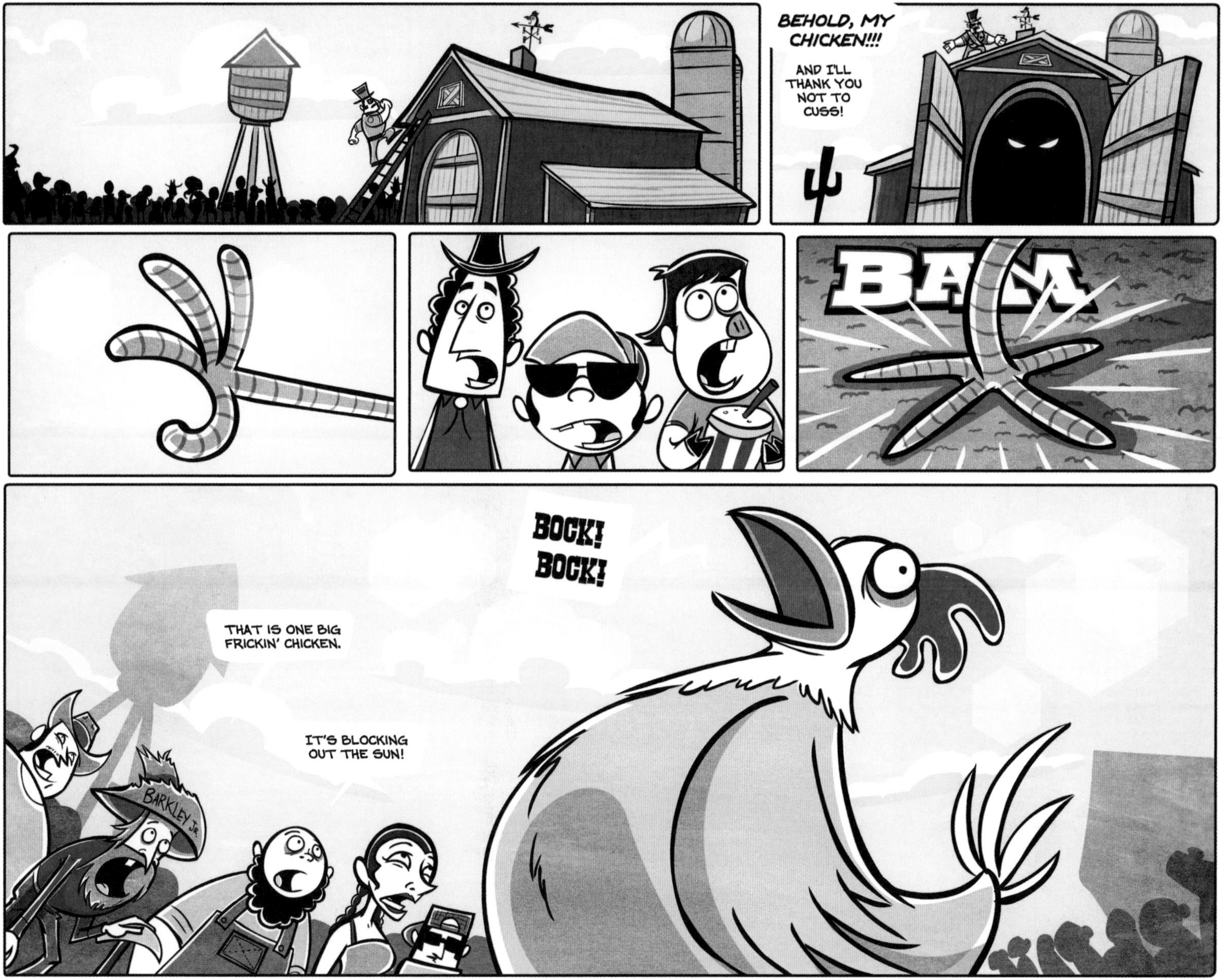
BEHOLD, MY CHICKEN!!!
AND I'LL THANK YOU NOT TO CUSS!
BAM
BOCK! BOCK!
THAT IS ONE BIG FRICKIN' CHICKEN.
IT'S BLOCKING OUT THE SUN!
BARKLEY JR.

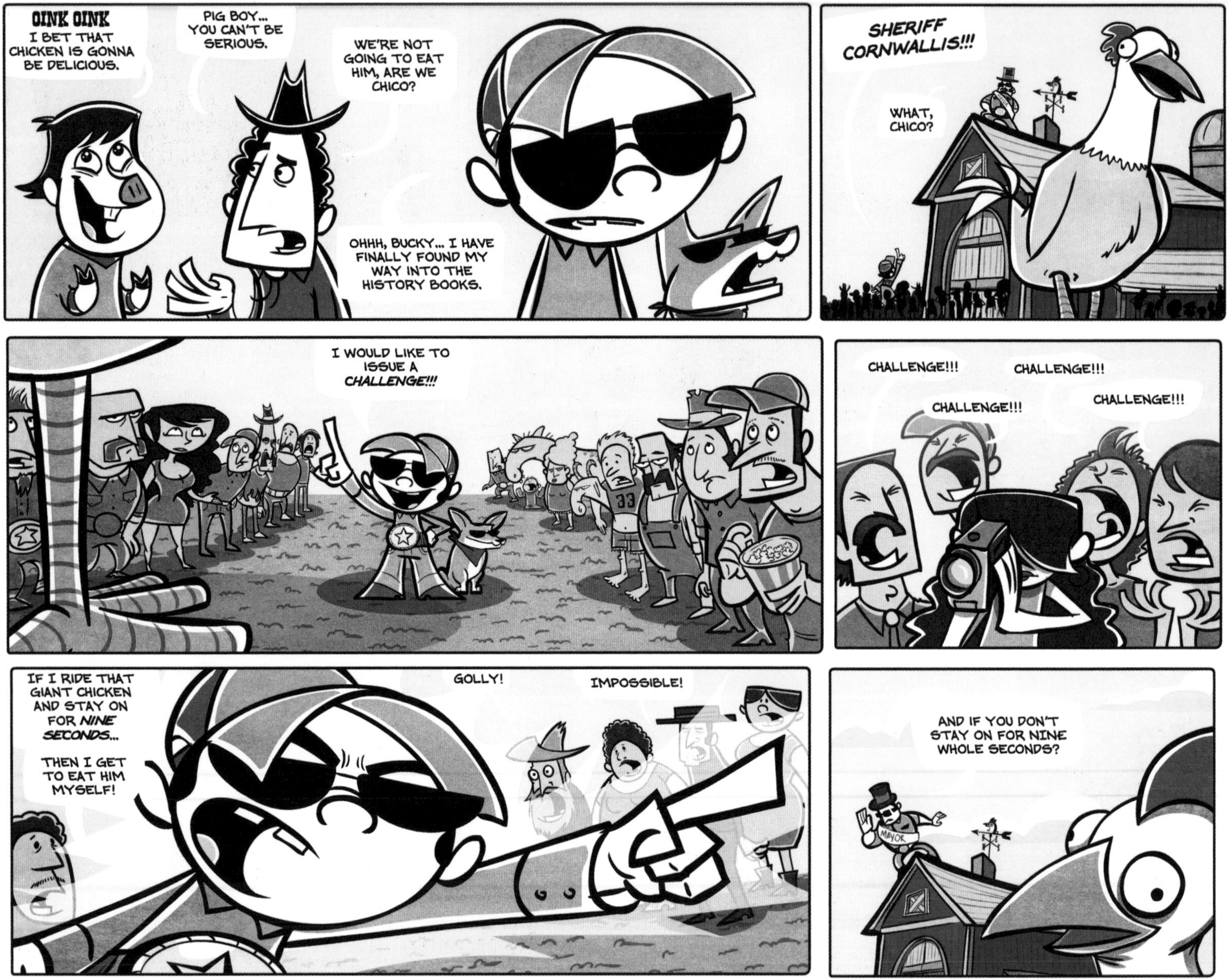
OINK OINK
I BET THAT CHICKEN IS GONNA BE DELICIOUS.
PIG BOY... YOU CAN'T BE SERIOUS.
WE'RE NOT GOING TO EAT HIM, ARE WE CHICO?
OHHH, BUCKY... I HAVE FINALLY FOUND MY WAY INTO THE HISTORY BOOKS.
SHERIFF CORNWALLIS!!!
WHAT, CHICO?
I WOULD LIKE TO ISSUE A CHALLENGE!!!
CHALLENGE!!!
CHALLENGE!!!
CHALLENGE!!!
CHALLENGE!!!
IF I RIDE THAT GIANT CHICKEN AND STAY ON FOR NINE SECONDS...
THEN I GET TO EAT HIM MYSELF!
GOLLY!
IMPOSSIBLE!
AND IF YOU DON'T STAY ON FOR NINE WHOLE SECONDS?
MAYOR

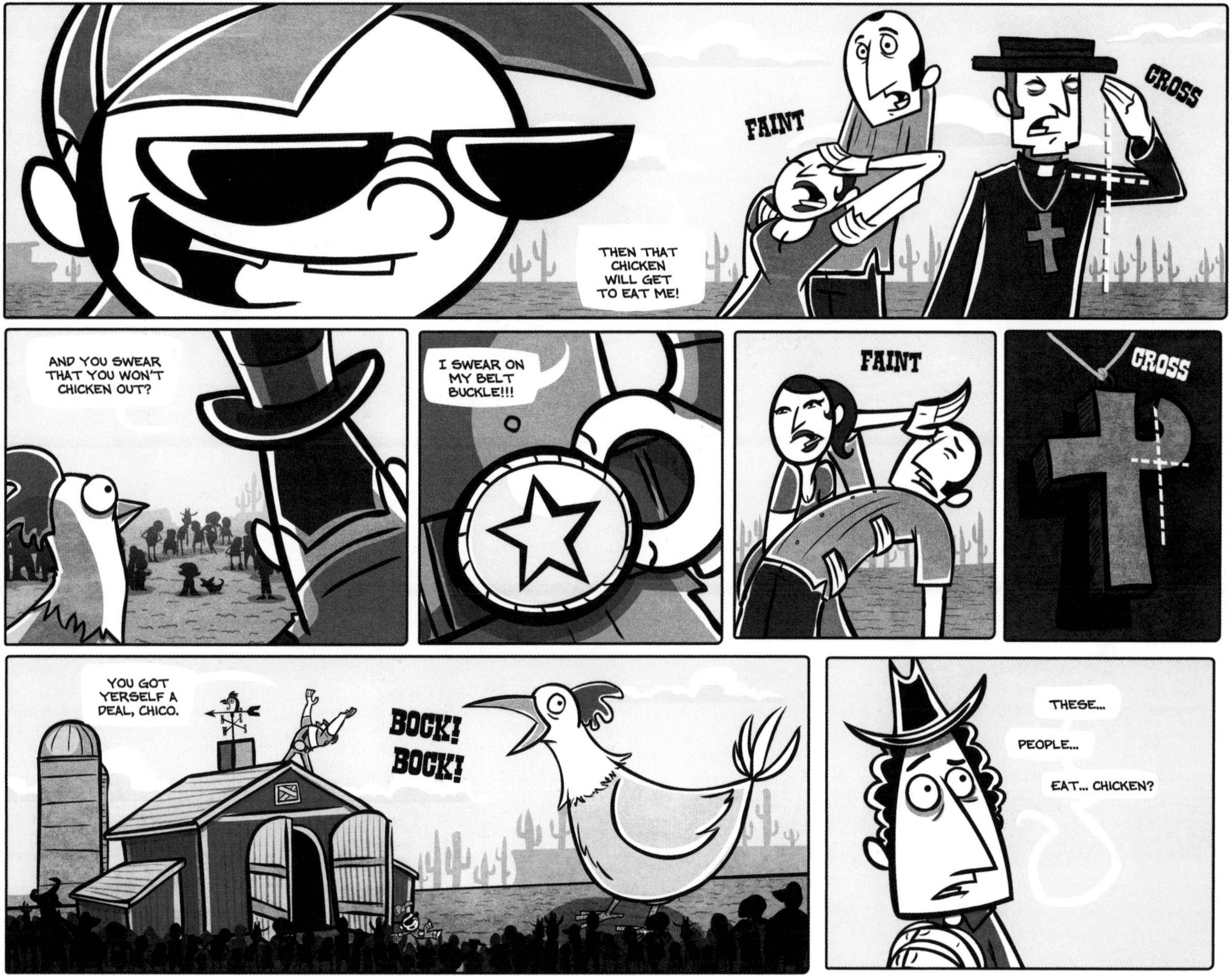
FAINT
CROSS
THEN THAT CHICKEN WILL GET TO EAT ME!
AND YOU SWEAR THAT YOU WON'T CHICKEN OUT?
I SWEAR ON MY BELT BUCKLE!!!
FAINT
CROSS
YOU GOT YERSELF A DEAL, CHICO.
BOCK! BOCK!
THESE...
PEOPLE...
EAT... CHICKEN?

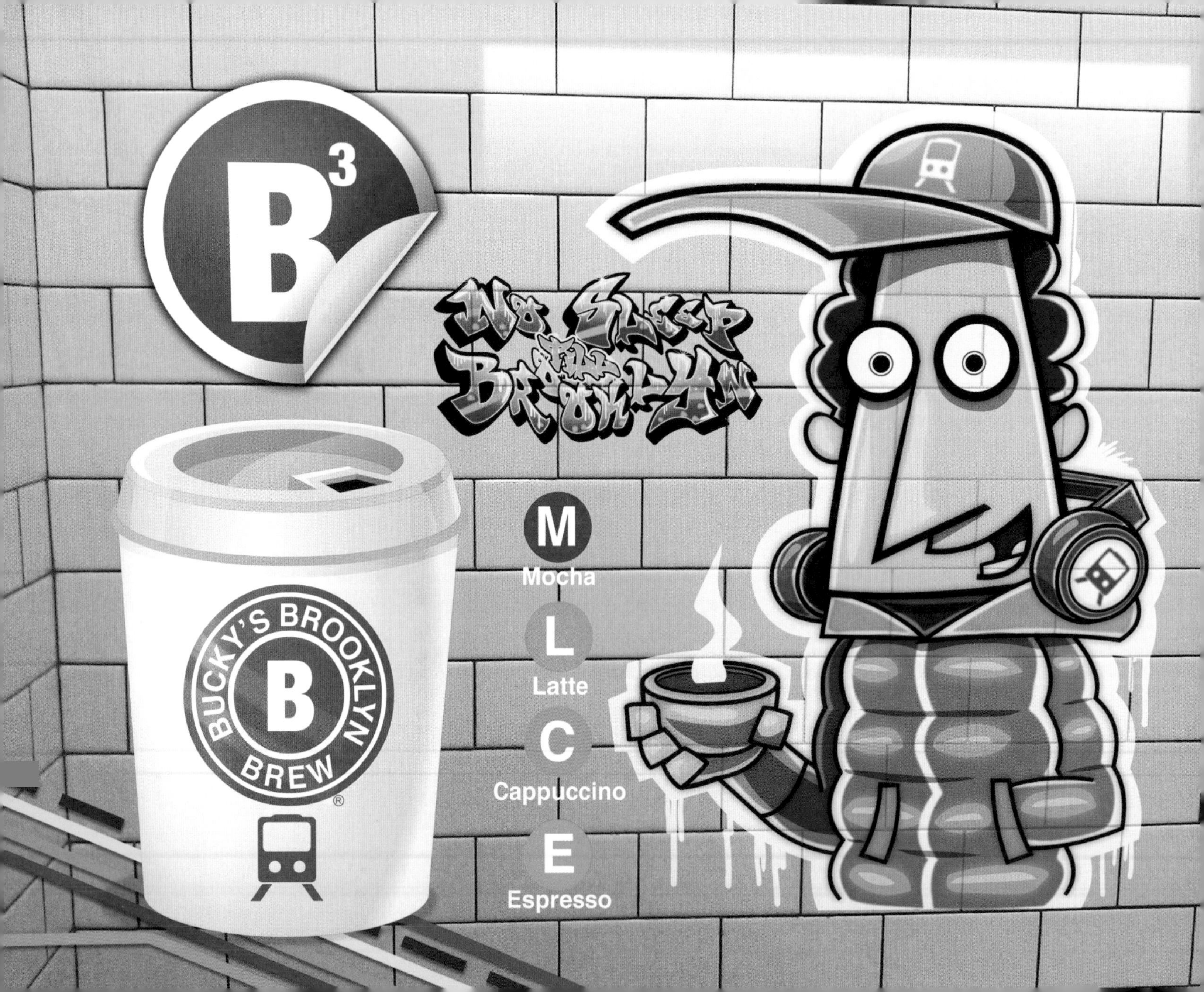
B3
BUCKY'S BROOKLYN BREW
B
M
Mocha
L
Latte
C
Cappuccino
E
Espresso

CHAPTER TRES

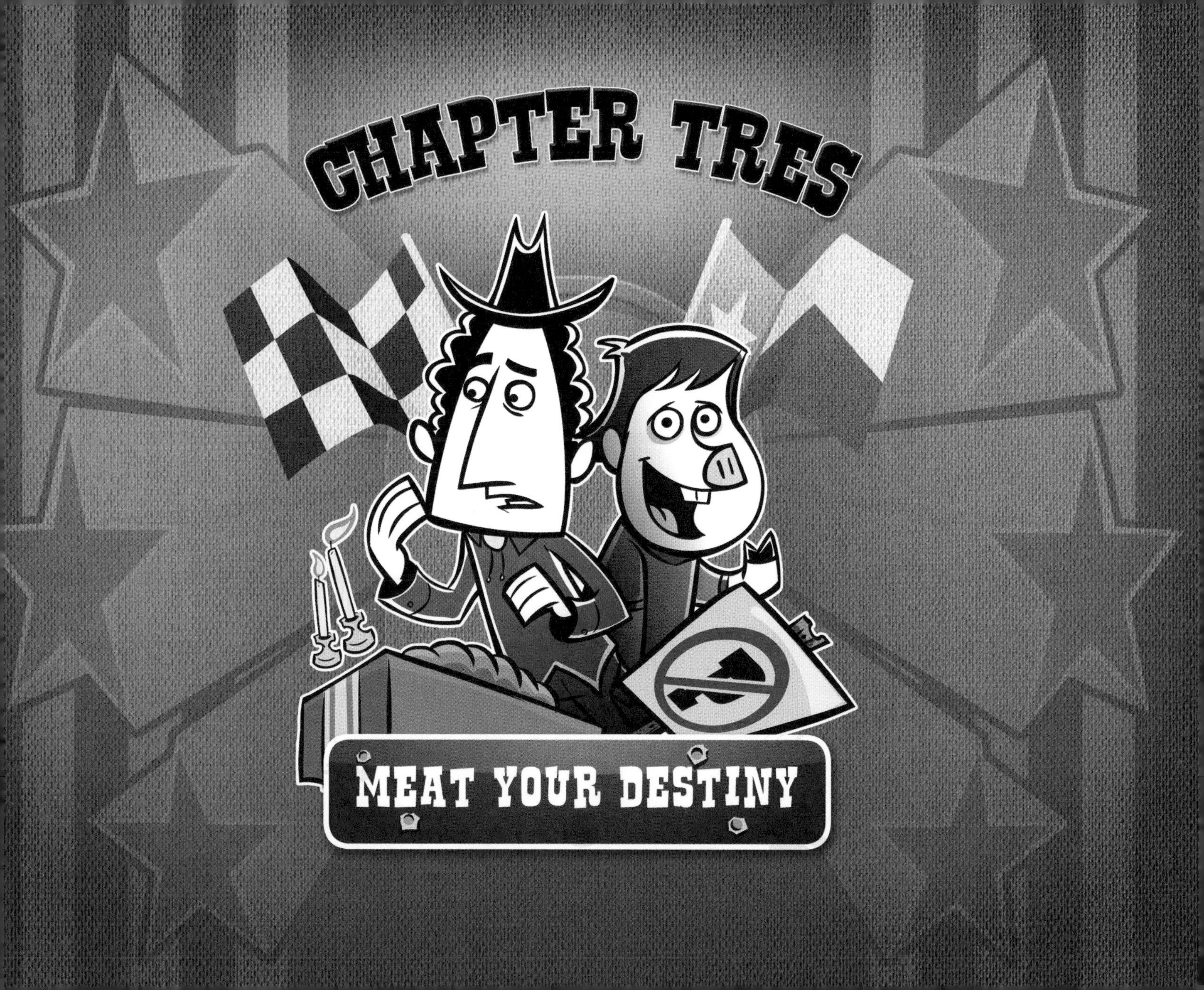

MEAT YOUR DESTINY

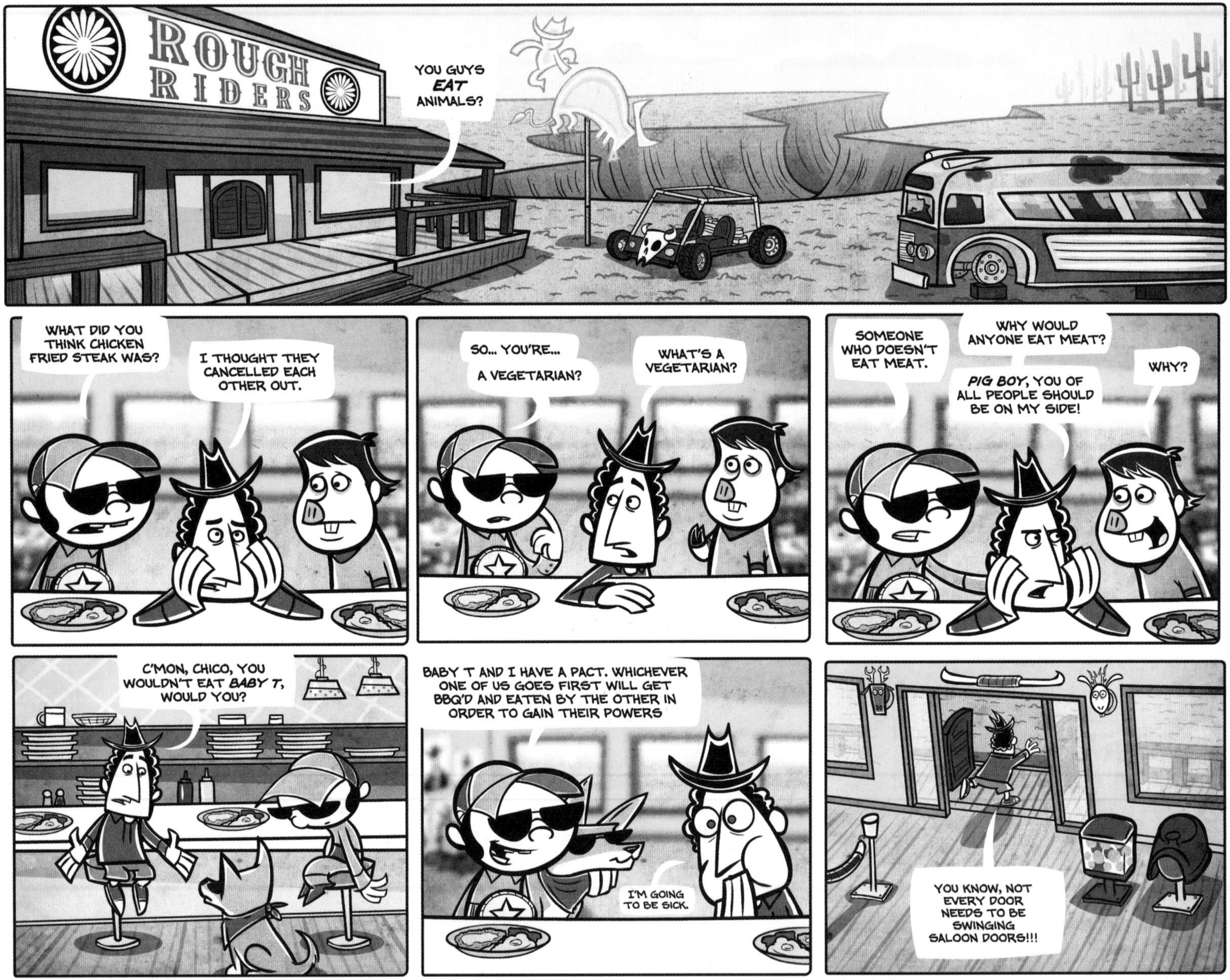
ROUGH RIDERS
YOU GUYS EAT ANIMALS?
WHAT DID YOU THINK CHICKEN FRIED STEAK WAS?
I THOUGHT THEY CANCELLED EACH OTHER OUT.
SO... YOU'RE...
A VEGETARIAN?
WHAT'S A VEGETARIAN?
SOMEONE WHO DOESN'T EAT MEAT.
WHY WOULD ANYONE EAT MEAT?
PIG BOY, YOU OF ALL PEOPLE SHOULD BE ON MY SIDE!
WHY?
C'MON, CHICO, YOU WOULDN'T EAT BABY T, WOULD YOU?
BABY T AND I HAVE A PACT. WHICHEVER ONE OF US GOES FIRST WILL GET BBQ'D AND EATEN BY THE OTHER IN ORDER TO GAIN THEIR POWERS
I'M GOING TO BE SICK.
YOU KNOW, NOT EVERY DOOR NEEDS TO BE SWINGING SALOON DOORS!!!

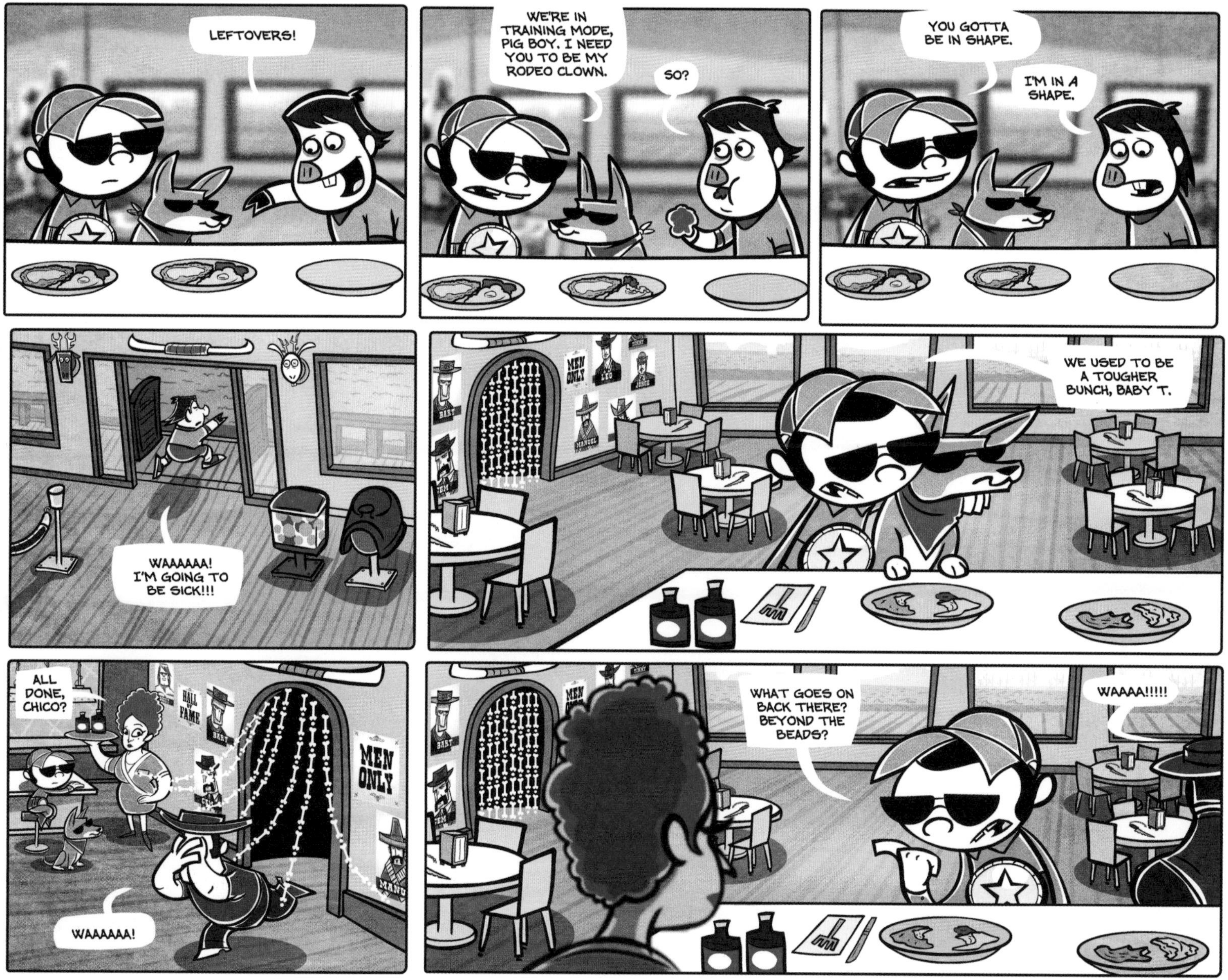
LEFTOVERS!
WE'RE IN TRAINING MODE, PIG BOY. I NEED YOU TO BE MY RODEO CLOWN.
SO?
YOU GOTTA BE IN SHAPE.
I'M IN A SHAPE.
WAAAAAA! I'M GOING TO BE SICK!!!
WE USED TO BE A TOUGHER BUNCH, BABY T.
ALL DONE, CHICO?
WAAAAAA!
MEN ONLY
HALL OF FAME
WHAT GOES ON BACK THERE? BEYOND THE BEADS?
WAAAA!!!!!

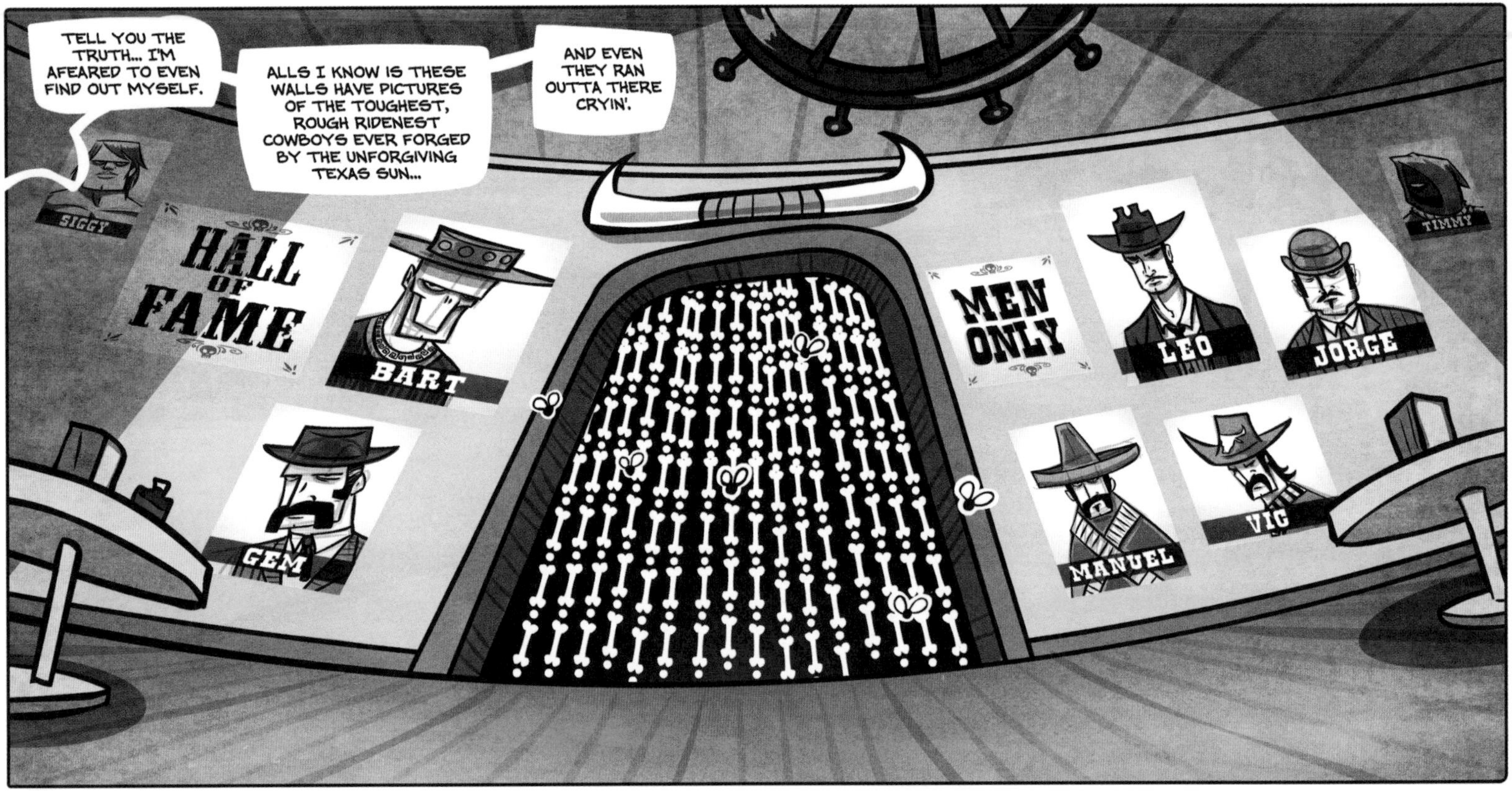
TELL YOU THE TRUTH... I'M AFEARED TO EVEN FIND OUT MYSELF.
ALLS I KNOW IS THESE WALLS HAVE PICTURES OF THE TOUGHEST, ROUGH RIDENEST COWBOYS EVER FORGED BY THE UNFORGIVING TEXAS SUN...
AND EVEN THEY RAN OUTTA THERE CRYIN'.
SIGGY
HALL OF FAME
BART
GEM
MEN ONLY
LEO
JORGE
TIMMY
MANUEL
VIC

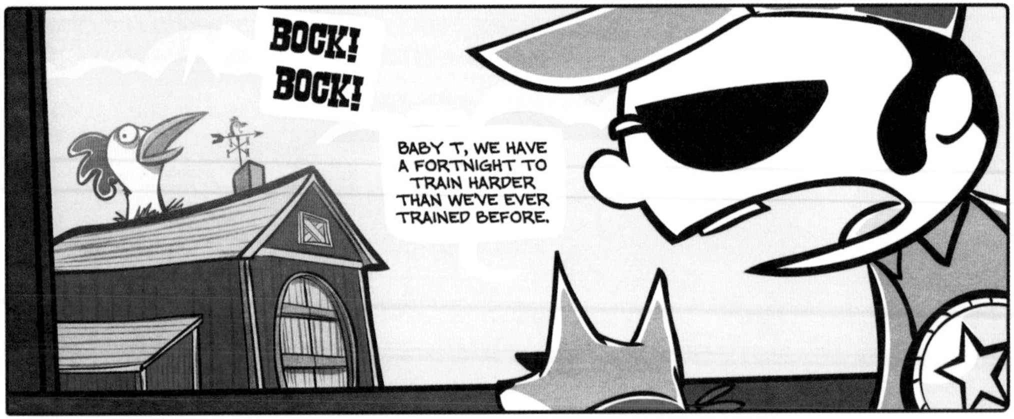
BOCK! BOCK!
BABY T, WE HAVE A FORTNIGHT TO TRAIN HARDER THAN WE'VE EVER TRAINED BEFORE.

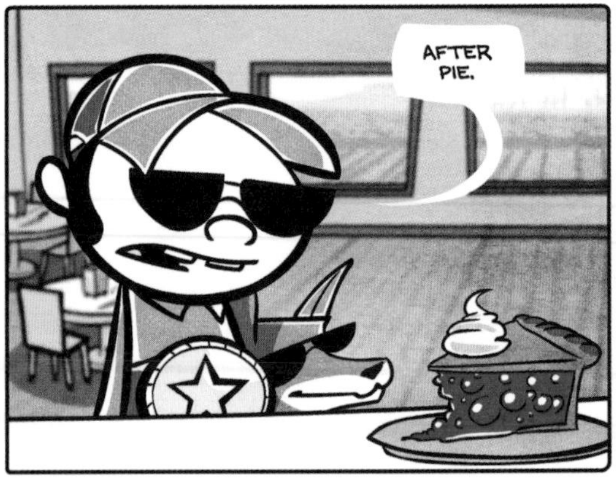
AFTER PIE.

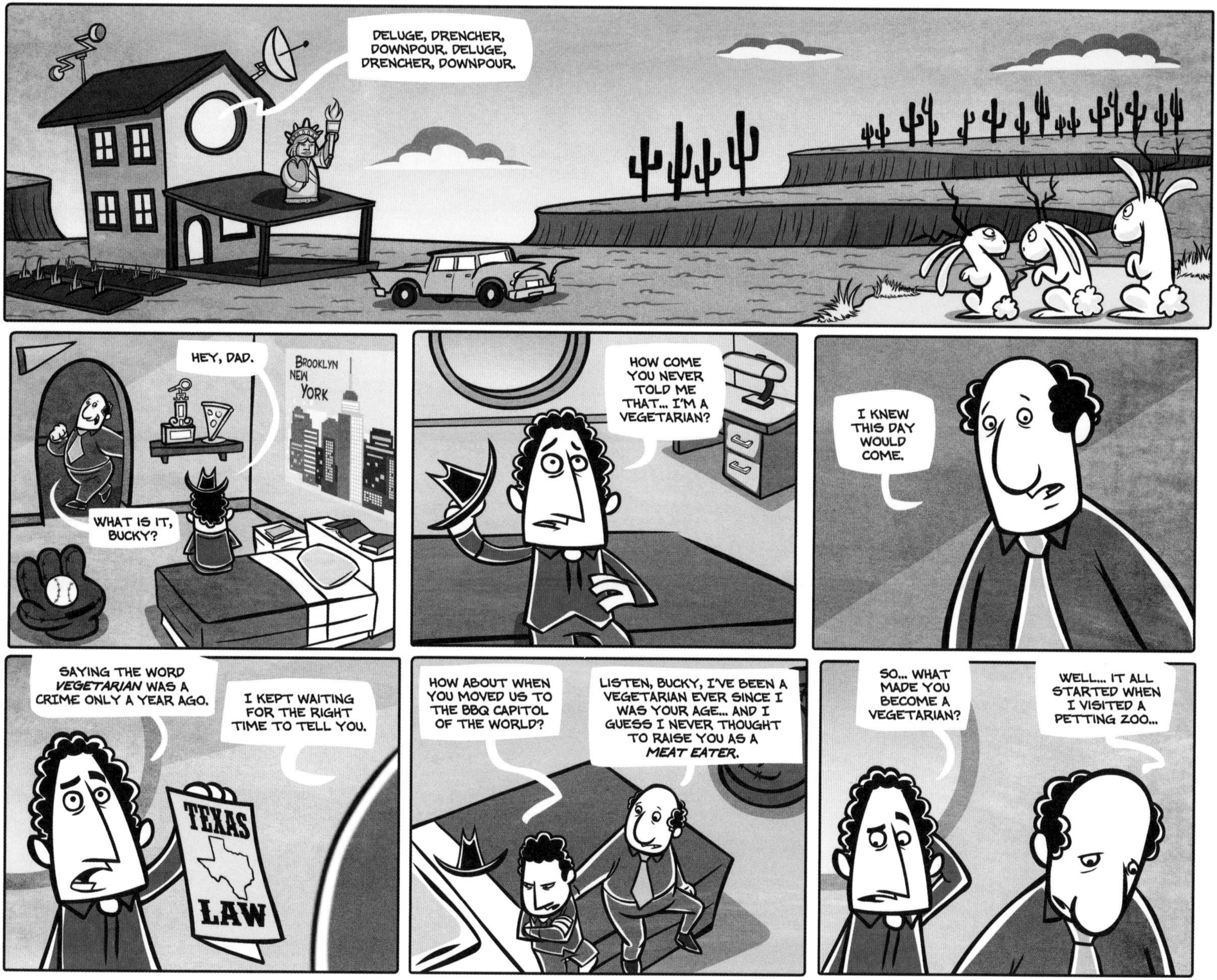
DELUGE, DRENCHER, DOWNPOUR. DELUGE, DRENCHER, DOWNPOUR.
HEY, DAD.
BROOKLYN NEW YORK
WHAT IS IT, BUCKY?
HOW COME YOU NEVER TOLD ME THAT... I'M A VEGETARIAN?
I KNEW THIS DAY WOULD COME.
SAYING THE WORD *VEGETARIAN* WAS A CRIME ONLY A YEAR AGO.
I KEPT WAITING FOR THE RIGHT TIME TO TELL YOU.
TEXAS LAW
HOW ABOUT WHEN YOU MOVED US TO THE BBQ CAPITOL OF THE WORLD?
LISTEN, BUCKY, I'VE BEEN A VEGETARIAN EVER SINCE I WAS YOUR AGE... AND I GUESS I NEVER THOUGHT TO RAISE YOU AS A *MEAT EATER*.
SO... WHAT MADE YOU BECOME A VEGETARIAN?
WELL... IT ALL STARTED WHEN I VISITED A PETTING ZOO...

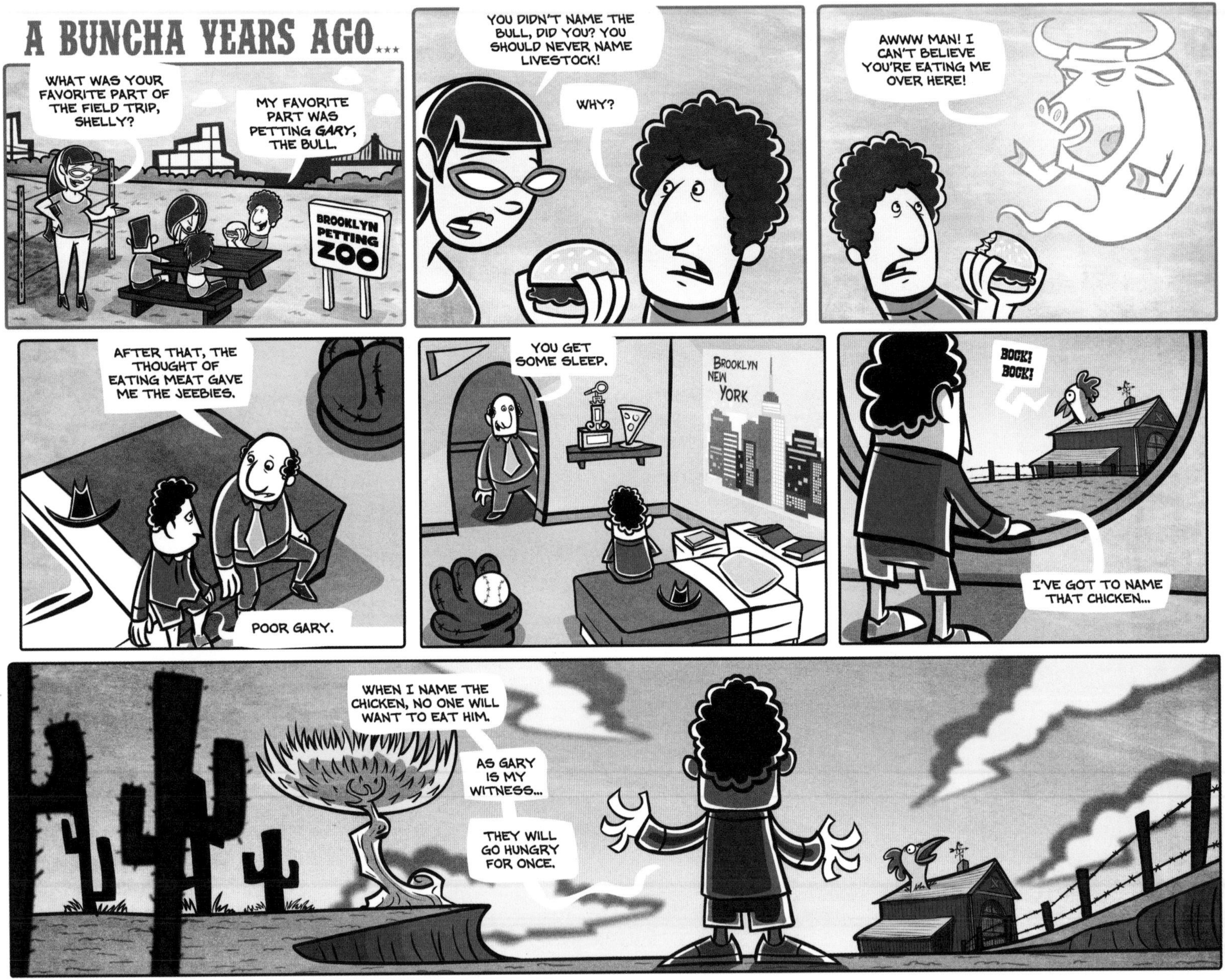
A BUNCHA YEARS AGO...
WHAT WAS YOUR FAVORITE PART OF THE FIELD TRIP, SHELLY?
MY FAVORITE PART WAS PETTING GARY, THE BULL.
BROOKLYN PETTING ZOO
YOU DIDN'T NAME THE BULL, DID YOU? YOU SHOULD NEVER NAME LIVESTOCK!
WHY?
AWWW MAN! I CAN'T BELIEVE YOU'RE EATING ME OVER HERE!
AFTER THAT, THE THOUGHT OF EATING MEAT GAVE ME THE JEEBIES.
POOR GARY.
YOU GET SOME SLEEP.
BROOKLYN NEW YORK
BOCK! BOCK!
I'VE GOT TO NAME THAT CHICKEN...
WHEN I NAME THE CHICKEN, NO ONE WILL WANT TO EAT HIM.
AS GARY IS MY WITNESS...
THEY WILL GO HUNGRY FOR ONCE.

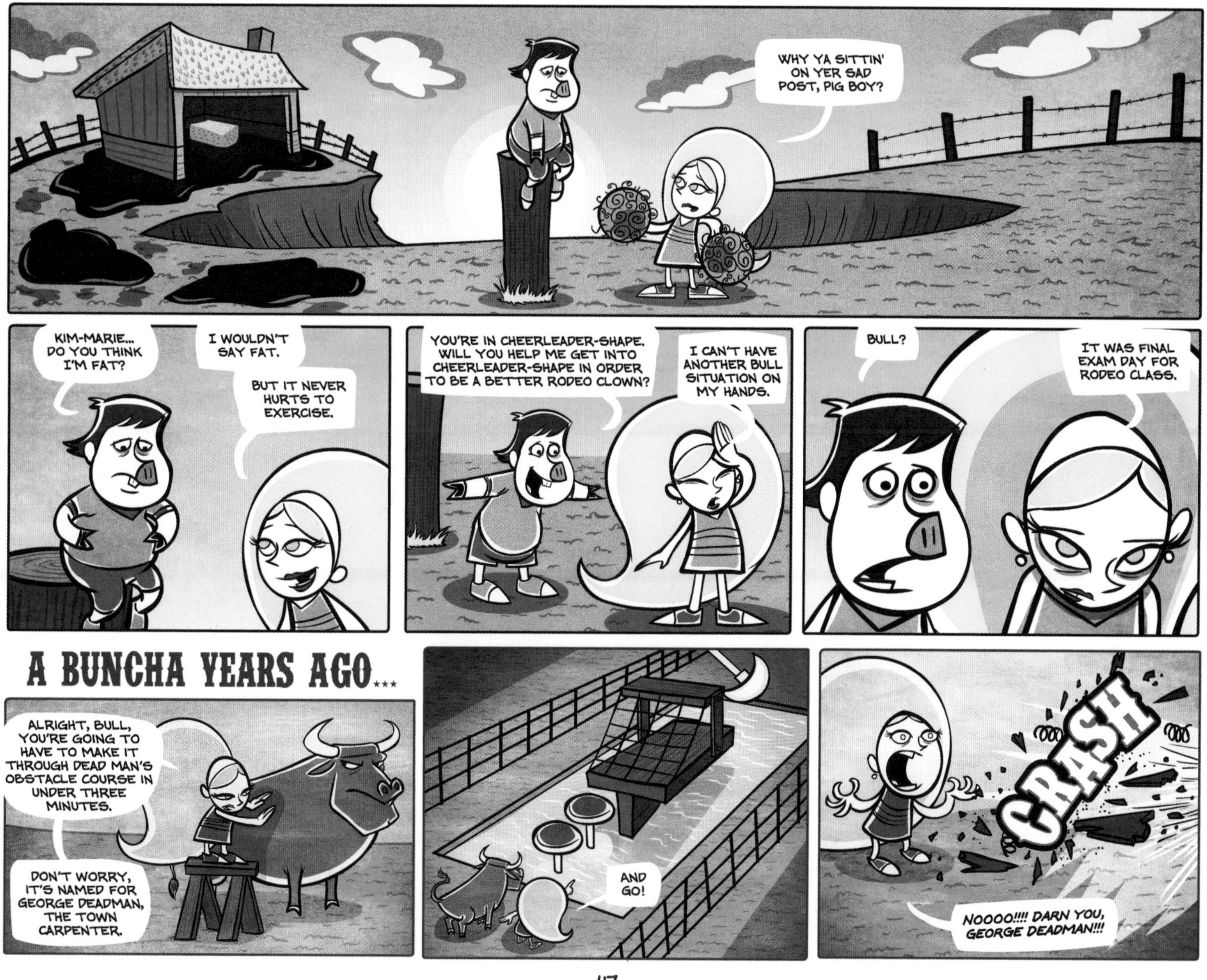
WHY YA SITTIN' ON YER SAD POST, PIG BOY?
KIM-MARIE... DO YOU THINK I'M FAT?
I WOULDN'T SAY FAT.
BUT IT NEVER HURTS TO EXERCISE.
YOU'RE IN CHEERLEADER-SHAPE. WILL YOU HELP ME GET INTO CHEERLEADER-SHAPE IN ORDER TO BE A BETTER RODEO CLOWN?
I CAN'T HAVE ANOTHER BULL SITUATION ON MY HANDS.
BULL?
IT WAS FINAL EXAM DAY FOR RODEO CLASS.
A BUNCHA YEARS AGO...
ALRIGHT, BULL, YOU'RE GOING TO HAVE TO MAKE IT THROUGH DEAD MAN'S OBSTACLE COURSE IN UNDER THREE MINUTES.
DON'T WORRY, IT'S NAMED FOR GEORGE DEADMAN, THE TOWN CARPENTER.
AND GO!
CRASH
NOOOO!!!! DARN YOU, GEORGE DEADMAN!!!

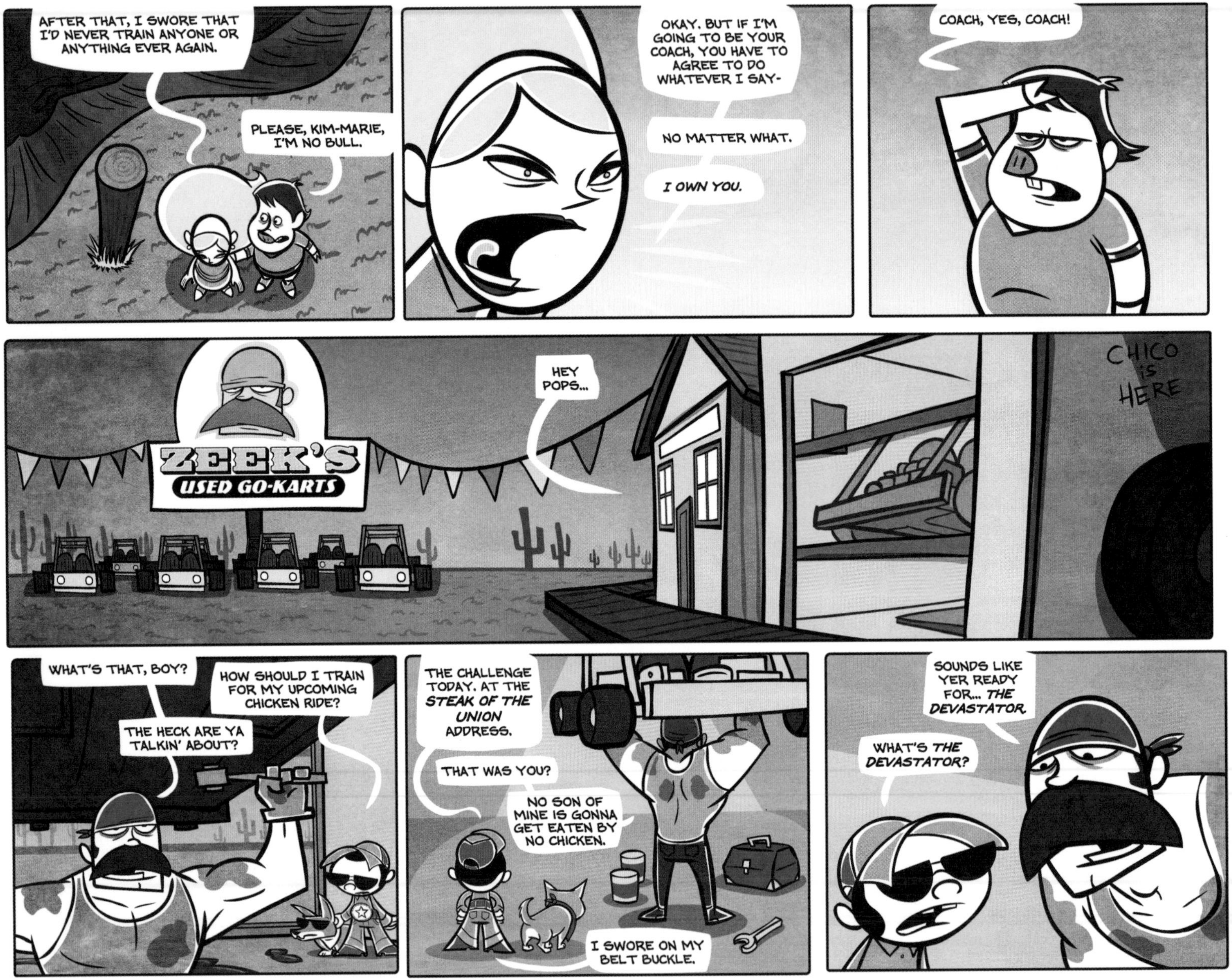
AFTER THAT, I SWORE THAT I'D NEVER TRAIN ANYONE OR ANYTHING EVER AGAIN.
PLEASE, KIM-MARIE, I'M NO BULL.
OKAY. BUT IF I'M GOING TO BE YOUR COACH, YOU HAVE TO AGREE TO DO WHATEVER I SAY-
NO MATTER WHAT.
I OWN YOU.
COACH, YES, COACH!
ZEEK'S
USED GO-KARTS
HEY POPS...
CHICO is HERE
WHAT'S THAT, BOY?
HOW SHOULD I TRAIN FOR MY UPCOMING CHICKEN RIDE?
THE HECK ARE YA TALKIN' ABOUT?
THE CHALLENGE TODAY. AT THE STEAK OF THE UNION ADDRESS.
THAT WAS YOU?
NO SON OF MINE IS GONNA GET EATEN BY NO CHICKEN.
I SWORE ON MY BELT BUCKLE.
SOUNDS LIKE YER READY FOR... THE DEVASTATOR.
WHAT'S THE DEVASTATOR?

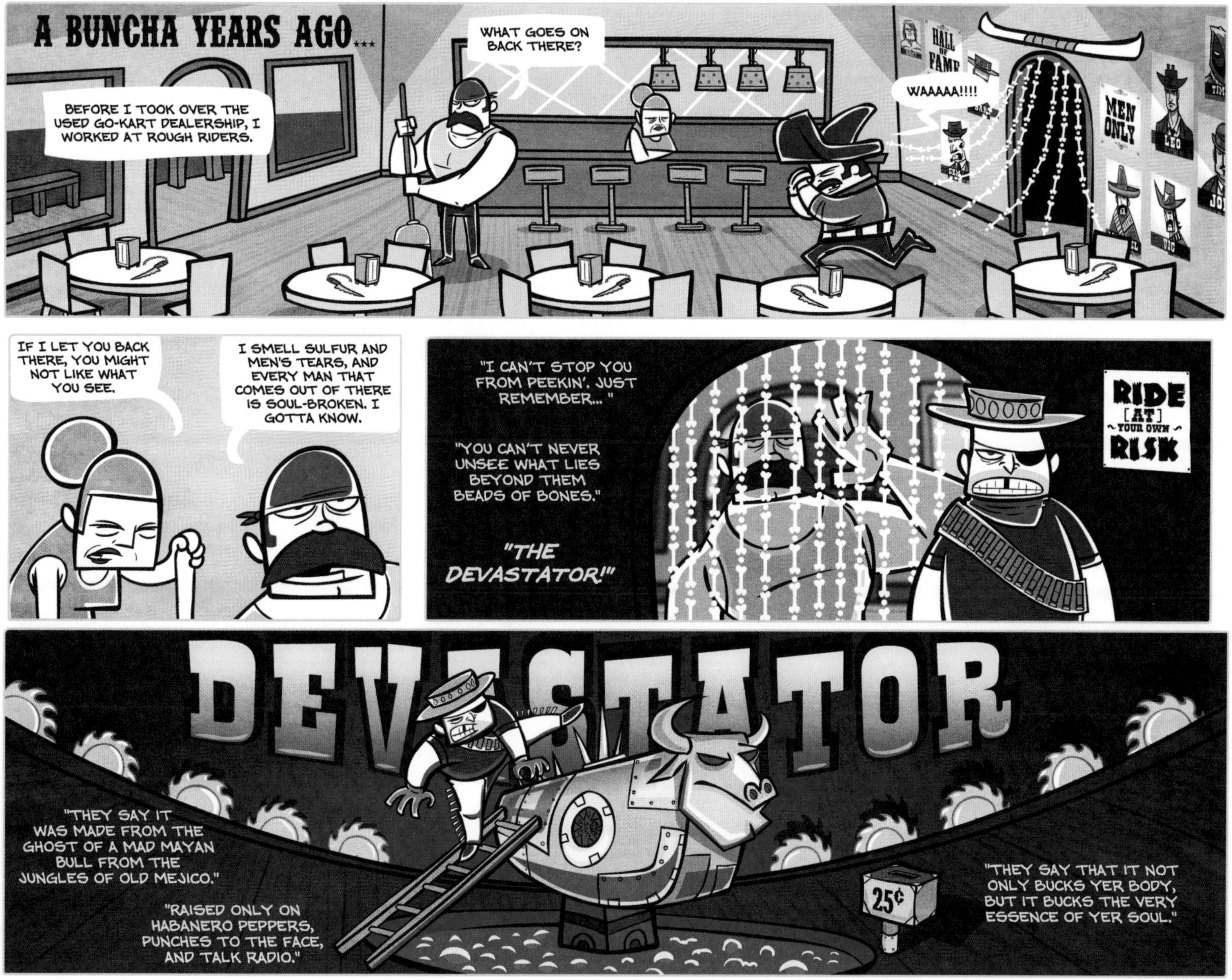
A BUNCHA YEARS AGO...
BEFORE I TOOK OVER THE USED GO-KART DEALERSHIP, I WORKED AT ROUGH RIDERS.
WHAT GOES ON BACK THERE?
WAAAAA!!!!
HALL OF FAME
MEN ONLY
LEO
IF I LET YOU BACK THERE, YOU MIGHT NOT LIKE WHAT YOU SEE.
I SMELL SULFUR AND MEN'S TEARS, AND EVERY MAN THAT COMES OUT OF THERE IS SOUL-BROKEN. I GOTTA KNOW.
"I CAN'T STOP YOU FROM PEEKIN'. JUST REMEMBER... "
"YOU CAN'T NEVER UNSEE WHAT LIES BEYOND THEM BEADS OF BONES."
"THE DEVASTATOR!"
RIDE [AT] YOUR OWN RISK
DEVASTATOR
"THEY SAY IT WAS MADE FROM THE GHOST OF A MAD MAYAN BULL FROM THE JUNGLES OF OLD MEJICO."
"RAISED ONLY ON HABANERO PEPPERS, PUNCHES TO THE FACE, AND TALK RADIO."
25¢
"THEY SAY THAT IT NOT ONLY BUCKS YER BODY, BUT IT BUCKS THE VERY ESSENCE OF YER SOUL."

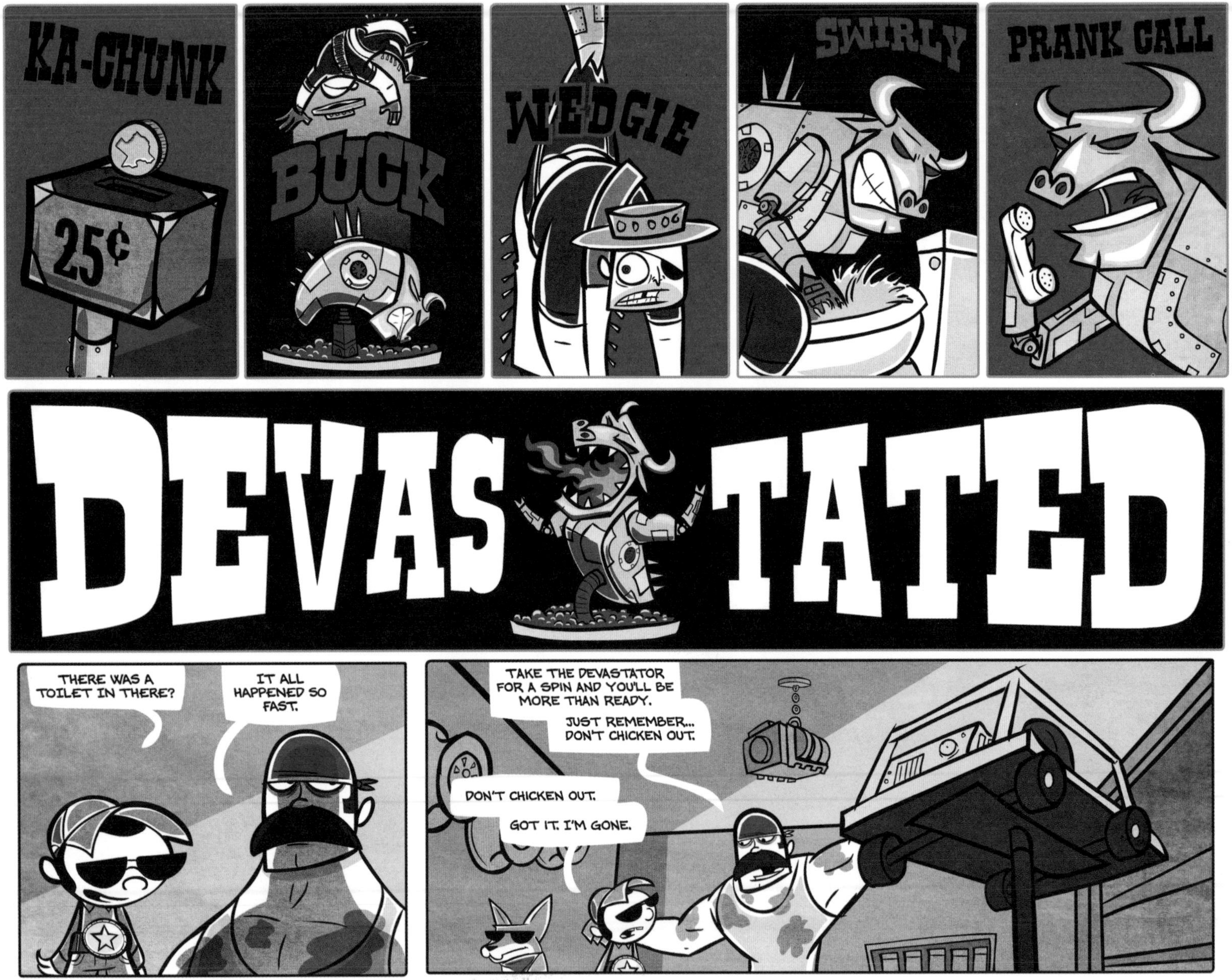
KA-CHUNK
25¢
BUCK
WEDGIE
SWIRLY
PRANK CALL
DEVAS TATED
THERE WAS A TOILET IN THERE?
IT ALL HAPPENED SO FAST.
TAKE THE DEVASTATOR FOR A SPIN AND YOU'LL BE MORE THAN READY.
JUST REMEMBER... DON'T CHICKEN OUT.
DON'T CHICKEN OUT.
GOT IT. I'M GONE.

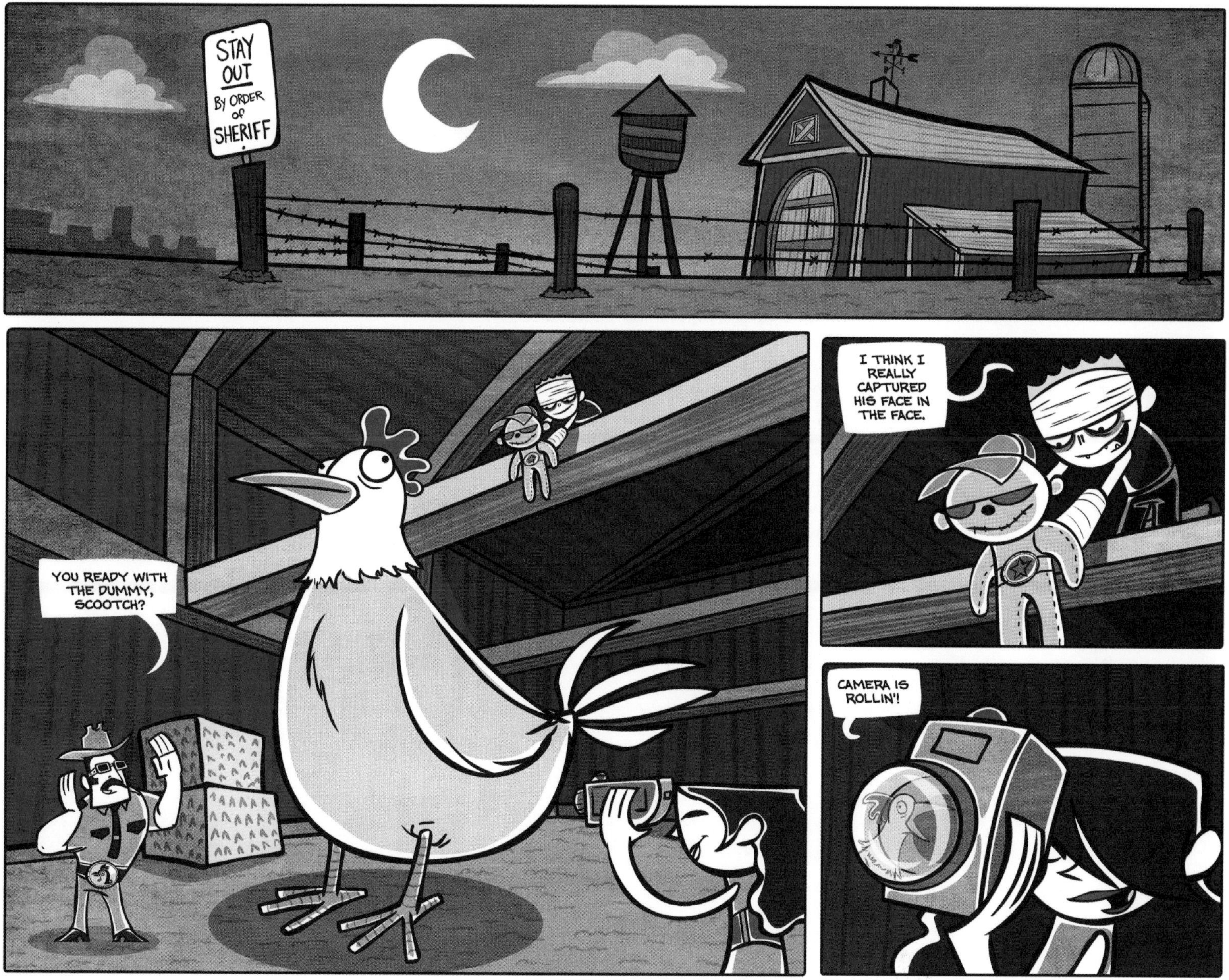
STAY OUT BY ORDER OF SHERIFF
YOU READY WITH THE DUMMY, SCOOTCH?
I THINK I REALLY CAPTURED HIS FACE IN THE FACE.
CAMERA IS ROLLIN'!

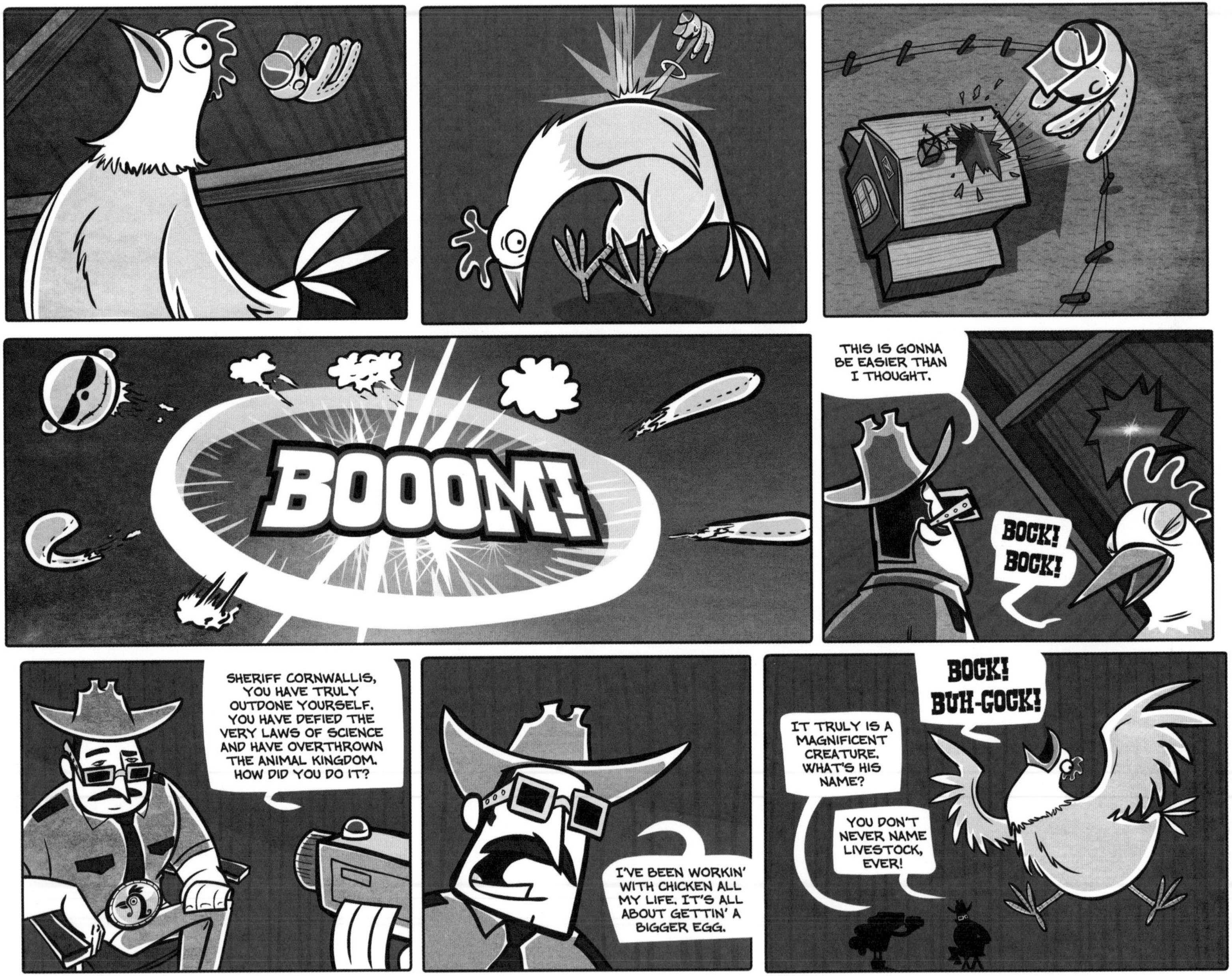
BOOOM!
THIS IS GONNA BE EASIER THAN I THOUGHT.
BOCK! BOCK!
SHERIFF CORNWALLIS, YOU HAVE TRULY OUTDONE YOURSELF. YOU HAVE DEFIED THE VERY LAWS OF SCIENCE AND HAVE OVERTHROWN THE ANIMAL KINGDOM. HOW DID YOU DO IT?
I'VE BEEN WORKIN' WITH CHICKEN ALL MY LIFE. IT'S ALL ABOUT GETTIN' A BIGGER EGG.
BOCK! BUH-GOCK!
IT TRULY IS A MAGNIFICENT CREATURE. WHAT'S HIS NAME?
YOU DON'T NEVER NAME LIVESTOCK, EVER!

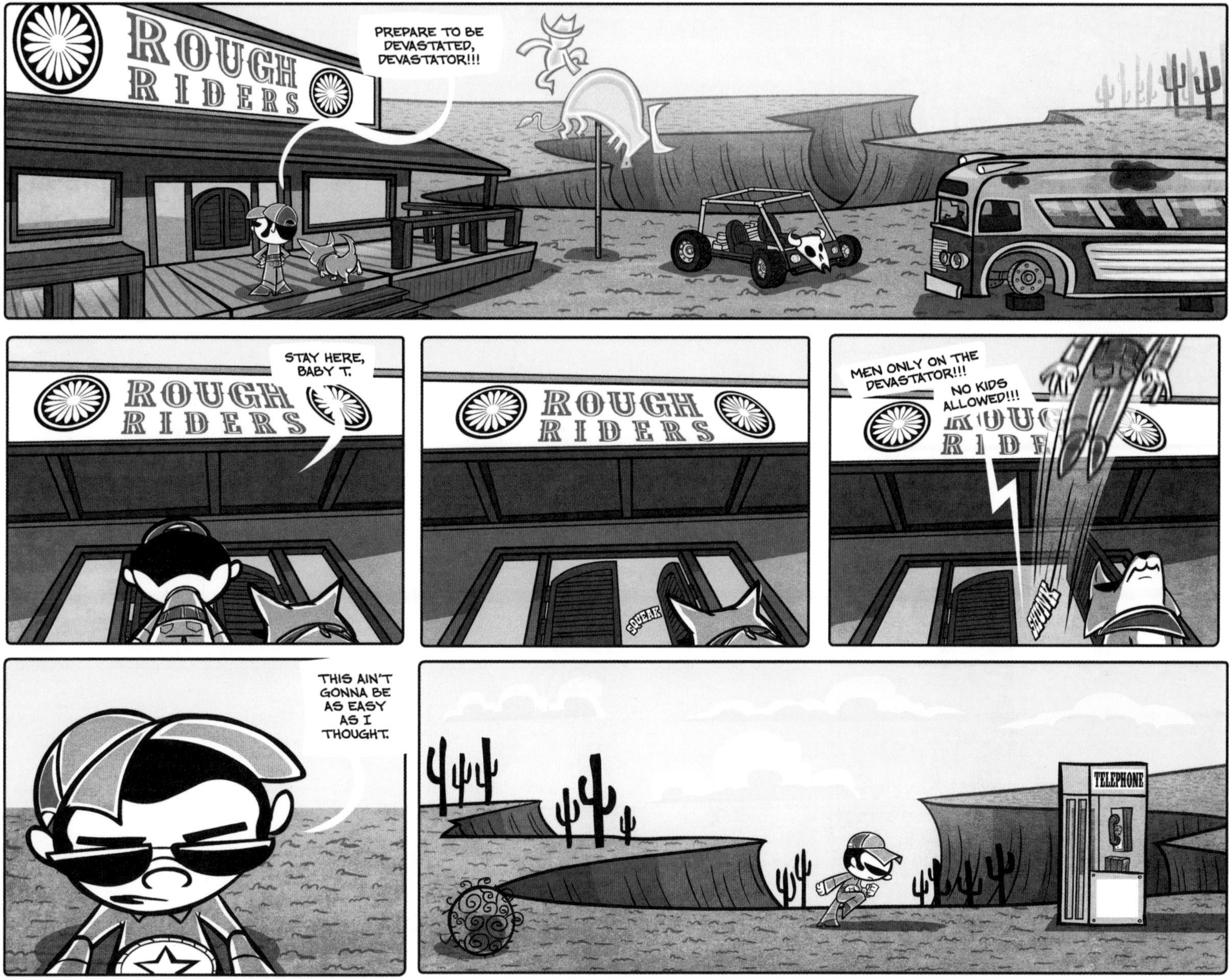
ROUGH RIDERS
PREPARE TO BE DEVASTATED, DEVASTATOR!!!
STAY HERE, BABY T.
SQUEAK
MEN ONLY ON THE DEVASTATOR!!!
NO KIDS ALLOWED!!!
THIS AIN'T GONNA BE AS EASY AS I THOUGHT.
TELEPHONE

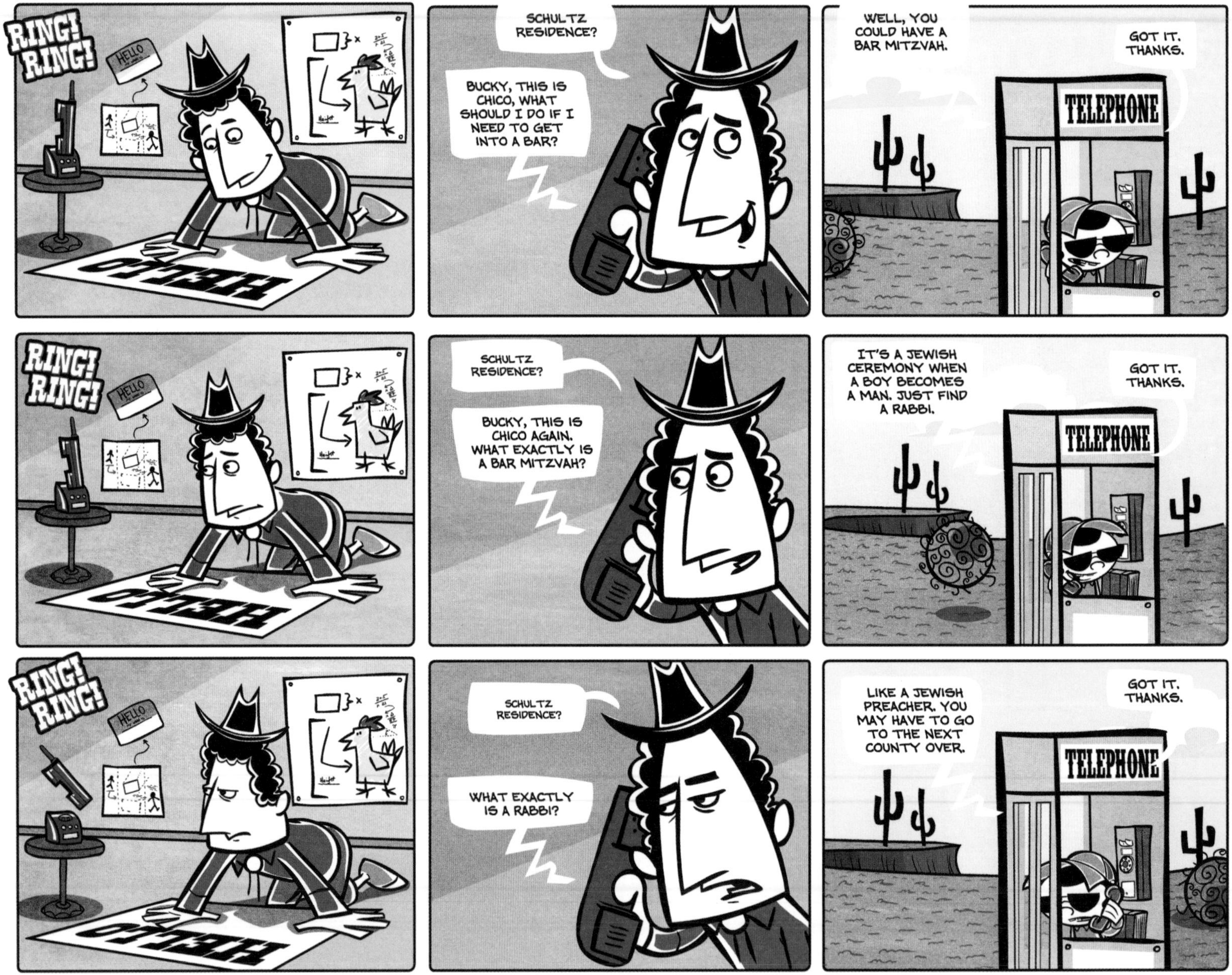
RING! RING!
HELLO
SCHULTZ RESIDENCE?
BUCKY, THIS IS CHICO, WHAT SHOULD I DO IF I NEED TO GET INTO A BAR?
WELL, YOU COULD HAVE A BAR MITZVAH.
GOT IT. THANKS.
TELEPHONE
RING! RING!
HELLO
SCHULTZ RESIDENCE?
BUCKY, THIS IS CHICO AGAIN. WHAT EXACTLY IS A BAR MITZVAH?
IT'S A JEWISH CEREMONY WHEN A BOY BECOMES A MAN. JUST FIND A RABBI.
GOT IT. THANKS.
TELEPHONE
RING! RING!
HELLO
SCHULTZ RESIDENCE?
WHAT EXACTLY IS A RABBI?
LIKE A JEWISH PREACHER. YOU MAY HAVE TO GO TO THE NEXT COUNTY OVER.
GOT IT. THANKS.
TELEPHONE

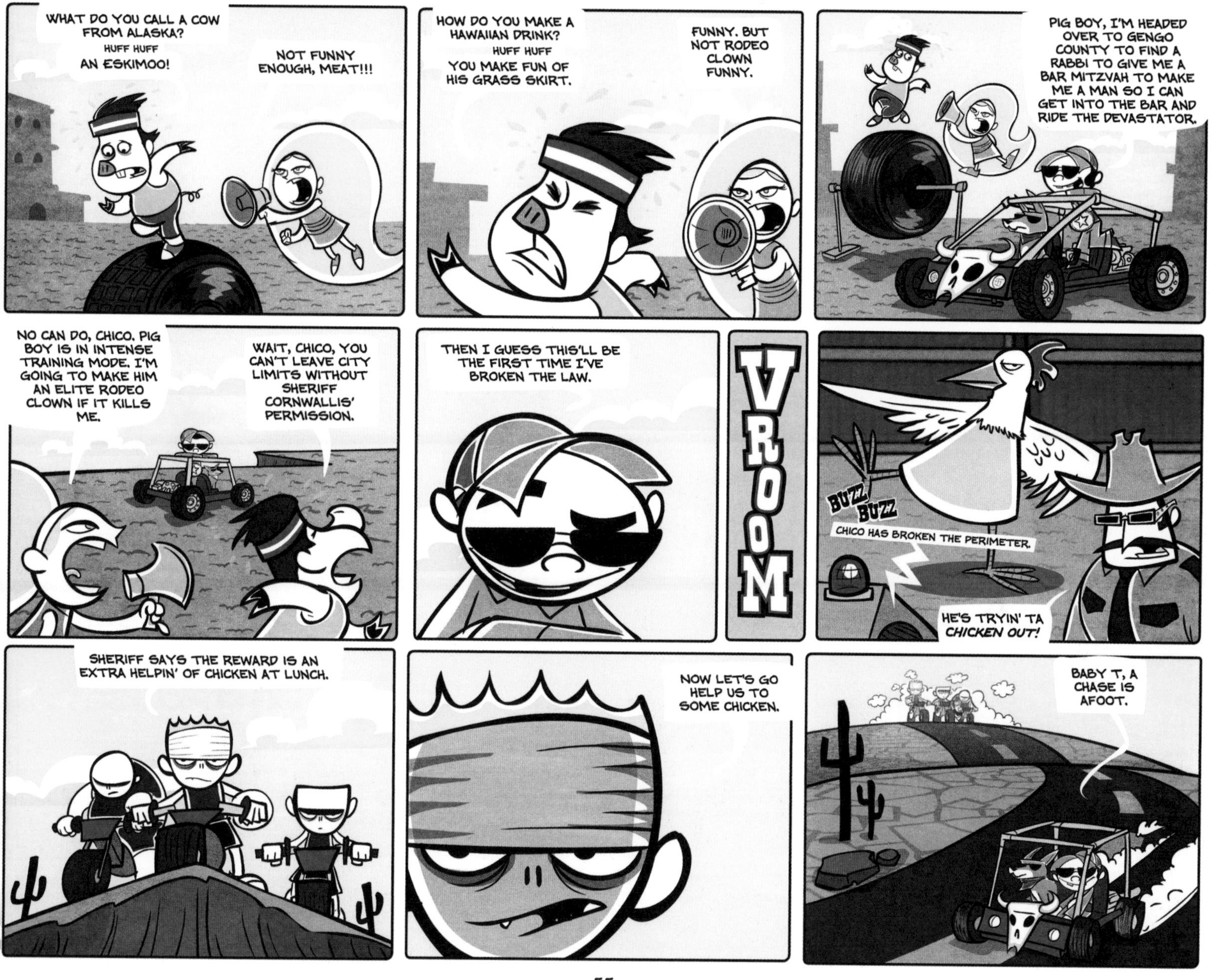
WHAT DO YOU CALL A COW FROM ALASKA?
HUFF HUFF
AN ESKIMOO!
NOT FUNNY ENOUGH, MEAT!!!
HOW DO YOU MAKE A HAWAIIAN DRINK?
HUFF HUFF
YOU MAKE FUN OF HIS GRASS SKIRT.
FUNNY. BUT NOT RODEO CLOWN FUNNY.
PIG BOY, I'M HEADED OVER TO GENGO COUNTY TO FIND A RABBI TO GIVE ME A BAR MITZVAH TO MAKE ME A MAN SO I CAN GET INTO THE BAR AND RIDE THE DEVASTATOR.
NO CAN DO, CHICO. PIG BOY IS IN INTENSE TRAINING MODE. I'M GOING TO MAKE HIM AN ELITE RODEO CLOWN IF IT KILLS ME.
WAIT, CHICO, YOU CAN'T LEAVE CITY LIMITS WITHOUT SHERIFF CORNWALLIS' PERMISSION.
THEN I GUESS THIS'LL BE THE FIRST TIME I'VE BROKEN THE LAW.
VROOM
BUZZ BUZZ
CHICO HAS BROKEN THE PERIMETER.
HE'S TRYIN' TA CHICKEN OUT!
SHERIFF SAYS THE REWARD IS AN EXTRA HELPIN' OF CHICKEN AT LUNCH.
NOW LET'S GO HELP US TO SOME CHICKEN.
BABY T, A CHASE IS AFOOT.

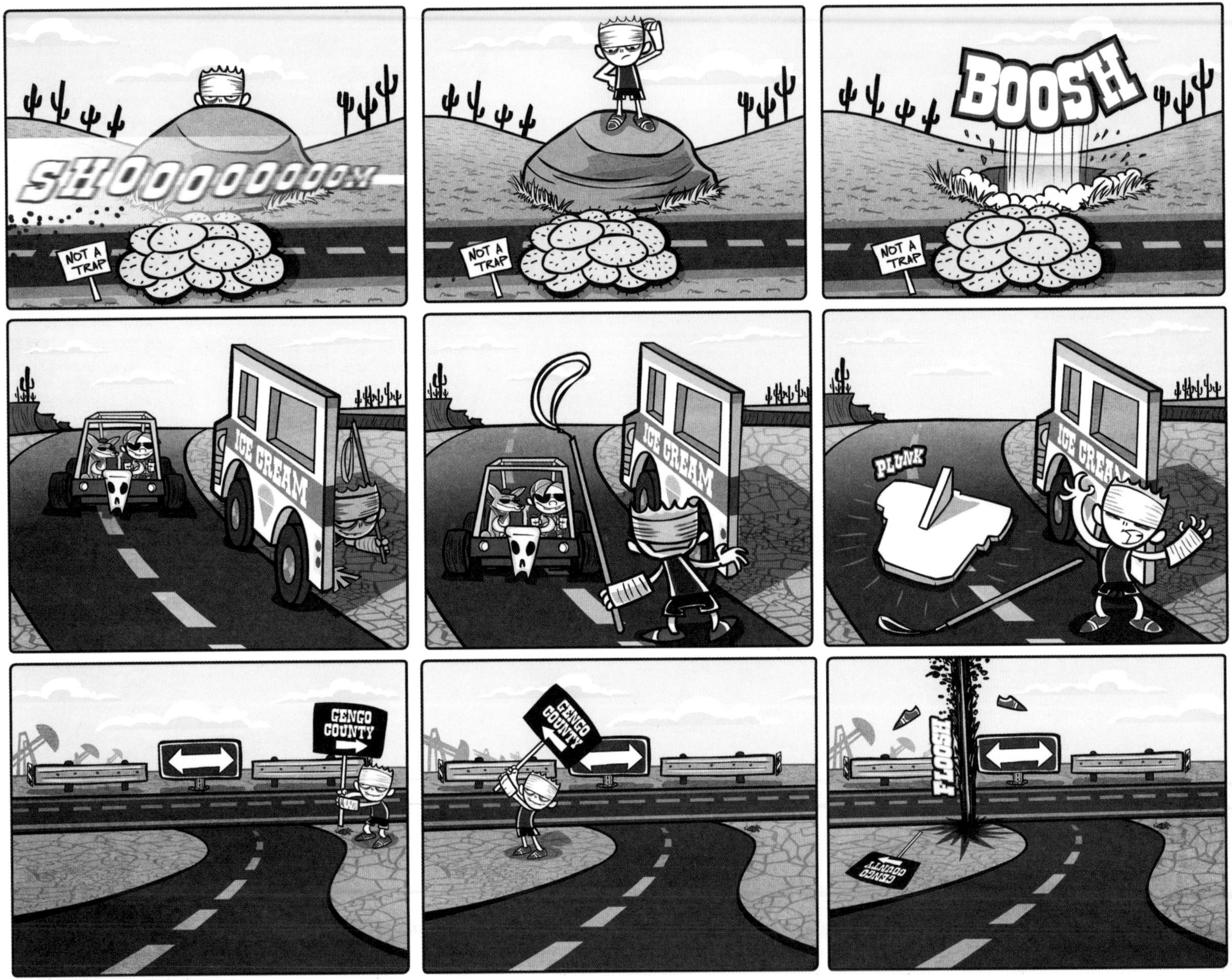
NOT A TRAP
NOT A TRAP
BOOSH
NOT A TRAP
ICE CREAM
ICE CREAM
PLUNK
ICE CREAM
GENGO COUNTY
GENGO COUNTY
FLOOSH
GENGO COUNTY

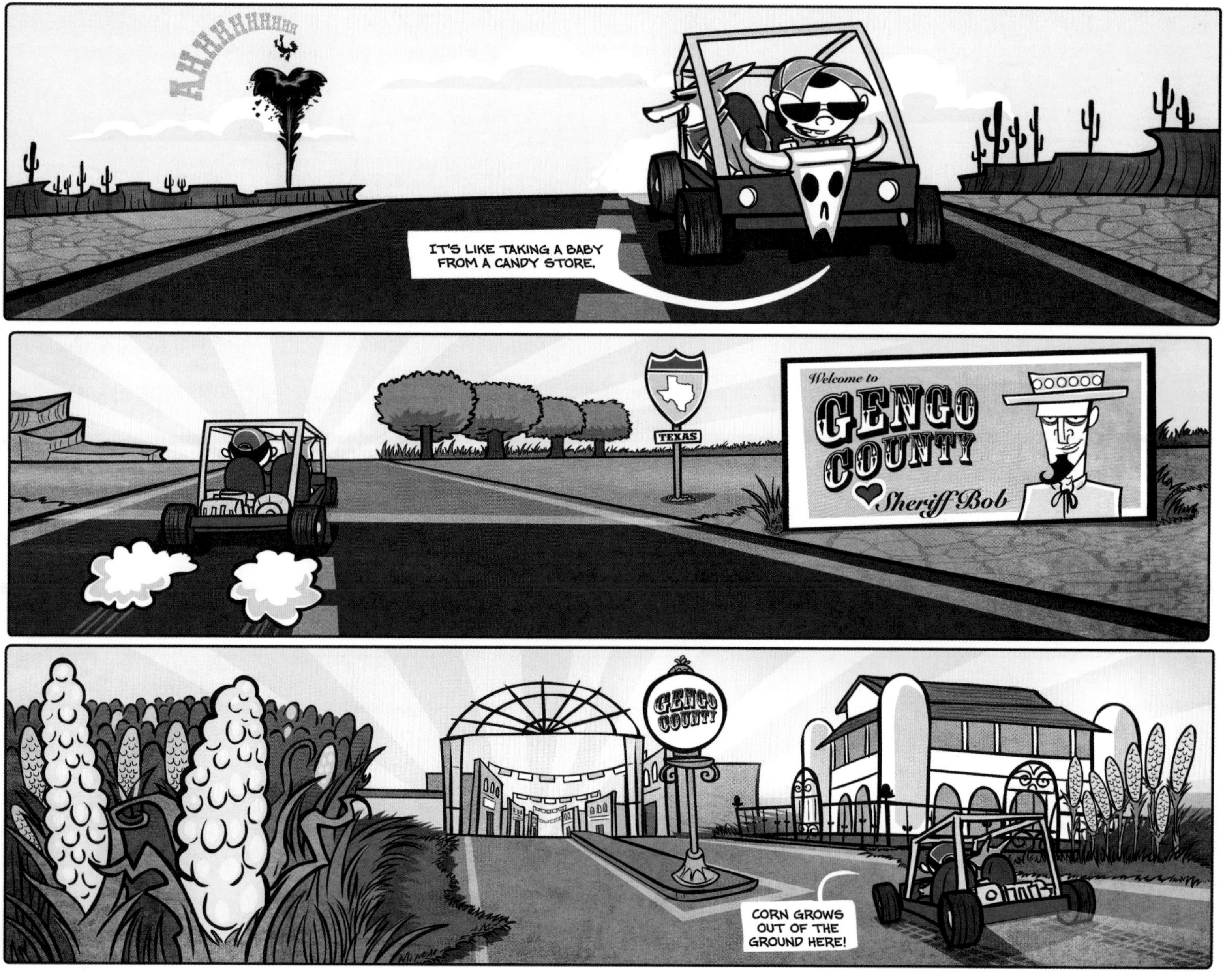
AHHHHHHHHH
IT'S LIKE TAKING A BABY FROM A CANDY STORE.
TEXAS
Welcome to
GENGO COUNTY
Sheriff Bob
GENGO COUNTY
CORN GROWS OUT OF THE GROUND HERE!

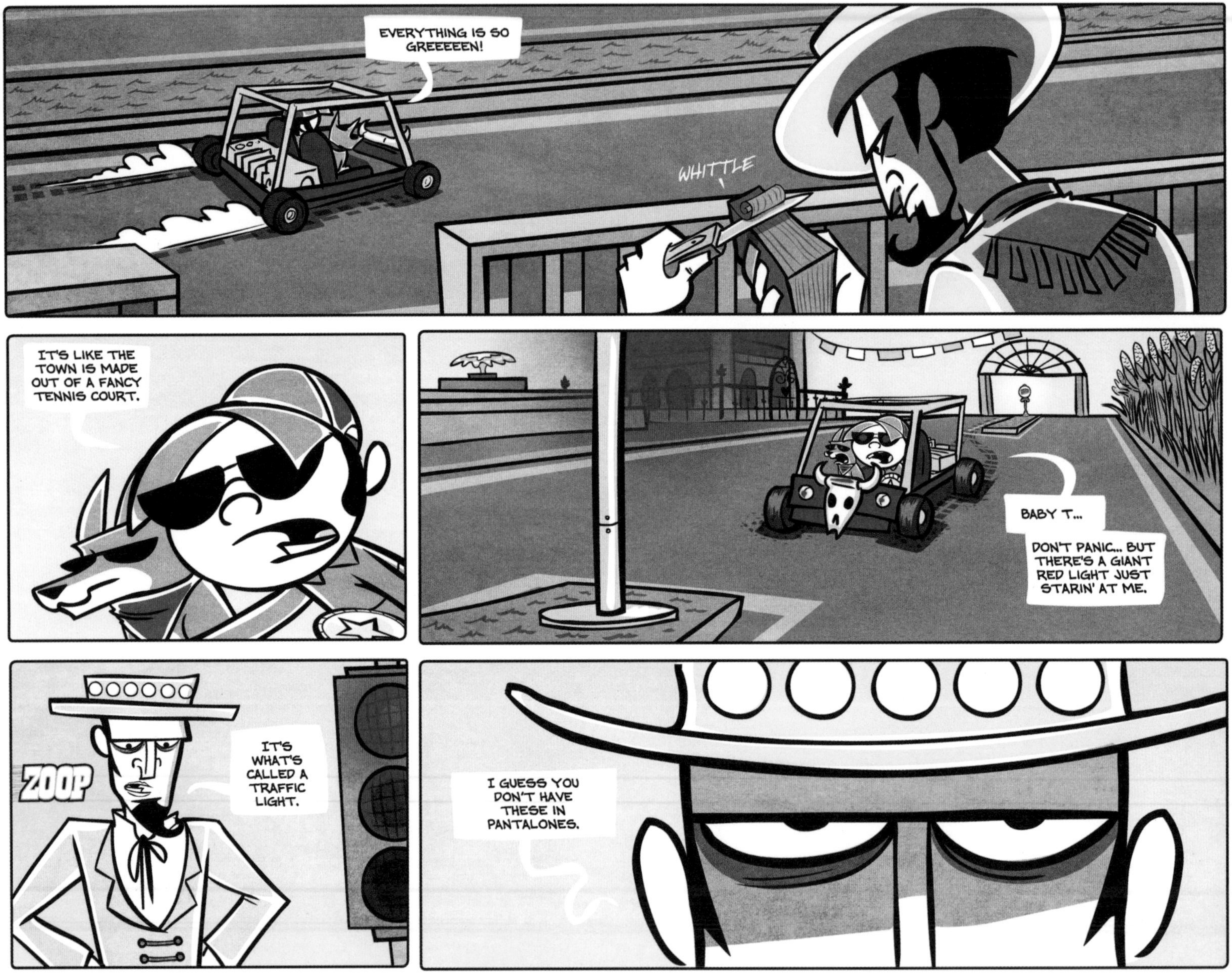
EVERYTHING IS SO GREEEEEN!
WHITTLE
IT'S LIKE THE TOWN IS MADE OUT OF A FANCY TENNIS COURT.
BABY T...
DON'T PANIC... BUT THERE'S A GIANT RED LIGHT JUST STARIN' AT ME.
ZOOP
IT'S WHAT'S CALLED A TRAFFIC LIGHT.
I GUESS YOU DON'T HAVE THESE IN PANTALONES.

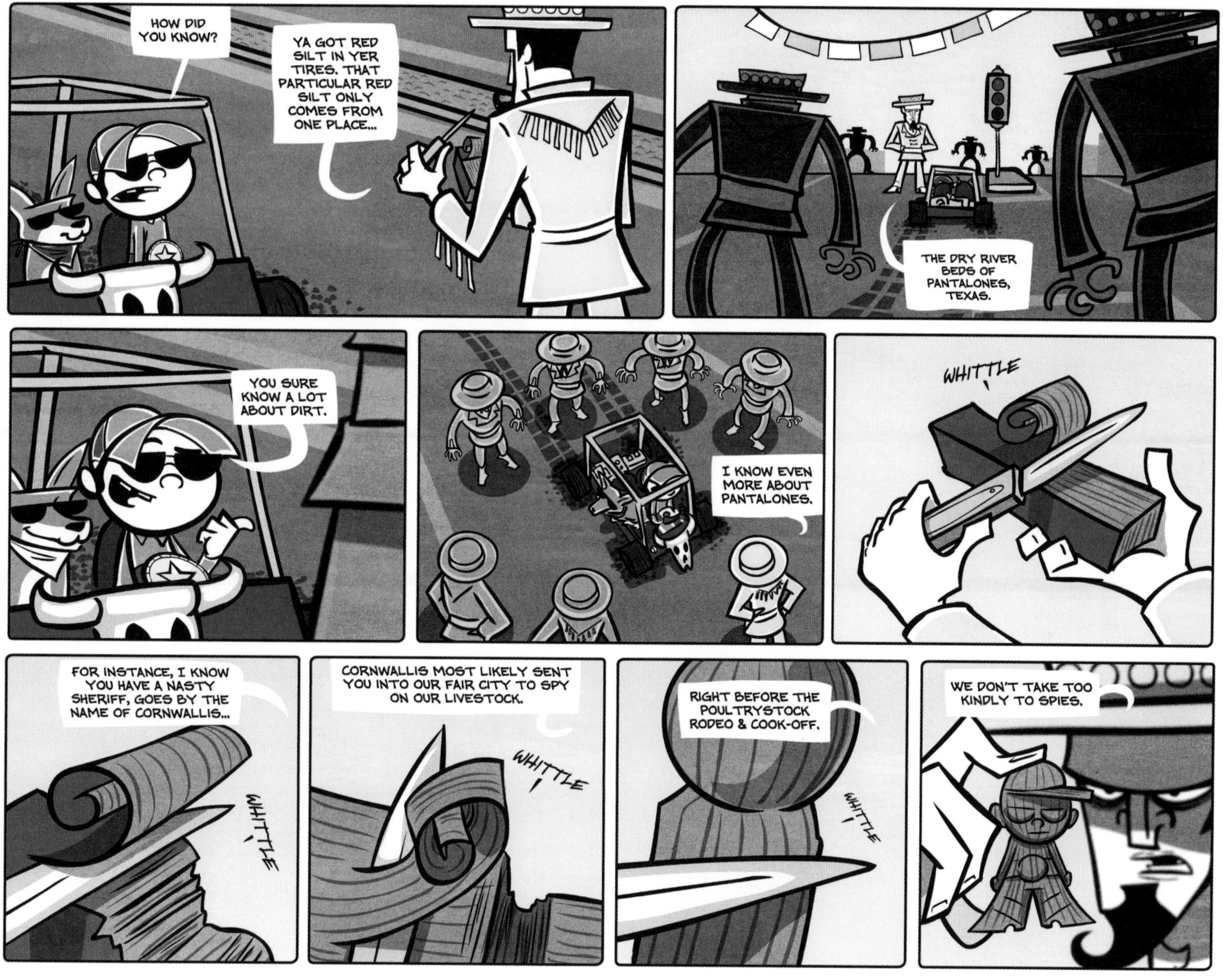
HOW DID YOU KNOW?
YA GOT RED SILT IN YER TIRES. THAT PARTICULAR RED SILT ONLY COMES FROM ONE PLACE...
THE DRY RIVER BEDS OF PANTALONES, TEXAS.
YOU SURE KNOW A LOT ABOUT DIRT.
I KNOW EVEN MORE ABOUT PANTALONES.
WHITTLE
FOR INSTANCE, I KNOW YOU HAVE A NASTY SHERIFF, GOES BY THE NAME OF CORNWALLIS...
WHITTLE
CORNWALLIS MOST LIKELY SENT YOU INTO OUR FAIR CITY TO SPY ON OUR LIVESTOCK.
WHITTLE
RIGHT BEFORE THE POULTRYSTOCK RODEO & COOK-OFF.
WHITTLE
WE DON'T TAKE TOO KINDLY TO SPIES.

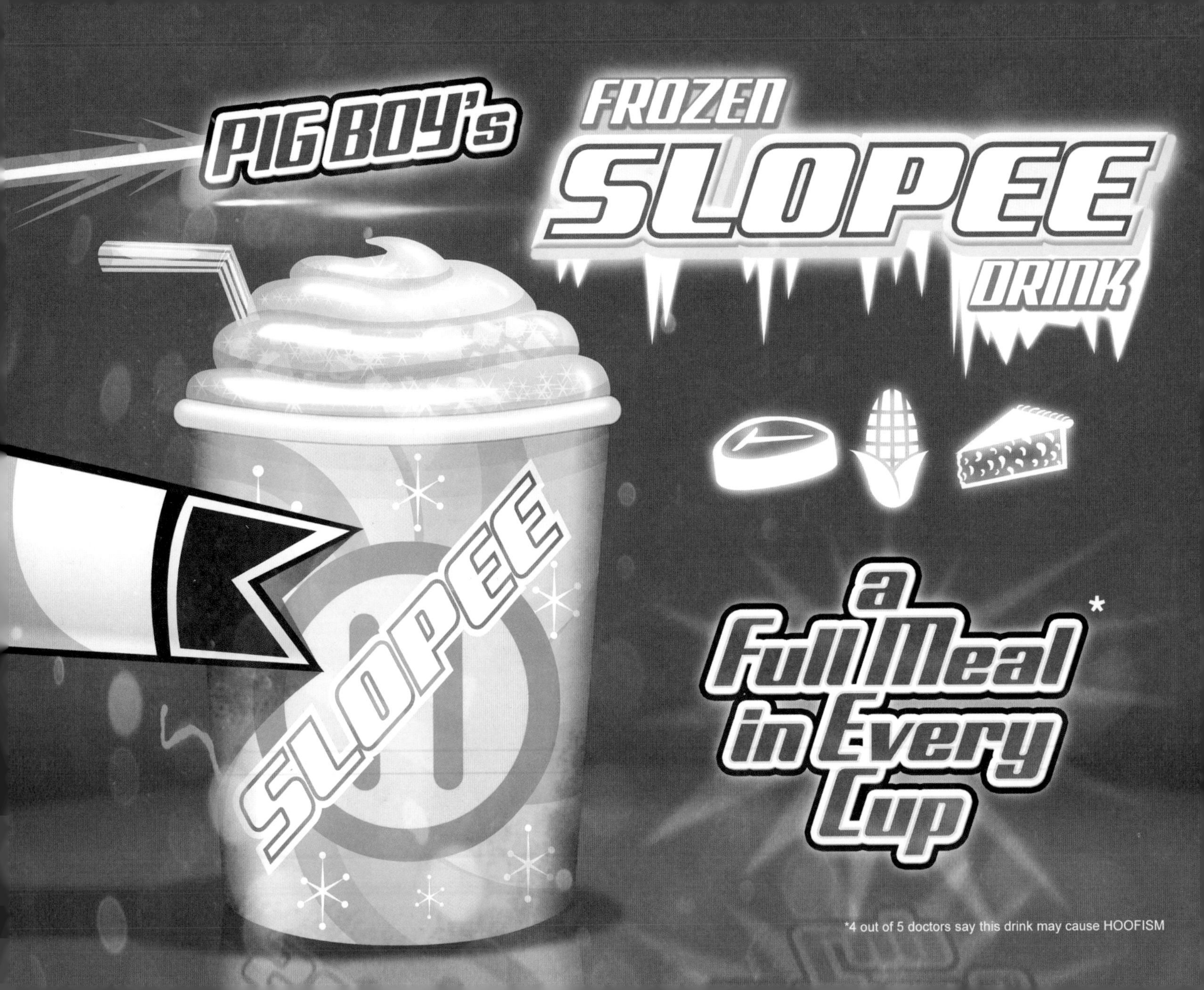
PIG BOY's
FROZEN
SLOPEE
DRINK
SLOPEE
a
Full Meal
in Every
Cup*
*4 out of 5 doctors say this drink may cause HOOFISM

CHAPTER CUATRO

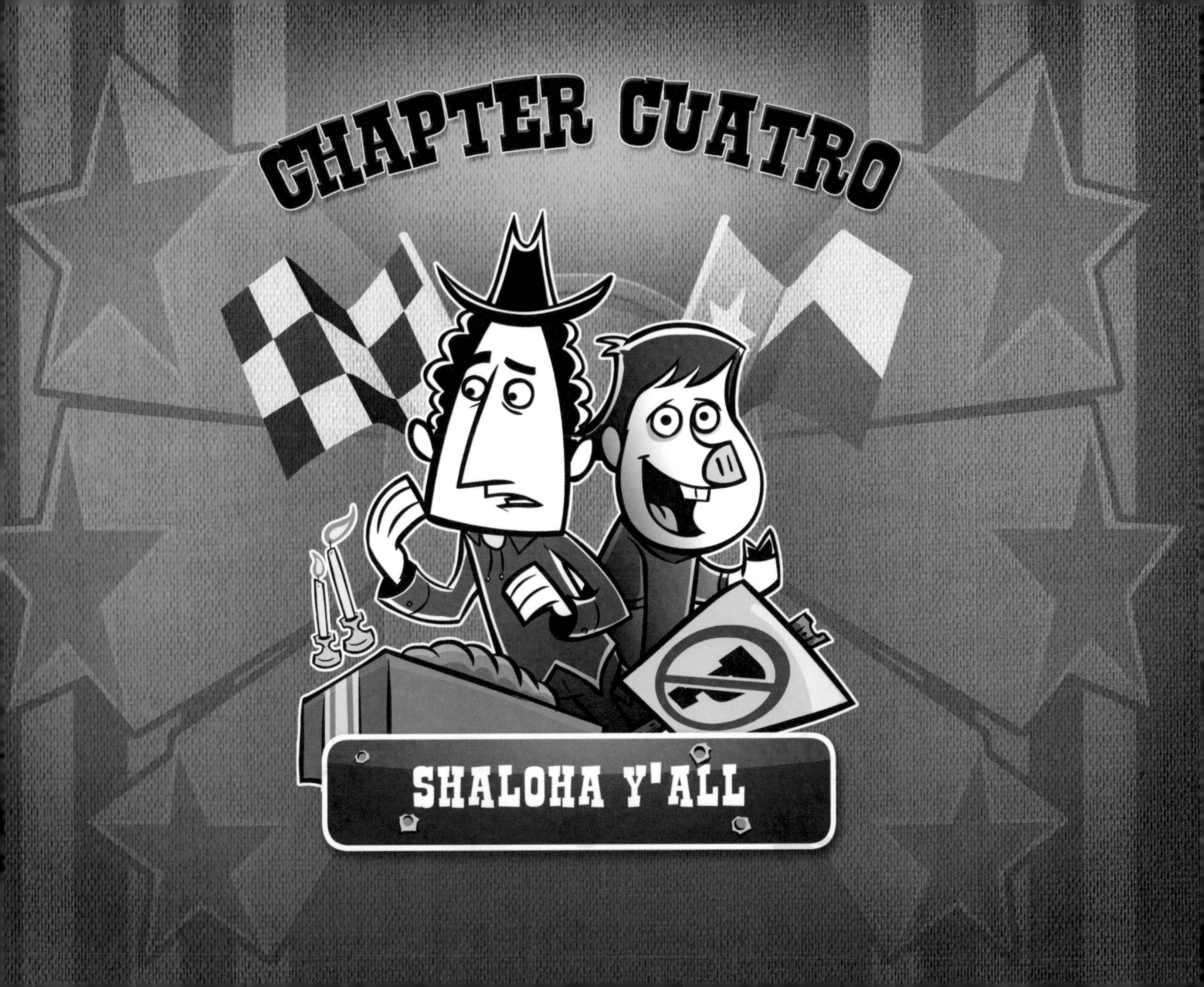

SHALOHA Y'ALL

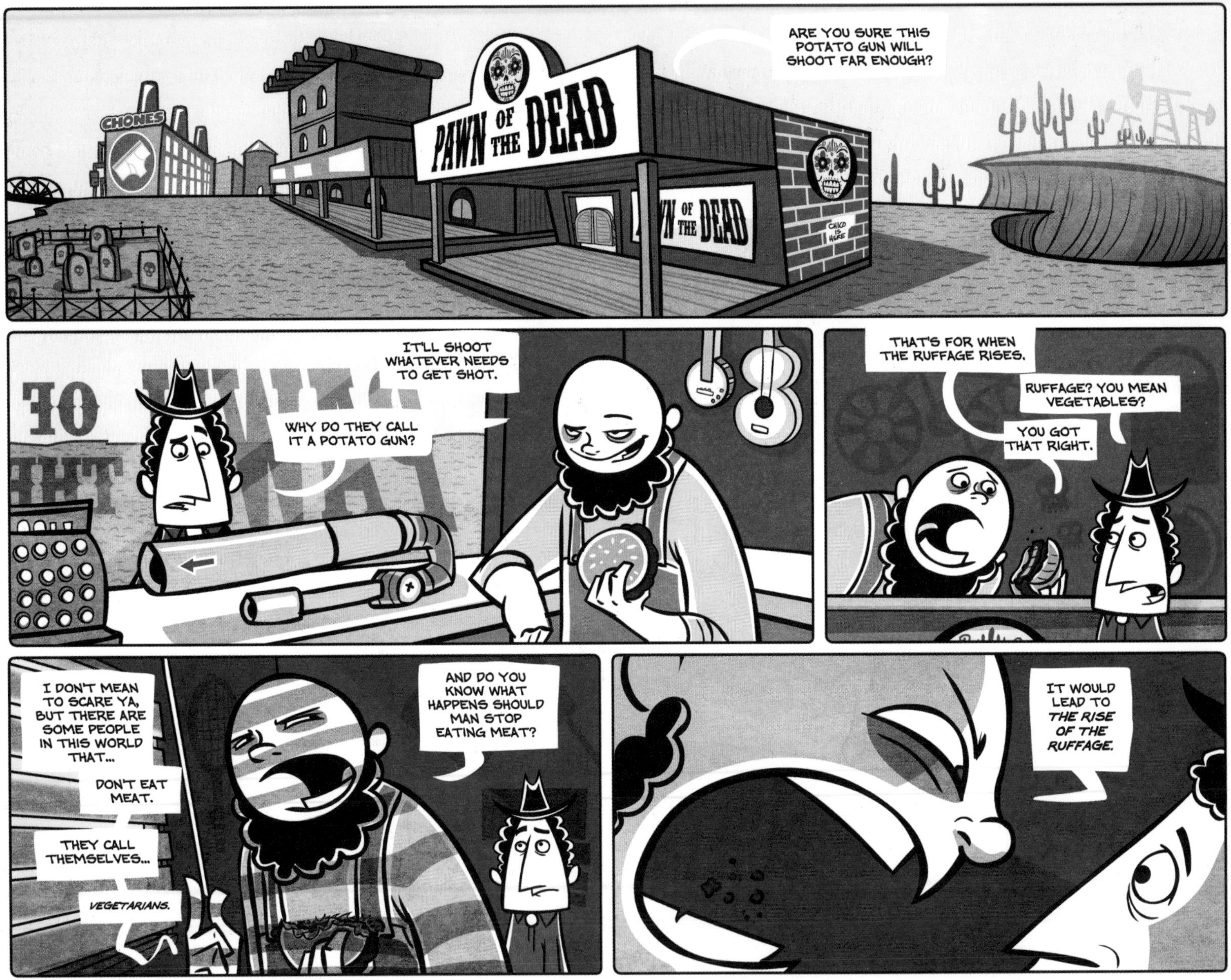
CHONES
PAWN OF THE DEAD
ARE YOU SURE THIS POTATO GUN WILL SHOOT FAR ENOUGH?
PAWN OF THE DEAD
CHICO IS HERE
IT'LL SHOOT WHATEVER NEEDS TO GET SHOT.
WHY DO THEY CALL IT A POTATO GUN?
THAT'S FOR WHEN THE RUFFAGE RISES.
RUFFAGE? YOU MEAN VEGETABLES?
YOU GOT THAT RIGHT.
I DON'T MEAN TO SCARE YA, BUT THERE ARE SOME PEOPLE IN THIS WORLD THAT...
DON'T EAT MEAT.
THEY CALL THEMSELVES...
VEGETARIANS.
AND DO YOU KNOW WHAT HAPPENS SHOULD MAN STOP EATING MEAT?
IT WOULD LEAD TO THE RISE OF THE RUFFAGE.

RISE OF THE RUFFAGE

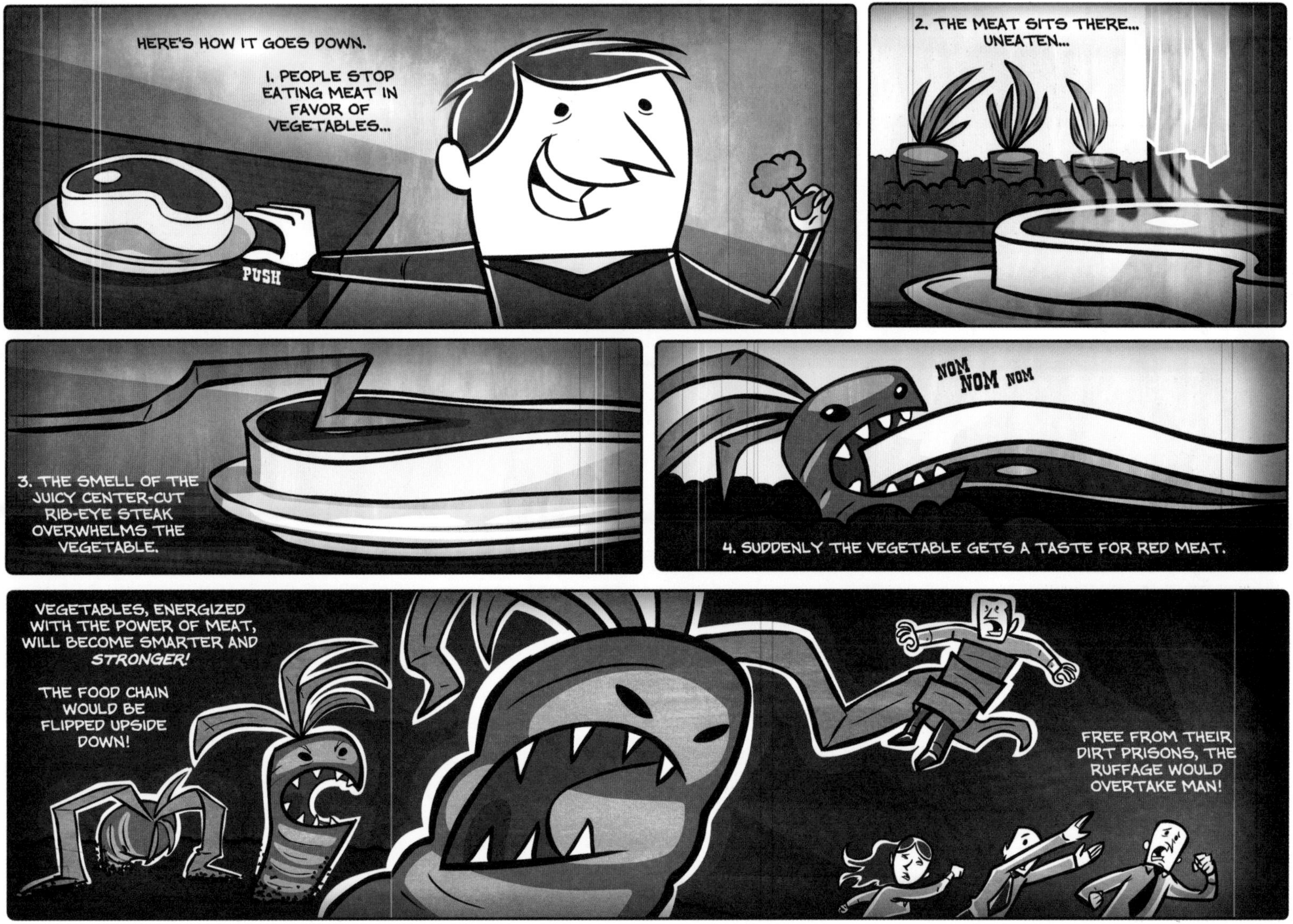
HERE'S HOW IT GOES DOWN.
1. PEOPLE STOP EATING MEAT IN FAVOR OF VEGETABLES...
PUSH
2. THE MEAT SITS THERE... UNEATEN...
3. THE SMELL OF THE JUICY CENTER-CUT RIB-EYE STEAK OVERWHELMS THE VEGETABLE.
NOM NOM NOM
4. SUDDENLY THE VEGETABLE GETS A TASTE FOR RED MEAT.
VEGETABLES, ENERGIZED WITH THE POWER OF MEAT, WILL BECOME SMARTER AND *STRONGER!*
THE FOOD CHAIN WOULD BE FLIPPED UPSIDE DOWN!
FREE FROM THEIR DIRT PRISONS, THE RUFFAGE WOULD OVERTAKE MAN!

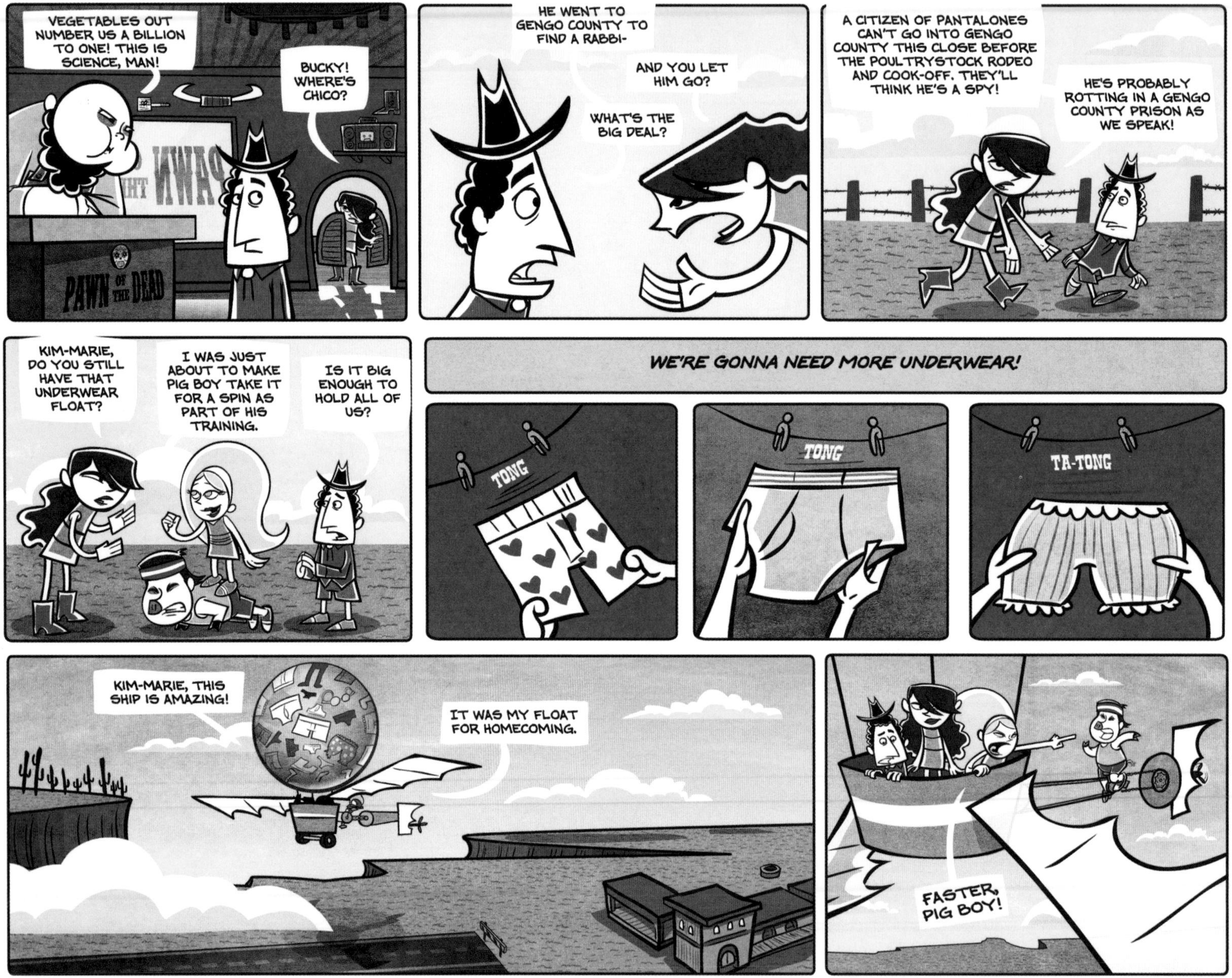
VEGETABLES OUT NUMBER US A BILLION TO ONE! THIS IS SCIENCE, MAN!
BUCKY! WHERE'S CHICO?
PAWN OF THE DEAD
HE WENT TO GENGO COUNTY TO FIND A RABBI-
AND YOU LET HIM GO?
WHAT'S THE BIG DEAL?
A CITIZEN OF PANTALONES CAN'T GO INTO GENGO COUNTY THIS CLOSE BEFORE THE POULTRYSTOCK RODEO AND COOK-OFF. THEY'LL THINK HE'S A SPY!
HE'S PROBABLY ROTTING IN A GENGO COUNTY PRISON AS WE SPEAK!
KIM-MARIE, DO YOU STILL HAVE THAT UNDERWEAR FLOAT?
I WAS JUST ABOUT TO MAKE PIG BOY TAKE IT FOR A SPIN AS PART OF HIS TRAINING.
IS IT BIG ENOUGH TO HOLD ALL OF US?
WE'RE GONNA NEED MORE UNDERWEAR!
TONG
TONG
TA-TONG
KIM-MARIE, THIS SHIP IS AMAZING!
IT WAS MY FLOAT FOR HOMECOMING.
FASTER, PIG BOY!

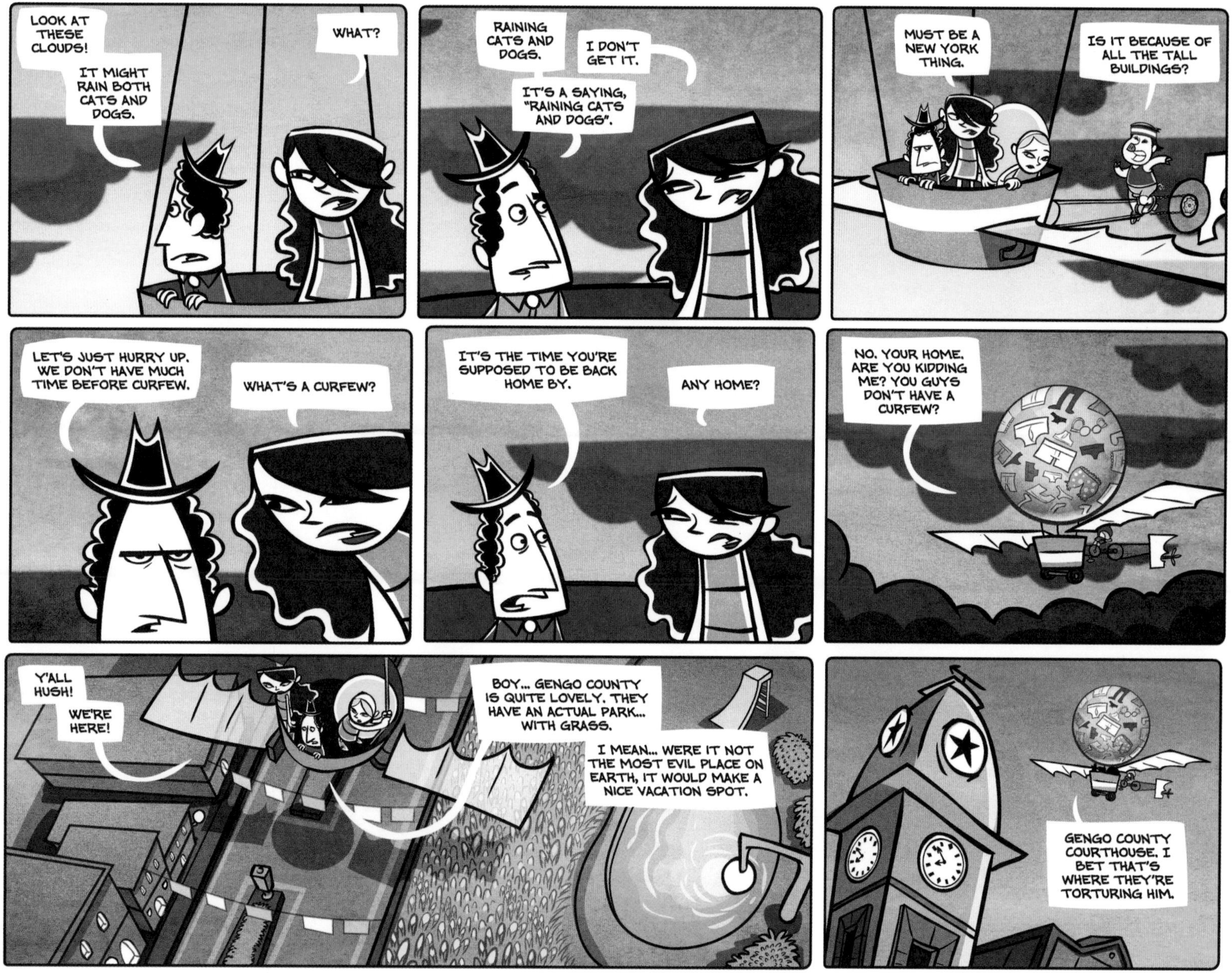
LOOK AT THESE CLOUDS!
IT MIGHT RAIN BOTH CATS AND DOGS.
WHAT?
RAINING CATS AND DOGS.
I DON'T GET IT.
IT'S A SAYING, "RAINING CATS AND DOGS".
MUST BE A NEW YORK THING.
IS IT BECAUSE OF ALL THE TALL BUILDINGS?
LET'S JUST HURRY UP. WE DON'T HAVE MUCH TIME BEFORE CURFEW.
WHAT'S A CURFEW?
IT'S THE TIME YOU'RE SUPPOSED TO BE BACK HOME BY.
ANY HOME?
NO. YOUR HOME. ARE YOU KIDDING ME? YOU GUYS DON'T HAVE A CURFEW?
Y'ALL HUSH!
WE'RE HERE!
BOY... GENGO COUNTY IS QUITE LOVELY. THEY HAVE AN ACTUAL PARK... WITH GRASS.
I MEAN... WERE IT NOT THE MOST EVIL PLACE ON EARTH, IT WOULD MAKE A NICE VACATION SPOT.
GENGO COUNTY COURTHOUSE. I BET THAT'S WHERE THEY'RE TORTURING HIM.

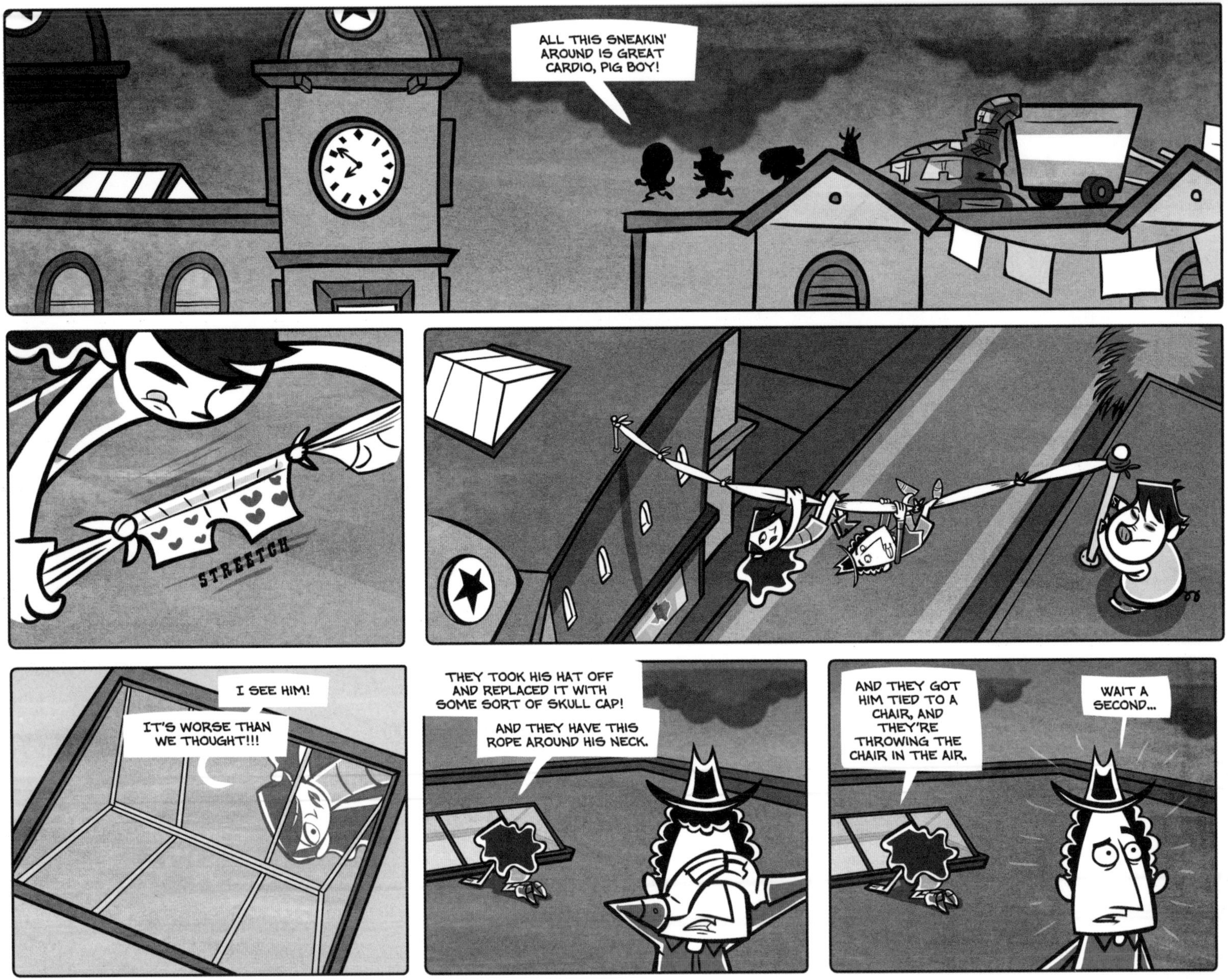

ALL THIS SNEAKIN' AROUND IS GREAT CARDIO, PIG BOY!
STREETCH
I SEE HIM!
IT'S WORSE THAN WE THOUGHT!!!
THEY TOOK HIS HAT OFF AND REPLACED IT WITH SOME SORT OF SKULL CAP!
AND THEY HAVE THIS ROPE AROUND HIS NECK.
AND THEY GOT HIM TIED TO A CHAIR, AND THEY'RE THROWING THE CHAIR IN THE AIR.
WAIT A SECOND...

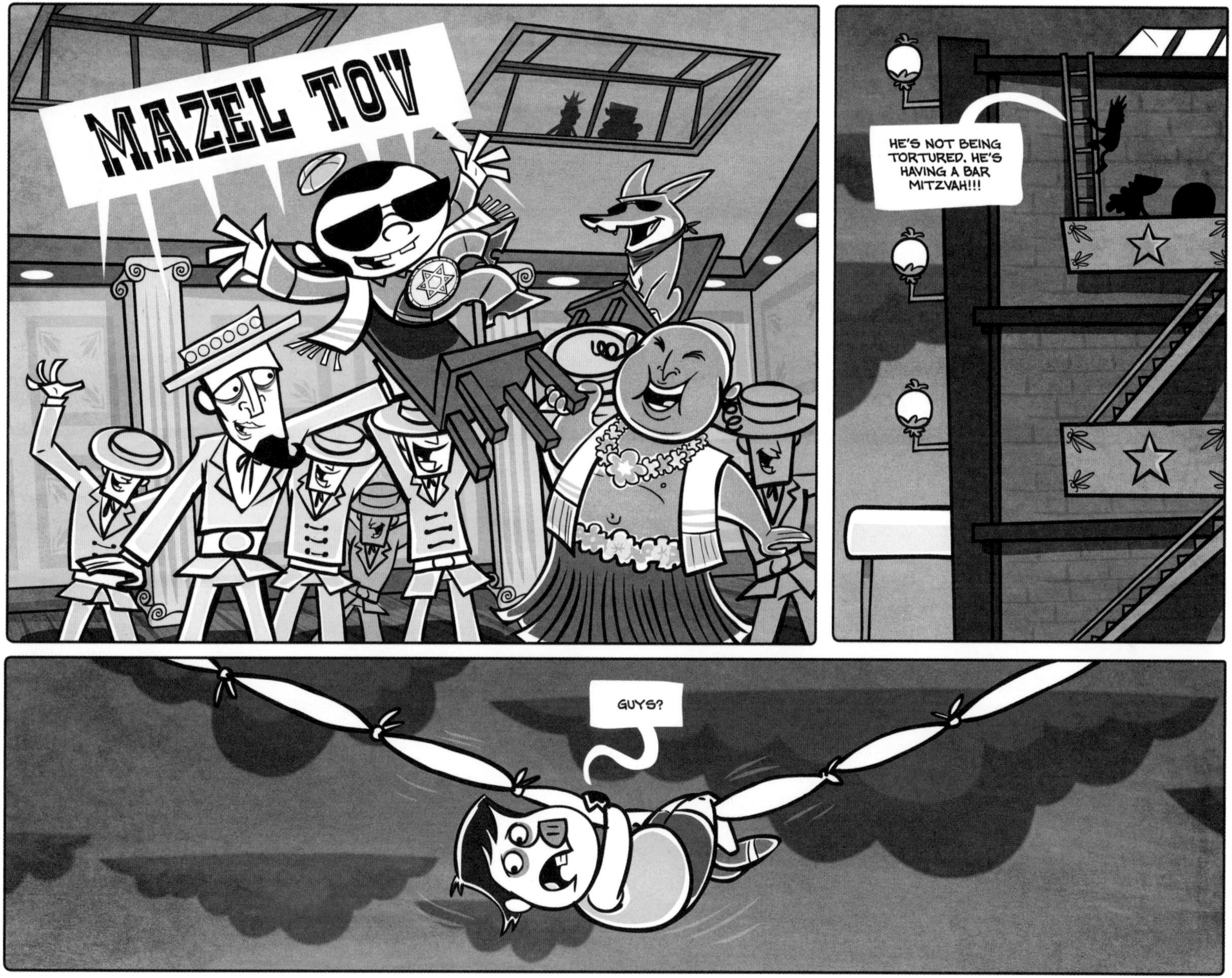
MAZEL TOV
HE'S NOT BEING TORTURED. HE'S HAVING A BAR MITZVAH!!!
GUYS?

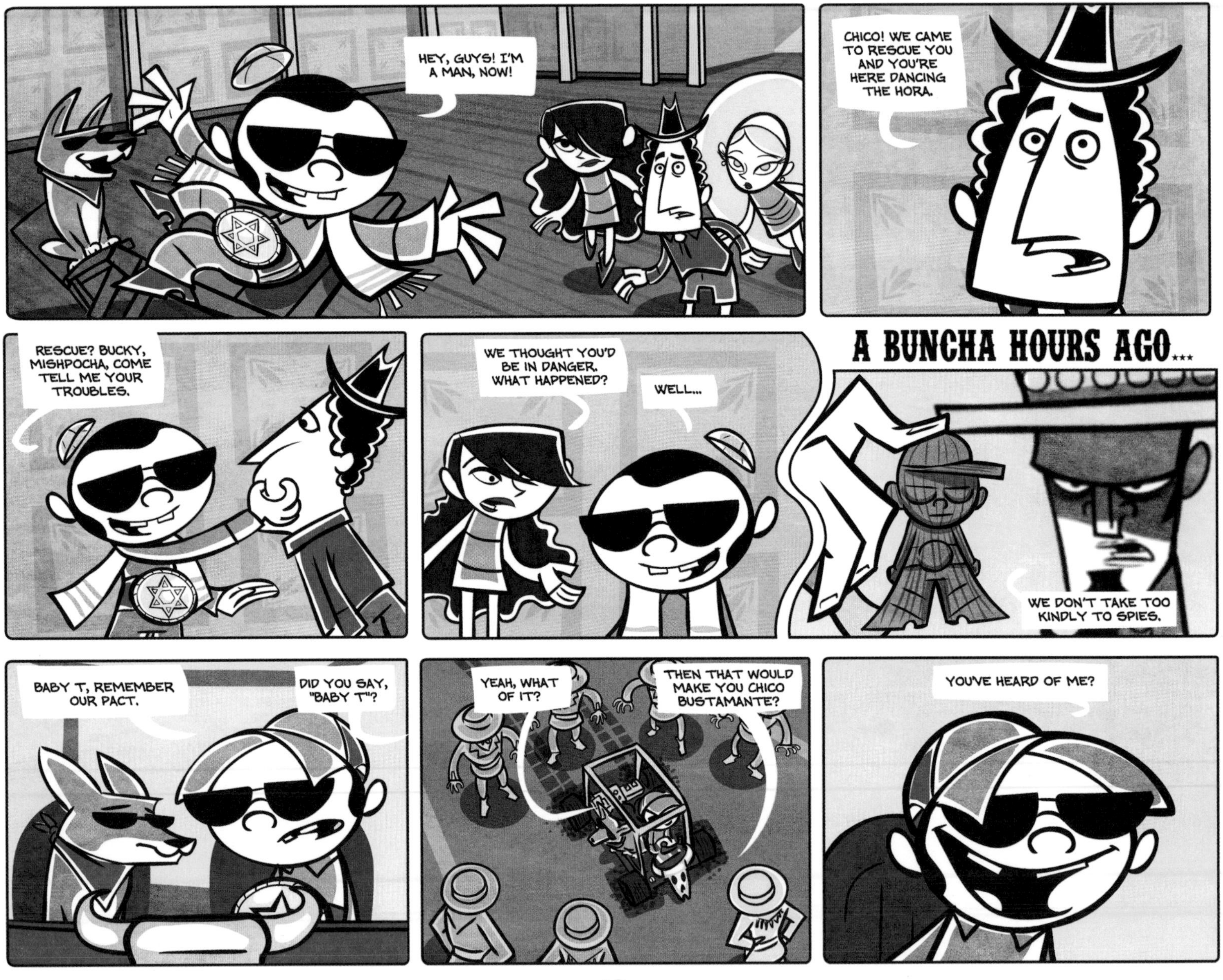
HEY, GUYS! I'M A MAN, NOW!
CHICO! WE CAME TO RESCUE YOU AND YOU'RE HERE DANCING THE HORA.
RESCUE? BUCKY, MISHPOCHA, COME TELL ME YOUR TROUBLES.
WE THOUGHT YOU'D BE IN DANGER. WHAT HAPPENED?
WELL...
A BUNCHA HOURS AGO...
WE DON'T TAKE TOO KINDLY TO SPIES.
BABY T, REMEMBER OUR PACT.
DID YOU SAY, "BABY T"?
YEAH, WHAT OF IT?
THEN THAT WOULD MAKE YOU CHICO BUSTAMANTE?
YOU'VE HEARD OF ME?

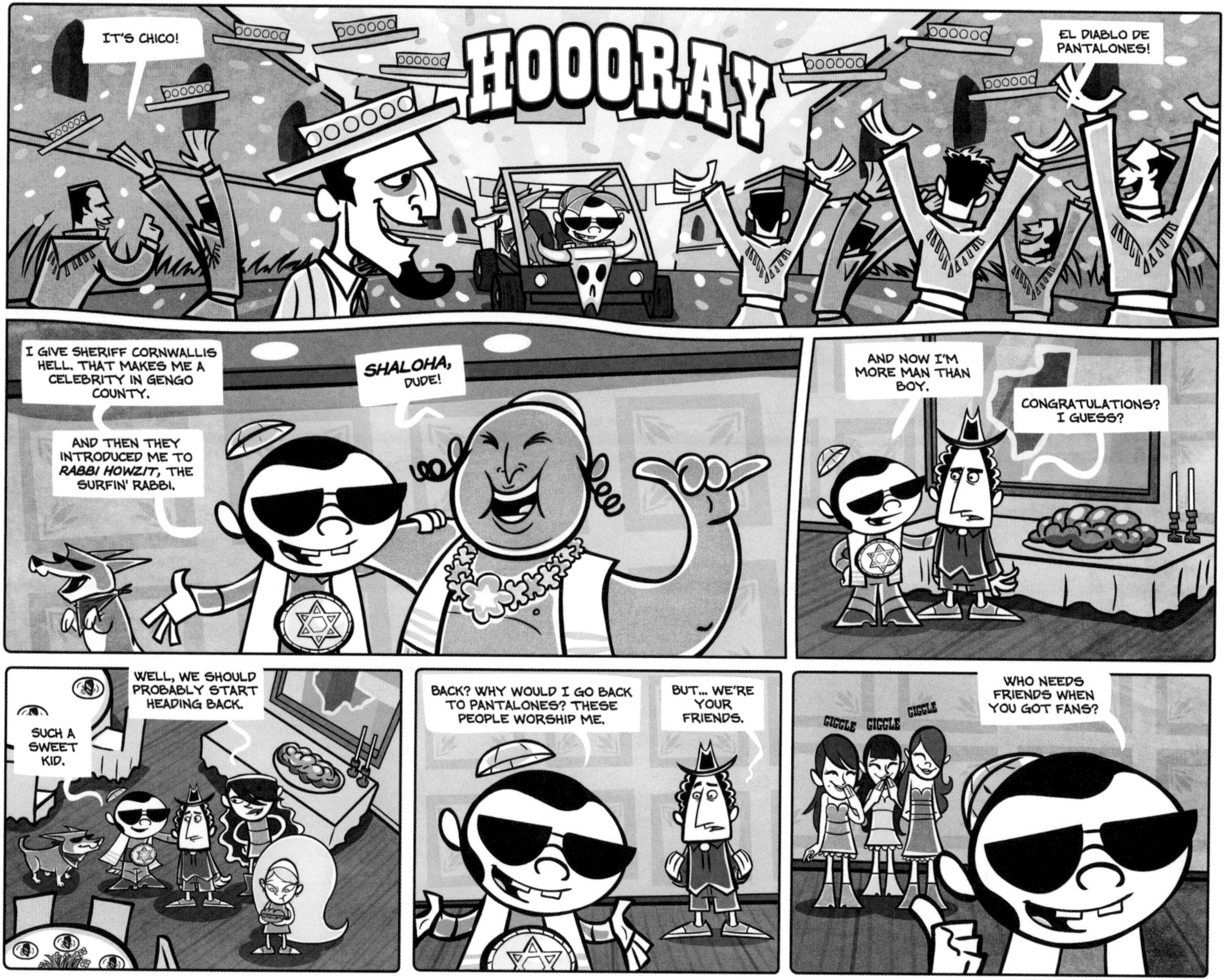
IT'S CHICO!
HOOORAY
EL DIABLO DE PANTALONES!
I GIVE SHERIFF CORNWALLIS HELL. THAT MAKES ME A CELEBRITY IN GENGO COUNTY.
AND THEN THEY INTRODUCED ME TO *RABBI HOWZIT*, THE SURFIN' RABBI.
SHALOHA, DUDE!
AND NOW I'M MORE MAN THAN BOY.
CONGRATULATIONS? I GUESS?
WELL, WE SHOULD PROBABLY START HEADING BACK.
SUCH A SWEET KID.
BACK? WHY WOULD I GO BACK TO PANTALONES? THESE PEOPLE WORSHIP ME.
BUT... WE'RE YOUR FRIENDS.
GIGGLE GIGGLE GIGGLE
WHO NEEDS FRIENDS WHEN YOU GOT FANS?

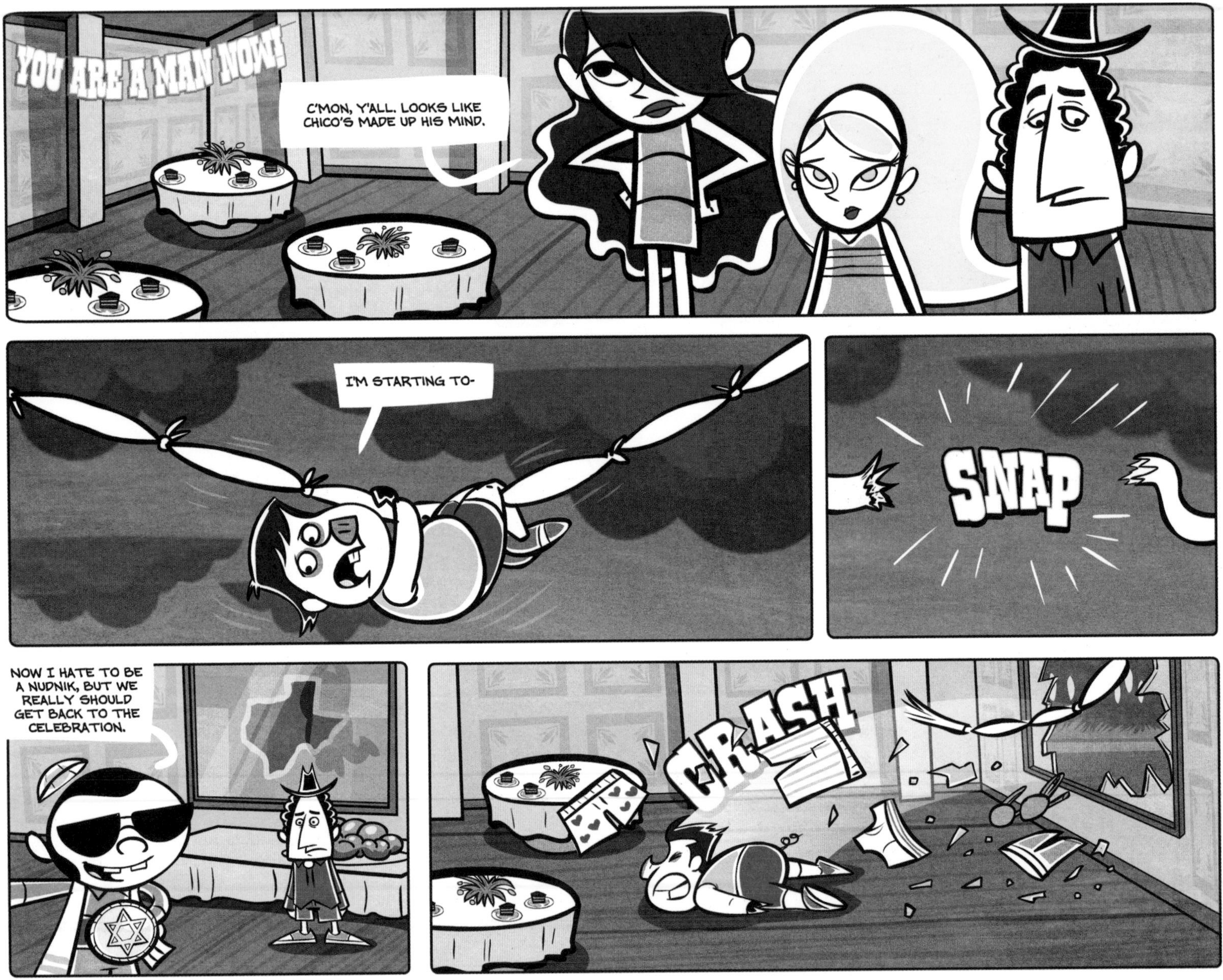
YOU ARE A MAN NOW!
C'MON, Y'ALL. LOOKS LIKE CHICO'S MADE UP HIS MIND.
I'M STARTING TO-
SNAP
NOW I HATE TO BE A NUDNIK, BUT WE REALLY SHOULD GET BACK TO THE CELEBRATION.
CRASH

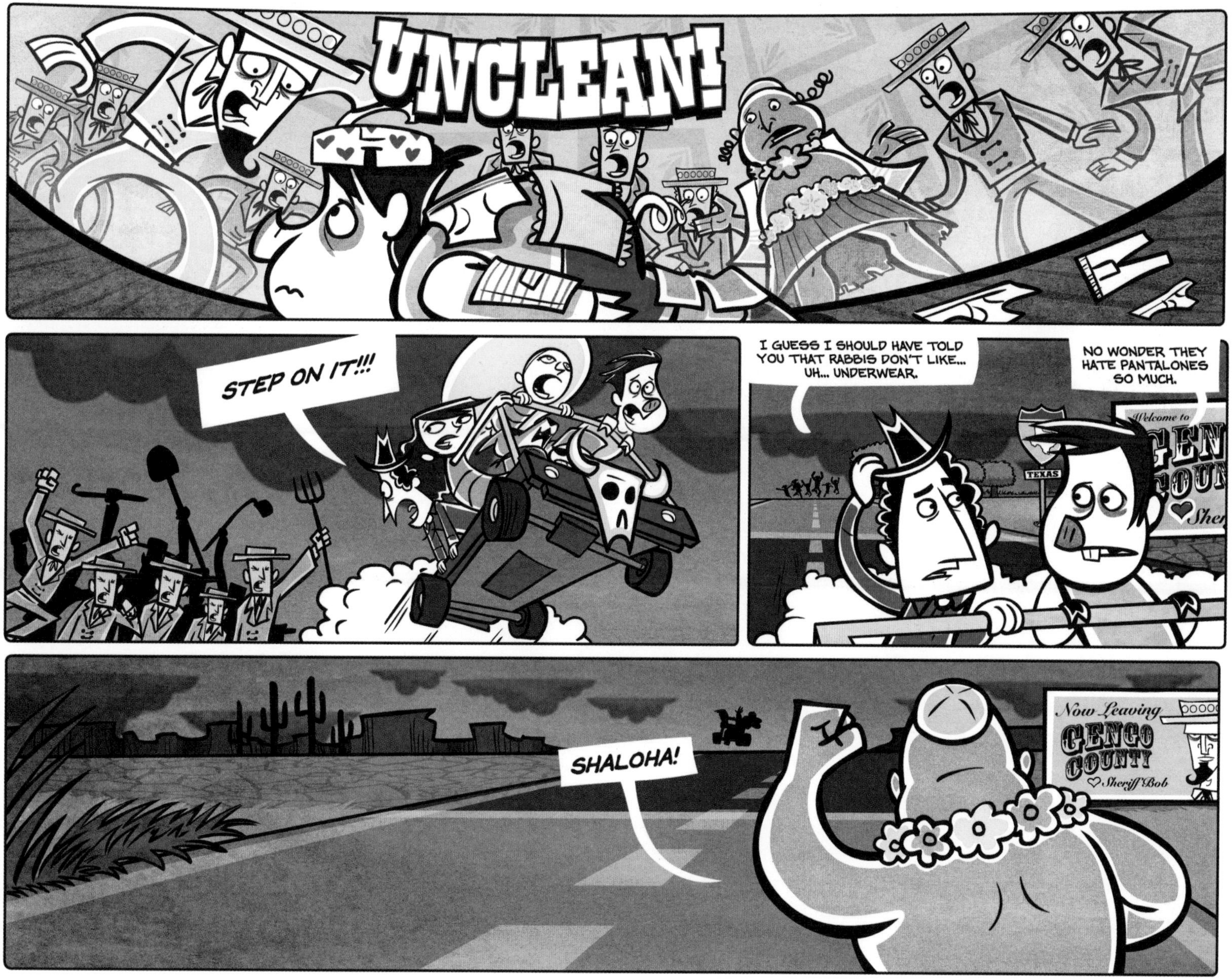
UNCLEAN!
STEP ON IT!!!
I GUESS I SHOULD HAVE TOLD YOU THAT RABBIS DON'T LIKE... UH... UNDERWEAR.
NO WONDER THEY HATE PANTALONES SO MUCH.
Welcome to
TEXAS
SHALOHA!
Now Leaving
GENGO COUNTY
♥ Sheriff Bob

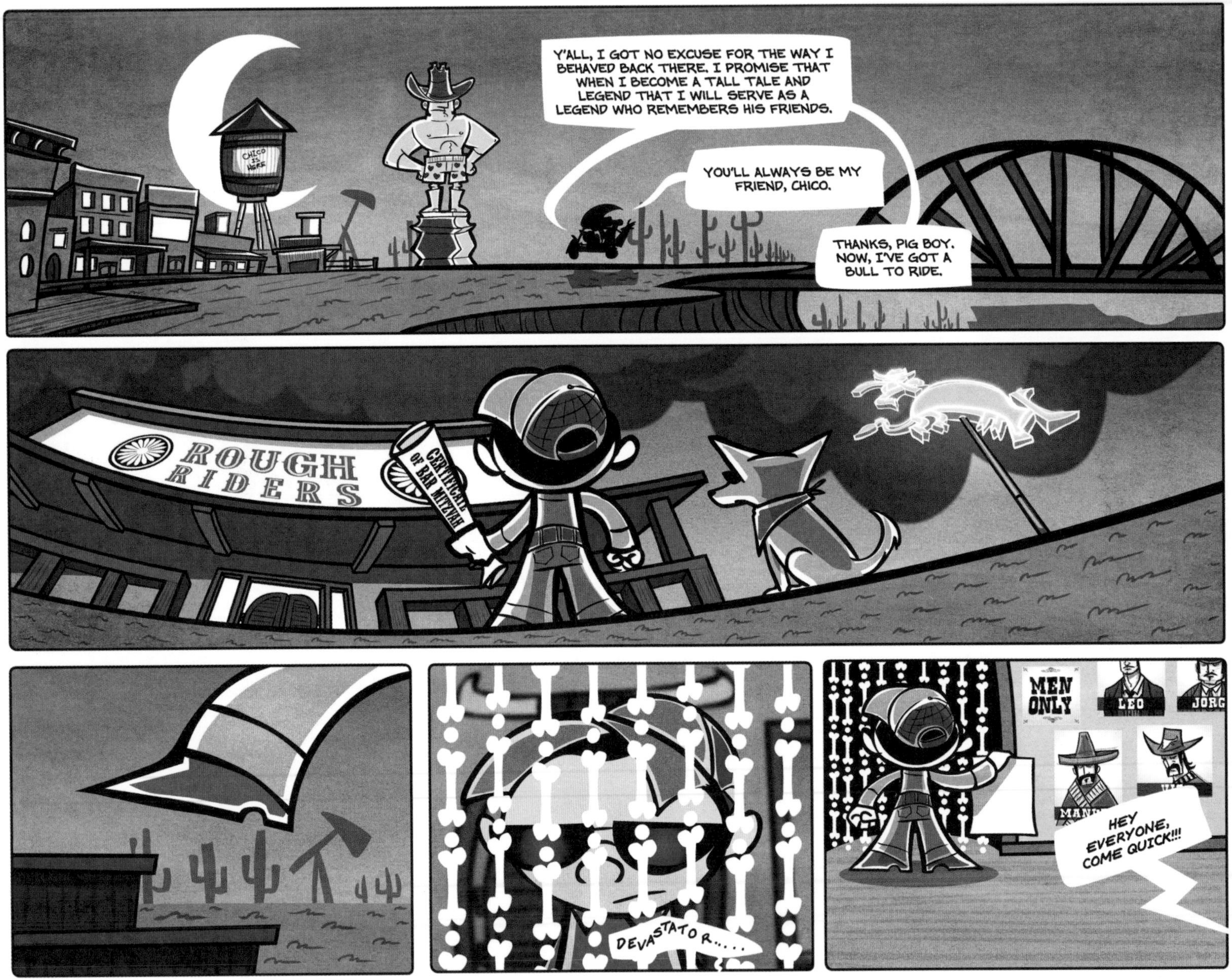
CHICO IS HERE
Y'ALL, I GOT NO EXCUSE FOR THE WAY I BEHAVED BACK THERE. I PROMISE THAT WHEN I BECOME A TALL TALE AND LEGEND THAT I WILL SERVE AS A LEGEND WHO REMEMBERS HIS FRIENDS.
YOU'LL ALWAYS BE MY FRIEND, CHICO.
THANKS, PIG BOY. NOW, I'VE GOT A BULL TO RIDE.
ROUGH RIDERS
CERTIFICATE OF BAR MITZVAH
DEVASTATOR.....
MEN ONLY
LEO
HEY EVERYONE, COME QUICK!!!

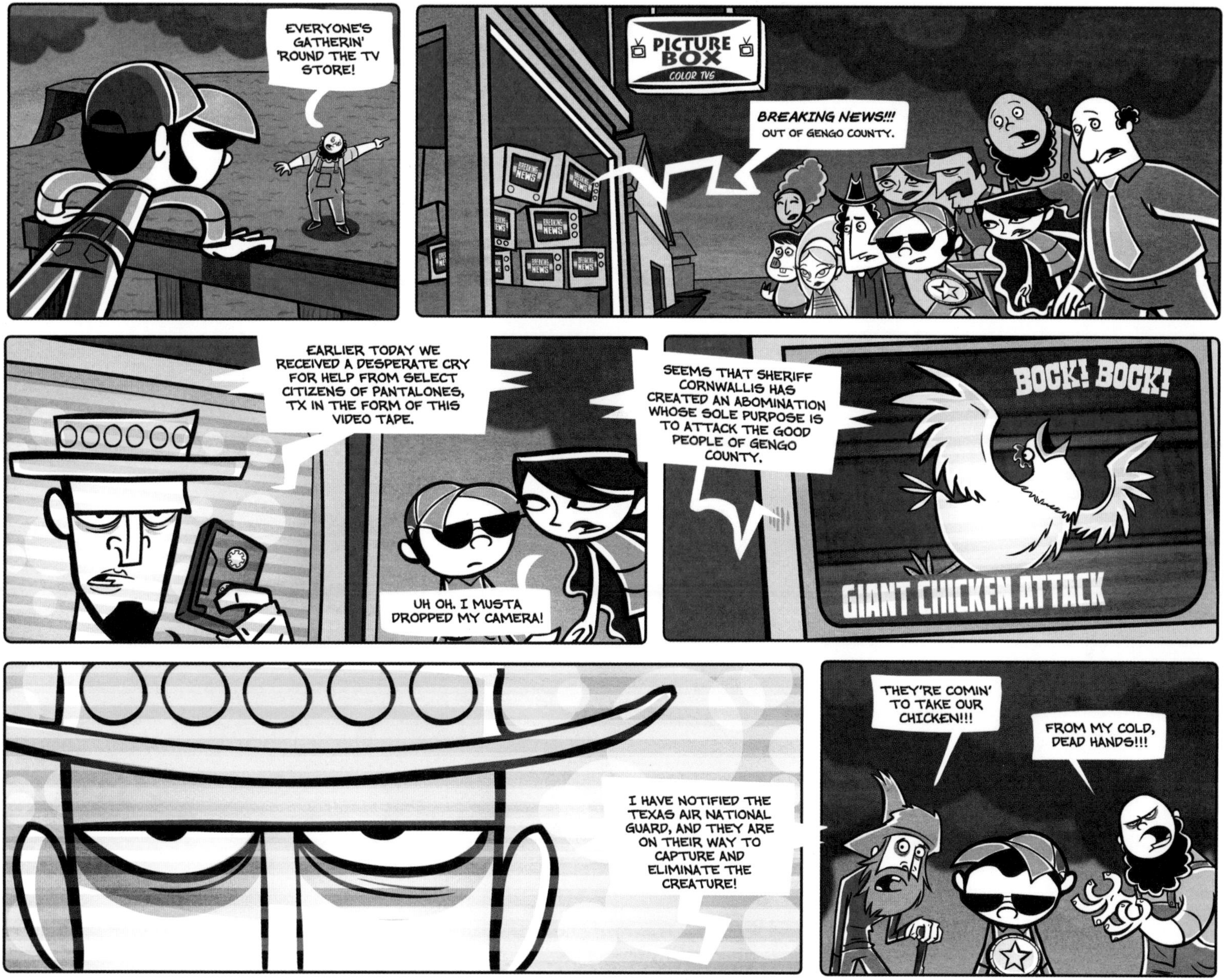
EVERYONE'S GATHERIN' 'ROUND THE TV STORE!
PICTURE BOX
COLOR TVS
BREAKING NEWS!!! OUT OF GENGO COUNTY.
EARLIER TODAY WE RECEIVED A DESPERATE CRY FOR HELP FROM SELECT CITIZENS OF PANTALONES, TX IN THE FORM OF THIS VIDEO TAPE.
UH OH. I MUSTA DROPPED MY CAMERA!
SEEMS THAT SHERIFF CORNWALLIS HAS CREATED AN ABOMINATION WHOSE SOLE PURPOSE IS TO ATTACK THE GOOD PEOPLE OF GENGO COUNTY.
BOCK! BOCK!
GIANT CHICKEN ATTACK
I HAVE NOTIFIED THE TEXAS AIR NATIONAL GUARD, AND THEY ARE ON THEIR WAY TO CAPTURE AND ELIMINATE THE CREATURE!
THEY'RE COMIN' TO TAKE OUR CHICKEN!!!
FROM MY COLD, DEAD HANDS!!!

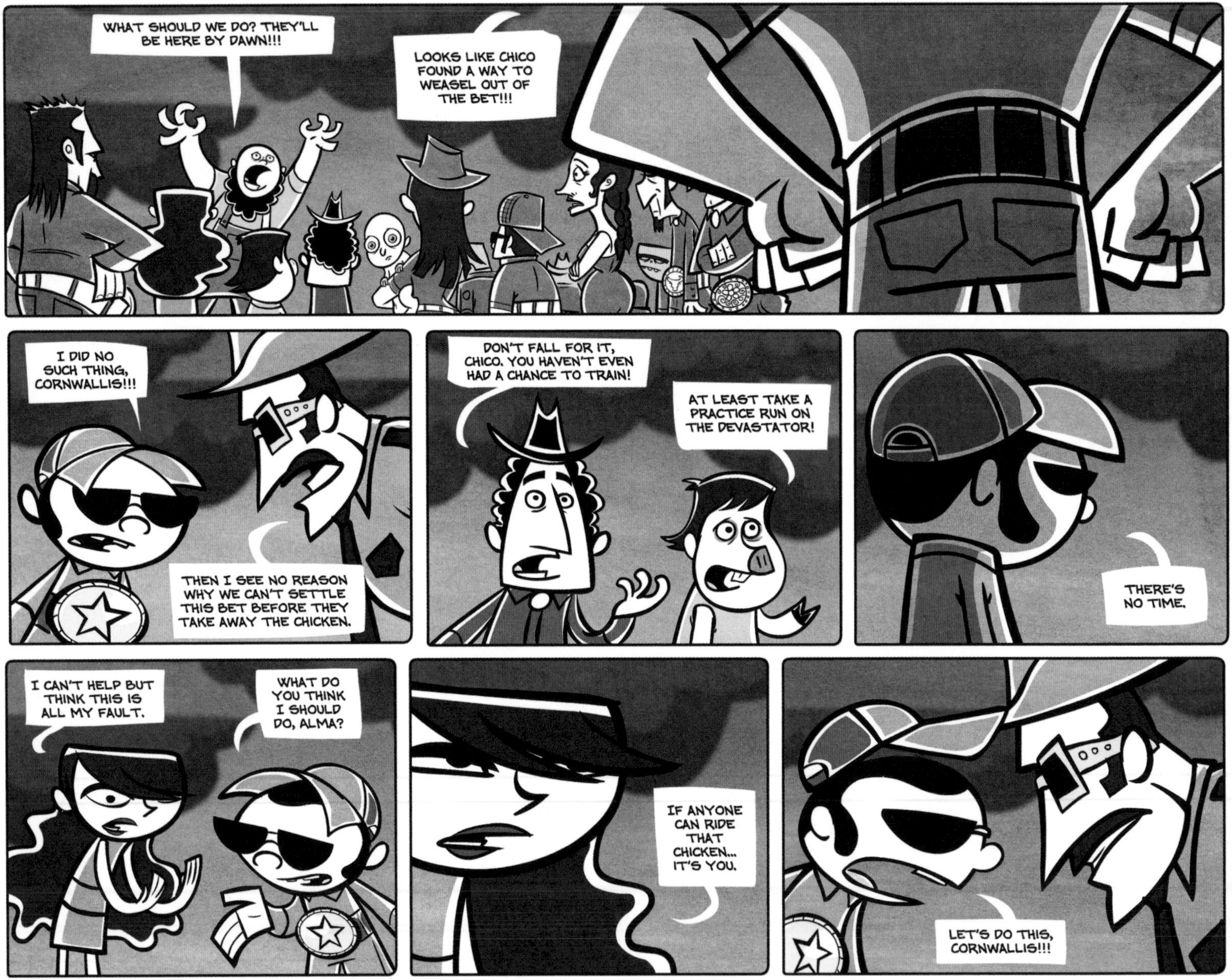
WHAT SHOULD WE DO? THEY'LL BE HERE BY DAWN!!!
LOOKS LIKE CHICO FOUND A WAY TO WEASEL OUT OF THE BET!!!
I DID NO SUCH THING, CORNWALLIS!!!
THEN I SEE NO REASON WHY WE CAN'T SETTLE THIS BET BEFORE THEY TAKE AWAY THE CHICKEN.
DON'T FALL FOR IT, CHICO. YOU HAVEN'T EVEN HAD A CHANCE TO TRAIN!
AT LEAST TAKE A PRACTICE RUN ON THE DEVASTATOR!
THERE'S NO TIME.
I CAN'T HELP BUT THINK THIS IS ALL MY FAULT.
WHAT DO YOU THINK I SHOULD DO, ALMA?
IF ANYONE CAN RIDE THAT CHICKEN... IT'S YOU.
LET'S DO THIS, CORNWALLIS!!!

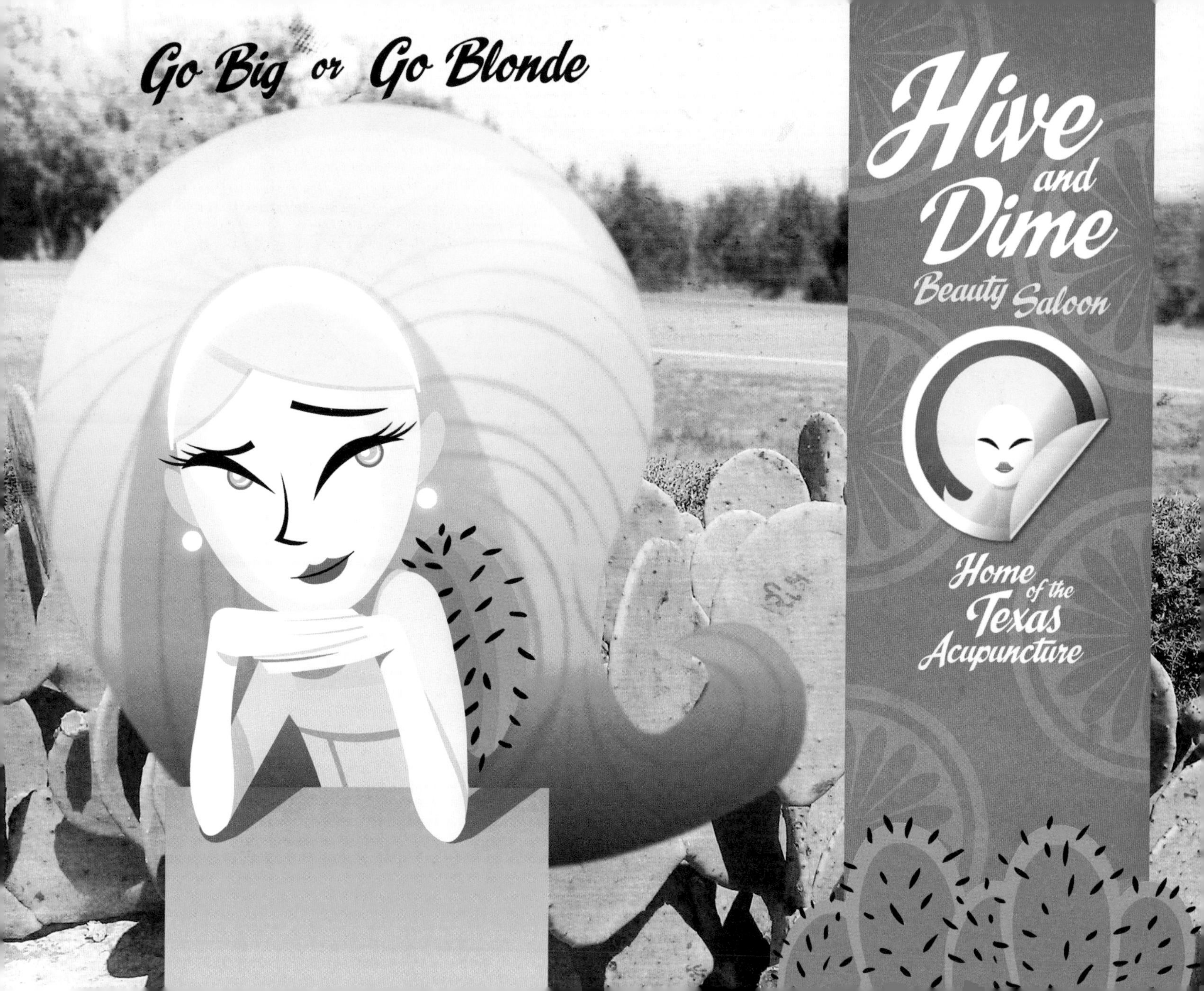
Go Big or Go Blonde
Hive and Dime
Beauty Saloon
Home of the Texas Acupuncture

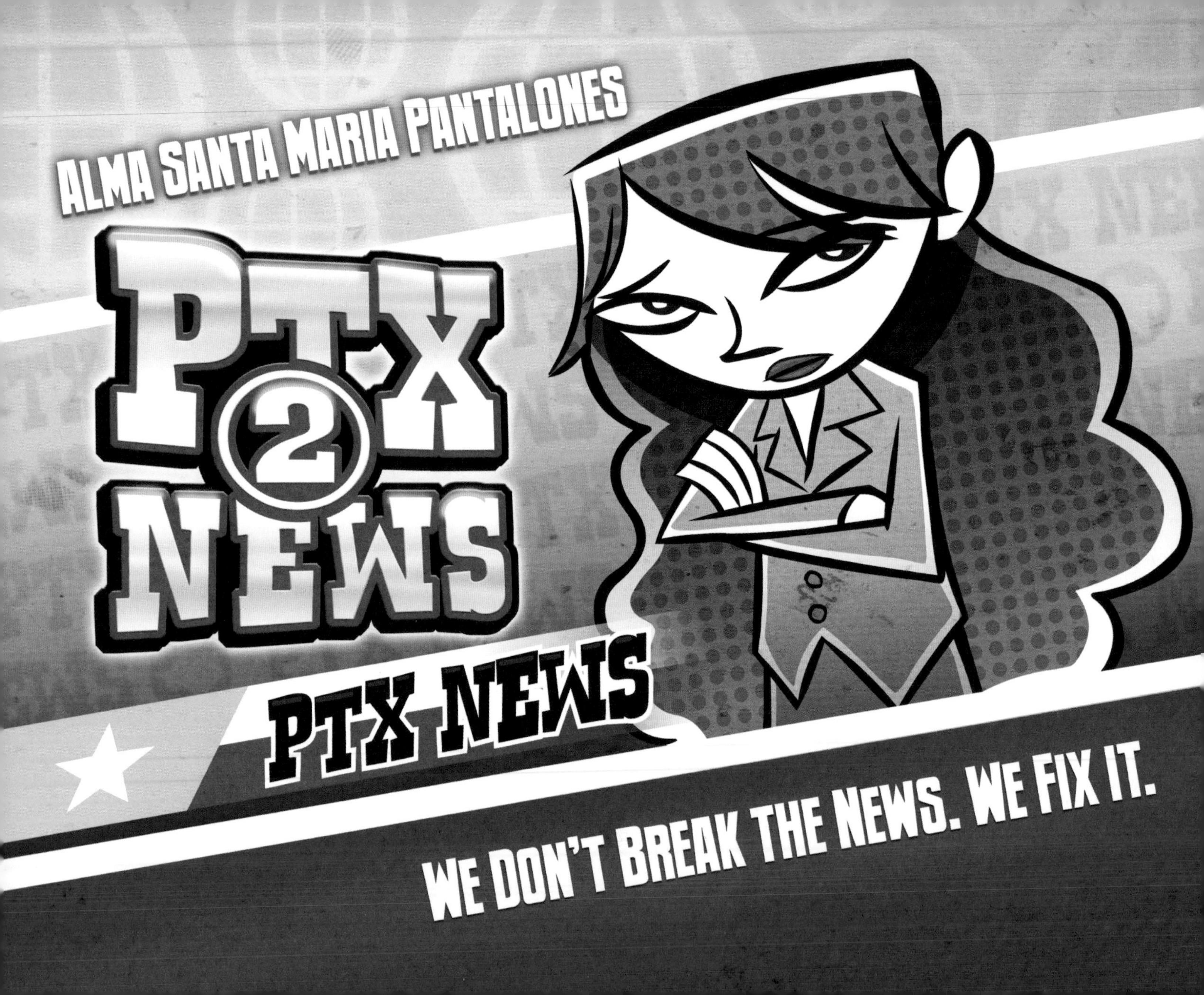
ALMA SANTA MARIA PANTALONES
PTX 2 NEWS
PTX NEWS
WE DON'T BREAK THE NEWS. WE FIX IT.

CHAPTER CINCO

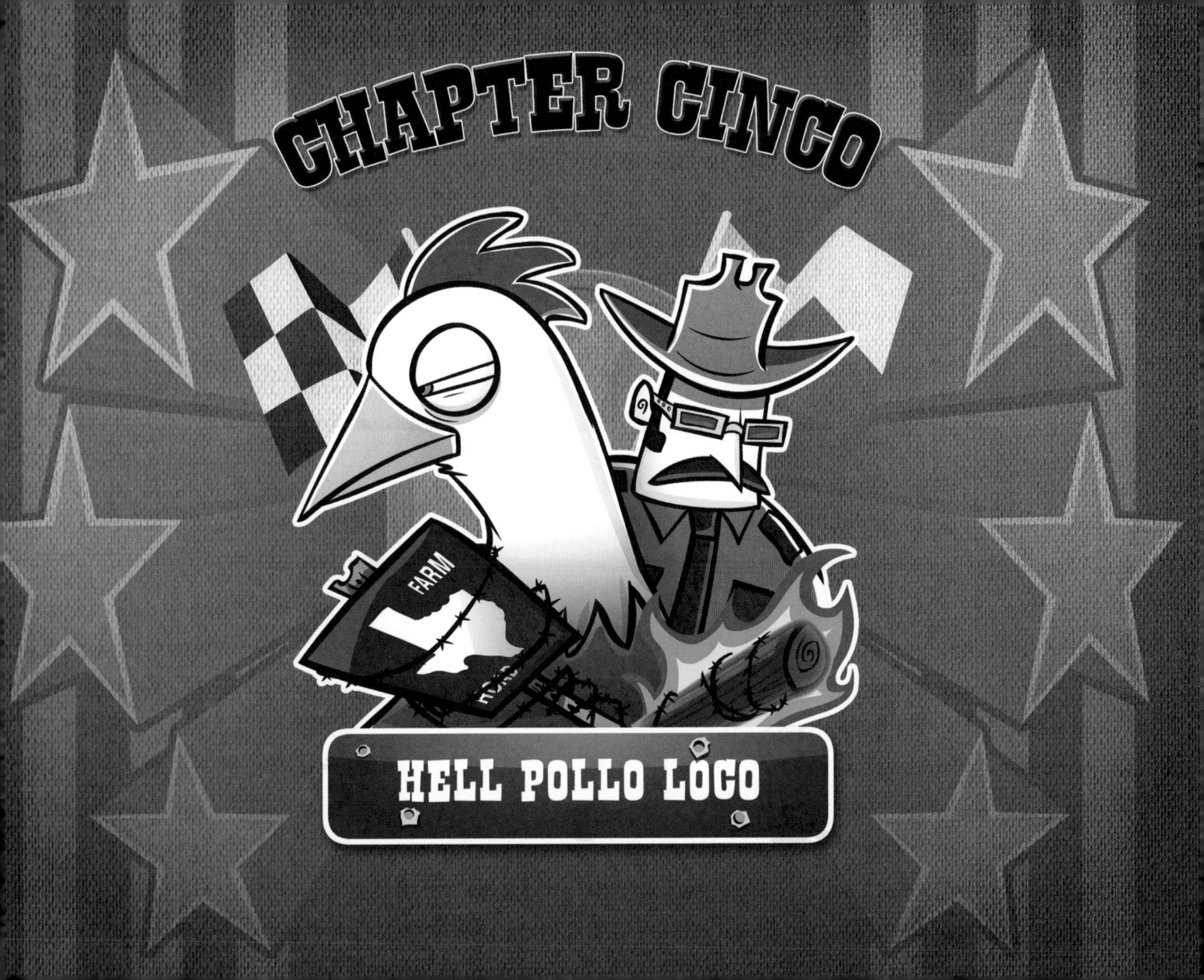
FARM

HELL POLLO LOCO

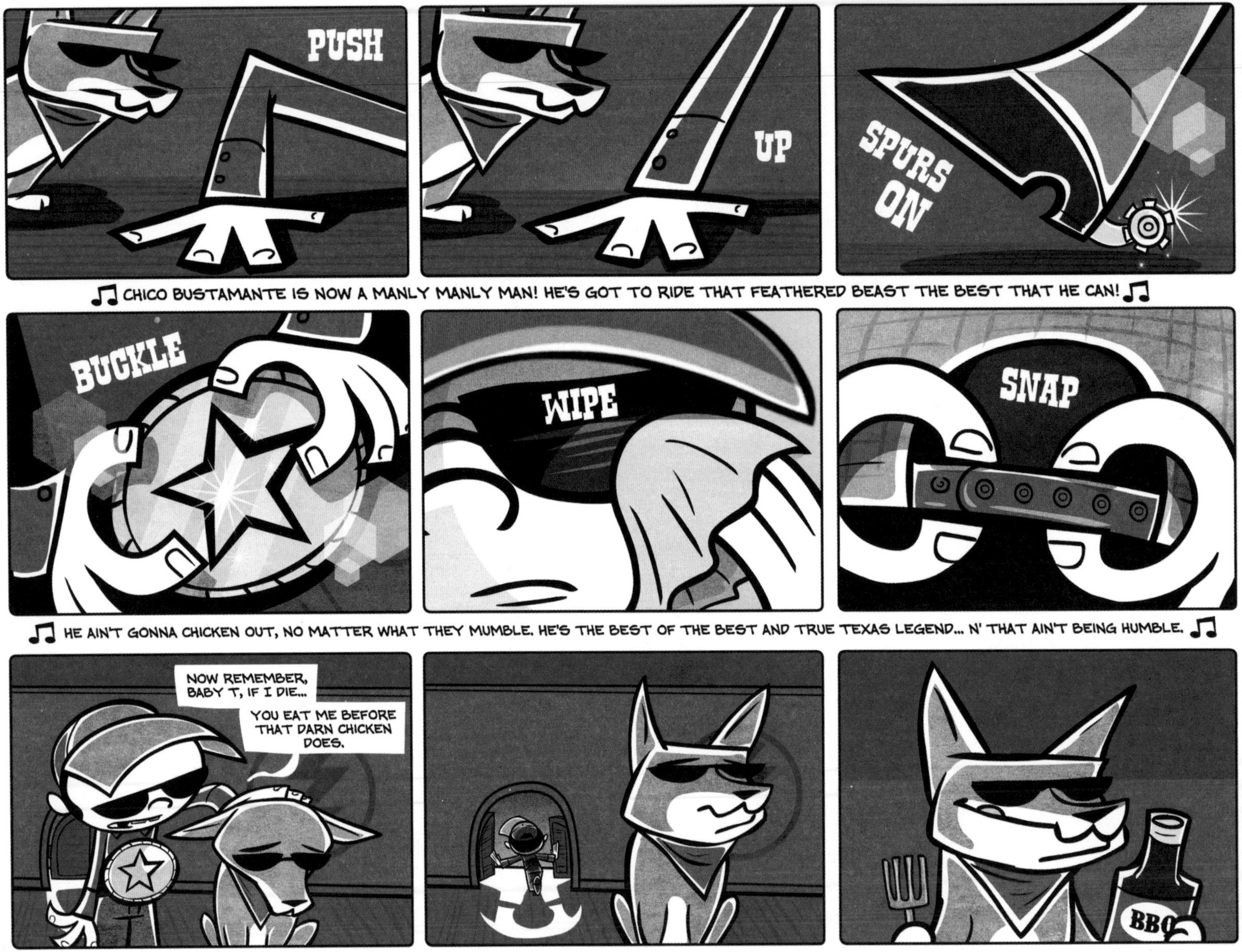
PUSH
UP
SPURS ON
♫ CHICO BUSTAMANTE IS NOW A MANLY MANLY MAN! HE'S GOT TO RIDE THAT FEATHERED BEAST THE BEST THAT HE CAN! ♫
BUCKLE
WIPE
SNAP
♫ HE AIN'T GONNA CHICKEN OUT, NO MATTER WHAT THEY MUMBLE. HE'S THE BEST OF THE BEST AND TRUE TEXAS LEGEND... N' THAT AIN'T BEING HUMBLE. ♫
NOW REMEMBER, BABY T, IF I DIE...
YOU EAT ME BEFORE THAT DARN CHICKEN DOES.
BBQ

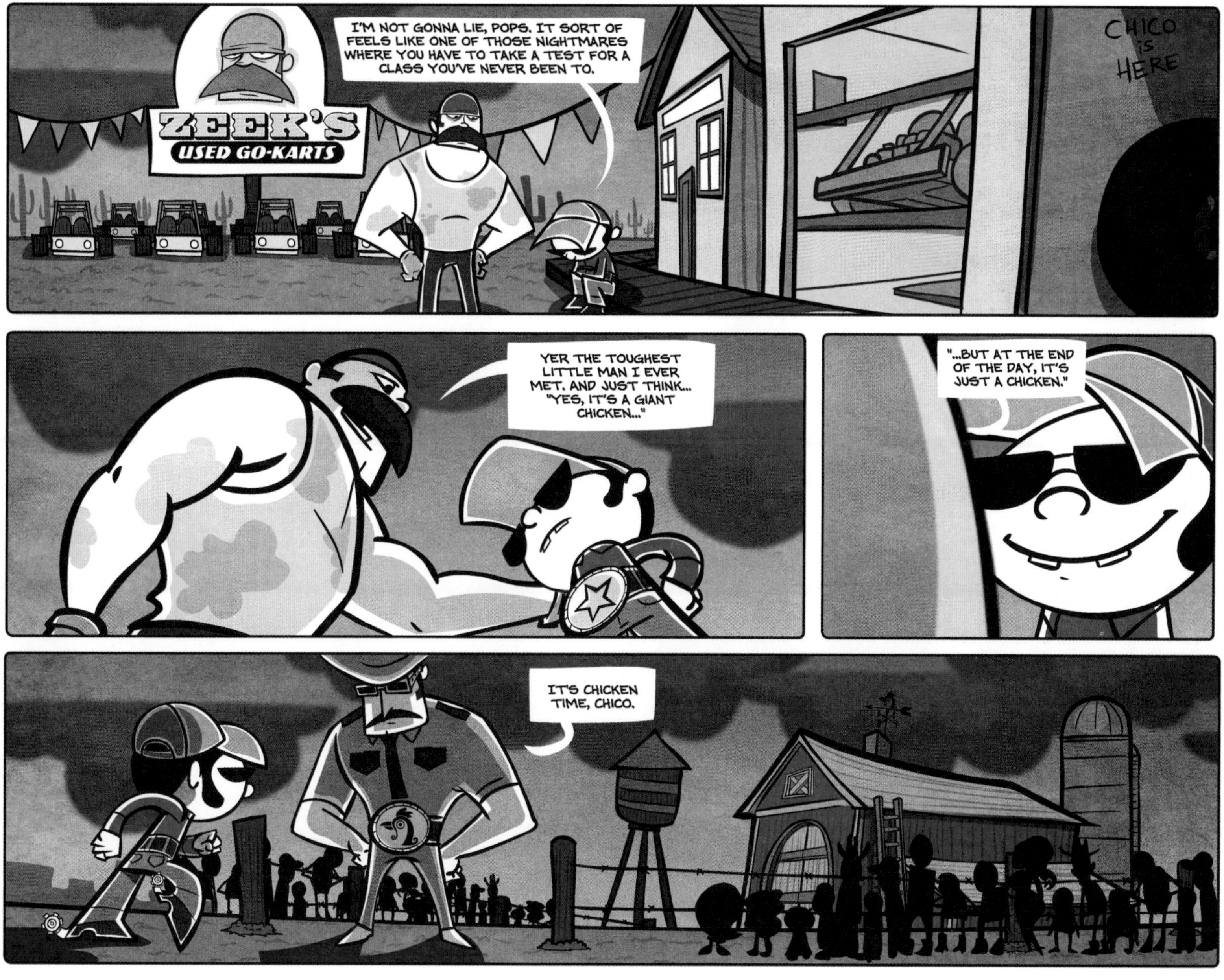
I'M NOT GONNA LIE, POPS. IT SORT OF FEELS LIKE ONE OF THOSE NIGHTMARES WHERE YOU HAVE TO TAKE A TEST FOR A CLASS YOU'VE NEVER BEEN TO.
ZEEK'S USED GO-KARTS
CHICO IS HERE
YER THE TOUGHEST LITTLE MAN I EVER MET. AND JUST THINK... "YES, IT'S A GIANT CHICKEN..."
"...BUT AT THE END OF THE DAY, IT'S JUST A CHICKEN."
IT'S CHICKEN TIME, CHICO.

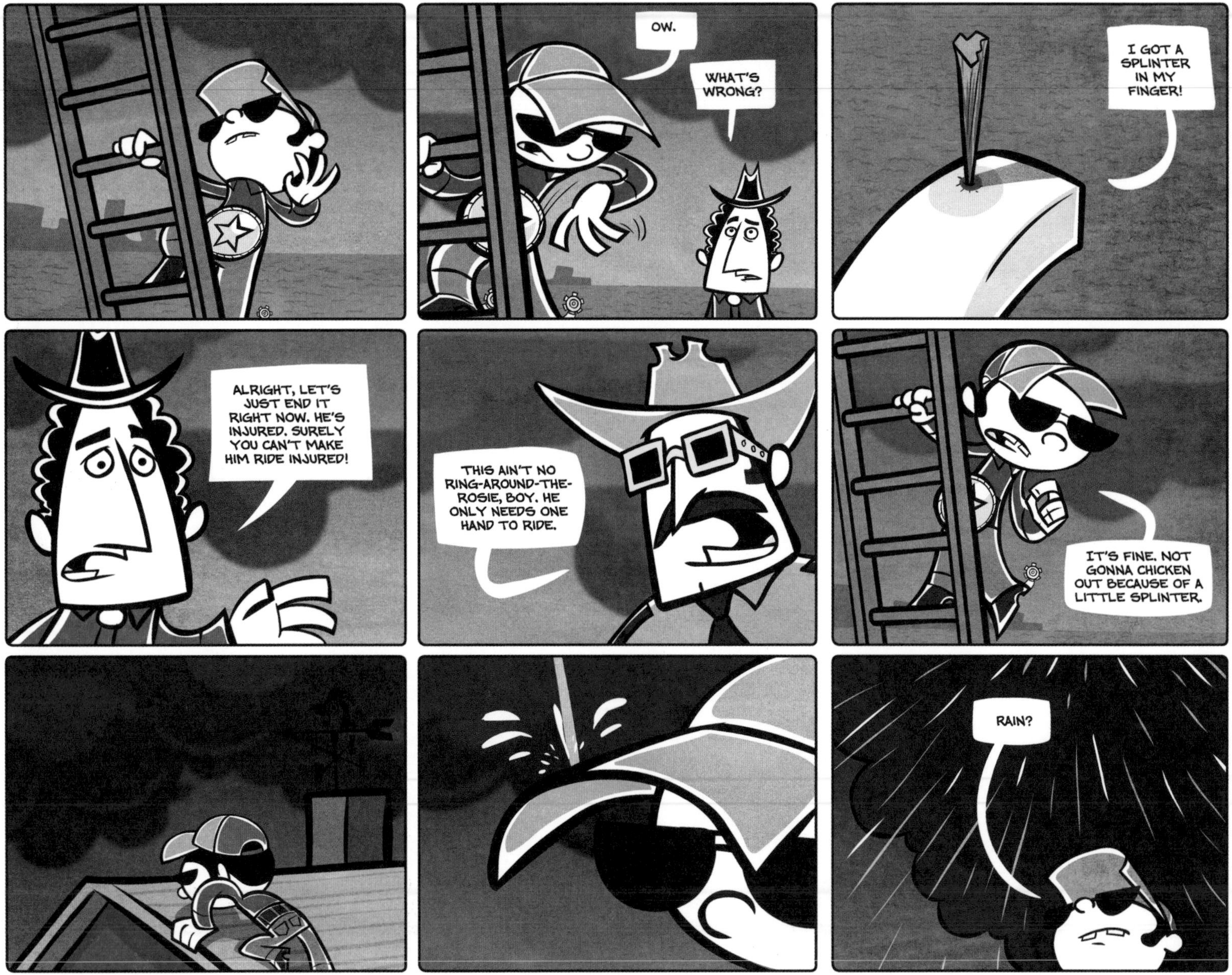
OW.
WHAT'S WRONG?
I GOT A SPLINTER IN MY FINGER!
ALRIGHT, LET'S JUST END IT RIGHT NOW. HE'S INJURED. SURELY YOU CAN'T MAKE HIM RIDE INJURED!
THIS AIN'T NO RING-AROUND-THE-ROSIE, BOY. HE ONLY NEEDS ONE HAND TO RIDE.
IT'S FINE. NOT GONNA CHICKEN OUT BECAUSE OF A LITTLE SPLINTER.
RAIN?

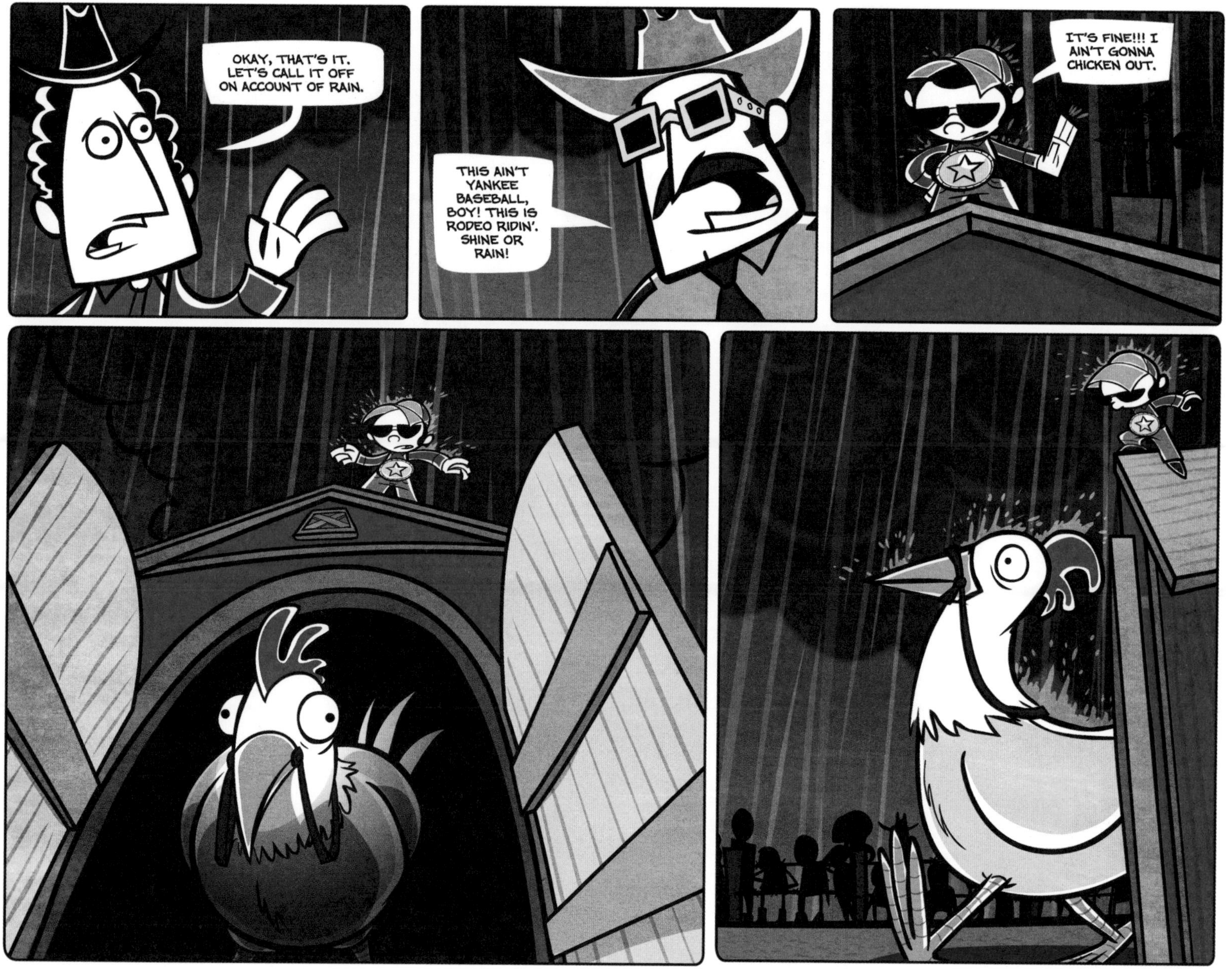
OKAY, THAT'S IT. LET'S CALL IT OFF ON ACCOUNT OF RAIN.
THIS AIN'T YANKEE BASEBALL, BOY! THIS IS RODEO RIDIN'. SHINE OR RAIN!
IT'S FINE!!! I AIN'T GONNA CHICKEN OUT.

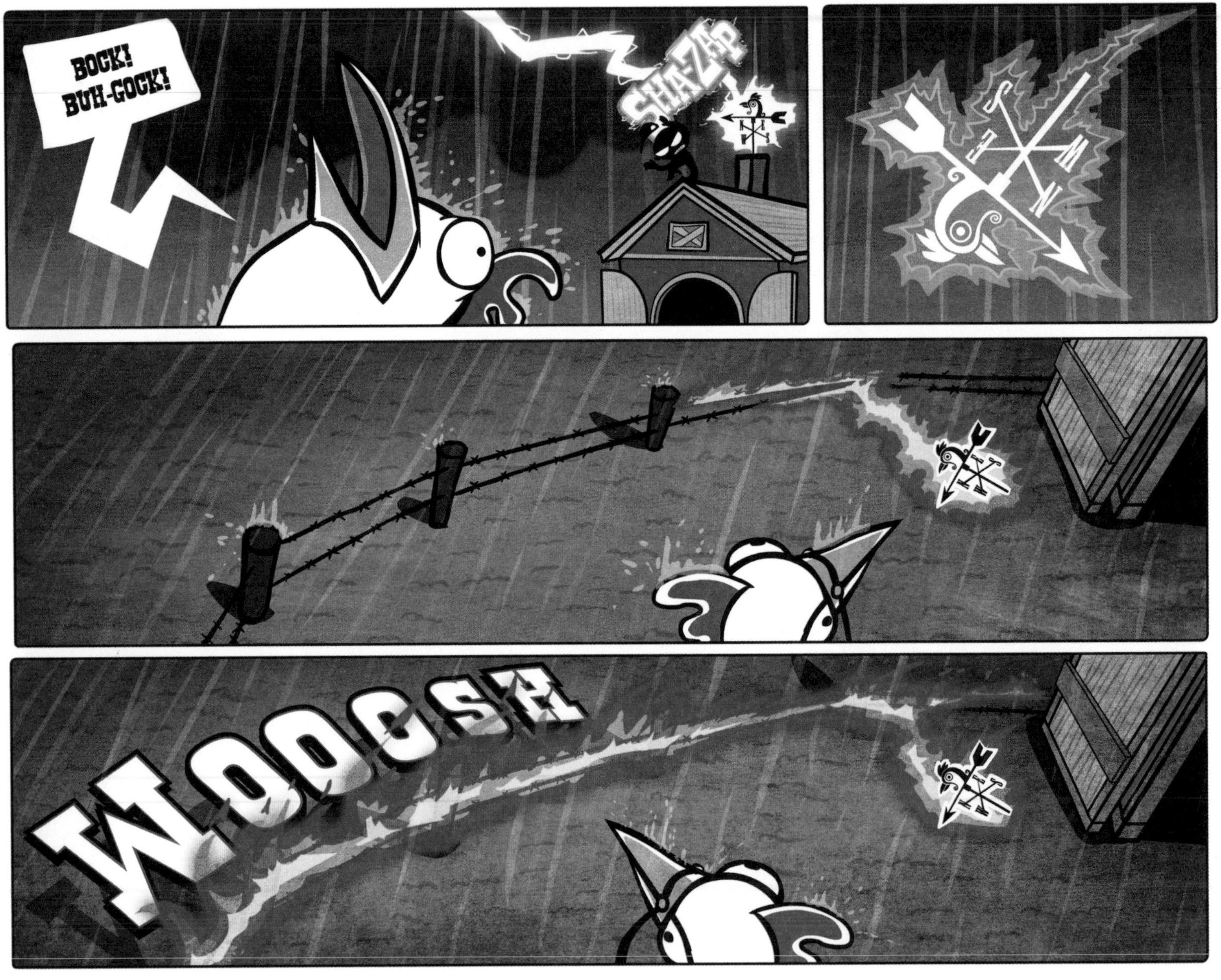
BOCK! BUH-GOCK!
SHA-ZAP
WOOOSH

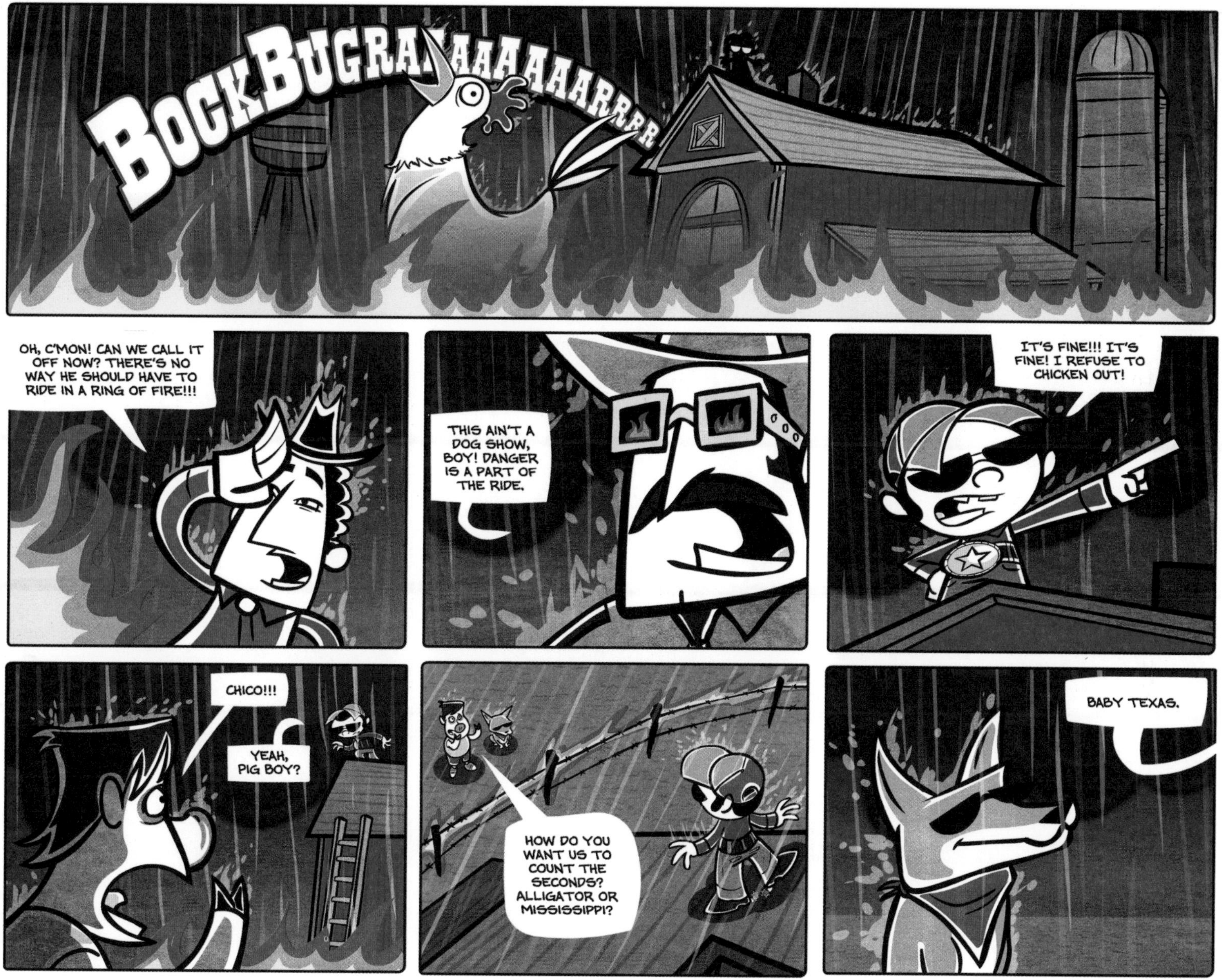
BOCKBUGRAAAAAAAARRRR
OH, C'MON! CAN WE CALL IT OFF NOW? THERE'S NO WAY HE SHOULD HAVE TO RIDE IN A RING OF FIRE!!!
THIS AIN'T A DOG SHOW, BOY! DANGER IS A PART OF THE RIDE.
IT'S FINE!!! IT'S FINE! I REFUSE TO CHICKEN OUT!
CHICO!!!
YEAH, PIG BOY?
HOW DO YOU WANT US TO COUNT THE SECONDS? ALLIGATOR OR MISSISSIPPI?
BABY TEXAS.

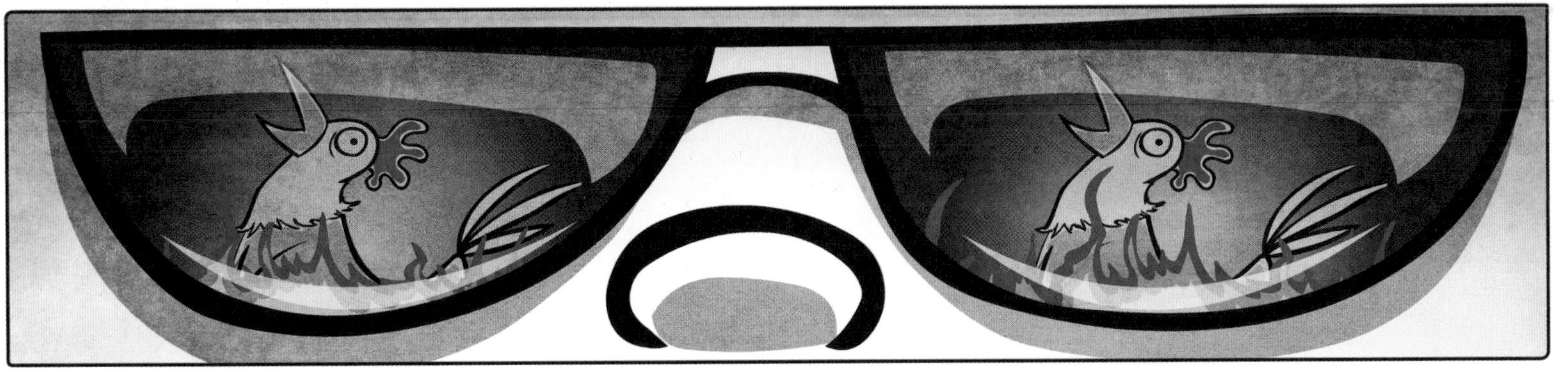

IT'S JUST A CHICKEN.

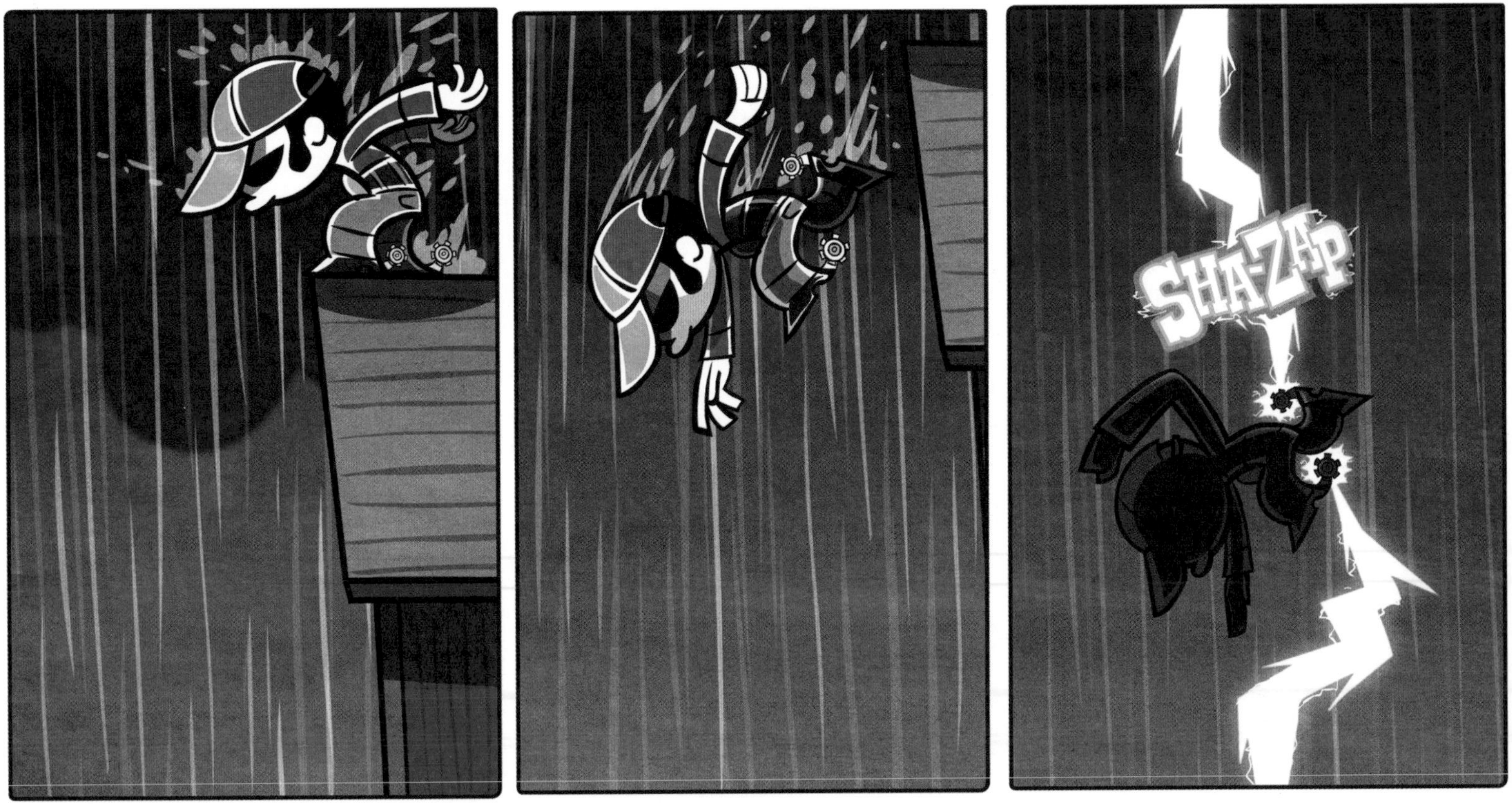
SHA-ZAP

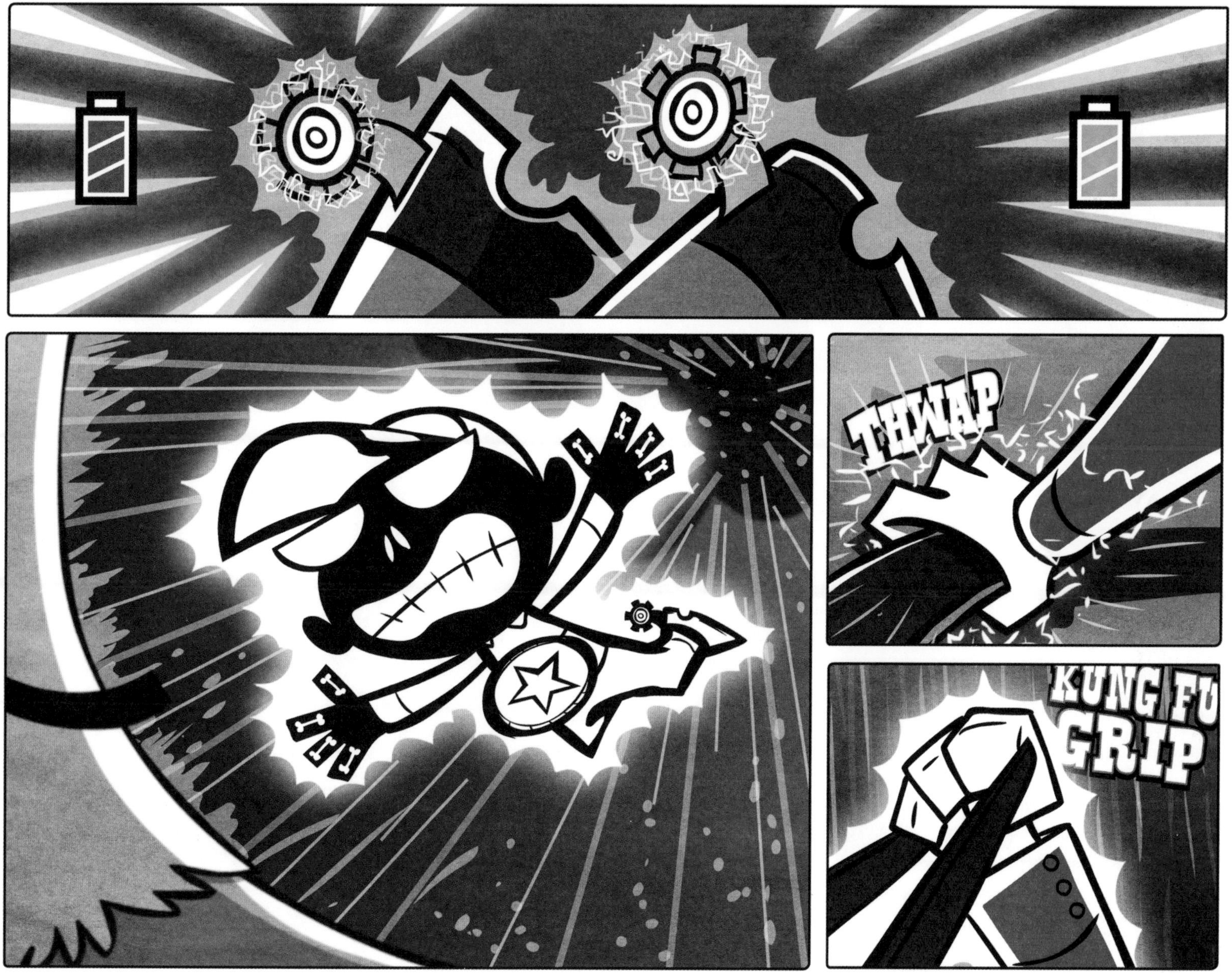
THWAP
KUNG FU
GRIP

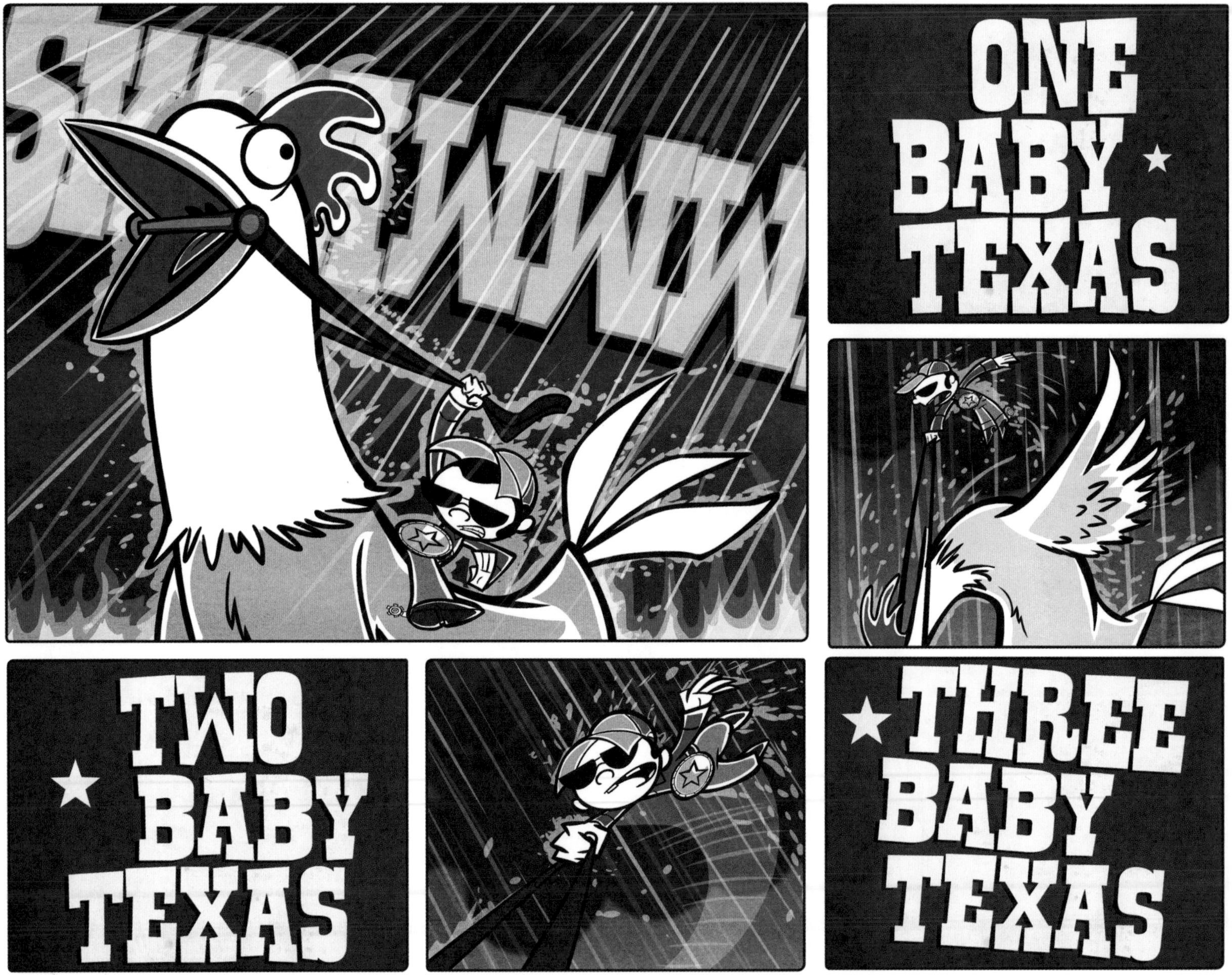
ONE BABY TEXAS
TWO BABY TEXAS
THREE BABY TEXAS

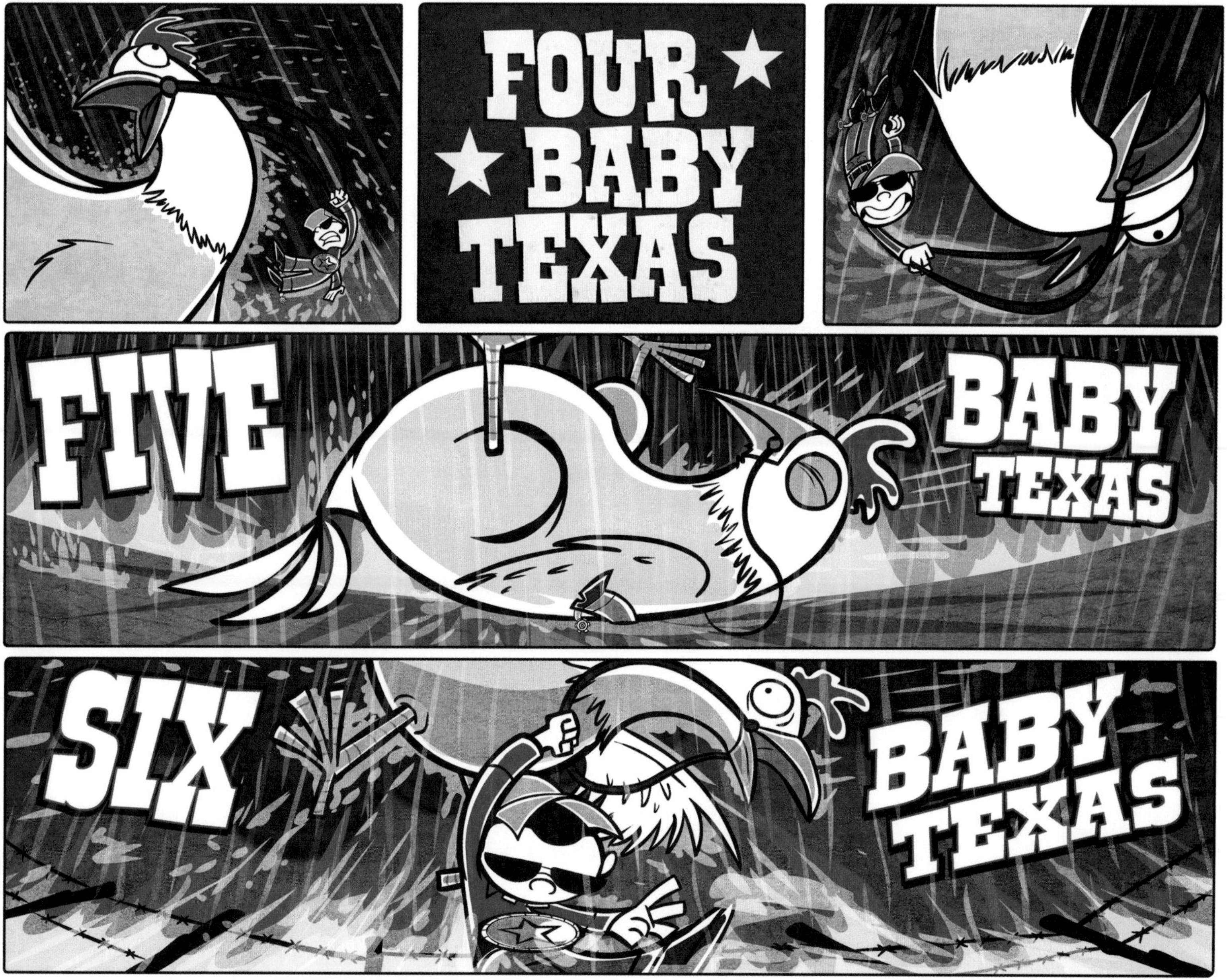
FOUR BABY TEXAS
FIVE BABY TEXAS
SIX BABY TEXAS

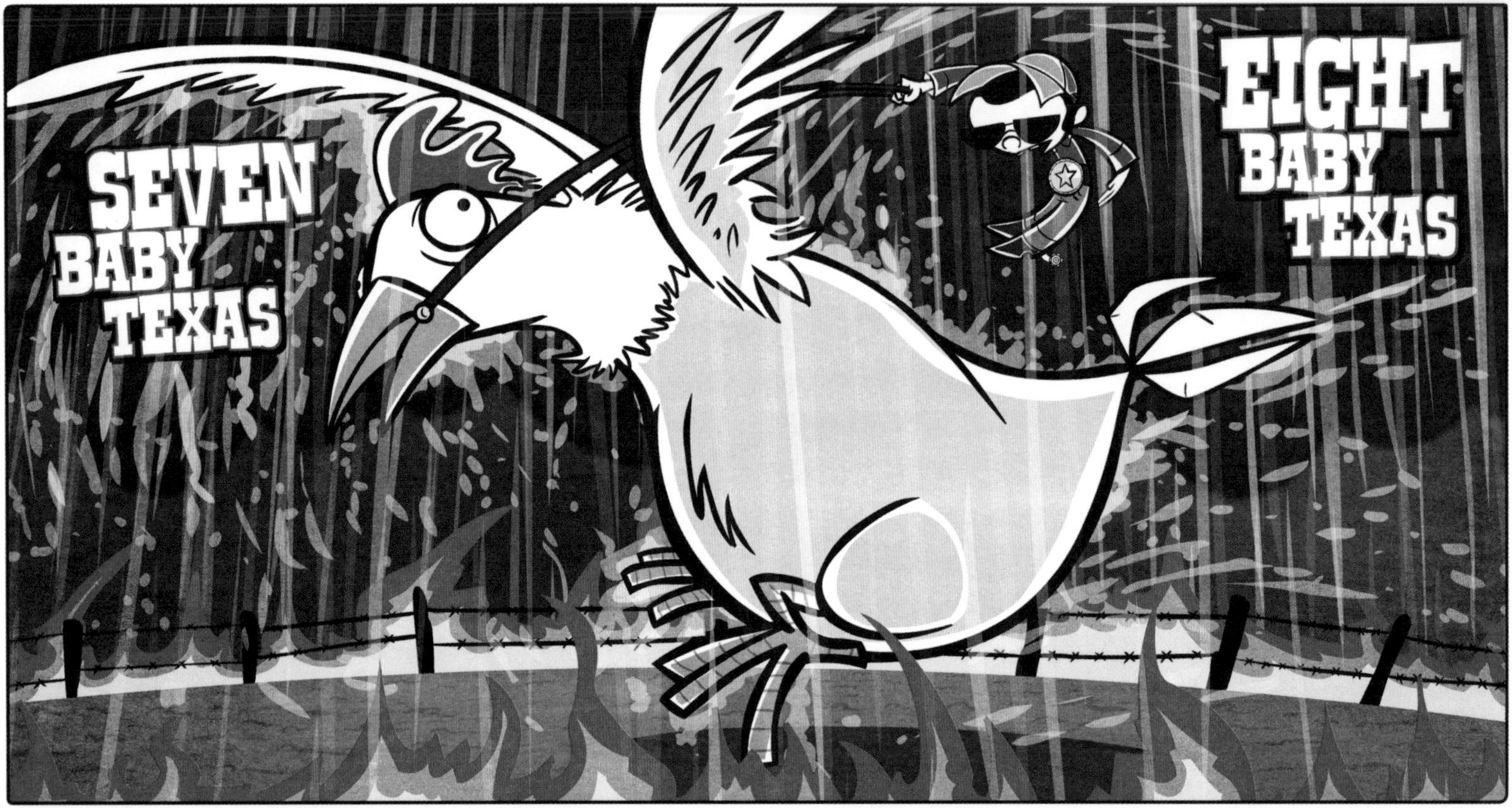
SEVEN BABY TEXAS
EIGHT BABY TEXAS

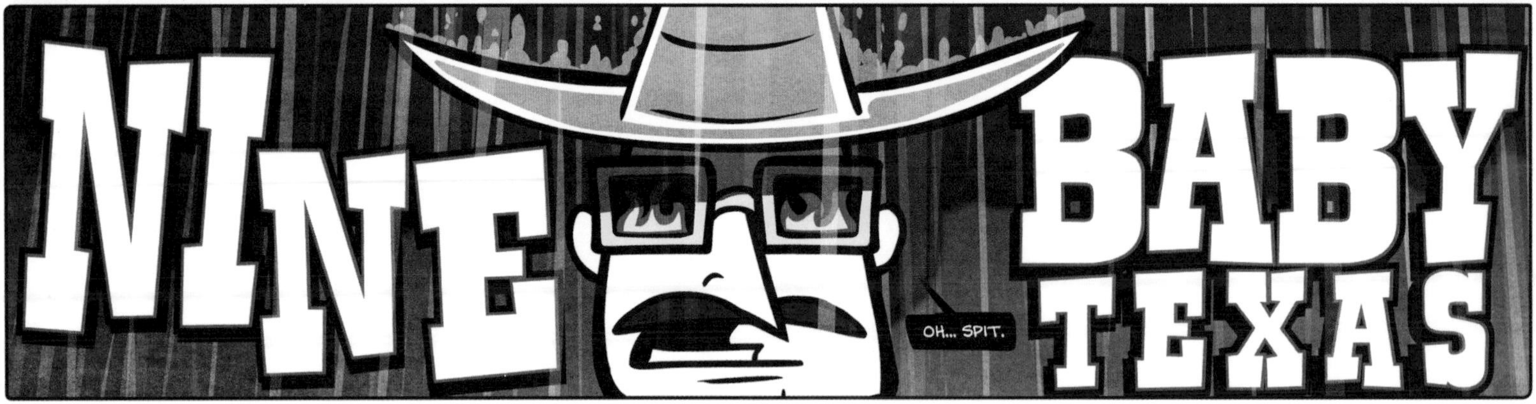
NINE BABY TEXAS
OH... SPIT.

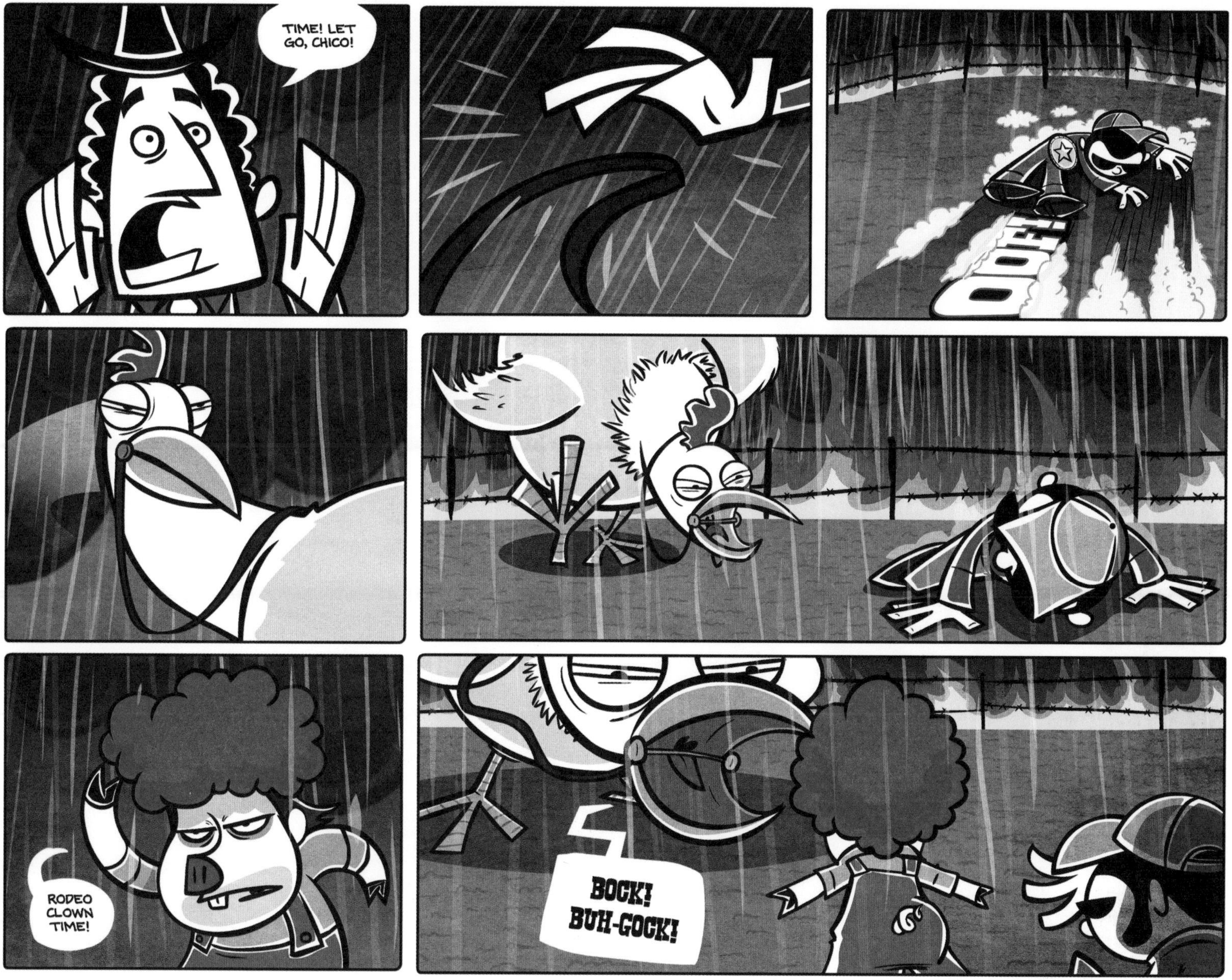
TIME! LET GO, CHICO!
OOF!
RODEO CLOWN TIME!
BOCK! BUH-GOCK!

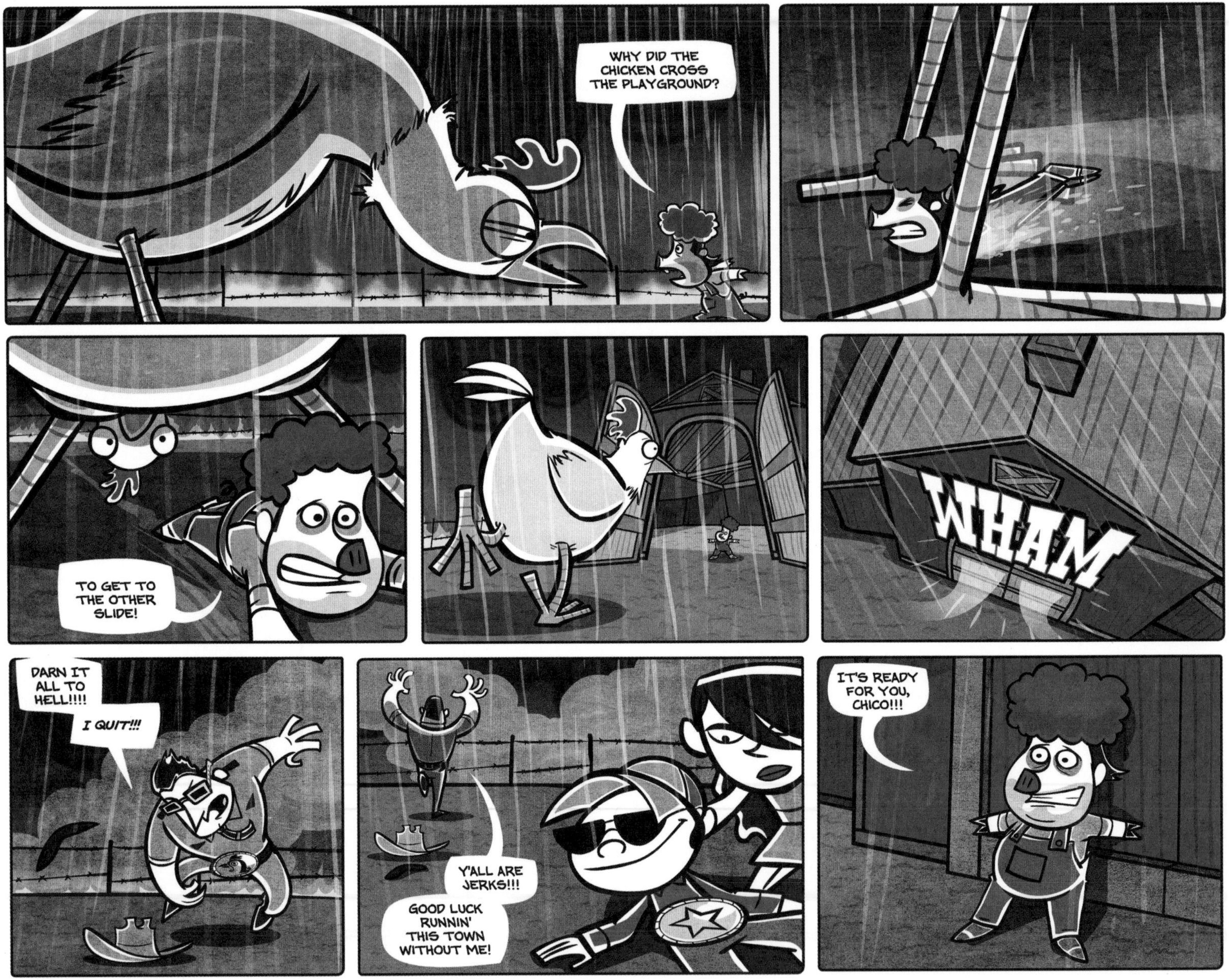
WHY DID THE CHICKEN CROSS THE PLAYGROUND?
TO GET TO THE OTHER SLIDE!
WHAM
DARN IT ALL TO HELL!!!!
I QUIT!!!
Y'ALL ARE JERKS!!!
GOOD LUCK RUNNIN' THIS TOWN WITHOUT ME!
IT'S READY FOR YOU, CHICO!!!

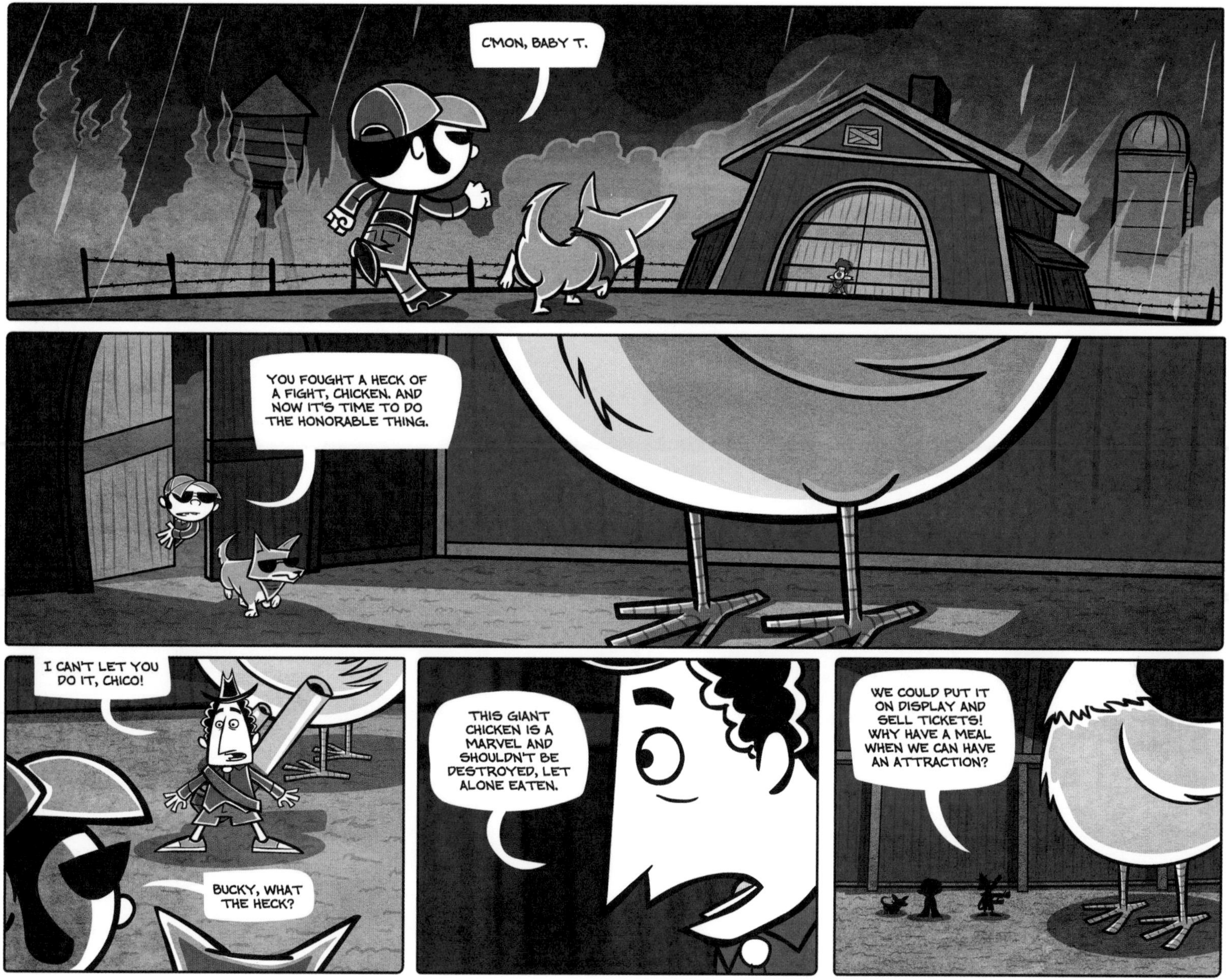

C'MON, BABY T.
YOU FOUGHT A HECK OF A FIGHT, CHICKEN. AND NOW IT'S TIME TO DO THE HONORABLE THING.
I CAN'T LET YOU DO IT, CHICO!
BUCKY, WHAT THE HECK?
THIS GIANT CHICKEN IS A MARVEL AND SHOULDN'T BE DESTROYED, LET ALONE EATEN.
WE COULD PUT IT ON DISPLAY AND SELL TICKETS! WHY HAVE A MEAL WHEN WE CAN HAVE AN ATTRACTION?

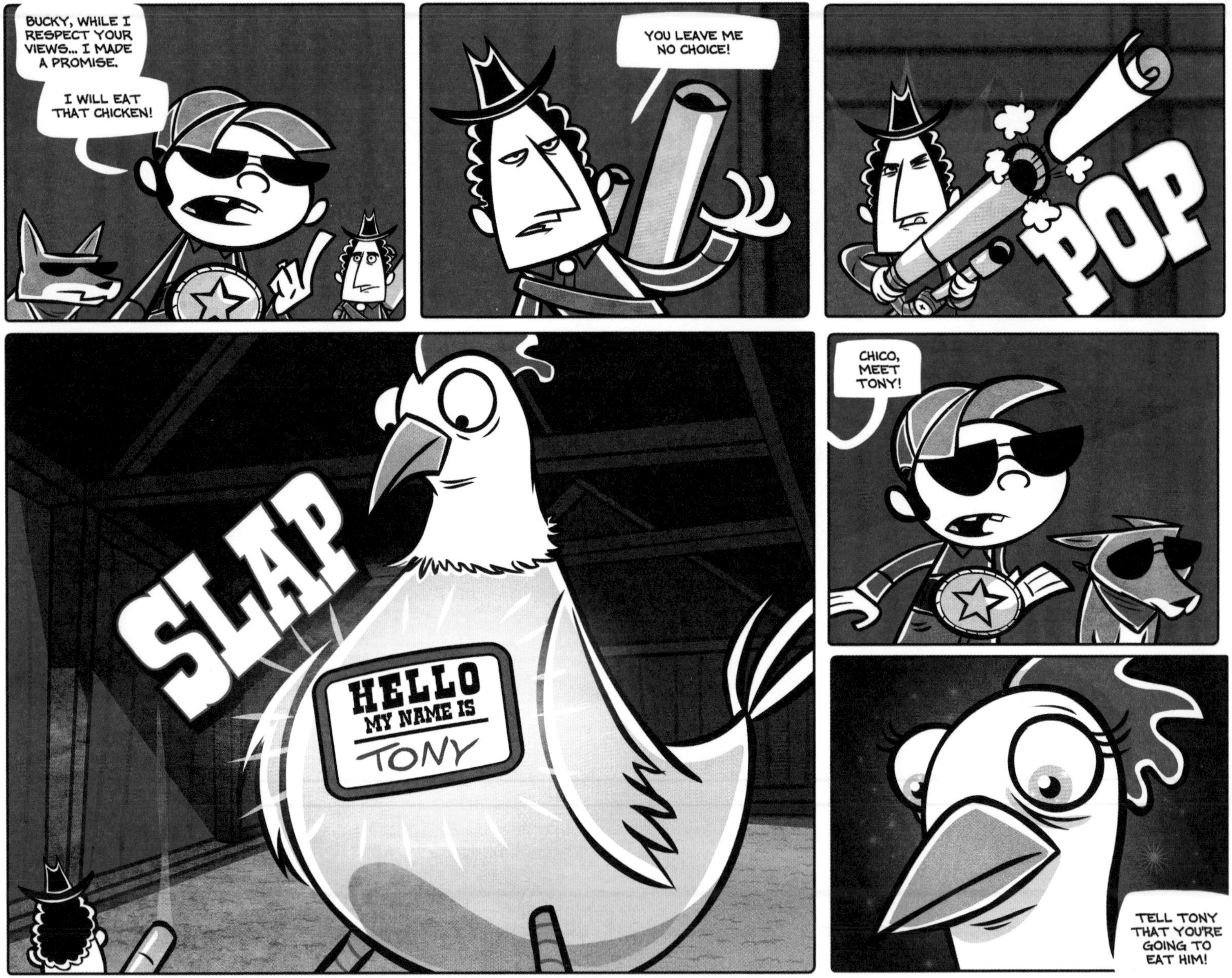
BUCKY, WHILE I RESPECT YOUR VIEWS... I MADE A PROMISE.
I WILL EAT THAT CHICKEN!
YOU LEAVE ME NO CHOICE!
POP
SLAP
HELLO MY NAME IS TONY
CHICO, MEET TONY!
TELL TONY THAT YOU'RE GOING TO EAT HIM!

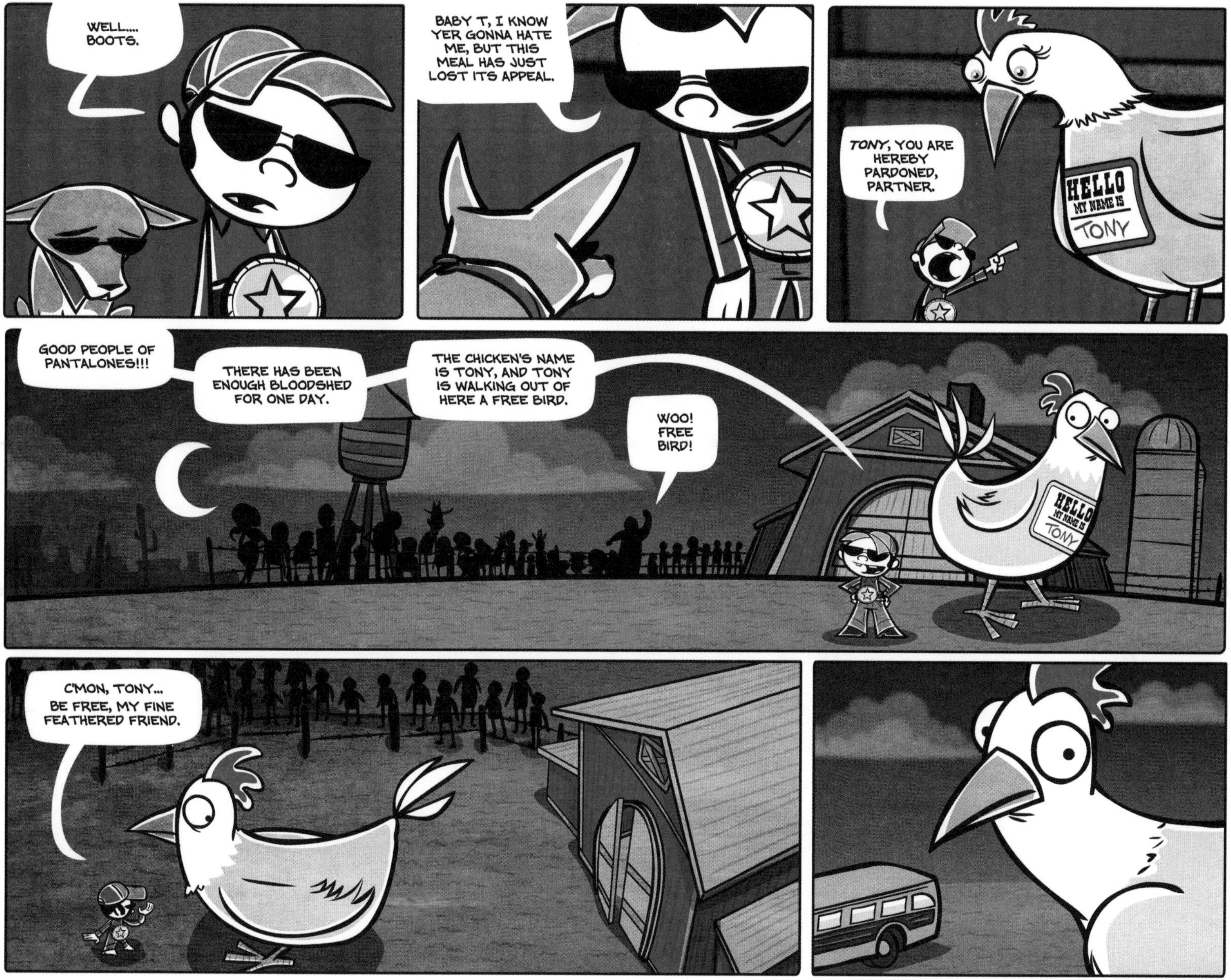
WELL.... BOOTS.
BABY T, I KNOW YER GONNA HATE ME, BUT THIS MEAL HAS JUST LOST ITS APPEAL.
TONY, YOU ARE HEREBY PARDONED, PARTNER.
HELLO MY NAME IS TONY
GOOD PEOPLE OF PANTALONES!!!
THERE HAS BEEN ENOUGH BLOODSHED FOR ONE DAY.
THE CHICKEN'S NAME IS TONY, AND TONY IS WALKING OUT OF HERE A FREE BIRD.
WOO! FREE BIRD!
HELLO MY NAME IS TONY
C'MON, TONY... BE FREE, MY FINE FEATHERED FRIEND.

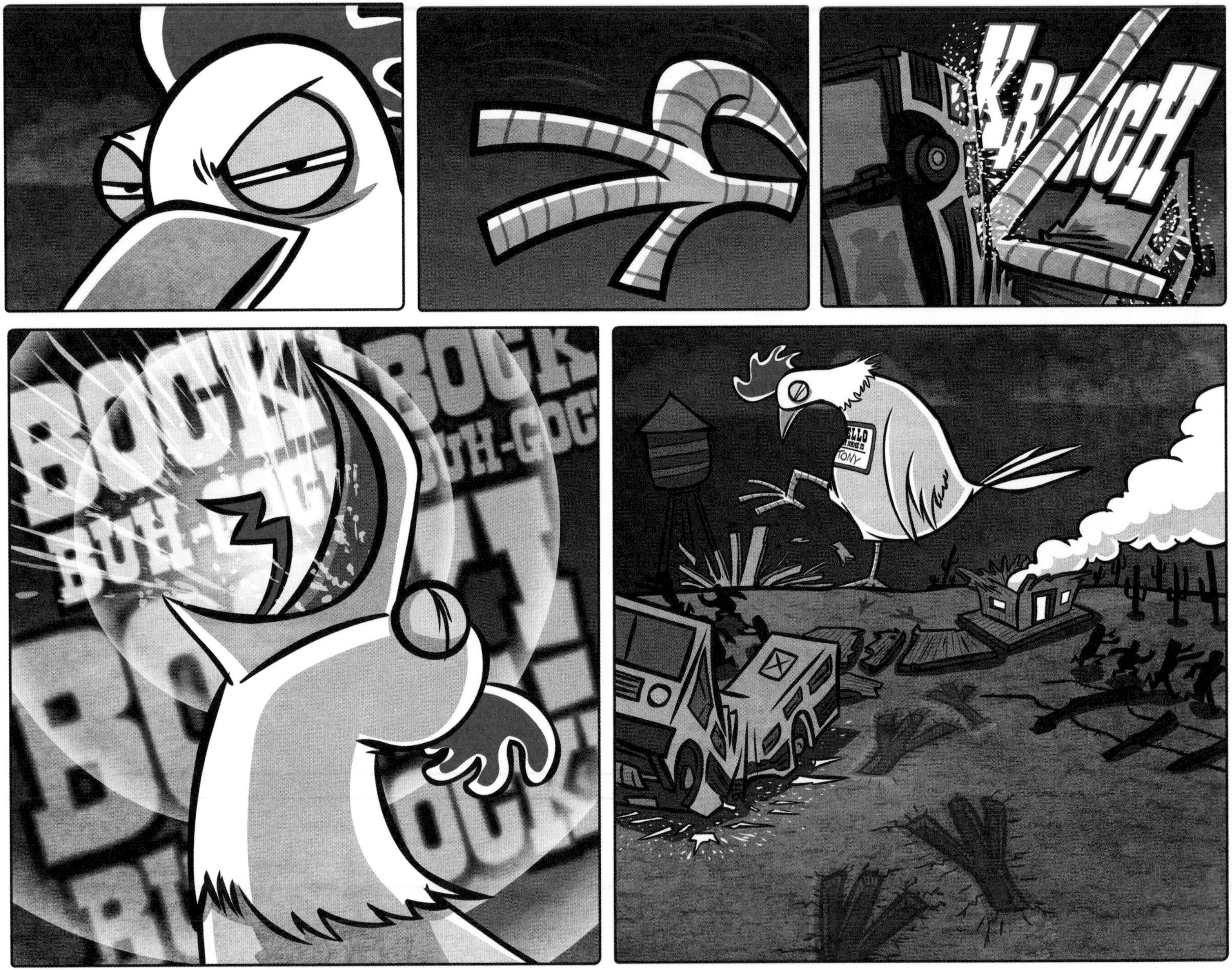
TONY

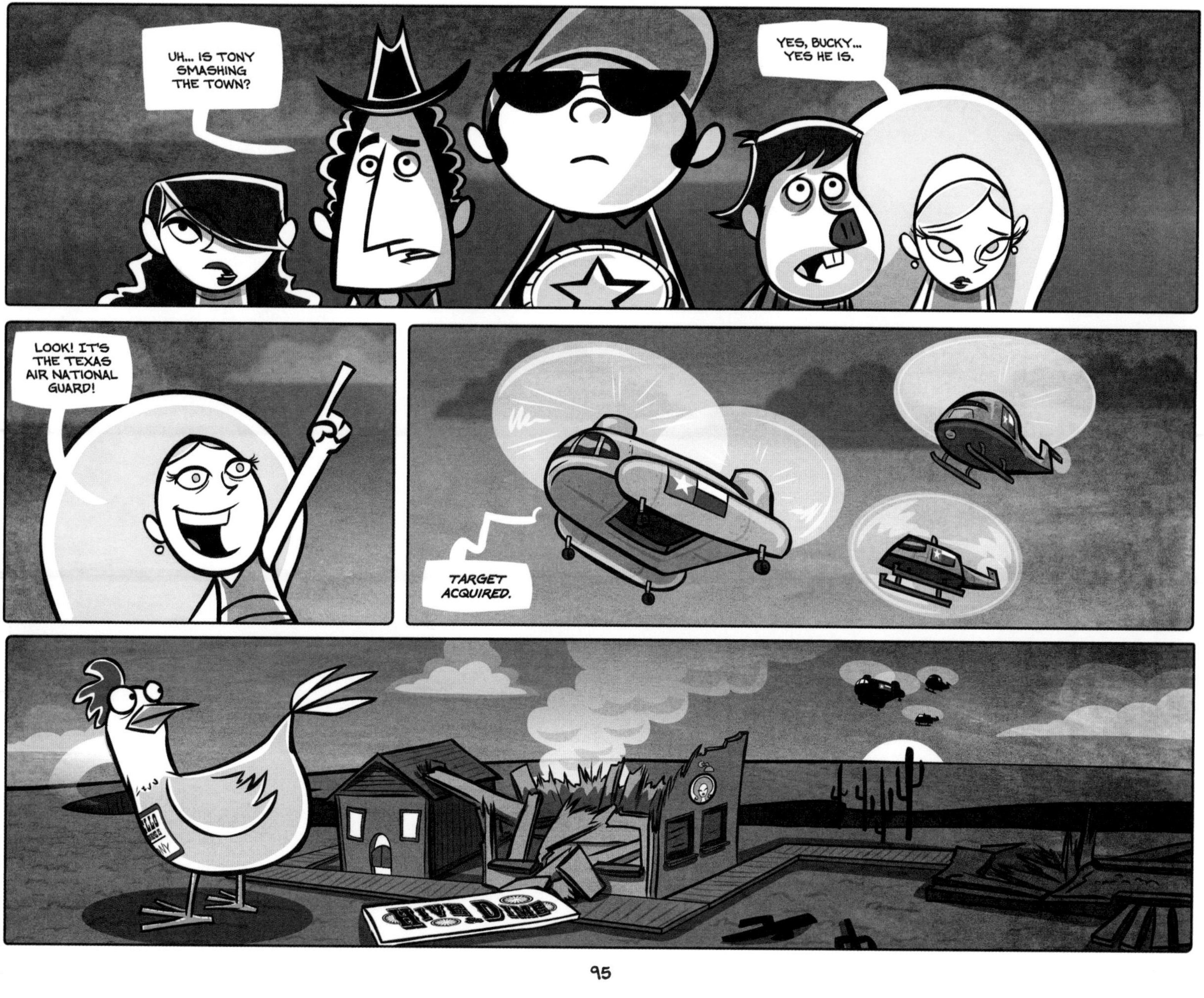
UH... IS TONY SMASHING THE TOWN?
YES, BUCKY... YES HE IS.
LOOK! IT'S THE TEXAS AIR NATIONAL GUARD!
TARGET ACQUIRED.
FIVE & DIME

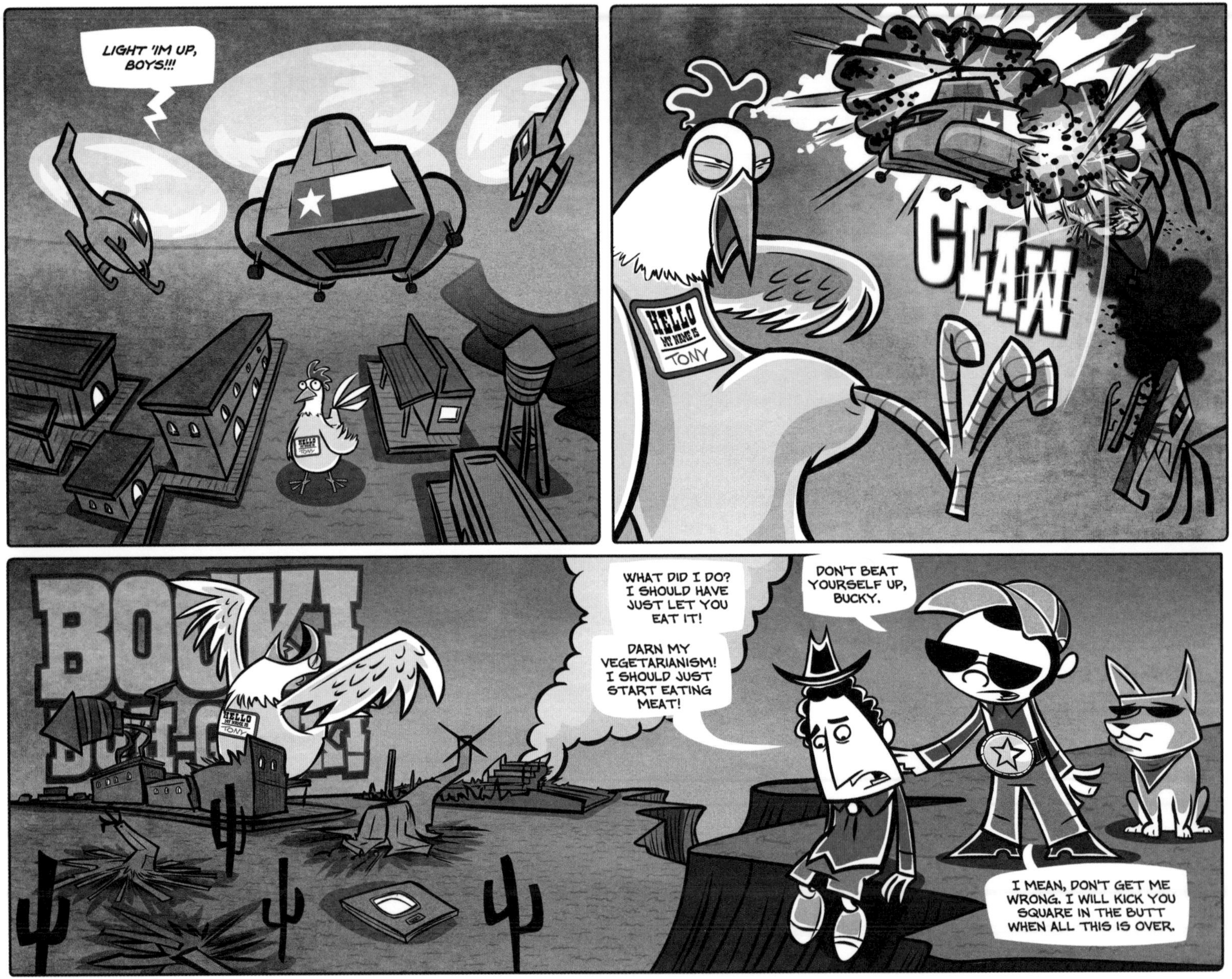
LIGHT 'IM UP, BOYS!!!
HELLO MY NAME IS TONY
CLAW
WHAT DID I DO? I SHOULD HAVE JUST LET YOU EAT IT!
DARN MY VEGETARIANISM! I SHOULD JUST START EATING MEAT!
DON'T BEAT YOURSELF UP, BUCKY.
I MEAN, DON'T GET ME WRONG. I WILL KICK YOU SQUARE IN THE BUTT WHEN ALL THIS IS OVER.

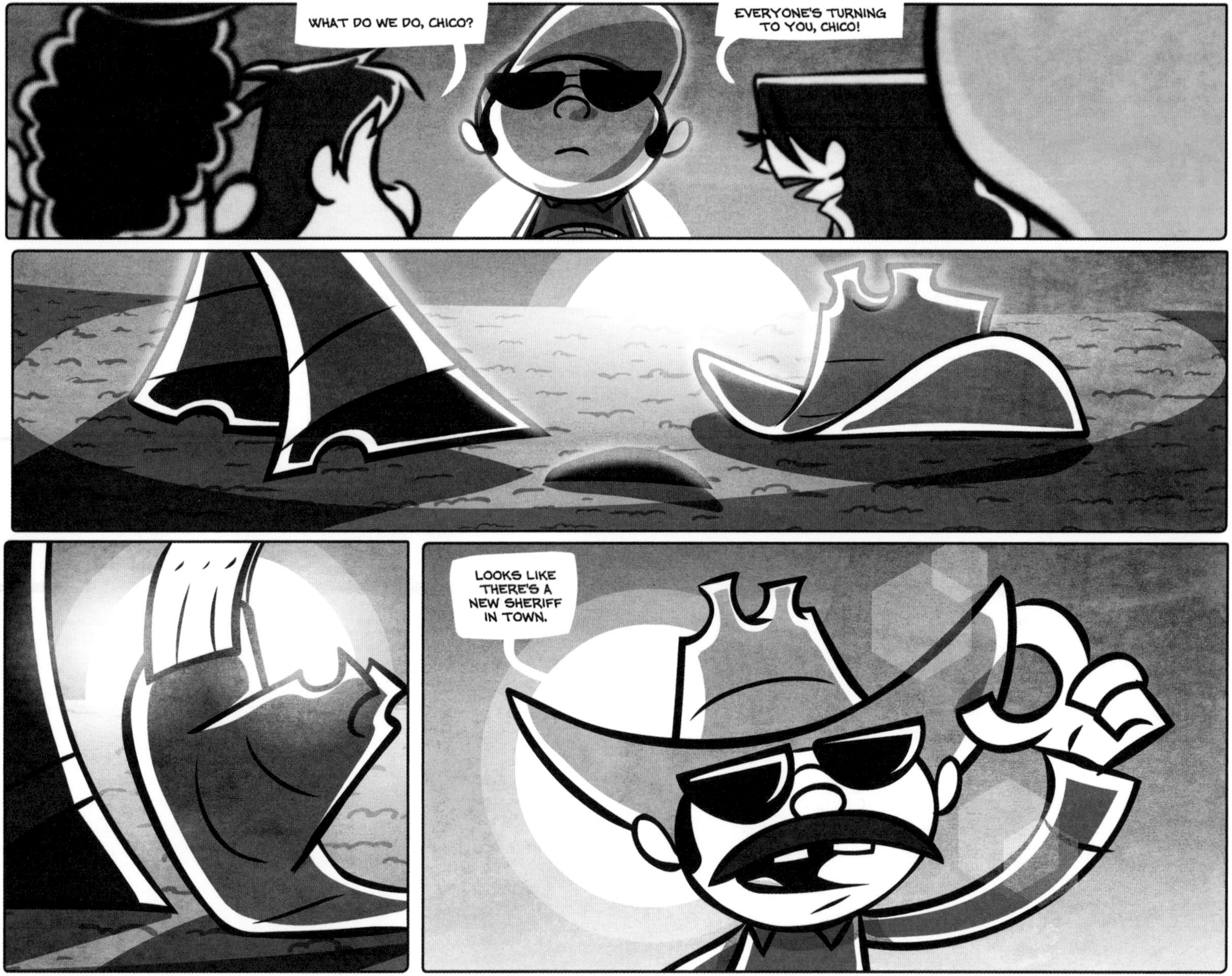
WHAT DO WE DO, CHICO?
EVERYONE'S TURNING TO YOU, CHICO!
LOOKS LIKE THERE'S A NEW SHERIFF IN TOWN.

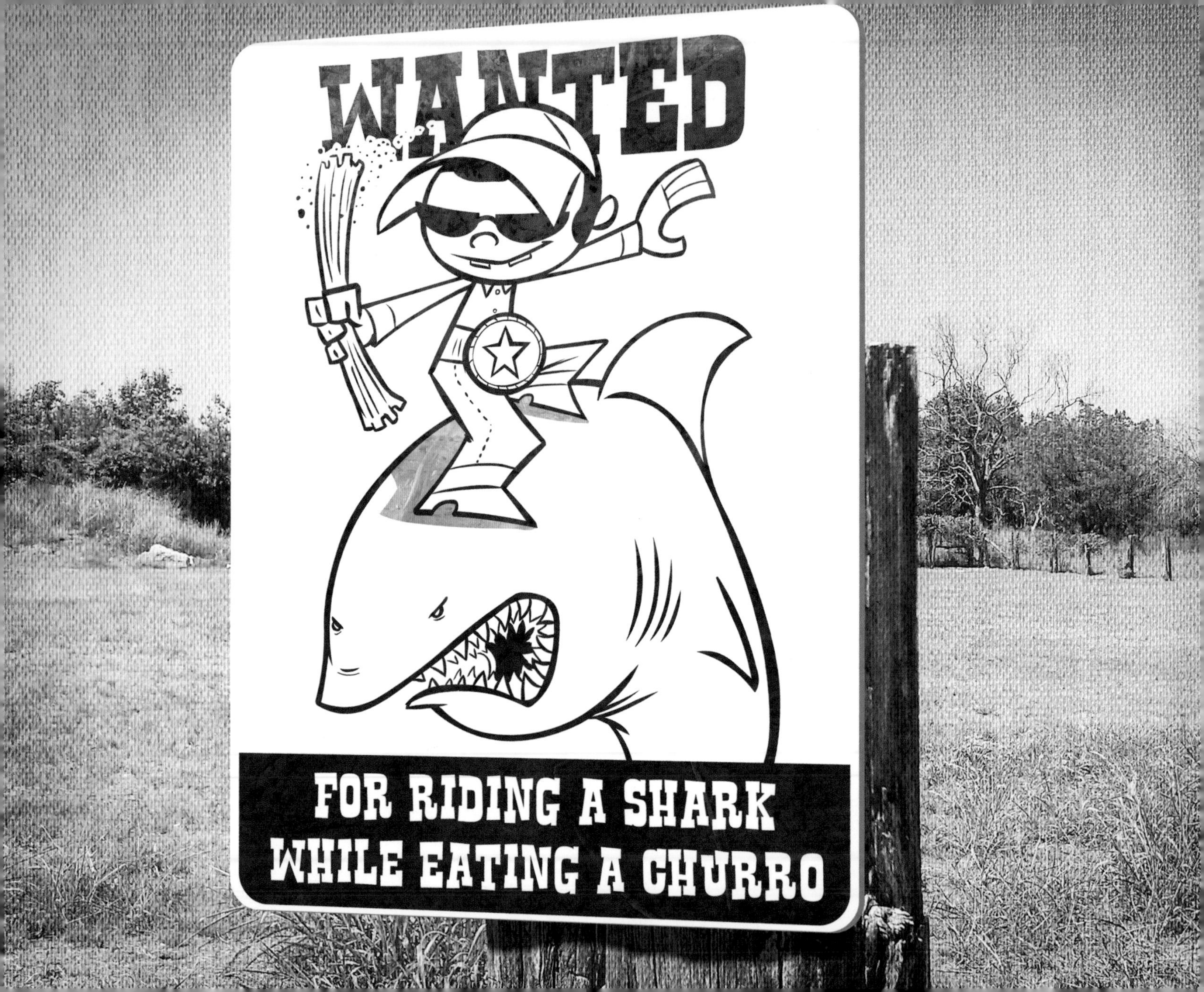
WANTED
FOR RIDING A SHARK
WHILE EATING A CHURRO

CHAPTER SEIS

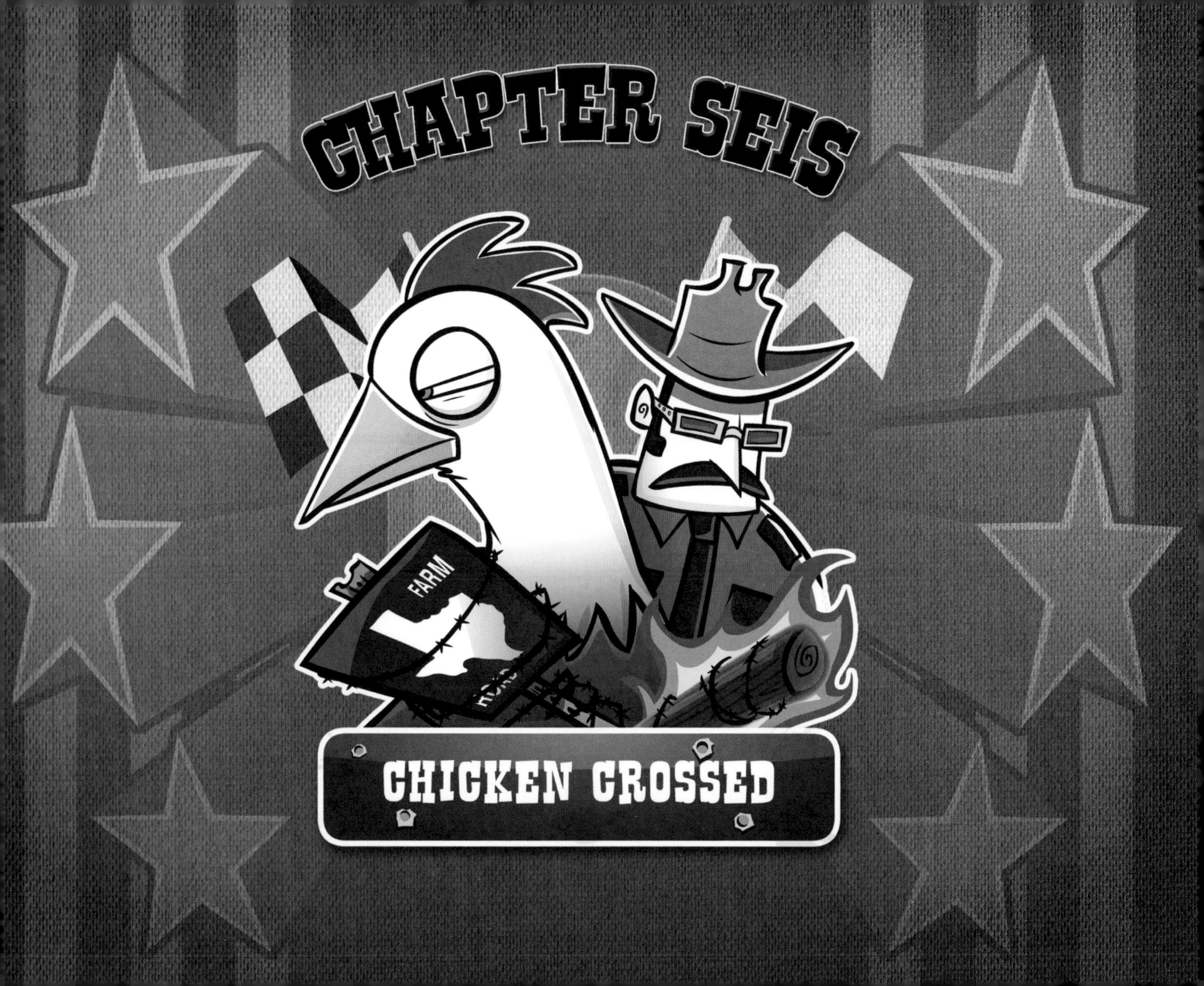
FARM

CHICKEN CROSSED

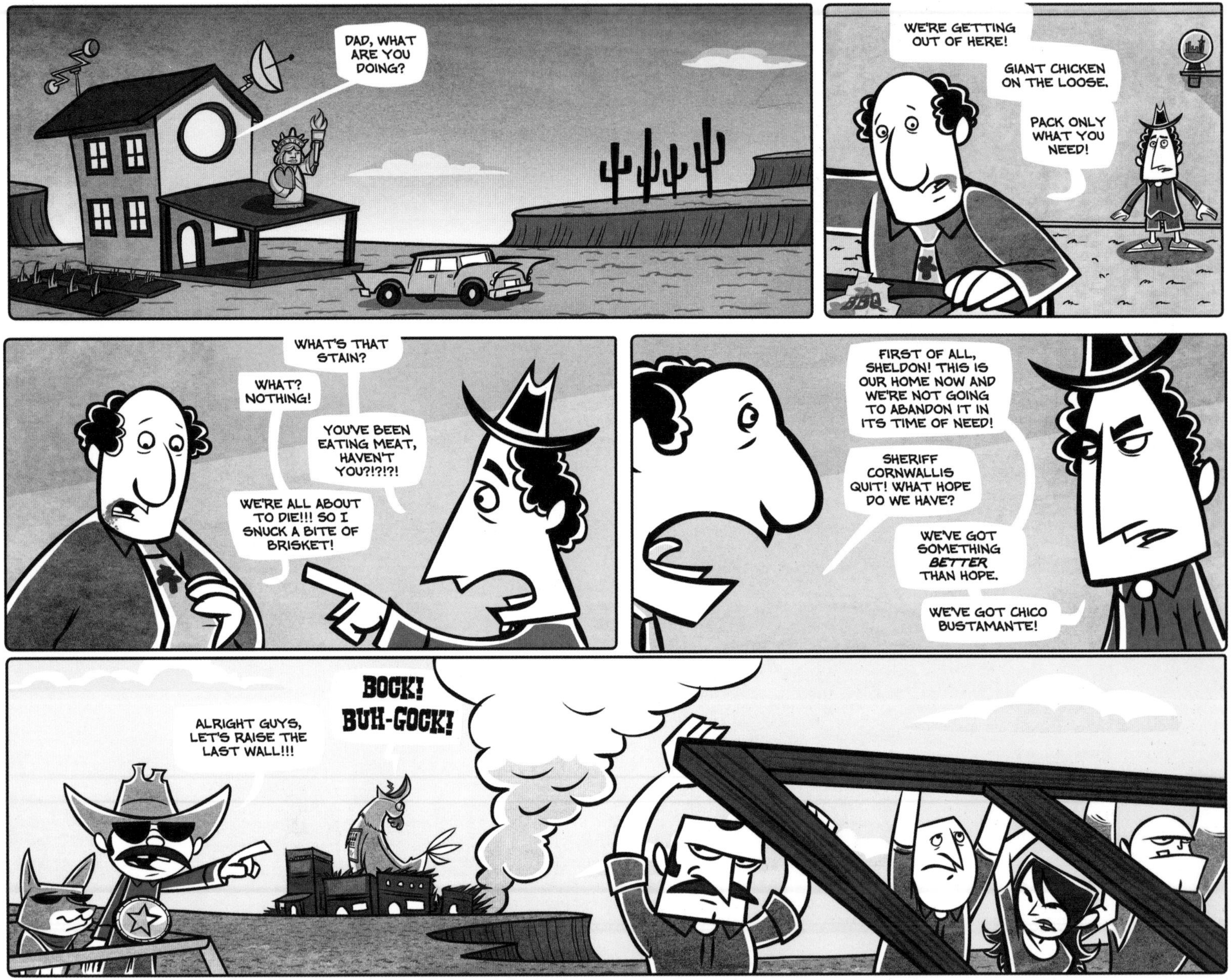
DAD, WHAT ARE YOU DOING?
WE'RE GETTING OUT OF HERE!
GIANT CHICKEN ON THE LOOSE.
PACK ONLY WHAT YOU NEED!
BBQ
WHAT'S THAT STAIN?
WHAT? NOTHING!
YOU'VE BEEN EATING MEAT, HAVEN'T YOU?!?!?!
WE'RE ALL ABOUT TO DIE!!! SO I SNUCK A BITE OF BRISKET!
FIRST OF ALL, SHELDON! THIS IS OUR HOME NOW AND WE'RE NOT GOING TO ABANDON IT IN ITS TIME OF NEED!
SHERIFF CORNWALLIS QUIT! WHAT HOPE DO WE HAVE?
WE'VE GOT SOMETHING *BETTER* THAN HOPE.
WE'VE GOT CHICO BUSTAMANTE!
ALRIGHT GUYS, LET'S RAISE THE LAST WALL!!!
BOCK! BUH-GOCK!

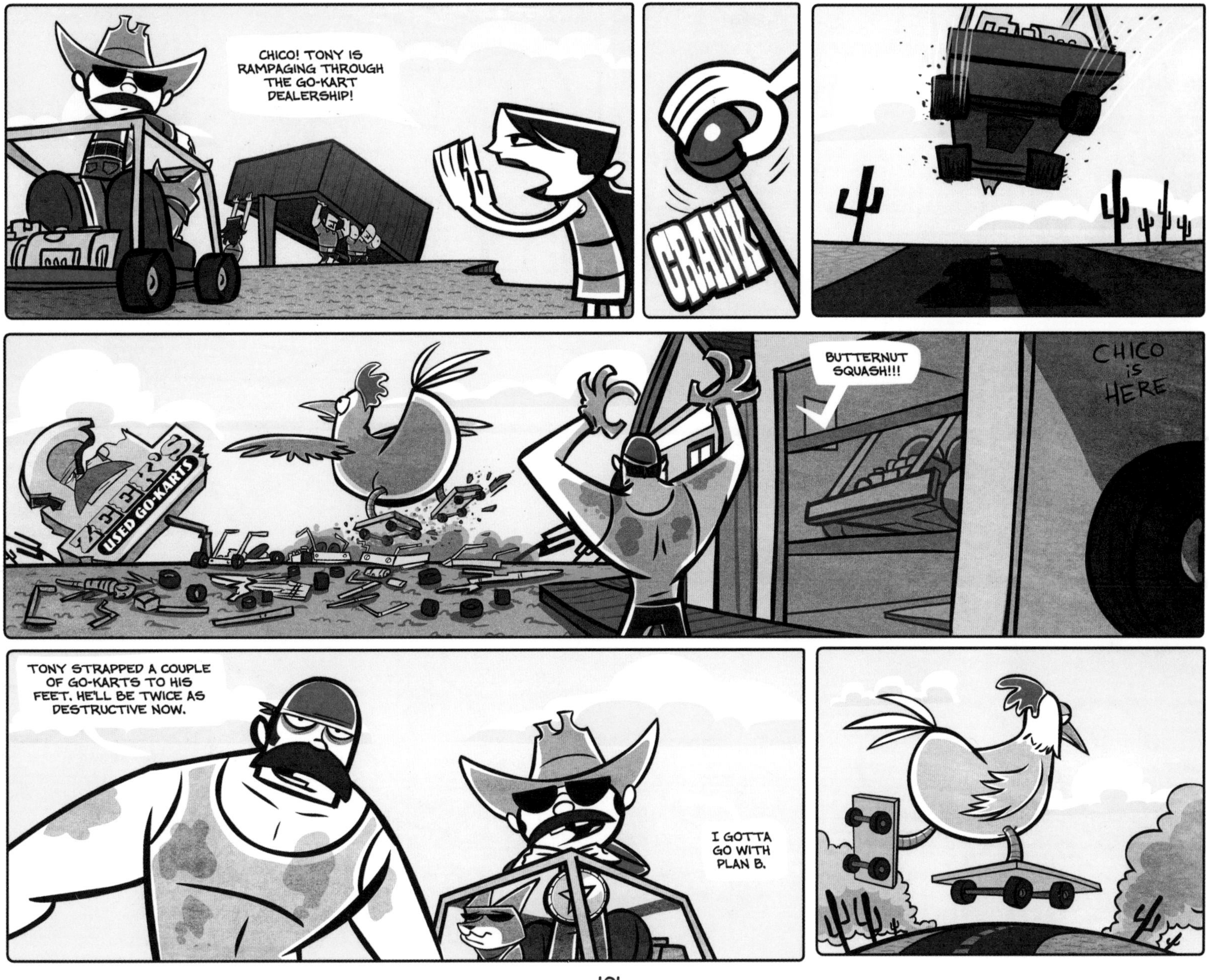
CHICO! TONY IS RAMPAGING THROUGH THE GO-KART DEALERSHIP!
CRANK
ZEEK'S
USED GO-KARTS
BUTTERNUT SQUASH!!!
CHICO is HERE
TONY STRAPPED A COUPLE OF GO-KARTS TO HIS FEET. HE'LL BE TWICE AS DESTRUCTIVE NOW.
I GOTTA GO WITH PLAN B.

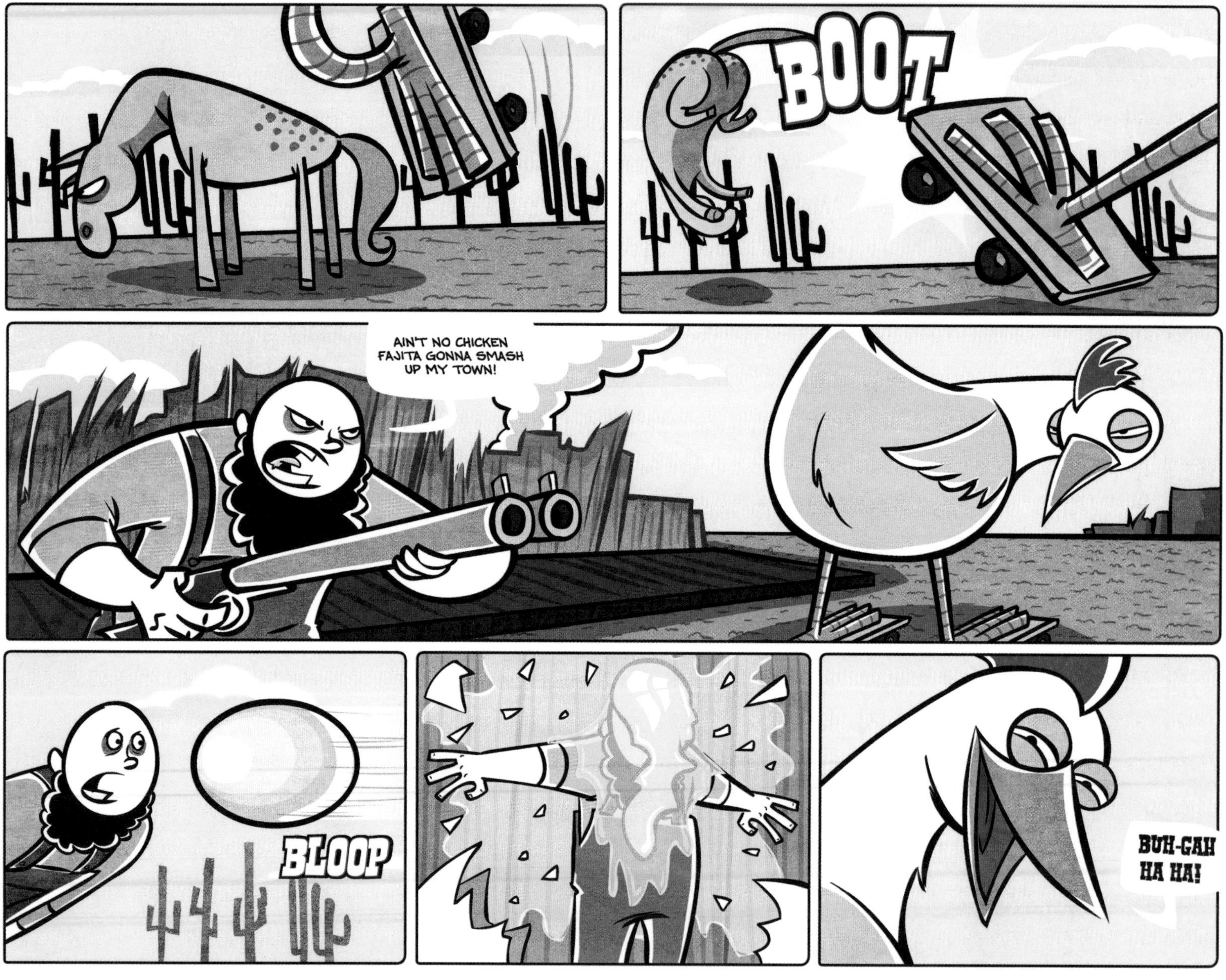
BOOT
AIN'T NO CHICKEN FAJITA GONNA SMASH UP MY TOWN!
BLOOP
BUH-GAH HA HA!

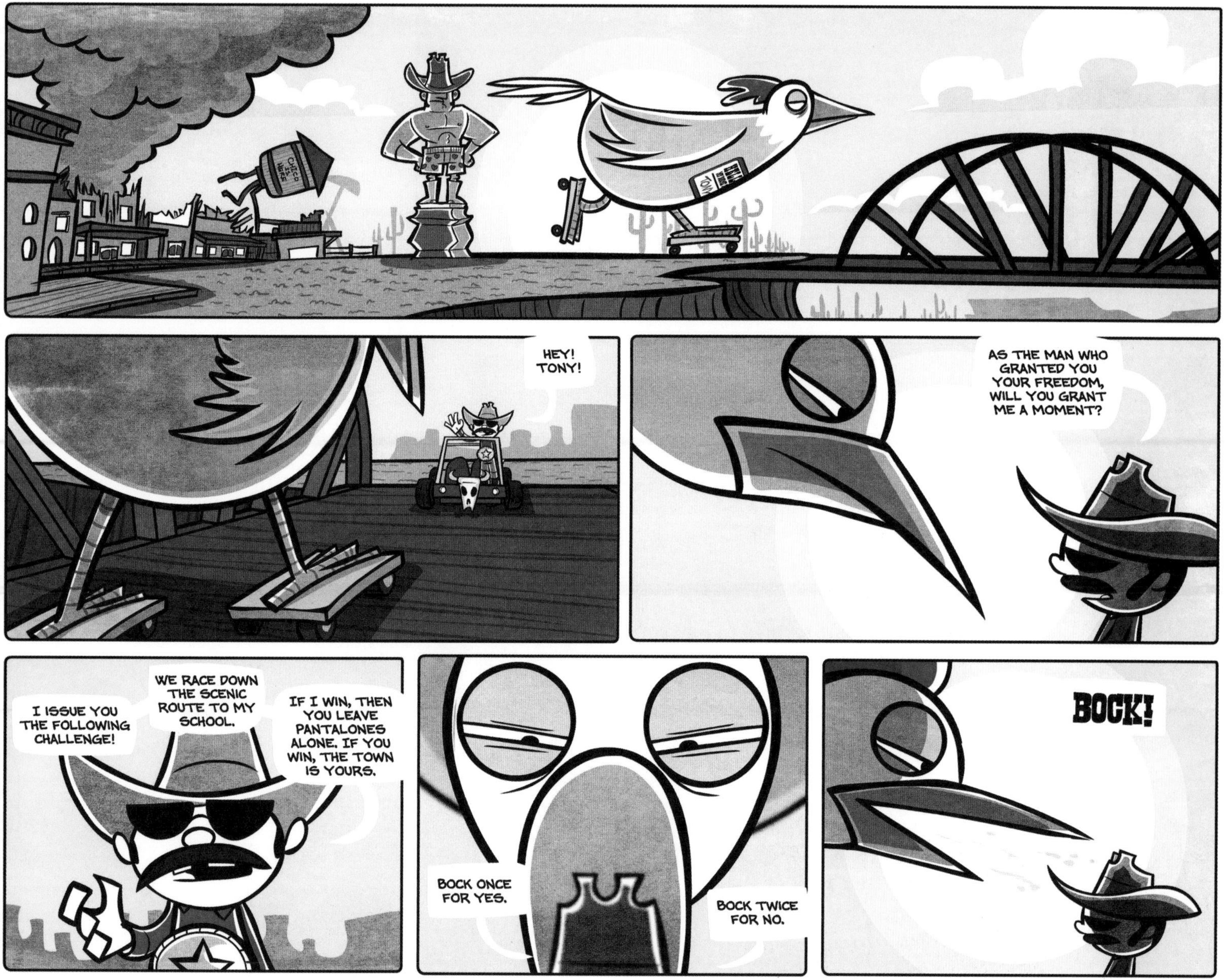
HEY! TONY!
AS THE MAN WHO GRANTED YOU YOUR FREEDOM, WILL YOU GRANT ME A MOMENT?
I ISSUE YOU THE FOLLOWING CHALLENGE!
WE RACE DOWN THE SCENIC ROUTE TO MY SCHOOL.
IF I WIN, THEN YOU LEAVE PANTALONES ALONE. IF YOU WIN, THE TOWN IS YOURS.
BOCK ONCE FOR YES.
BOCK TWICE FOR NO.
BOCK!

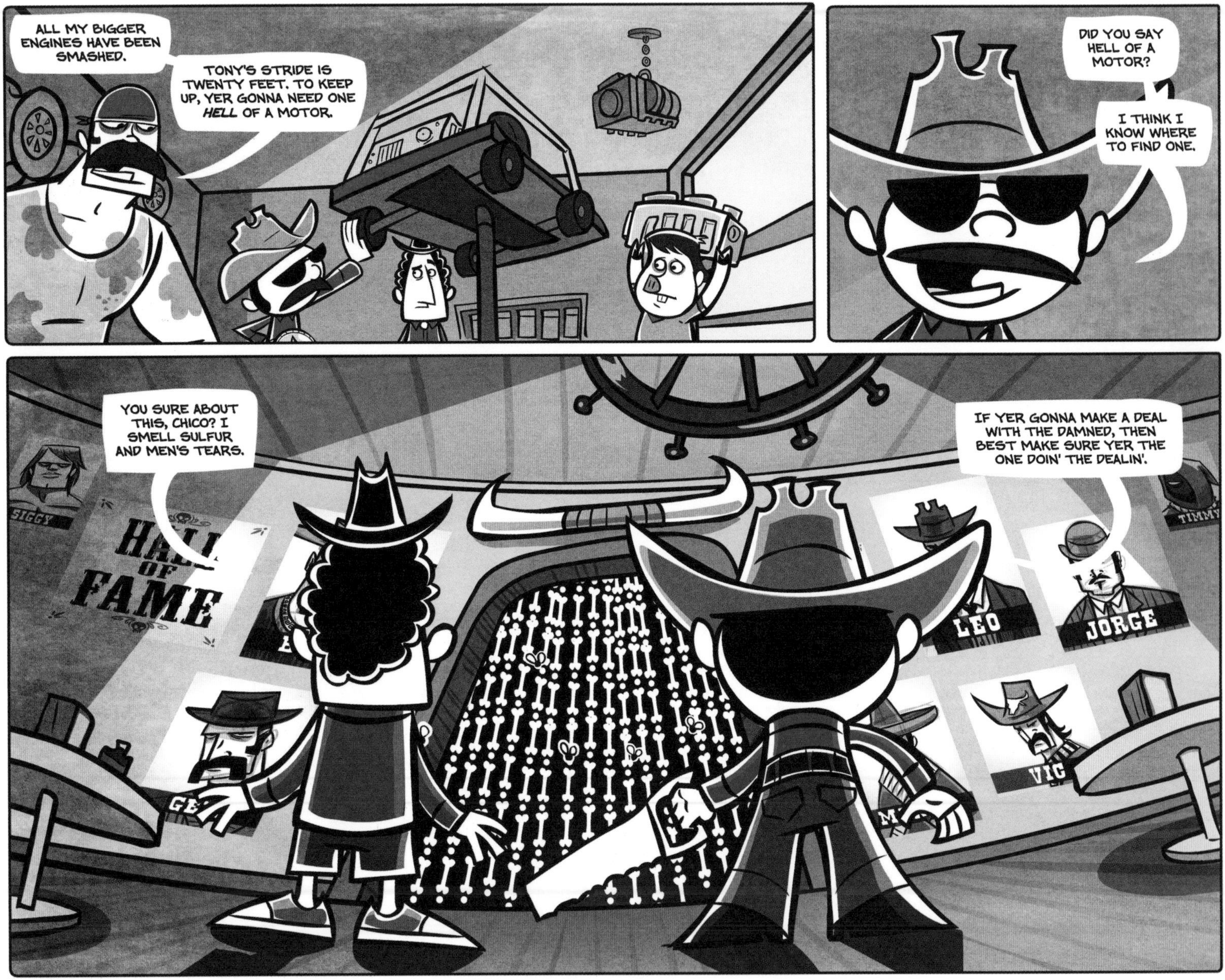
ALL MY BIGGER ENGINES HAVE BEEN SMASHED.
TONY'S STRIDE IS TWENTY FEET. TO KEEP UP, YER GONNA NEED ONE *HELL* OF A MOTOR.
DID YOU SAY HELL OF A MOTOR?
I THINK I KNOW WHERE TO FIND ONE.
YOU SURE ABOUT THIS, CHICO? I SMELL SULFUR AND MEN'S TEARS.
IF YER GONNA MAKE A DEAL WITH THE DAMNED, THEN BEST MAKE SURE YER THE ONE DOIN' THE DEALIN'.
SIGGY
FAME
LEO
JORGE
VIC
TIMMY

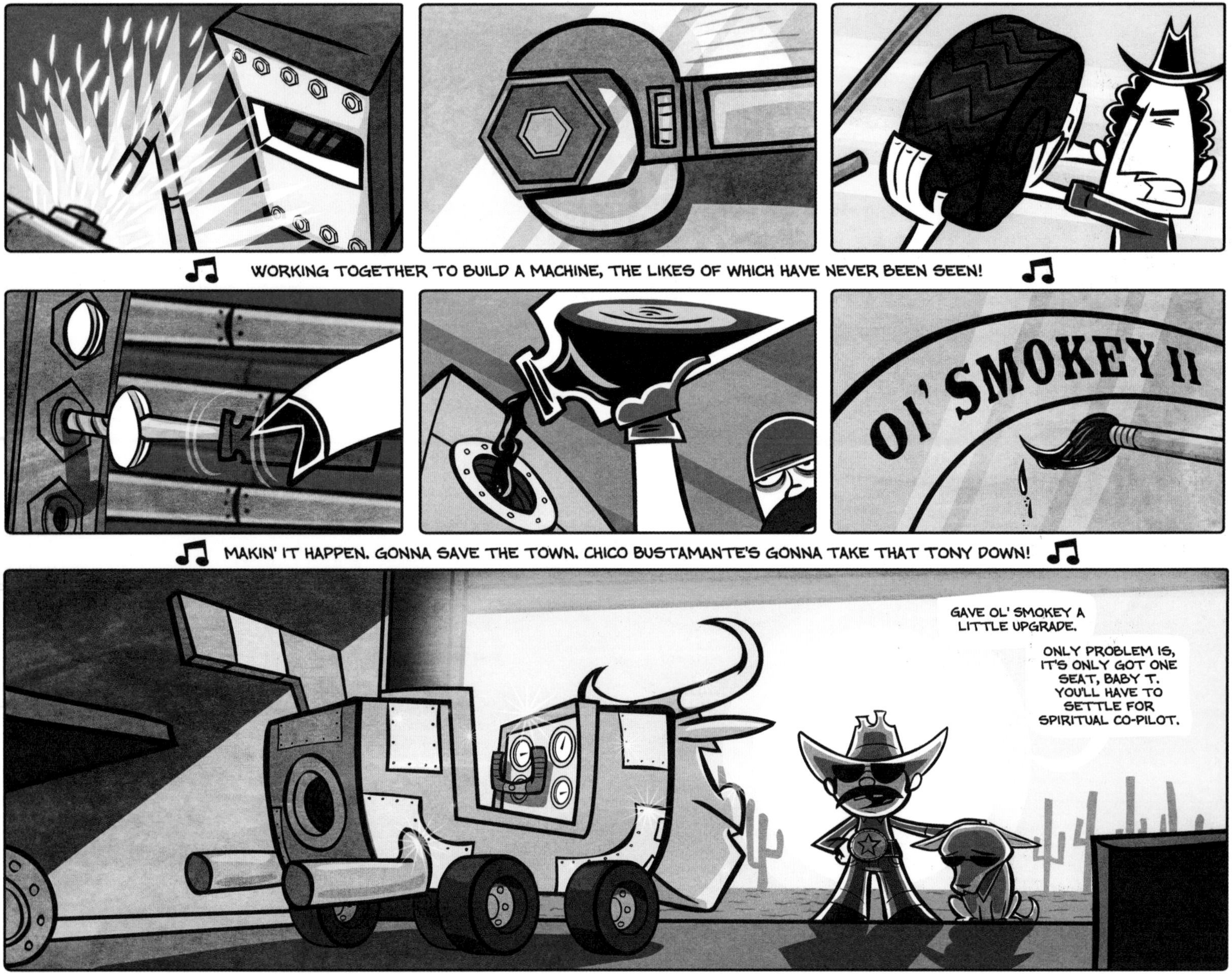
♫ WORKING TOGETHER TO BUILD A MACHINE, THE LIKES OF WHICH HAVE NEVER BEEN SEEN! ♫
OL' SMOKEY II
♫ MAKIN' IT HAPPEN. GONNA SAVE THE TOWN. CHICO BUSTAMANTE'S GONNA TAKE THAT TONY DOWN! ♫
GAVE OL' SMOKEY A LITTLE UPGRADE.
ONLY PROBLEM IS, IT'S ONLY GOT ONE SEAT, BABY T. YOU'LL HAVE TO SETTLE FOR SPIRITUAL CO-PILOT.

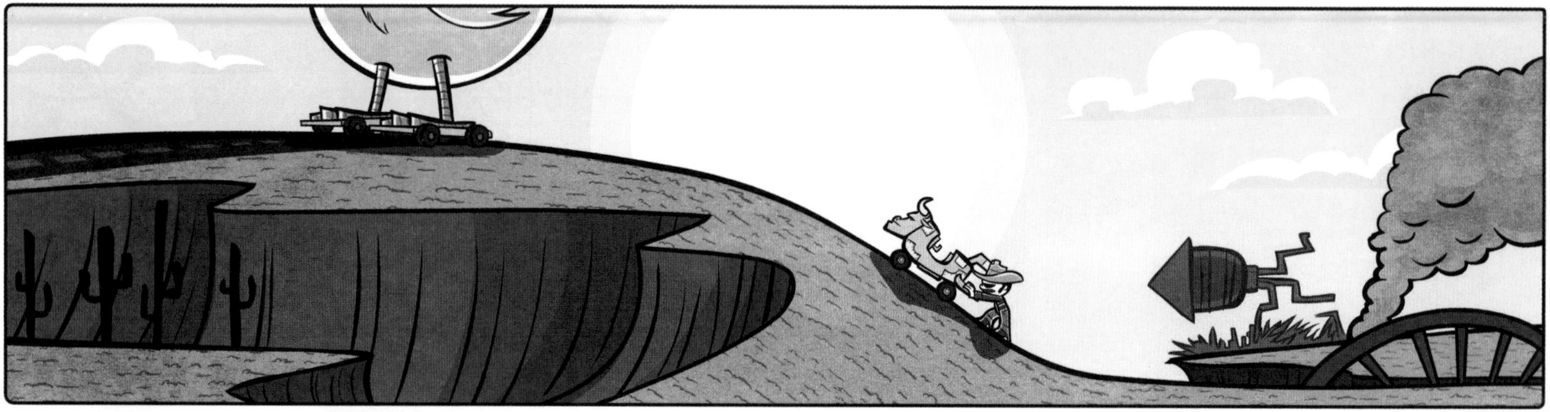

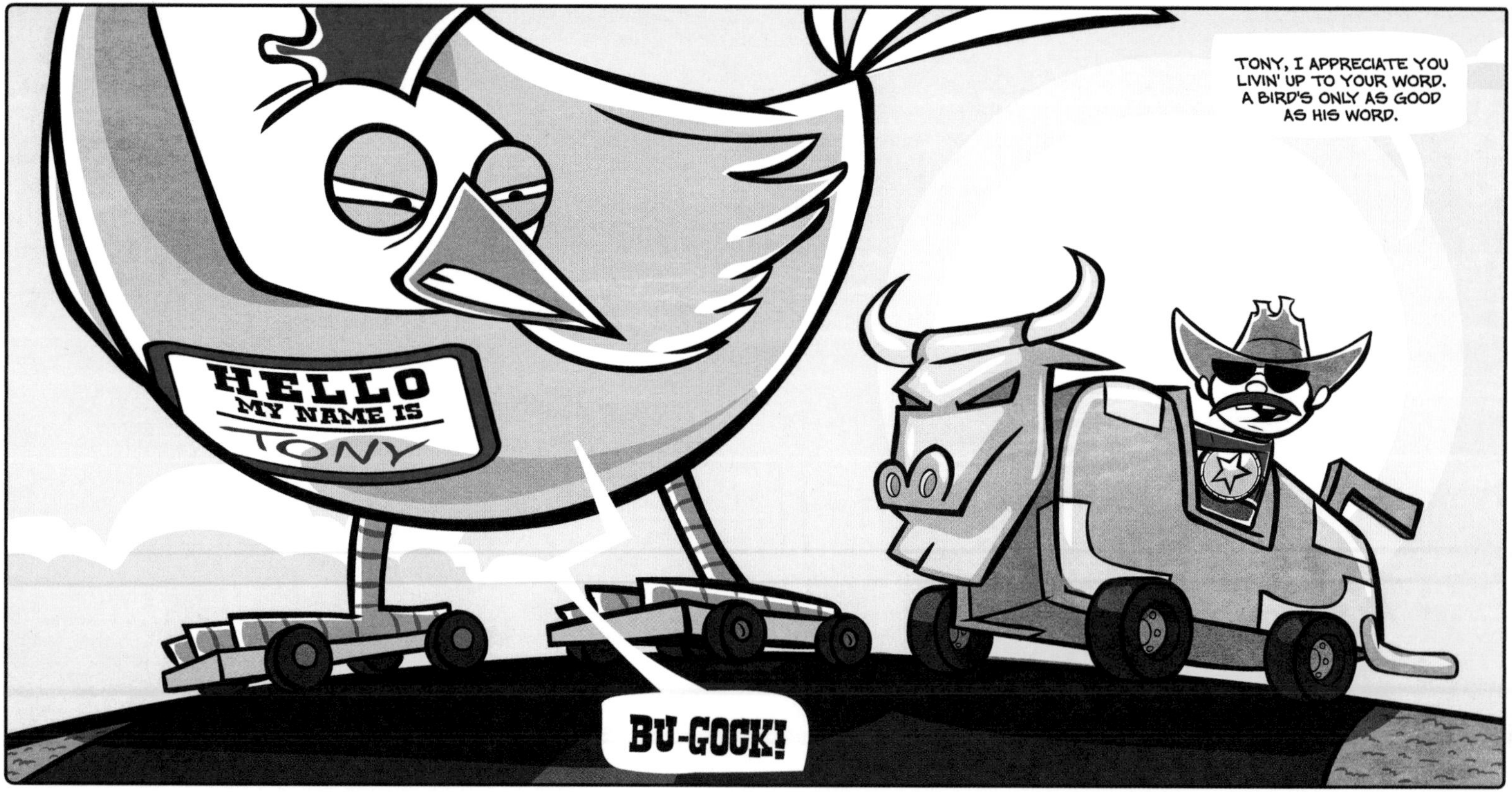
TONY, I APPRECIATE YOU LIVIN' UP TO YOUR WORD. A BIRD'S ONLY AS GOOD AS HIS WORD.
HELLO
MY NAME IS
TONY
BU-GOCK!

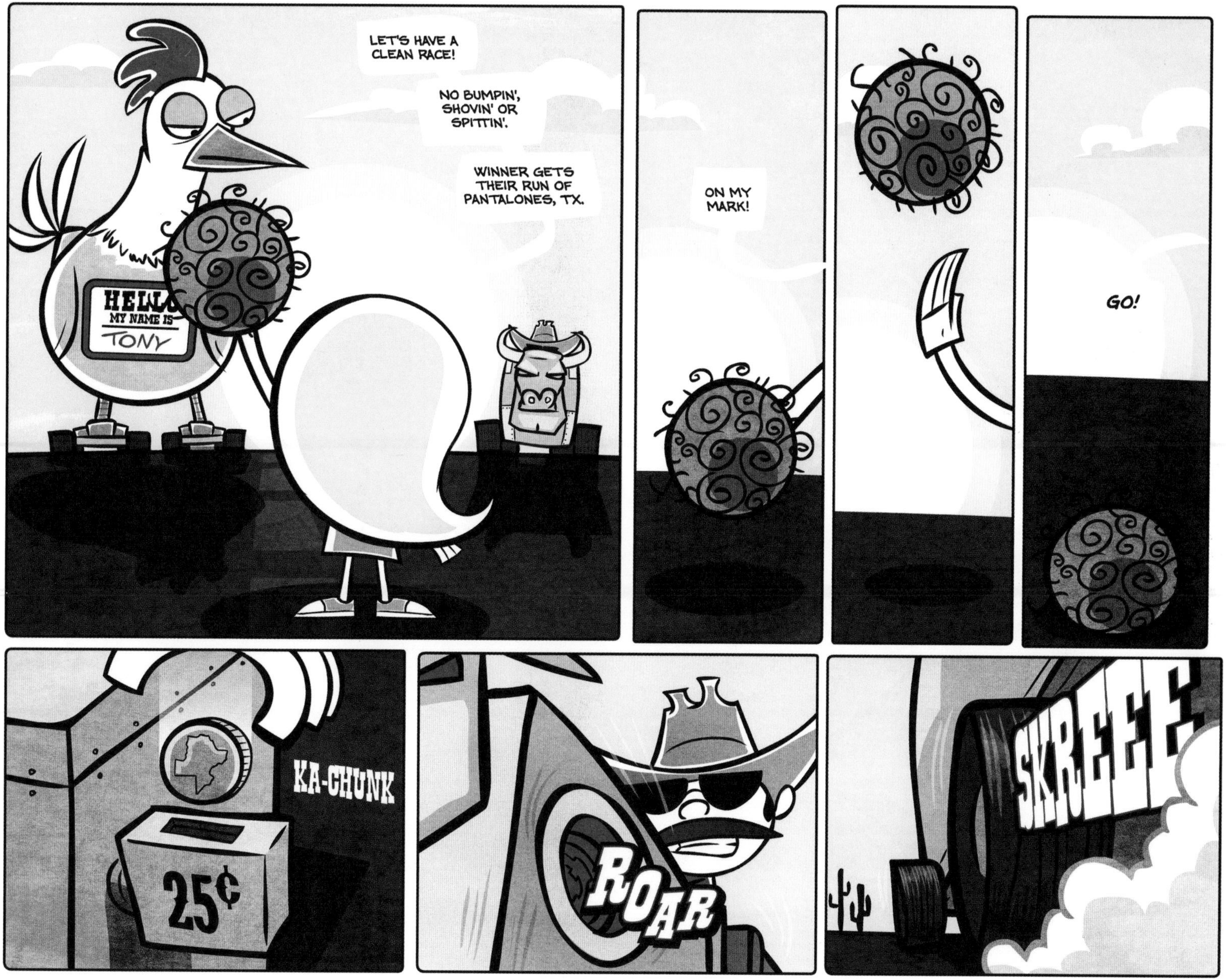
LET'S HAVE A CLEAN RACE!
NO BUMPIN', SHOVIN' OR SPITTIN'.
WINNER GETS THEIR RUN OF PANTALONES, TX.
HELLO MY NAME IS
TONY
ON MY MARK!
GO!
25¢
KA-CHUNK
ROAR
SKREEE

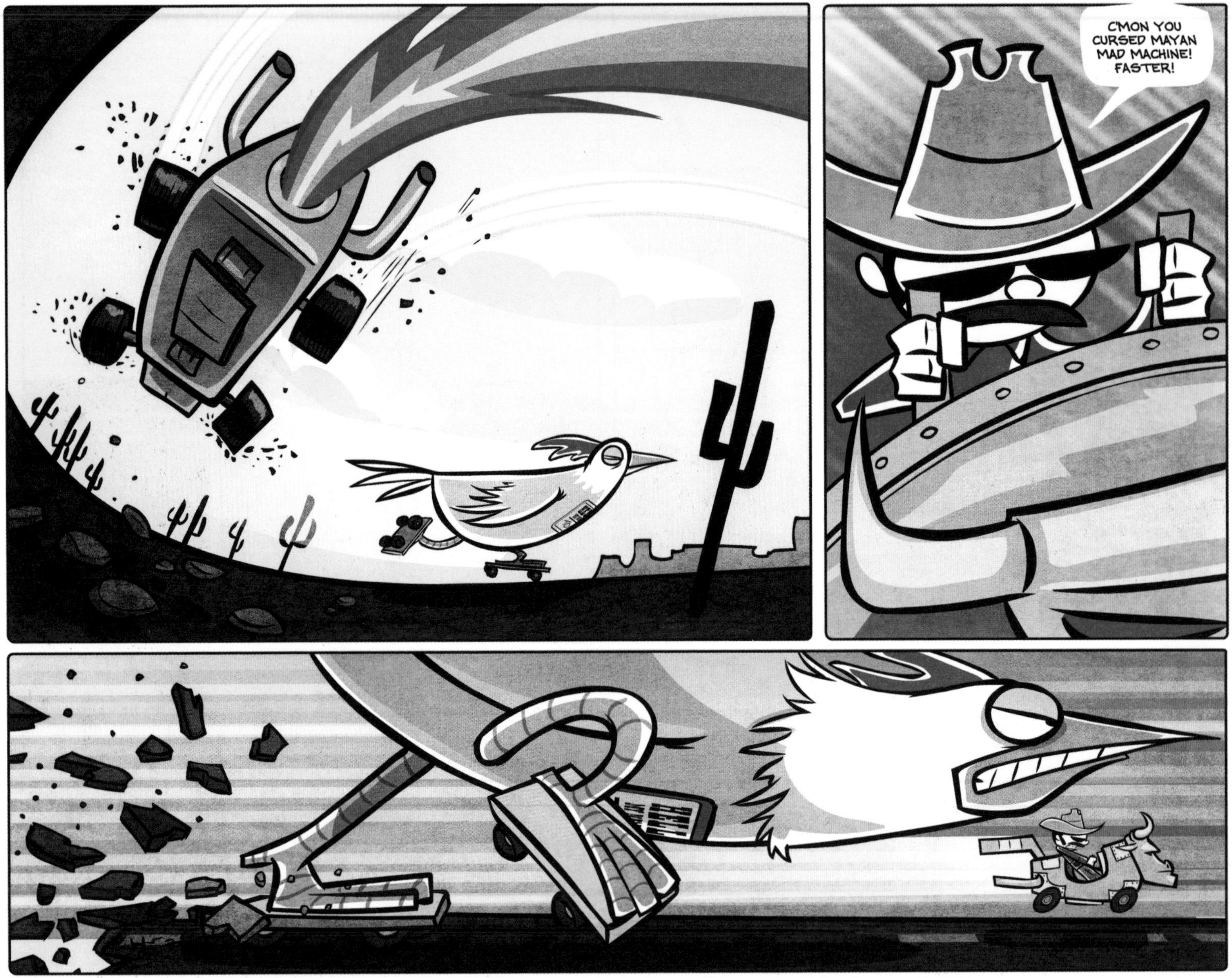
C'MON YOU CURSED MAYAN MAD MACHINE! FASTER!

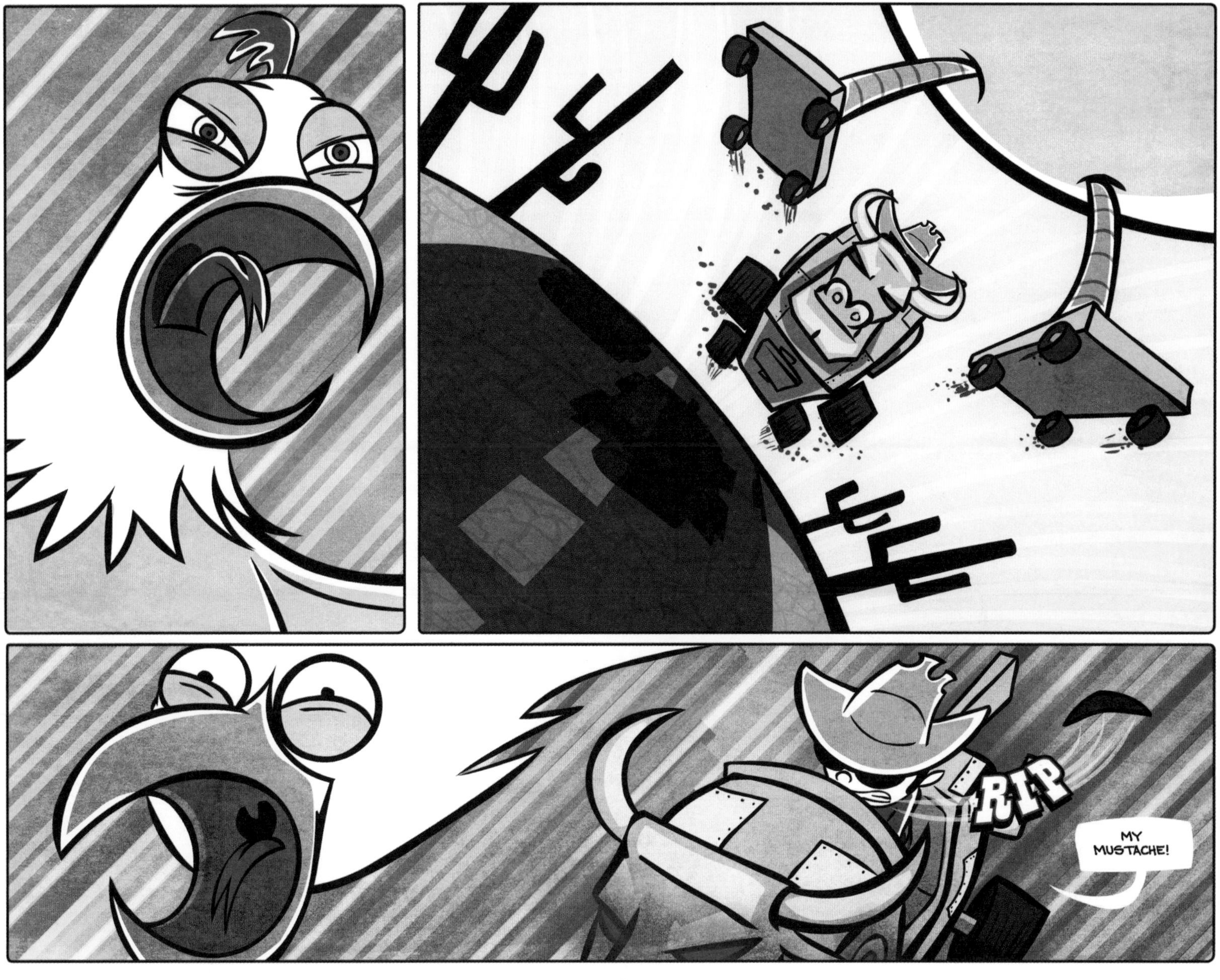
RIP
MY MUSTACHE!

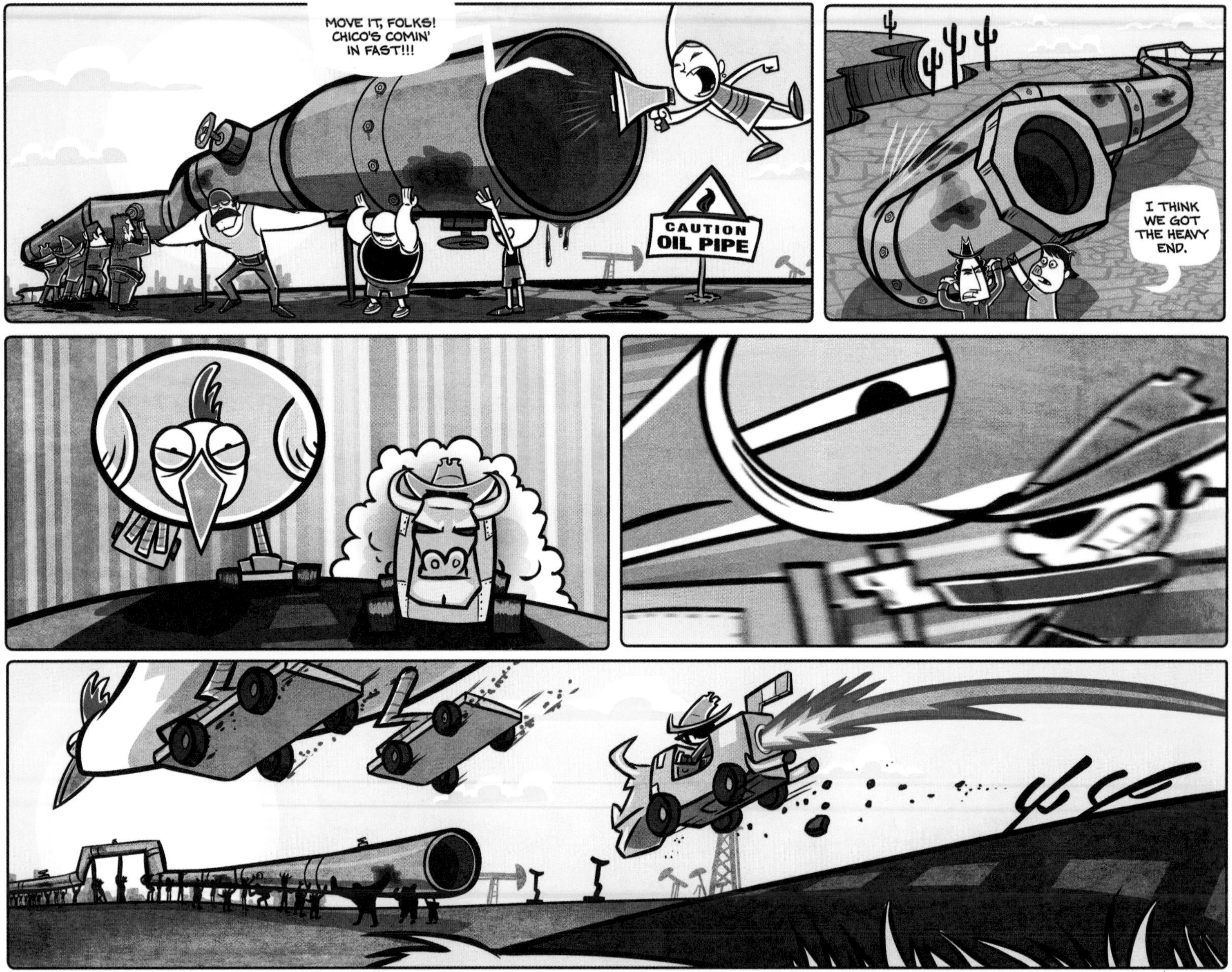
MOVE IT, FOLKS! CHICO'S COMIN' IN FAST!!!
CAUTION OIL PIPE
I THINK WE GOT THE HEAVY END.

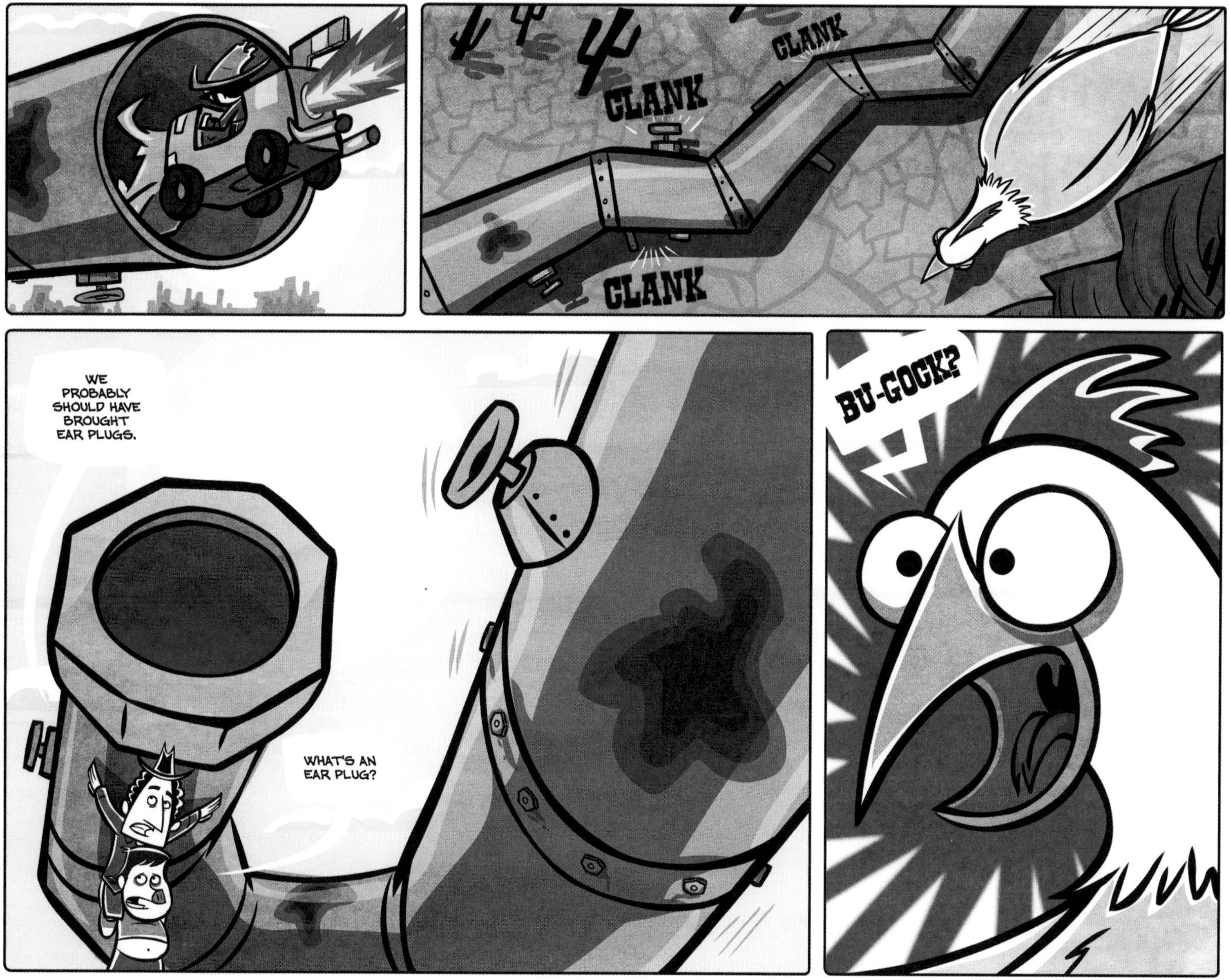
CLANK
CLANK
CLANK
WE PROBABLY SHOULD HAVE BROUGHT EAR PLUGS.
WHAT'S AN EAR PLUG?
BU-GOCK?

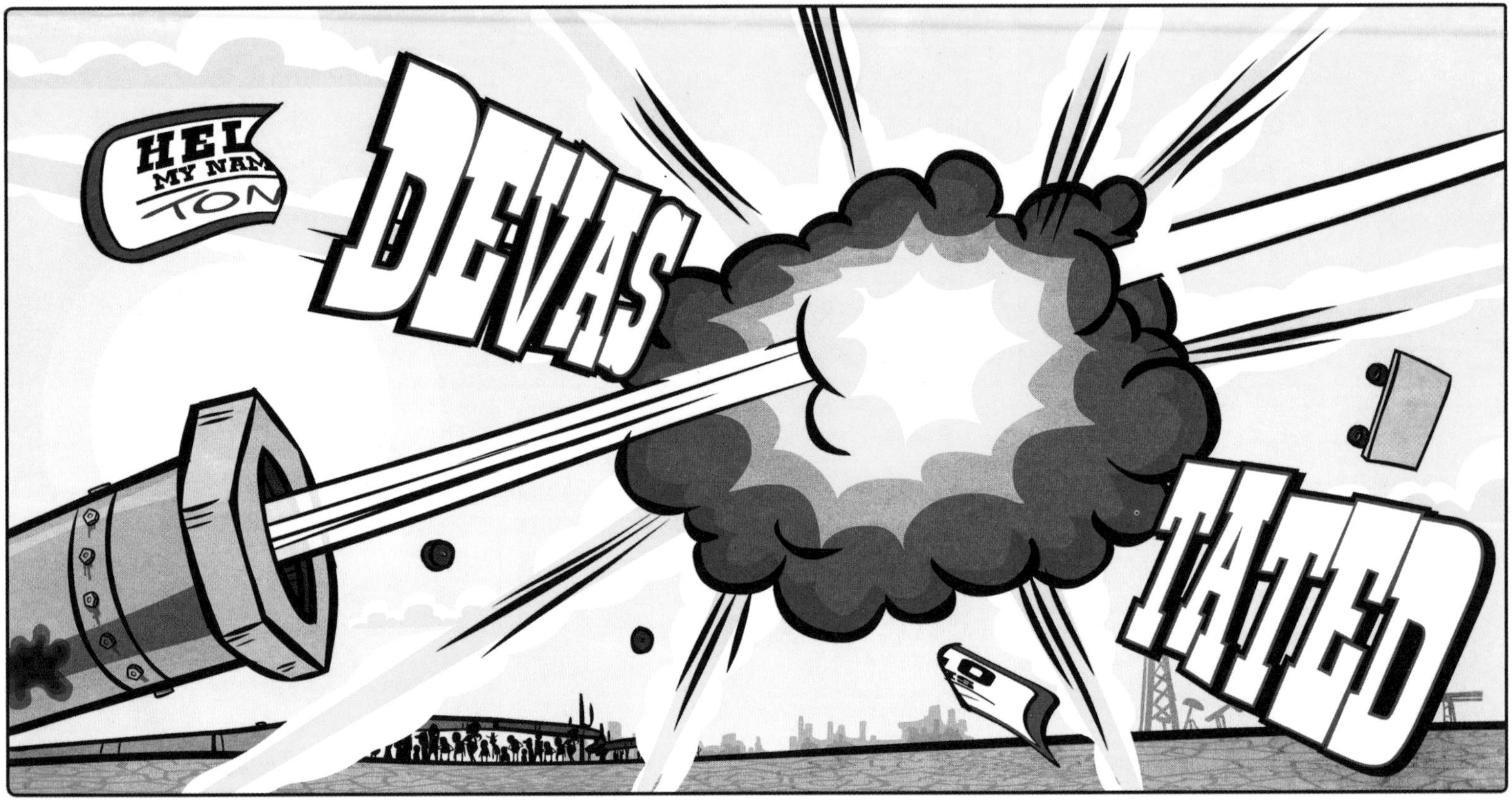
HEL
MY NAM
TON
DEVAS
TATED

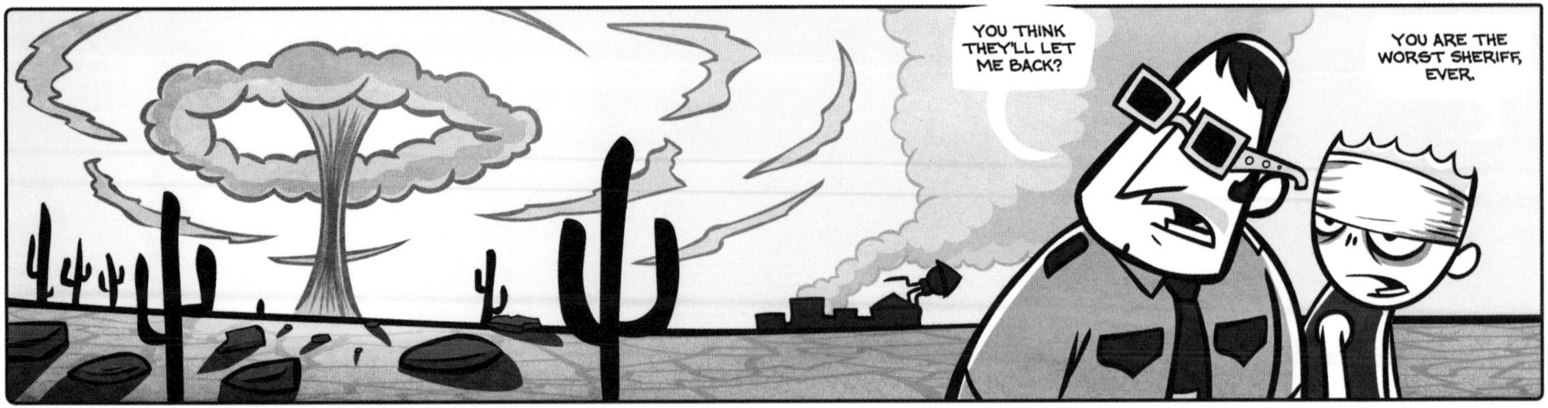
YOU THINK THEY'LL LET ME BACK?
YOU ARE THE WORST SHERIFF, EVER.

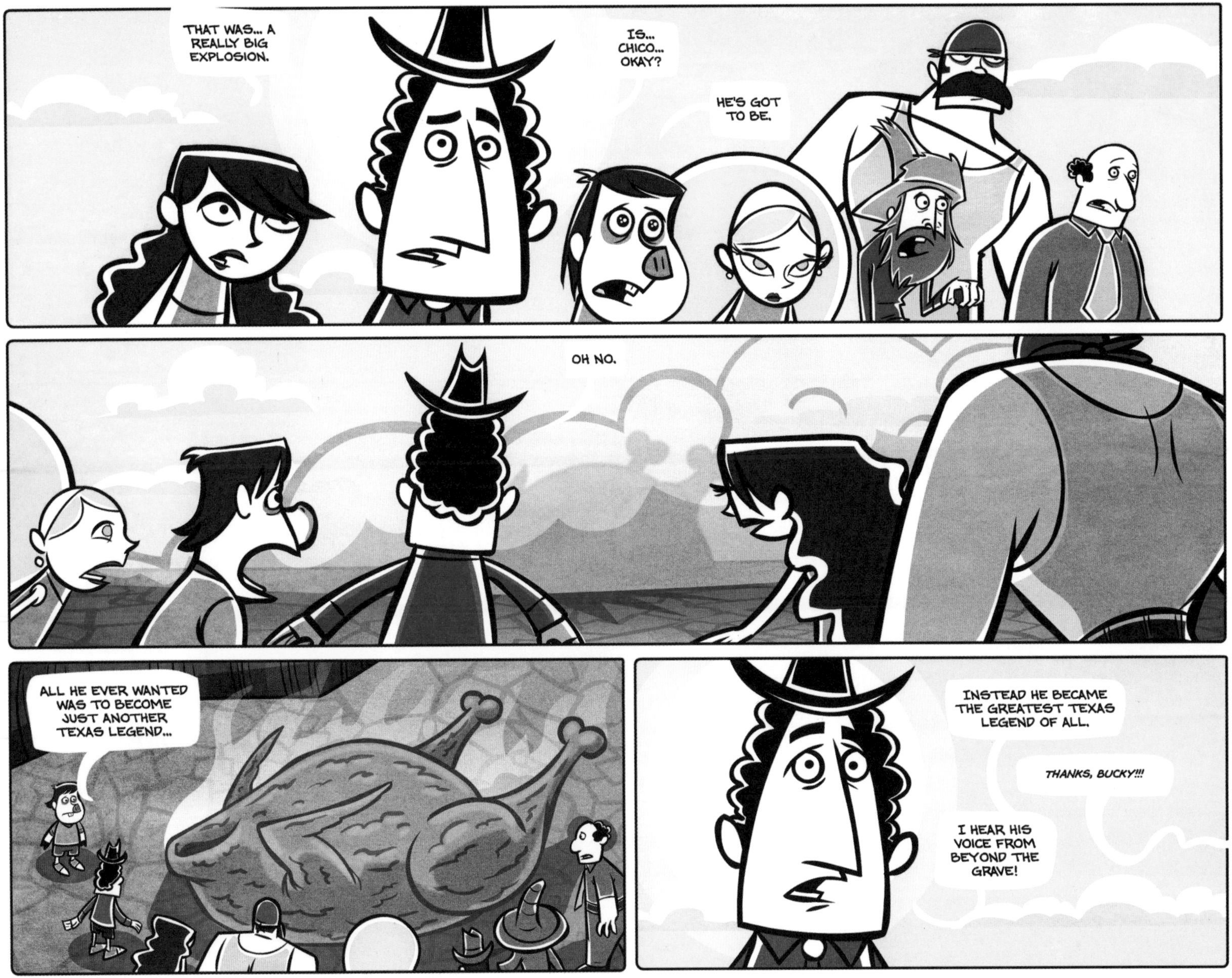
THAT WAS... A REALLY BIG EXPLOSION.
IS... CHICO... OKAY?
HE'S GOT TO BE.
OH NO.
ALL HE EVER WANTED WAS TO BECOME JUST ANOTHER TEXAS LEGEND...
INSTEAD HE BECAME THE GREATEST TEXAS LEGEND OF ALL.
THANKS, BUCKY!!!
I HEAR HIS VOICE FROM BEYOND THE GRAVE!

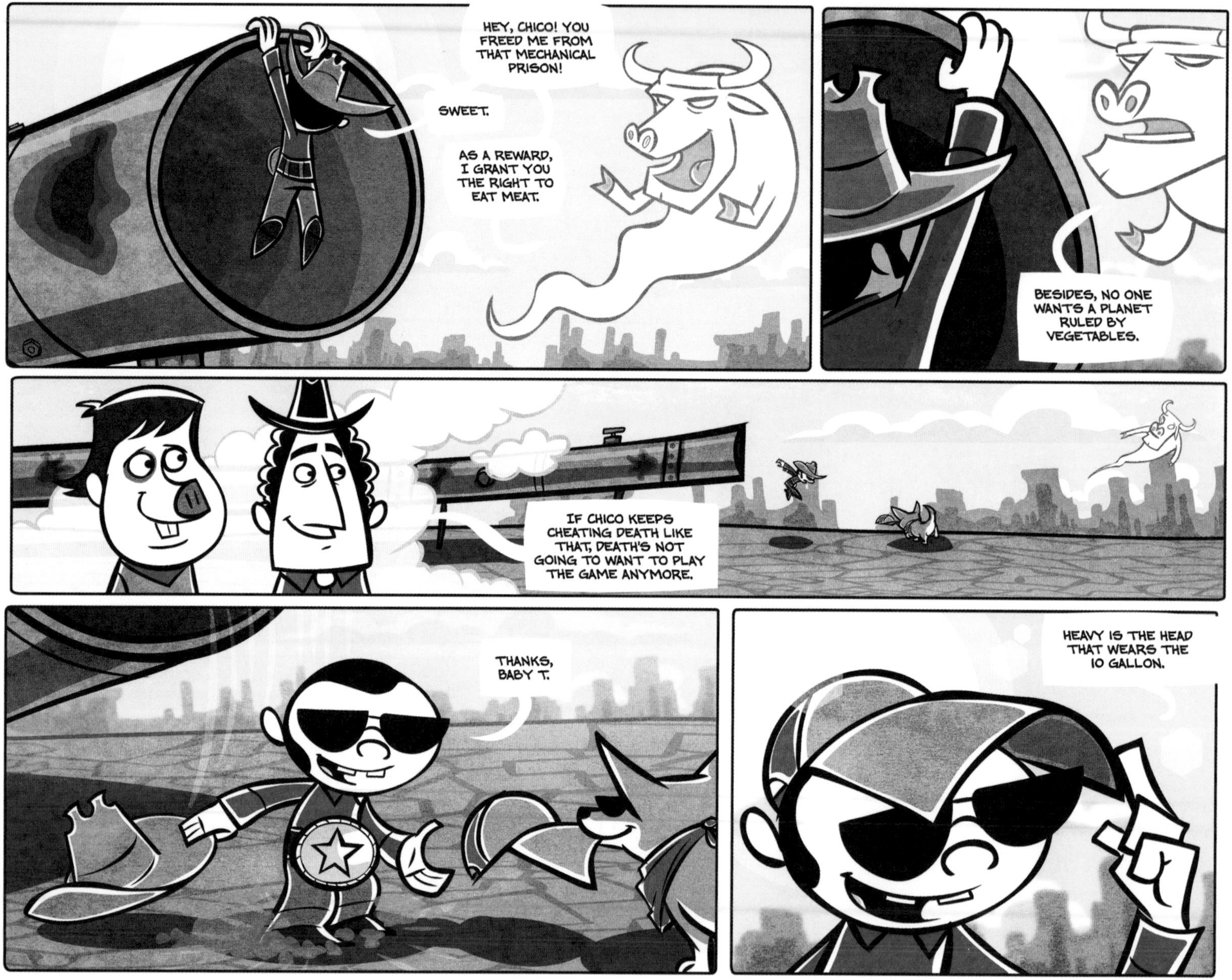
HEY, CHICO! YOU FREED ME FROM THAT MECHANICAL PRISON!
SWEET.
AS A REWARD, I GRANT YOU THE RIGHT TO EAT MEAT.
BESIDES, NO ONE WANTS A PLANET RULED BY VEGETABLES.
IF CHICO KEEPS CHEATING DEATH LIKE THAT, DEATH'S NOT GOING TO WANT TO PLAY THE GAME ANYMORE.
THANKS, BABY T.
HEAVY IS THE HEAD THAT WEARS THE 10 GALLON.

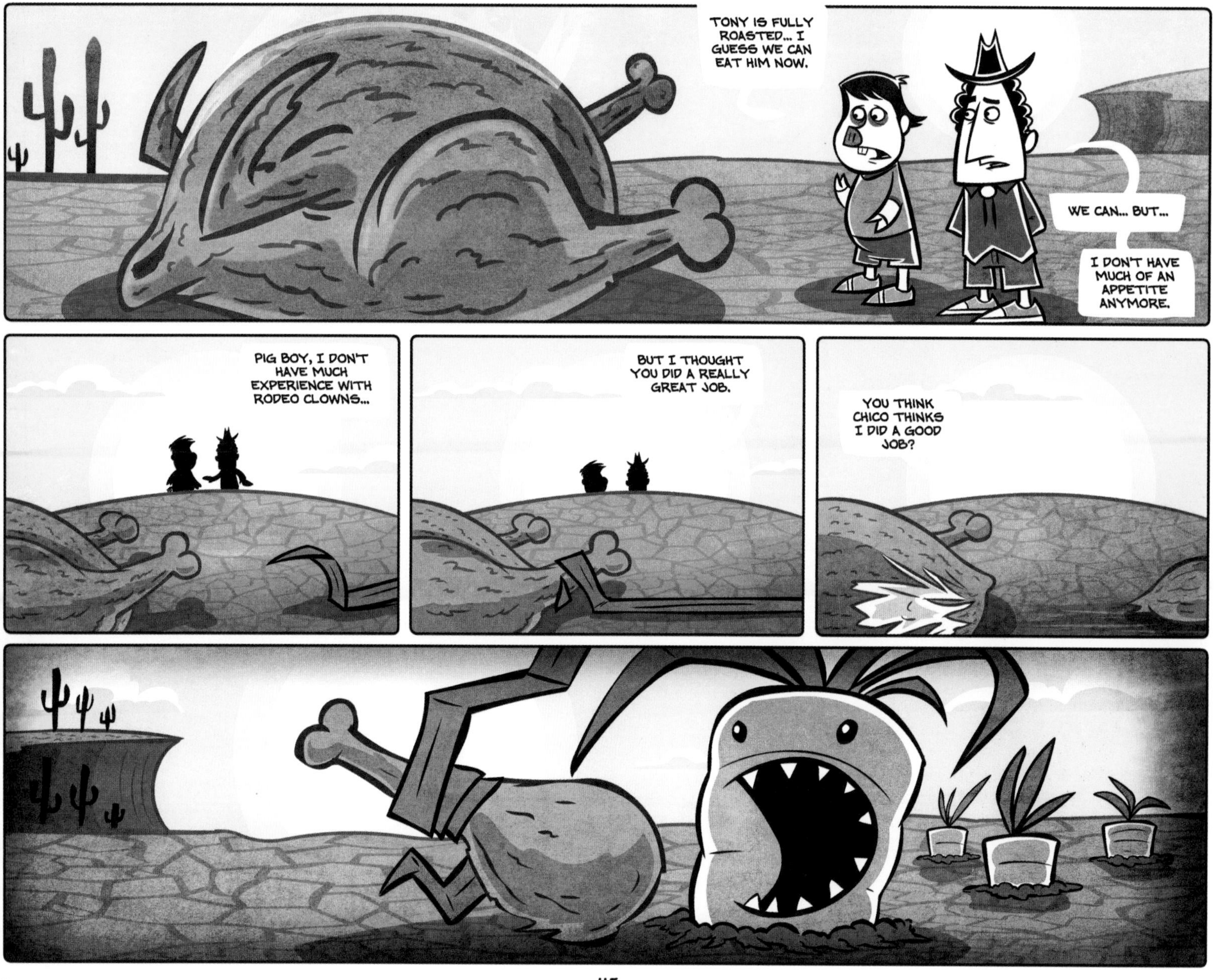

TONY IS FULLY ROASTED... I GUESS WE CAN EAT HIM NOW.
WE CAN... BUT...
I DON'T HAVE MUCH OF AN APPETITE ANYMORE.
PIG BOY, I DON'T HAVE MUCH EXPERIENCE WITH RODEO CLOWNS...
BUT I THOUGHT YOU DID A REALLY GREAT JOB.
YOU THINK CHICO THINKS I DID A GOOD JOB?

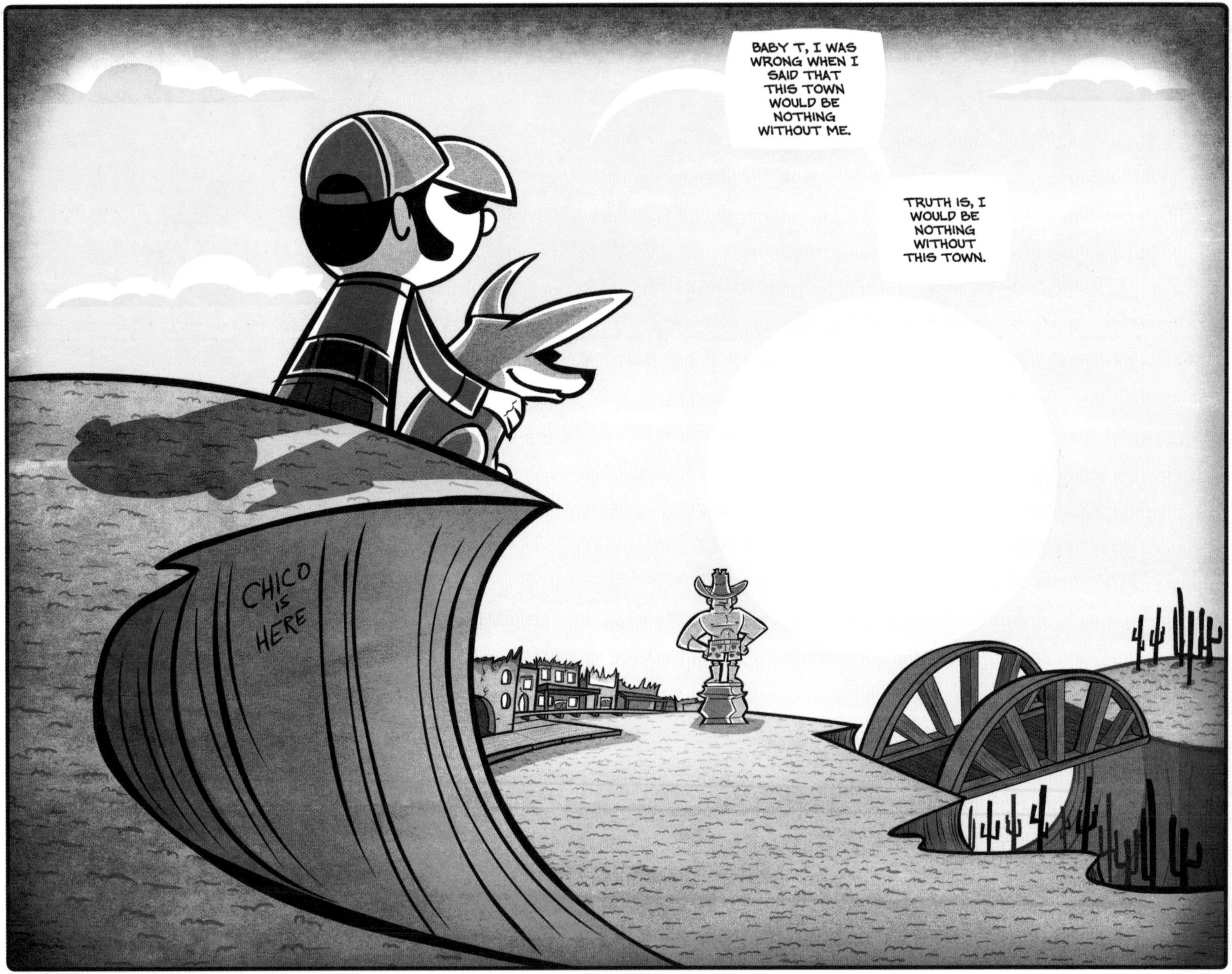
BABY T, I WAS WRONG WHEN I SAID THAT THIS TOWN WOULD BE NOTHING WITHOUT ME.
TRUTH IS, I WOULD BE NOTHING WITHOUT THIS TOWN.
CHICO IS HERE

MMXII a SuperMercado Joint. Made in Austin, USA

EARLY SKETCHES

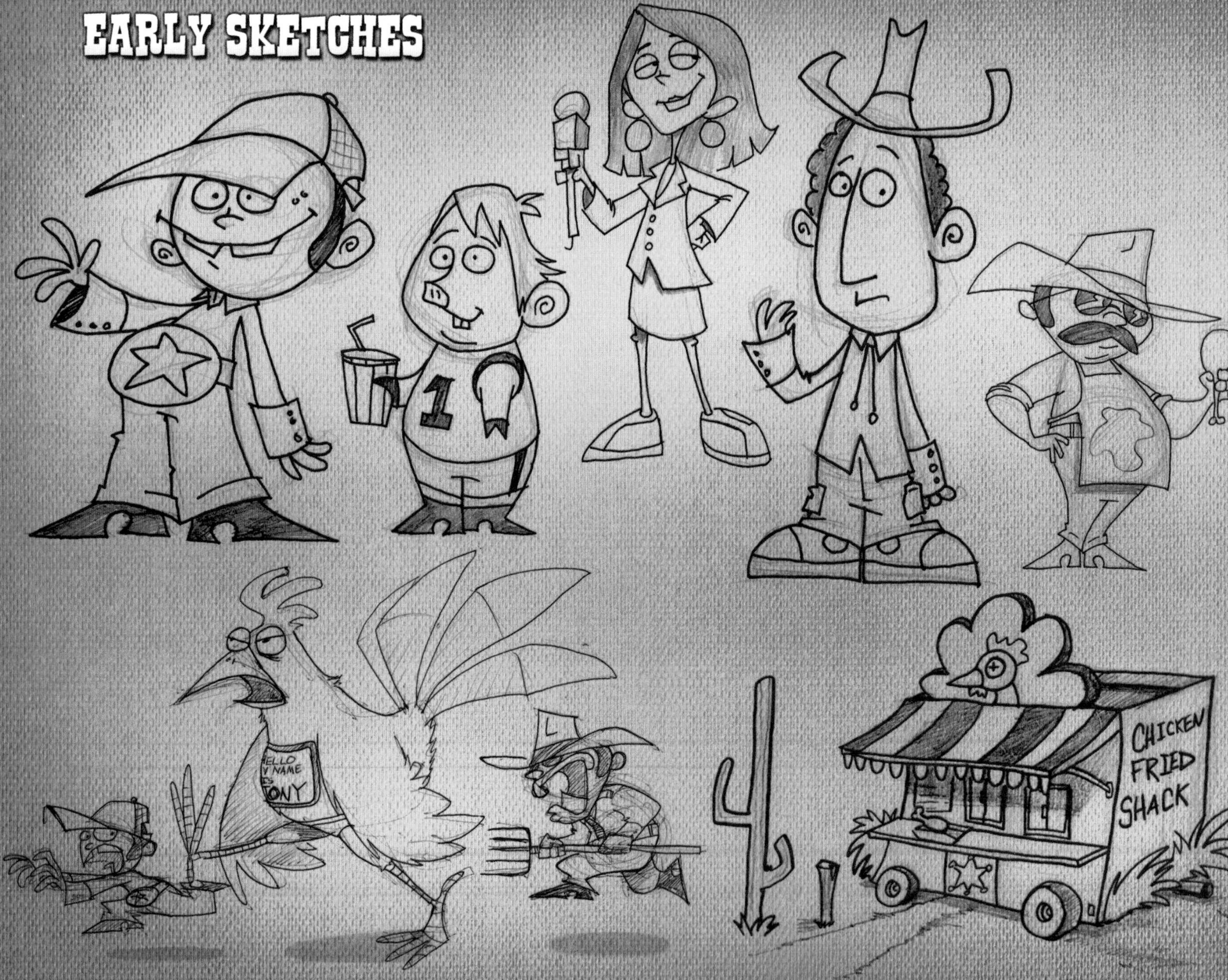
HELLO
CHICKEN
FRIED
SHACK

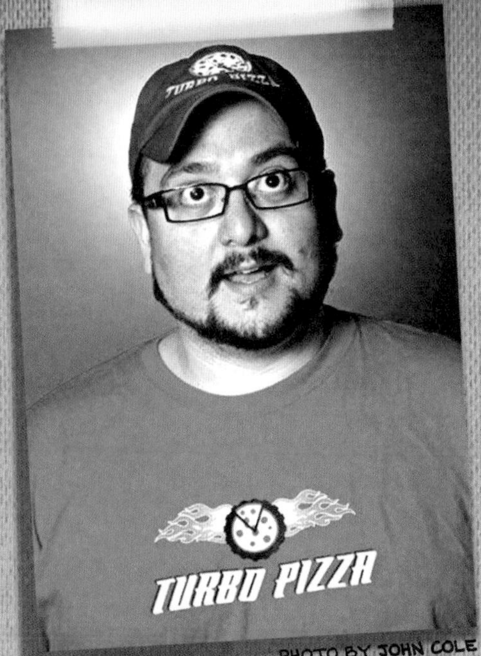
TURBO PIZZA

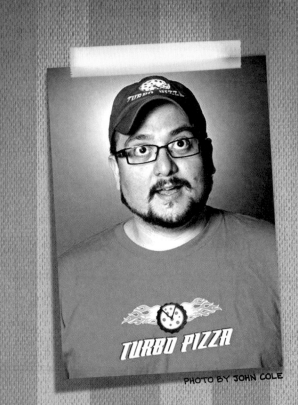

PHOTO BY JOHN COLE

YEHUDI MERCADO

YEHUDI WAS A PIZZA DELIVERY DRIVER BUT NOW DRAWS AND WRITES FOR A LIVING. HE'S DONE VIDEO GAMES, MUSIC VIDEOS, SHORT FILMS, SCREENPLAYS, COMMERCIALS, AN ANIMATED SERIES AND GRAPHIC NOVELS. AS A CHILD, YEHUDI WOULD THROW HIMSELF DOWN SEVERAL FLIGHTS OF STAIRS IN ORDER TO PREPARE HIMSELF TO BE A STUNT MAN. BRUISING AND BREAKING EASILY, YEHUDI TOOK THE EASY WAY OUT AND CHOSE TO DRAW AND FILM STUNTS INSTEAD. HE LIVES WITH HIS GIRLFRIEND, EILEEN, IN AUSTIN, TX.

FIND MORE OF YEHUDI'S WORK AT **SUPERMERCADOCOMICS.COM.**

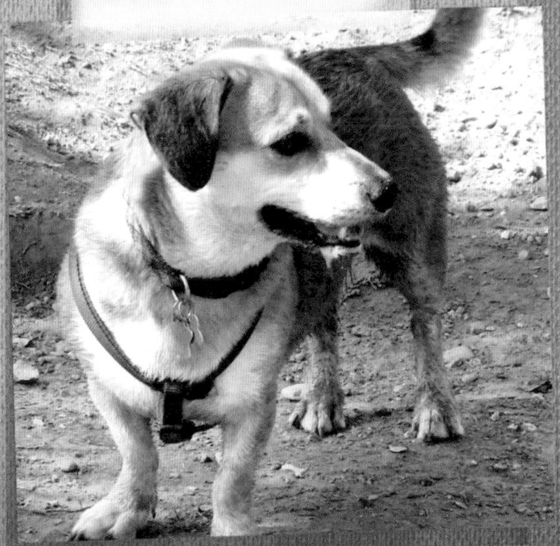

TEXAS THE DOG

TEXAS MET YEHUDI IN THE SUMMER OF 2005 WHEN HIS ORIGINAL FAMILY WAS PREPARING TO MOVE TO AFRICA. TEXAS' FIRST OUTING WAS TO A MUSIC VIDEO SHOOT FOR COUNTRY MUSIC STAR PAT GREEN. FROM THAT DAY ON, TEXAS AND YEHUDI BECOME FAST FRIENDS. HE LIKES TO BE CALLED BABY T AND HE TOLERATES HIS YOUNGER BROTHER, ROCKET, BUT HATES HIS OLDER BROTHER, FINSTER THE CAT.

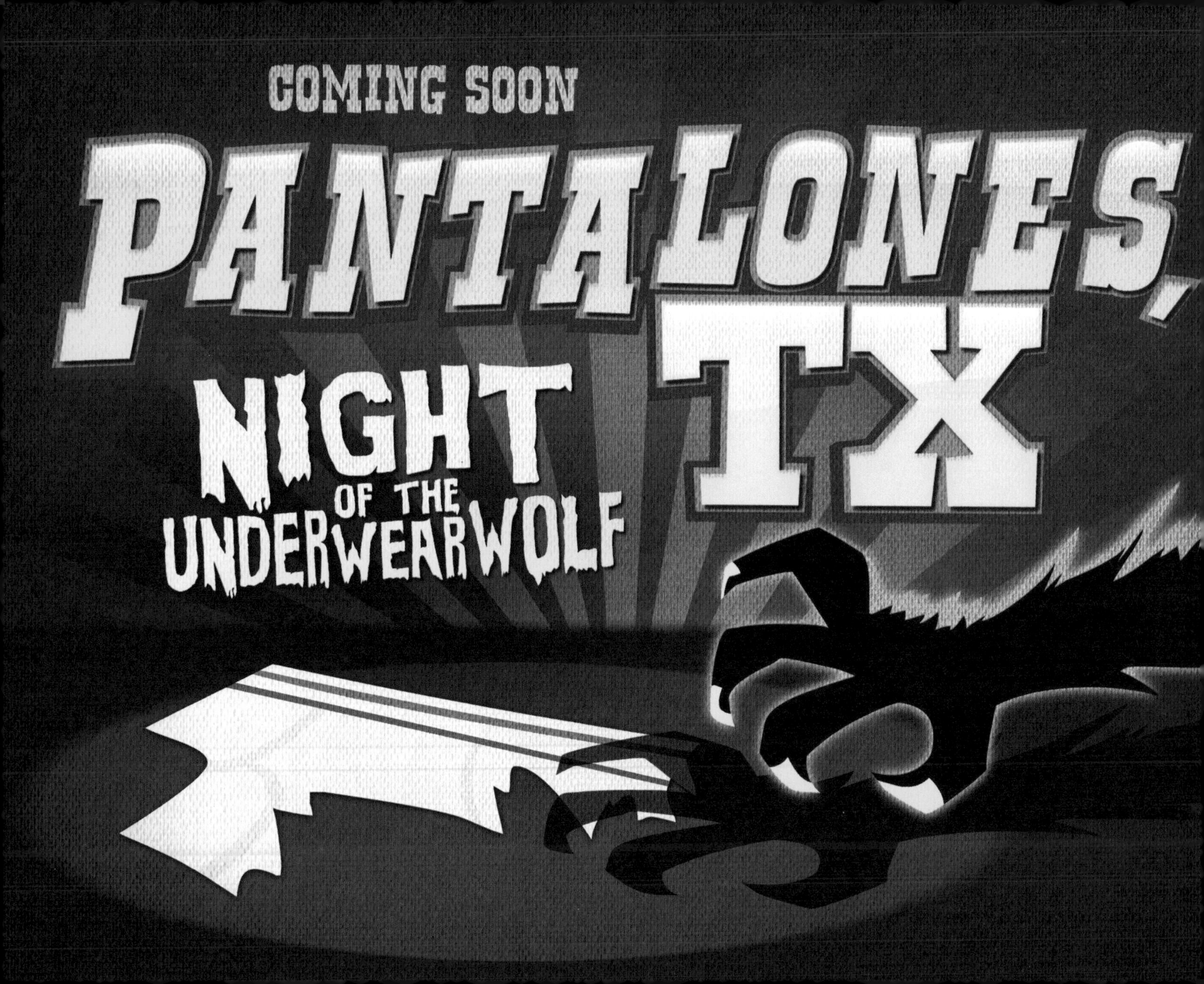

COMING SOON
PANTALONES, TX
NIGHT OF THE UNDERWEARWOLF

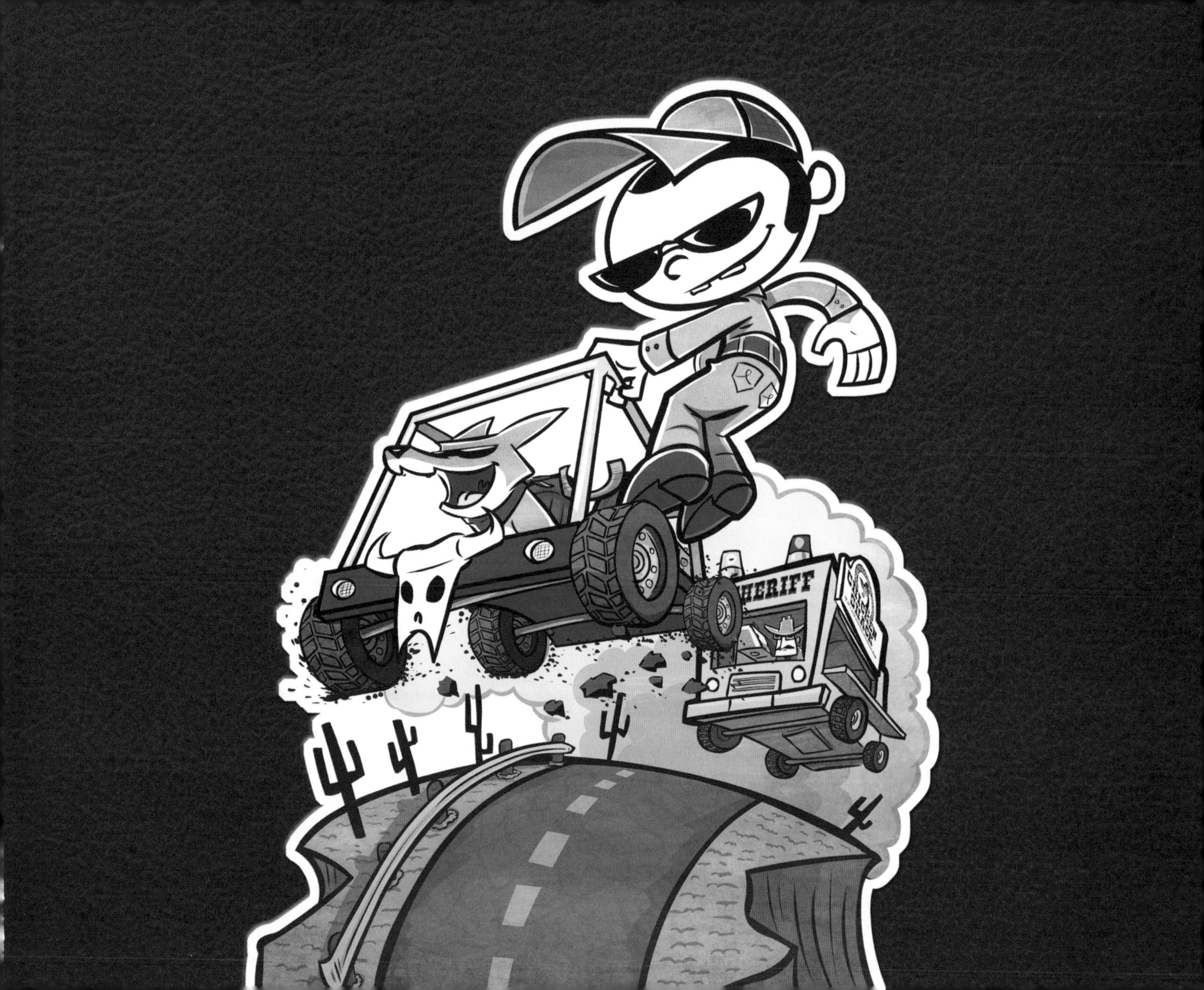
HERIFF